P9-DCJ-672
Millis, Mass. 02054
SEP 2 2 2009

MURDER AT LONGBOURN

MURDER AT LONGBOURN

A Mystery

TRACY KIELY

MINOTAUR BOOKS
NEW YORK

This is a work of fiction. All of the characters, organizations, and events portrayed in this novel are either products of the author's imagination or are used fictitiously.

A THOMAS DUNNE BOOK FOR MINOTAUR BOOKS.
An imprint of St. Martin's Publishing Group.

MURDER AT LONGBOURN. Copyright © 2009 by Tracy Kiely. All rights reserved.
Printed in the United States of America. For information, address St. Martin's Press, 175 Fifth Avenue, New York, N.Y. 10010.

www.thomasdunnebooks.com
www.minotaurbooks.com

Library of Congress Cataloging-in-Publication Data

Kiely, Tracy.
Murder at Longbourn / Tracy Kiely.—1st ed.
p. cm.
"A Thomas Dunne book for Minotaur Books"—T.p. verso.
ISBN 978-0-312-53756-2
1. Bed and breakfast accommodations—Fiction. 2. Cape Cod (Mass.)—Fiction. I. Title.
PS3611.I4453M87 2009
813'.6—dc22

2009012724

First Edition: September 2009

10 9 8 7 6 5 4 3 2 1

For my mother, Elizabeth

ACKNOWLEDGMENTS

INASMUCH AS THIS may be my only opportunity to write an acknowledgment, I am taking full advantage of the space allotted me here. Besides, I owe many thanks to many people. First, I must pay homage to Jane Austen; without her wonderful works the world would be a little duller and I would have no hook. Barbara Kiely, Shirley Shevlin, Mary Doyle, Terry Mullen Sweeney, Mary Melanson, Robin Decker, Elizabeth Cush, Lisa Beagan, and Mary Ann Kingsly were all kind enough to read early versions of my book (after I cornered them and rudely foisted it upon them), and they provided invaluable input and suggestions in spite of my pushy behavior. I also need to thank the Bunco "Ladies" for their endless support (sorry, girls, they balked at the other term). I also owe a great deal to Judith O'Neill for her excellent teaching and editing. I thank my wonderful agent, Barbara Poelle, who stuck with me despite a rather silly idea involving a bullmastiff, and my editor, Toni Plummer, who suggested several excellent improvements. But the person I need to thank most is Bridget Kiely. Without her unflagging support and wonderful suggestions, this all would be nothing more than idle cocktail-party chatter. (So, if upon finishing this book you find that you hate it, please direct all complaints/correspondence to her.)

And last, but certainly not least, I thank my wonderful husband,

Matt. While initially reluctant, he actually grew to enjoy my numerous viewings of *Pride & Prejudice* and put up with hours of bizarre conversations, which usually began, "So, if you were going to kill someone . . ." His patience, humor, and common sense were invaluable. He is simply 最佳 (*ding how*).

"The whole of this unfortunate business," said Dr. Lyster, "has been the result of Pride and Prejudice.*"*

—*FANNY BURNEY*, CECILIA

MURDER AT LONGBOURN

CHAPTER 1

When fate's got it in for you there's no limit
to what you may have to put up with.
—GEORGETTE HEYER

IT WOULD BE dramatic to say that as soon as I saw Aunt Winnie's letter I had a premonition of danger—a shiver of apprehension, perhaps, or even a sudden feeling of dread. In reality, the only thing I felt was mild amusement, not so much at the message but at the mode of its delivery. I'm not so romantic as to expect correspondence from elderly spinsters to be limited to lavender-scented paper, but by this same token, I certainly didn't expect a hastily scrawled note on a yellow Post-it, cheerfully inviting me to a murder.

Of course, it wasn't an actual murder, only one of those How-to-Host-a-Murder parties. Aunt Winnie's eccentricities, while trying at times, rarely lent themselves to actual felonies. From the scrawl on the Post-it, which resembled something an acrobatic spider might create if left alone with an ink pot, I deduced that the "murder" was to take place on New Year's Eve at Aunt Winnie's new Cape Cod bed-and-breakfast.

I set the Post-it on the hall table with the rest of the mail, while I shrugged out of my damp overcoat. The weather outside was beastly, much like my mood. It was December 29, so you'd think that any precipitation would mean light, fluffy snow. But this was northern

Virginia, which meant it was cold, hard rain. Rubbing my arms for warmth, I kicked off my wet boots and headed for the kitchen. Yanking open the cupboard, I reached for the bag of Oreos, belatedly remembered that I was on a diet, and flung the package back untouched.

Some 56.3 hours before—but who was counting?—I had gotten a jump start on my New Year's resolution to lead a healthier lifestyle by giving up fatty foods and a two-timing lobbyist. Unfortunately, the only thing my health kick had earned me was a grumbling stomach, the prospect of a lonely weekend yawning out in front of me, and a crabby mood. As a result, I'd spent the better part of the week slumped in front of the television, watching various adaptations of Dickens's *A Christmas Carol* and heckling the poor Cratchit family, whose single-minded cheerfulness struck me as more than a little inane.

From upstairs, Bridget, my best friend and roommate, yelled down, "Elizabeth? Thank God you're home. I need you."

I trudged up the stairs to her room, pausing in the doorway. On her bed lay a suitcase haphazardly crammed with a mishmash of clothes; Bridget's taste was eclectic or god-awful, depending on how you characterized bright green cowboy boots and purple sequined tops. Bridget stood with her back to me, sucking in her already flat stomach and frowning at her reflection in the floor-length mirror. She was wearing a turquoise leather miniskirt, a silky orange blouse, and purple suede boots. Bridget is only five three, even in the spiked heels she considers mandatory. She believes that bold outfits offset her diminutive stature.

She can say that's why she dresses the way she does all she wants, but I've known Bridget since we were little. I saw how she dressed her Barbie dolls. I mention this because Barbie's vital statistics are such that, were she a real woman, she'd be something like seven feet tall. Therefore, not in any sense diminutive. Yet her dolls were always clad like some bizarre cross between Joan Collins and Liberace.

Still eyeing herself critically, Bridget asked, "Tell me the truth. Does this outfit make me look fat?"

I rolled my eyes. "Fat? No. Color-blind, maybe. But not fat."

At my response she swung around, almost losing her balance in the process. Four-inch heels can do that to a girl. Peering at me from underneath her spiky red bangs, she stared at me aghast. "Color-blind? Are you serious? These colors are hot this season."

"That may be so, but I find it hard to believe that you're supposed to wear them at the same time."

"That's because you have no fashion sense." She glanced disparagingly at my tan corduroy skirt and blue cable-knit sweater. "You really should let me give you a makeover."

"I thank you for the favor, but no. The last time you gave me a makeover, some guy kept trying to shove dollar bills down my skirt."

"That's not true!" Bridget said, laughing.

"Okay, maybe so," I admitted with a grin, "but you're still not giving me a makeover."

"Why not? Come to New York with me and Colin. We can update your look and start the New Year off right."

Colin is Bridget's boyfriend. For New Year's, the two of them are going to New York for the weekend. Bridget has been trying to convince me to go with them, especially now that I am, as she delicately put it, "without plans."

"Come on, it'll be fun!" she continued excitedly. "You know nobody does New Year's better than Times Square! We could go shopping! We could try new restaurants! And more important, we can celebrate your freedom from a man who is, let's face it, the soul-sucking spawn of Satan. And don't even get me started about his obsession with argyle."

I pushed aside the suitcase and flopped across her bed. The soul-sucking, argyle-wearing spawn of Satan is my ex-boyfriend Mark. To say that Bridget had never liked him was a gross understatement—over the past few months she'd developed a small facial tic at the sound of his name.

"Bridget, you know I love you and Colin, and you're sweet to invite me, but for the thousandth time, no. I'd be a third wheel—and on New Year's Eve of all nights!"

"You wouldn't be a third wheel," she countered. "You'd be with friends."

"Friends who are a couple. Which would make me the third wheel. No offense, but I'd rather stick glass in my eyes."

"Offense? Don't be silly. Who could take offense at that? You simply prefer self-mutilation to a weekend with friends."

"Only figuratively. The truth is, it's been a long week and all I want to do is relax and catch up on some reading." While that was true, I was also refusing for more altruistic reasons. I knew something she didn't: Colin was planning to propose at the stroke of midnight on New Year's.

"Reading?"

"Yes, reading," I replied with a lofty wave of my hand. "I have decided to devote myself to the improvement of my mind by extensive reading."

Bridget narrowed her eyes. "That's from *Pride and Prejudice,* isn't it? Damn it, Elizabeth, whenever you start quoting from *P&P* I know you're in a mood. I swear, that book is your security blanket when you're upset."

Luckily the chime of the doorbell saved me from a response. "Oh, God!" cried Bridget. "It's Colin. Can you let him in? Tell him I'll just be a minute."

I rolled off the bed and went downstairs to let Colin in. Colin is six two, with curly brown hair and large brown eyes. To me, he's always resembled an enormous teddy bear come to life. That pretty much sums up his personality, too. He's like the big brother every girl wishes she had. He was still stamping his wet feet on the doormat when Bridget poked her head out of her room and hollered down, "Colin, I'll be ready in two seconds. Try to convince Elizabeth to come with us. She needs cheering up."

Colin glanced quizzically at me. "Is that true?"

"No. She will most certainly *not* be ready in two seconds."

"I meant about your needing cheering up."

"I'm fine. She's referring to Mark."

"Oh, that's right," said Colin, rearranging his face into a somber expression. "I was sorry to hear you two broke up."

"Liar."

He grinned and dipped his head in acknowledgment. "Okay, you're right. The news made my day. The guy was a jackass." Pulling me into a quick hug, he added, "You deserve nothing but the best, Elizabeth. Don't forget that."

See why I love Colin?

Eventually Bridget emerged from her room, dragging a bulging suitcase. Ignoring her pleas that I join them, I resolutely settled down on our couch with a copy of Faulkner's *The Sound and the Fury,* finally convincing her that all I wanted to do was stay home and read. With Colin looking grateful and Bridget looking concerned, they left me to tackle the novel.

However, with their exit, the apartment seemed unnaturally

quiet, and I had trouble concentrating on the text. Our landlord didn't allow animals, so I didn't even have the warmth of a furry friend to comfort me. Our only pets, if you could even call them that, were two goldfish purchased during a rare fit of domesticity. Unfortunately, our local pet store didn't stock a particularly hardy variety, resulting in bimonthly replacement visits. As a result, I'd named each new pair Rosencrantz and Guildenstern. It didn't change their fate, but it added a little drama when I had to announce it.

Forty-five minutes later, after having read the first twelve pages of Benjy's narrative a total of eight times, I flung the book down, now feeling hungry, lonely, *and* stupid. Deciding that I could alleviate at least one of those problems, I grabbed the bag of Oreos just as the phone rang. Seeing the caller ID, my mood went from bad to worse.

It was my sister Kit. I knew what was coming. One of her goals in life is to see me married—and while I'm in no way opposed to the idea, it's not my driving force in life. As I expected, no sooner did she hear my voice than she launched into rapid-fire speech. She had heard the news of my breakup from our mother and was clearly dumbfounded. How could I let a "catch" like Mark "slip away"? Didn't I understand that with each passing year my chances of getting married diminished? (I'm all of twenty-six.) Didn't I know that I had to "reel them in" while I was still young? (The way Kit tossed around the fishing jargon you'd think she was a seasoned angler. But the closest she ever got to fish was in her grocer's freezer section.)

I didn't want to tell her the real reason for the breakup—that Mark had been seeing at least two other women behind my back. So I did what any reasonable person in my position would do. I lied.

Unfortunately, it's not a skill that I'm adept at and the reason I gave her—that he smoked—sounded silly even to me. I know Kit found it funny, because she laughed for a good thirty seconds. Loudly. Then she launched into a lecture, the point of which was that unless I stopped being so picky, I was going to end up *alone.*

She said this last bit in the whispery kind of voice some people reserve for revealing a stint in prison or a terminal illness. As she continued to scoff at my "pickiness," something inside me snapped. Candidly I volunteered, "He cheated on me, Kit, okay?"

Silence answered.

"Kit, are you there?"

Finally, all in one breath I got, "Oh, you poor, poor thing. What a *terrible* thing to have to go through. No *wonder* you didn't want to tell me! How awful! Not that I have any *personal* experience, of course. Well, don't worry about it, I won't mention it again. Except to say that I always *thought* there was something untrustworthy about him. His eyes are too close together for one. And he really could be a pompous jackass at times. But there's no point in going into all of that *now.* Are you alone? You shouldn't be alone. Where's Bridget? Oh, that's right, Colin's proposing this weekend, isn't he? Well, *don't* let that get you down. I know what you're probably thinking. You're thinking that you're going to end up some lonely old woman who lives with cats, but that's not *true*!"

"Actually, Kit, I wasn't thinking that . . ."

"Good, *that's* the spirit! Okay, here's what we'll do. I'll come down. No, that won't work. Tom and I are having a huge party this weekend for some clients. It's been unbelievably stressful. You'll just have to come here."

My brother-in-law sells hot tubs. It wasn't hard to imagine where the night would end with a party composed of fellow enthusiasts in a house with the deluxe model.

She continued on. "You come here and we'll forget all about Mark. We won't even mention him. Do you know who he was seeing? Is she pretty? You poor, poor thing."

The thing about my sister is that she does mean well. However, her idea of well and my idea of well are on opposite ends of the spectrum. I knew she wouldn't stop about the party until I either agreed to come or produced a reasonable excuse. Panic set in as my brain frantically struggled to generate the latter. Happily, my eyes landed on Aunt Winnie's Post-it. With a heroic effort to keep any trace of relief out of my voice, I told her that, sadly, I couldn't possibly go to her party as I was already going to Aunt Winnie's.

There was a brief pause as Kit absorbed this information. "Aunt Winnie's having a party?" she asked, a note of hurt in her voice.

"Um, well, it's more of a work weekend, really," I fibbed. "I think she just needs my help getting the inn ready."

"Oh, I see—*that* makes sense. Well, as long as she doesn't let you cook, everything should be fine," she said, breaking out into the overly hearty laugh she employed whenever she insulted me. It was meant to imply "we're all just one big, happy, teasing family and if you don't get that, then you're *way* too sensitive." All it did was set my teeth on edge.

Thanking her for the invitation and promising that I would call if I needed to talk, I hung up on another, "Oh, you poor, poor thing."

I looked at the Oreos. After my third one, I realized I needed something stronger. I needed a large glass of chardonnay and a larger dose of Cary Grant. Pulling my woolly cardigan around me, I went to ransack Bridget's DVD collection. Passing the hall table, I reread Aunt Winnie's invitation. I realized that I really did want to go, and not just so that I wouldn't end up in a hot tub with my brother-in-law's single clients. No, I thought with a smile, a visit with Aunt Winnie was just what I needed. Right after *North by Northwest*.

My goal to get an early start was thwarted. I am not an early riser and Kit called me six more times to try to convince me to come to her party instead. Just as I was leaving, call number seven came in. I let the answering machine deal with it. Pushing my black suitcase out the door, I heard her say that if I was worried about not having a nice dress, she had an old one I could borrow. I slammed the door with more force than was strictly necessary and headed for my car.

By late afternoon, I was on the Cape. Directions in hand, I drove along the narrow, winding roads past scruffy pine trees and low walls of smooth gray stone, occasionally catching sight of the icy blue waters of Nantucket Sound. Above me, gnarled tree branches intermingled with power lines, both having been there so long it was hard to tell where one began and the other ended. My spirits rose at the sights, and some of my melancholy over Mark's betrayal faded. After all, what are men to trees and rocks? Finally, I pulled into a curved tree-lined drive. At the end was a rambling two-story house. Hanging over the door was a freshly painted white sign. In large green letters it proclaimed: THE INN AT LONGBOURN. I smiled. Aunt Winnie was a dedicated, some might say an obsessed, fan of *Pride and Prejudice.*

As picturesque as it was, I had to admit that I had thought Aunt Winnie was crazy when she bought it several months earlier. She had seen the property while on a tour of Cape Cod and had impulsively decided to buy it, renovate it, and turn it into a B and B—regardless of the fact that she had absolutely no experience in anything of the sort. But Aunt Winnie seldom let logic interfere with her plans.

My aunt came bustling out the door just as I switched off the car's engine. If your idea of a woman of seventy-odd years is of the genteel, blue-haired variety, then Aunt Winnie might be something of a shock. Her short, round figure was covered by a long coat that appeared to have been purloined from some off-off-Broadway production of *Joseph and the Amazing Technicolor Dreamcoat*. But bright as her coat was, it was nothing compared to her short, curly hair, currently colored an outrageous shade of red.

Aunt Winnie had never married, but that's not to say that she hadn't had offers. She used to joke that she thought marriage was a great institution, but that she didn't want to be in an institution. I think her reluctance had more to do with her childhood than anything else. Her mother had died when she was young, and her father was a demanding hypochondriac who was convinced that his death was right around the corner. He withdrew to his room, where he fussed and moaned in glorious seclusion.

With his retreat, Aunt Winnie had been forced to run the family's hardware store. Her two older brothers had left home years earlier and by then had their own careers to run. When her father finally did die six years later from pneumonia, no one was more surprised than he. But with his death, Aunt Winnie was free to live her own life. Taking her not insignificant inheritance to an investor, she ended up impressing that man with her business savvy and received a job offer instead. Over the next several years, Aunt Winnie worked and learned and continued to grow her inheritance until she was an extremely wealthy woman. The men who wanted to marry her always promised to "take her away from all of this," a promise she found unappealing. She liked her work and she was good at it. So she turned them all down, had affairs instead, traveled, and made even more money.

"Elizabeth! Oh, it's so good to see you," she said now, giving me a tight hug. I happily returned it, breathing in the familiar scent of Chanel No. 5 that clung to her. "Let me get a look at you!" She held me at arm's length and took a quick inventory. "You're too thin, of course, but I guess that's the style nowadays. I'm glad that in my day women were expected to have some curves." Here she stopped to pat her own ample supply. "But you still look lovely—I've always said you've got the map of Ireland stamped on your face." I laughed. The first time Aunt Winnie said that to me I was six years old and I instantly ran to the mirror to see if my freckles actually did form some sort of geographical pattern. As she helped me bring in my bag, she said, "So, I hear that you and your latest beau have broken up. Do I offer condolences or congratulations?"

"Definitely the latter," I said. "To tell you the truth, I'm beginning to think that Mr. Darcy is just a fictional character."

Aunt Winnie laughed. "He's out there; you just haven't met him. Yet."

Something in her tone made me peer suspiciously at her. "What do you mean, *yet*? Aunt Winnie, please, please tell me you haven't planned any surprises for this weekend. I'm really not in the mood for a blind date."

"Blind date! Please! What sort of meddler do you think I am? A blind date, indeed!"

A contrite apology hovered on my lips until I realized that she was stressing the "blind" part a bit much. "Aunt Winnie," I said, coming to an abrupt halt in the gravel driveway, "tell me now or I swear I will turn around this instant and go home."

An expression of defiance tinged with guilt crossed her face.

Finally, she tossed her chin, the movement sending her tight red curls quivering. "Well, now that you mention it," she said casually, "there is someone here you know. Peter McGowan."

At the sound of his name my stomach lurched. I think most people are emotionally frozen about someone or something—it may be that they are still intimidated by their third-grade teacher or continue to harbor a secret terror of clowns—but whatever it is, neither time nor maturity can break its power. For me that thing was Peter Emmett McGowan, intimidating elder and evil clown all rolled into one.

I met Peter the summer I turned ten. It was also the summer I obtained glasses, braces, and an extra fifteen pounds brought on by overeating to comfort myself about the aforementioned glasses and braces. Peter was fourteen going on seven and heir to a hugely successful hotel business. He had the easy confidence that money and good looks usually bring. He was also sneaky, cruel, and sadistic. I can't count the number of hours I spent locked in some dark basement by his hands or the number of slimy bugs that "mysteriously" found their way down the back of my shirt. And, although the braces were gone, laser surgery had removed my need for glasses, and the weight problem was (more or less) under control, I still found myself pulling my coat tightly around my neck in a gesture that had nothing to do with the blustery weather.

"Aunt Winnie," I began.

"Now, don't squawk. Save your breath to cool your porridge. I asked him here to help me start up the inn. I needed somebody with experience in running this kind of business and Peter was kind enough to offer his services."

Thinking that his experience would be far more suitable for a house of horrors, I made no reply and focused on keeping my face neutral. Apparently my mother was right when she told me that I didn't have a poker face because Aunt Winnie continued as if I had spoken aloud.

"Peter's a grown man now, Elizabeth. Besides, his parents are two of my dearest friends. You shouldn't judge him for a few boyish pranks that happened more than fifteen years ago."

"Don't try to paint him as some Gilbert Blythe innocent. He locked me in a basement for two hours!"

"And you put a dead fish in his bed."

I squelched my old familiar cry of "He started it!" and forced myself to act mature. When I saw Peter I would be polite and self-assured. I would have inner poise.

Right after I threw up.

To distract my mind from my roiling stomach, I took a restorative breath of the cold, salty air and turned my attention to the house. It really was quite perfect. Gray cedar shingles blanketed the large façade, including the veranda and bay windows, giving the impression of friendly bulges rather than separate features. Wide stone steps led to a deep porch that ran across the front. A few Adirondack chairs, painted cherry red, sat in cozy groupings. It made a charming and pretty picture. It was also totally useless in calming my nerves.

We walked onto the porch and inside to a simple reception area. In one corner, a Christmas tree covered in thousands of tiny white lights loomed. In the other corner, two very disapproving blue eyes stared out at me from the comfort of a green brocade chair.

Startled, I blurted out a blasphemy that had little to do with my reverence for the season. Aunt Winnie also noticed the room's other inhabitant. "Elizabeth," she said formally, "I'd like to introduce you to Lady Catherine."

It was a cat, a regal-looking Persian with preposterously fluffy white fur. Under her breath, Aunt Winnie added, "I briefly considered calling her Mrs. Danvers, but she's clearly above domestic service."

The cat's pale blue eyes surveyed me with what could only be described as an expression of distaste, and I whispered back, "But she may not be above the crazed behavior."

I thought I detected a faint hiss. Good God, was the cat actually scowling? Great. Apparently, I inspired a visceral loathing in cats. This did not bode well should Kit's dire prediction for my future prove true. I had a sudden vision of myself as a sad, lonely woman trapped in a tiny apartment, surrounded by hissing cats. A noise from the back office interrupted this bleak picture and I steeled myself for the inevitable meeting with Peter. Instead, a petite woman in her mid- to late fifties emerged. She was trim and conservatively dressed in an A-line tweed skirt and black turtleneck. The only jarring note in her otherwise demure appearance was her hair. It was thick and curly and bright red—naturally red, not like Aunt Winnie's hue. She had pulled it back into a tight bun, but it still gave the impression that it was fighting to break free. Her gray eyes widened in surprise at seeing us. "Oh, Ms. Reynolds," she said quickly. "I hope you don't mind, but I couldn't get a signal on my cell, so I used your phone. Just a local call, though." She peered anxiously at us from behind thin wire-framed glasses.

Aunt Winnie waved away her apologies and made the introductions. "Elizabeth, this is Joan Anderson. She and her husband, Henry, are also guests at the inn for New Year's. Joan, this is my grandniece, Elizabeth."

Joan chatted pleasantly with us for a few moments, telling us how much she and her husband liked the inn and how they were looking forward to tomorrow night's show. Almost on cue, a tall, heavyset man with receding brown hair walked down the stairs. There was a formal air to his demeanor that was at odds with Joan's easiness. Seeing us, he made his way over. Joan quickly introduced me.

"It's very nice to meet you," Henry said. He enveloped my hand with both of his, in a firm, albeit clammy, grip. "Joan and I are quite impressed with your aunt's inn, especially the decor." Turning to Aunt Winnie, he said, "You have some very nice pieces here, Ms. Reynolds. Really, it's quite above your average B and B." With a glance in my direction, he added, "I don't know if Joan told you, but we own an antiques business in New York called Old Things—perhaps you've heard of it?"

"I don't think I have . . ."

"Well, surely you've heard of Mrs. Kristell Dubois," he said, his voice deepening almost reverently. "The widow of Marshall Dubois? She is New York's most generous patron of the arts. I was able to find her a rare first edition of *Fordyce's Sermons* and she was most grateful. As a result we were lucky enough to secure her as a client—she is *very* particular. Although she has become much more than just a client. She's almost a benefactress. Her generosity is endless. We have been invited—twice—to her estate on Martha's Vineyard, and her improvements to our humble store have been most invaluable."

Henry paused, turning to Joan so that she could add her own praise. She haltingly added, "She has been a very conscientious client." Henry waited impressively for my response, and I was forced once again to admit my ignorance. The glowing light in his eyes was quickly replaced by faint disapproval.

"I doubt if Mrs. Dubois's reputation extends beyond New York, Henry," Joan said timidly.

"Yes, well, perhaps," Henry admitted reluctantly. Then brightening, he added, "Mrs. Dubois introduced Joan and me to bridge recently and I must say we're hooked. We're hoping to get a foursome together this weekend—do you play? If not, I'd be happy to teach you and further acquaint you with Mrs. Dubois's excellent work."

"Oh, thank you," I said, "but I'm afraid I'm not very good at cards. I was actually hoping to catch up on some reading this weekend. But I appreciate the offer."

Henry received my excuse with obvious incredulity, finally murmuring, "I see. Well, in any case, we shouldn't keep you. I'm sure you have much to prepare for." Turning to his wife, he added, "Joan, have you seen my watch? I can't find it anywhere."

"Really, Henry. You've got to get that clasp fixed. That's the third time this week you've lost it. It's probably in the room somewhere. Come on, I'll help you find it."

"You prefer reading to cards?" Aunt Winnie whispered with mock disdain once they moved out of earshot. "That is rather singular."

I smirked. "I deserve neither such praise nor such censure. I just suspect that tales of Mrs. Kristell Dubois are one of those delights of which a little goes a long way. Which brings me to my next point—who *is* she, anyway?"

"Weren't you listening, silly? She's one of New York's most generous patrons. And I may have this all wrong, but I *think* Mrs. Dubois frequents his shop."

I giggled. "Well, she could not have bestowed this honor on a more grateful recipient."

Aunt Winnie grimaced. "You have no idea *how* grateful. But by tomorrow I suspect you will. In fact, by tomorrow I suspect we'll all wish that it's Mrs. Kristell Dubois who gets knocked off during the show."

"Speaking of the show, what exactly is the plan?"

"Grab your bag and I'll tell you as I show you your room." She preceded me up a steep, curving staircase. "Cocktails start at eight and dinner is at nine. The actors will pose as guests and mingle with everyone else. Sometime during the evening, the 'murder' takes place. Our guests then try to solve it with the help of the actors. Once we have a solution, we'll have some dancing and then ring in the New Year."

"Sounds fun." I puffed as I lugged my increasingly heavy suitcase up the maple-stained stairs. I mentally added "working out more" to my ever-growing list of resolutions, even though the "more" part was technically a lie. I also added, "stop lying to self." We finally reached the top landing. Gleaming white bead board ran along the lower half of the hallway walls. The upper half was painted a misty blue. Aunt Winnie flung open a white paneled door to the left of the stairs.

"This is you," she said, as she gave the room a final once-over. "There are ten bedrooms. They are all pretty much the same, although I think this is the nicest." I had to smile my thanks. I was sadly out of breath. The room's furnishings were simple but inviting—a large gray-and-white braided rug, a tall wooden bureau, a wingback chair upholstered in a pattern of faded pink and green cabbage roses, a standing floor mirror, and an antique nightstand. The only luxurious item was the large mahogany four-poster bed, its white down comforter floating like a soft layer of meringue.

"What a lovely room!" I cried. "It's perfect!" As Aunt Winnie peered at her reflection in the mirror, patting an errant curl into place, I opened the closet to hang up my coat. Teasingly, I stood back and said, "What? No shelves in the closet? I'm all astonishment!" Laughing, Aunt Winnie turned away from the mirror. "Don't be a smart-ass. But I *am* glad you like it. And thanks again for coming, sweetheart." She gave me a quick hug. "I really appreciate it. Now, why don't you freshen up and meet me in the dining room in about half an hour? On Friday nights, some of the locals come in for a drink. It's our version of happy hour. You can meet everyone . . . and see Peter again." Giving me a wink, she moved out into the hall, shutting the heavy door behind her.

I sank into the wingback chair and frowned at the cabbage roses. What had I gotten myself into? I loved Aunt Winnie and wanted to help her with the weekend, but I wondered if I'd made a mistake in coming. The last thing my battered ego needed was Peter McGowan. Repeatedly telling myself that I was a mature woman now, not some insecure kid, seemed to be of little avail.

I added new resolutions for the weekend and repeated them over and over as a mantra:

- I will have inner poise.
- I will not let Peter McGowan get under my skin.
- I will not allow myself to be locked in a dark basement.
- I will have a calm and relaxing New Year's.

I couldn't have been more off the mark if I had tried.

CHAPTER 2

For what do we live, but to make sport for our neighbors, and laugh at them in our turn?

—JANE AUSTEN, *PRIDE AND PREJUDICE*

"What I want to know is, who is he exactly? Lauren *says* he's an old friend of the family, but then why is he staying here and not with them? No, there's something fishy going on there. I may be old-fashioned, but you just can't discount appearances." This from an elderly woman wearing an enormous maroon velvet hat liberally festooned with silk flowers. A large yellow mum near the top quivered in delighted disapproval.

Beside me, Joan Anderson leaned forward, her glasses slipping down her nose. "What is she like, anyway? I've never seen her."

The couple at the center of this speculation was Lauren Ramsey and Daniel Simms. She was the wife of wealthy local, Gerald Ramsey; he, the purported old family friend. Daniel's unexpected visit had apparently provided hours of conjecture for the town's avid gossips, the undisputed leader being the woman in the velvet hat, Miss Jacqueline Tanner, known as Jackie.

"Oh, she's pretty, in a kind of obvious way, you know, blond, perpetually tan. She tends to keep to herself." Jackie's expression indicated a deep suspicion of people who enjoyed privacy.

"But why do you think he isn't staying with them?" Joan asked.

Jackie's only response to this was a slight raising of her eyebrow. It spoke volumes.

"But wouldn't it make more sense to stay there if . . . I mean . . ." Joan broke off, blushing. Henry's round face radiated discomfort, not only at the sordid direction the conversation was taking but at his wife's participation in it. His long fingers played with the stem of his wineglass.

"Maybe they didn't have enough room," I offered.

Jackie scoffed. "Clearly you haven't seen their house. Lack of room is not the reason. There's another reason, or I'll eat my hat." Momentarily distracted by that bizarre image, I lost the thread of conversation. "If you ask me," she continued, "there's no fool like an old fool and Gerald is not a man who invites much sympathy. His first wife died, you know. From what I understand, she found death a refuge."

Beside me, I heard Joan's quick intake of breath at this callous remark. Jackie continued unawares. "No, the one I feel sorry for is the girl, Polly. She's a bit of an odd duck, but who wouldn't be, growing up in that house? Rumor has it Gerald practically keeps her a prisoner. Won't let her live on her own, which is just absurd. I gather that she was accepted to Oxford for some art history program, but he won't let her go. And until she inherits her trust fund—which won't be until she's twenty-five—she's stuck."

Any sympathy I might have felt for Polly markedly diminished at this. Call me insensitive, but the woes of trust-fund babies failed to stir any real sympathy in me. Jackie was still talking. "I wonder if Polly resents Lauren," she mused, before adding, "not, of course, that it's any of my business." She said this last bit without a trace of irony and it was hard not to be impressed. Suddenly, her head swiveled, sending her droplet earrings swinging. Something behind me held her attention; her eyes darkened with interest. "Well, speak of the devil," she said softly.

I've heard of people described as "exuding sex appeal," but I don't think I ever understood what it meant until I saw Daniel Simms. It wasn't merely that he was incredibly good-looking—think of a contemporary Greek god with slightly tousled, dark ash hair and keen blue eyes, and you get the picture. But as I said, it wasn't just his looks. It was the way his tailored shirt hugged his shoulders, his wolfish grin, his slightly predatory way of moving that all added up to "it"—honest-to-God sex appeal. He paused for a moment in the narrow doorway and, seeing our little group, ambled toward us. From the smile on his face, I was sure that he not only knew we had just been talking about him, but that he found it amusing.

"Good evening, ladies," he said.

Oh, my God, he was British! I let the sound of his vocal cords—all suggestive of crumpets and Burberry tweed—wash over me. I admit to a certain weakness for an English accent. Which is a polite way of saying that the man could read the phone book to me and I would lose all capacity for rational thought.

After politely greeting Aunt Winnie, he turned his attention to Jackie, saying, "Miss Tanner, it's always a pleasure to see you."

In spite of her unflattering gossip, Jackie was clearly not immune to his charm. A girlish blush stained the little bit of face that was visible underneath her hat. "We were just saying, Mr. Simms," she said in a chirpy voice, "how much we're all looking forward to tomorrow night. I only hope the weather holds. What's it like now?"

"A bit rotten, actually." He enunciated both *t*'s in *rotten* like an art lover discussing Giotto. Heaven.

Aunt Winnie introduced me to Daniel and quickly pulled the

others away under the flimsy pretext of showing them a flower arrangement. Subtlety is not her strong point. "I feel a bit at a disadvantage," Daniel said to me, once they moved away. "I don't know anything about you. But I suspect that you can't say the same of me." He finished with a nod at Jackie's retreating back.

"She did provide a pretty thorough biography." I matched his light tone. "Although, I must confess, the years between your tenth and thirteenth birthdays are somewhat murky."

"Ah, yes. The dark years, as I like to call them." Jackie returned now. An outmaneuvered Aunt Winnie joined us a split second later, her mouth twisted in an annoyed grimace.

"The dark years? Whatever are you two talking about?" Jackie asked, with a small birdlike tilt of her head.

Daniel's voice dropped an octave. "I don't usually tell people about that part of my life, but that's what I call the time when I was sent away." He discreetly winked at me. "It was a horrible place. Cold. Impersonal. Terrible food. Filled with other lads just like me."

"Prison?" Jackie gasped eagerly.

Daniel shook his head. "Boarding school."

After a brief pause, Jackie burst out laughing. "Terrible man! Go on, laugh at an old woman. At my age I can't drink or smoke. Gossiping is the only vice I have left!"

As we continued talking, the knot in my stomach slowly unfurled. This might be a good weekend after all. Aunt Winnie could be maddening at times and she definitely was an interfering matchmaker, but she had struck gold. Daniel was wonderful—good-looking, smart, and funny. From the way he kept directing bits of conversation my way, it seemed that he was interested as well. All was right with my world. Then I heard the voice. His voice. "Aunt Winnie, have you seen the inventory list for tomorrow night?" My effervescent feeling evaporated so quickly it felt like someone had sucked all the air out of my lungs. I turned and there he stood, the nemesis of my youth—Peter Emmett McGowan.

He looked pretty much the same, which was damned unfair. I believe that intrinsically evil people should manifest those traits physically. But he seemed untouched. He was still tall, his brown hair was still thick and curly, and his eyes were still that unusual shade of amber. I consoled myself by thinking that he must have a portrait of himself—one that showed him covered in boils and lesions—hidden away somewhere. The past fifteen years dropped away. I was once again a gawky, overweight girl with buckteeth and glasses. So real was the feeling that I gave myself a quick mental shake and took a generous sip of wine, mainly to reassure myself that it wasn't a glass of Ovaltine that I held in my hands. Then he saw me. It was clear that it didn't register who I was at first, but soon recognition dawned in his eyes. "Oh, my God!" he said. "Cocoa Puff! Is that really you?"

Cocoa Puff! That stupid, hateful nickname! I couldn't believe he had just called me that! And in front of Daniel, no less! The blood rushed to my face and I saw red.

"Worm face!" I heard myself retort. No! Inner poise! Inner poise, I mentally screamed at myself too late. Peter burst out laughing. "Worm face? God, I haven't heard that one in years. You might look different, but you're the same old Elizabeth. How have you been?"

"Fine," I muttered, my dignity in tatters. Oh, yes, I thought. I'm just fine. I just called a grown man "worm face" in front of people I barely knew. Inner poise, my ass!

An hour later I was with Aunt Winnie in the kitchen. The cocktail party had broken up shortly after my outburst. Daniel was eating at the Ramseys' house; Joan and Henry had reservations at a local restaurant; and Peter had wandered off with his inventory in hand, apparently oblivious to the churning emotions he'd stirred up in me. But as black as my mood had been, it was hard to maintain it in the kitchen's almost relentlessly cheerful atmosphere. Aunt Winnie had compensated for the coldness of the necessarily industrial stainless-steel appliances with a seemingly endless amount of red toile. It was the fabric for the curtains. It was the tablecloth. It was the seat cushions. It was even papered on the back wall. The wide pine planks of the floor were still bare, but I suspected the future held . . . something.

Aunt Winnie sat at the long farmhouse-style table while I cooked us both omelets—the only hot meal I could make with any real success. "You're not going to stay mad at Peter for the whole weekend, are you?" she asked.

"I am in no humor to give consequence to the young man who delighted in tormenting me as a child," I groused.

She laughed. "Don't you think you might be misjudging him?"

I threw some mushrooms and onions into the pan. "I think he's arrogant, immature, and self-centered, and I have no opinion of him."

Aunt Winnie rolled her eyes upward. "Fine. Have it your way. New subject. What did you think of Daniel?"

"*Him* I like." I shook the pan and flipped the omelet over. "But why does everyone think there's something odd about his being here?"

"You'd have to know the Ramseys to understand." I slid the fluffy yellow omelet onto her plate. "Thank you, sweetie," she said before continuing. "Gerald is a singularly unpleasant man. It makes it hard to believe that Lauren fell in love with him and not his money. But I suppose whenever a wealthy older man marries a beautiful and much younger woman, tongues are bound to wag."

I sat down across from her. "But to suggest that she'd bring her lover to town under her husband's nose is pretty outrageous."

Aunt Winnie nodded. "Well, that's Jackie for you. She is a horrible gossip, but there's something endearing about her all the same. I met her down at the gym—we both take that senior fitness program, and she's in amazing shape." Aunt Winnie paused. "Somehow I get the impression that she hasn't had a particularly happy life. Although truth be told, I really don't know her all that well. They only moved here last month."

"They?" I said through a mouthful.

"She and Linnet Westin. Apparently she's an old school friend of Jackie's. Jackie lives with her as a sort of companion."

"What's she like?"

"I've never met her, actually. I guess we'll find out tomorrow night," Aunt Winnie said. "Oh! I forgot to show you the invitations for the party." She reached into a toile-lined basket on the countertop behind her, pulled out the invitation, and handed it to me. Printed on heavy white card stock, the invitation read:

HELP US RING IN THE NEW YEAR
WITH A NIGHT OF DINNER, DANCING, AND DEATH!
BE PREPARED FOR INTRIGUE,
SCREAMS IN THE DARK,
AND RED HERRINGS.
AND REMEMBER, MANY WILL COME,
BUT ONE WON'T BE GOING HOME!

"So, what do you think? Don't you just love it?"

"It's very nice," I agreed before adding pointedly, "I got a Post-it."

Aunt Winnie leaned forward and took back the invitation. "Yes,

I know, dear. Remember, I'm the one who sent it. Now don't pout. I ran out of the printed ones, except this one, of course. I wanted one for the memory books. So," she continued as she leaned back in the wooden chair, "you haven't told me what you think of the place." She paused dramatically. "How do you like the house, Lizzy?"

I grinned. "I like it very much. I don't think I've ever seen a house so happily situated."

Aunt Winnie laughed. "God, you've no idea how long I've been waiting to ask you that."

"Glad to oblige. Seriously, though, it's wonderful. I'm still amazed that you bought it."

Aunt Winnie's lips curled up in a self-satisfied smile. "Yes. And I suspect there are a few others who feel that way as well."

"Meaning?"

"Meaning this place was in the middle of a nasty bidding war when I first saw it. Actually, one of the bidders was Gerald Ramsey. Oh, he was fit to be tied when the owner sold it to me and not him. I heard he turned eight shades of purple when he found out. He's been a real pain in the ass ever since."

"How so?"

"Well, he is something of a bigwig around here, and as such he does wield a lot of influence. Unfortunately, one of his cronies—Ted Marshall—is on the zoning board. Lately Mr. Marshall has pushed through several new B and B requirements that seem designed solely to make my life miserable."

"Such as?"

"Oh, things like septic tank upgrades, proper fencing, adequate parking facilities, random Board of Health inspections, you name it. I wouldn't be surprised to see him out front measuring the length of the grass come summer."

"Can't you do anything to fight back?"

"Oh, don't worry about me," she said with a smile. "I've dealt with the likes of Gerald Ramsey before. I know what to do with him. I have a friend who writes for the local paper. He'd be more than happy to do a piece on town council corruption. But it'll probably never even get to that. I'm sure Gerald will eventually move on to some other obsession. Right now his pride is hurt because he lost this place—and he's not used to losing."

"How did you manage to get the house, then?"

"As luck would have it, the woman who was selling it was a fan of Jane Austen as well. When I told her my plan to turn it into a B and B and name it the Inn at Longbourn, the dear woman's eyes practically misted over. We became good friends. I invited her to the party tomorrow but she's visiting her grandchildren in California and can't make it. Now, enough about me. How are you doing?"

"The truth?" I asked, pushing my empty plate away from me. She nodded. "Well, I hate my job, my boyfriend turned out to be a two-timing creep, Kit calls me weekly to inform me that my chances of ever getting married are rapidly deteriorating, and George seems well on his way to becoming a permanent fixture in Mom's life."

George is my mother's boyfriend. They started dating a few years after my father died, apparently during a fit of loneliness on my mom's part. My mother is an English professor who I thought would be attracted to men capable of multisyllabic speech. With George she opted for brawn over brains. And while George is a nice enough fellow, he needs to be watered once a week.

"Well, then, this weekend is just what you need. And who knows? You just might find that Peter improves on closer acquaintance."

I rolled my eyes. "I'd sooner call George a wit."

Aunt Winnie laughed. "Oh, cheer up. I can't fix George's ignorance, or your job, or even Kit, for that matter. But I can show you a good time tomorrow night." She yawned. "And, speaking of tomorrow, I really should get a head start on the muffins for breakfast."

"You go to bed," I said, clearing the dishes. "I can handle the muffins." Aunt Winnie protested, but in the end I won out. After mixing the batter for the banana-nut muffins and setting out the blue-and-white breakfast dishes on the dining room sideboard, I was still wide awake. I shut off the lights in the dining room, made myself a mug of hot Earl Grey, and headed for the reading room. Just off the reception area, it was a cozy, comfortable room, decorated in varying shades of yellow and blue. There were several overstuffed club chairs, and the built-in bookshelves that ran along the far wall were filled to capacity. In the middle of the far wall was a large brick fireplace. I had just settled contentedly into one of the fireside chairs with a copy of *Rebecca* when I heard a noise. It seemed to be coming from the dining room.

As I made my way there, I passed Aunt Winnie's office. From behind its closed door I could hear movement. Peter, no doubt. The last thing I wanted to do was ask for his help, so I gamely continued on toward the dining room.

Peering into that room's inky darkness, I couldn't make anything out, but the noise was definitely coming from the back corner. "Hello?" I called out softly. No one answered, but the noise continued and was now moving in my direction. Goose bumps danced down my arms as the uneasy sensation of being watched overcame me. Spooked, I fumbled for the light switch, finding it just as something heavy hit my shoulder, briefly dug in, and launched off of me. The accompanying hissing sound gave me little doubt as to the identity of my attacker. But the combination of the sudden, blinding light and Lady Catherine's crazed behavior left me disoriented. I took an unsteady step backward. The form I came into contact with this time, however, was definitely not feline and I screamed as a pair of arms came up around me.

"Whoa! I didn't mean to frighten! Are you all right?" asked Daniel.

My legs felt like jelly and I leaned against him for support. "Sorry," I said with a weak smile. "That damned cat scared me."

I heard running footsteps on the staircase and a second later Peter stood in the doorway. When he saw me in Daniel's arms, his dark brows lowered in an ominous line, transforming his original expression of concern into one of mild disgust. "Excuse me," he said stiffly. "I didn't mean to interrupt."

I opened my mouth to explain, but Daniel spoke first. "Quite all right. Sorry to disturb." Peter shot me an annoyed look before disappearing back into the foyer. Daniel turned back to me. "What's his problem?"

"Who knows," I muttered, reluctantly detaching myself from his arms. "As you can see, Peter and I are not the best of friends."

"Ah, yes. That would explain the worm-face remark."

Averting my face to hide my blush, I saw the reason for Lady Catherine's nocturnal visit to the dining room. My carefully laid out sideboard was trampled. The cereal canisters lay on their sides, their contents spread out every which way. A mass of pink flowers lay in a pool of water, their stems twisted and broken. I uttered a very unladylike oath. Daniel glanced at me in surprise. "Sorry," I said, embarrassed. "By-product of four years at an all-girls boarding school."

"Please, don't apologize," he said with a grin. "There's something a little sexy about a fresh-faced girl with a filthy mouth."

Unsure how to respond, I instead focused on cleaning up the

mess. Daniel stayed and helped. Sometime during the process, Lady Catherine nonchalantly returned. With an incurious glance in our direction, she languidly settled herself in her bed. It was a large wicker basket filled with soft white pillows, embroidered with frolicking mice. Situated underneath the mahogany sideboard, it not only gave Lady Catherine an excellent vantage point of the room but also put her in close proximity to the food.

After we reset everything, Daniel walked me to the door of my room, almost as if it were the end of a date. I thanked him again. "It was my pleasure," he said with an exaggerated bow.

Once inside my room, the sleep that had eluded me before now overtook me. I quickly changed into my pajamas and gratefully sank into the soft featherbed. As I leaned over to turn out the light, I saw that Aunt Winnie had hung a framed quote of Woody Allen's over the nightstand: *"The lion will lay down with the lamb, but the lamb won't get much sleep."* Unbidden, Peter's annoyed face swam before my eyes. The two of us were just not destined to get along, although for Aunt Winnie's sake, I would try. Refusing to let my last thoughts before sleep center on Peter, I concentrated instead on Daniel. It certainly was nice of him to help me clean up the dining room, I thought sleepily. But just as I was drifting off, I realized Peter had come from upstairs when he heard me scream. So who had been in Aunt Winnie's office? And why hadn't whoever it was come, too?

CHAPTER 3

The trouble with trouble is that it always starts out like fun.

—ANONYMOUS

I DO NOT function properly until I've had at least two cups of coffee, so the next morning was a bit of a blur. I got up early to help Aunt Winnie with the breakfast, which was a yeoman's task, given that my bed was warm, the room was chilly, and I had a faint headache. Somehow I forced myself out of the bed, threw on some clothes, and headed downstairs. Hearing movement in the kitchen, and assuming it was Aunt Winnie, I pushed the heavy door open with a greeting that, while not exactly cheerful, was as close as I was going to get at this hour of the morning. To my surprise, it was Peter who stood before me. Whatever his greeting might have been, it caught in his throat at the sight of my feet. I followed his gaze. Brilliant. I was wearing my bunny slippers. I stuck my chin out, silently daring him to say something. "Late night?" he finally choked out.

"Not in the way you think," I shot back.

"Actually, I have no thoughts on the matter one way or another," he said. "But, next time you might want to keep it down. This is a B and B, after all, not a frat house."

"I thought you had no thoughts on the matter," I said tartly. There was no point in trying to explain that I had been attacked by a crazed cat. Not without coffee, anyway.

Thankfully, Aunt Winnie entered the kitchen, putting a halt to our conversation. Other than a brief hello to Peter and a casual "Nice slippers, babe," to me, nothing much more was said by any of us until I heard Peter humming "These Boots Are Made for Walkin'." I retaliated by humming "If I Only Had a Brain." Finally, Aunt Winnie had enough of our dueling and began belting out the lyrics to Ozzy Osbourne's "Crazy Train."

After that we all worked quickly, getting the simple breakfast of coffee, banana-nut muffins, and sliced melon and strawberries ready. At some point, Lady Catherine wandered in, no doubt lured by the smell of food. By tacit agreement, I ignored her and she me. Instead, she wound her furry little body sinuously around Aunt Winnie's ankles and purred like a locomotive.

Aunt Winnie loaded the first breakfast tray and, deftly pushing the door ajar with her foot, breezed through the open doorway with it. Minutes later, with slightly less flourish, I followed her out with my own tray. As I passed into the dining room, I heard Joan and Henry talking, their voices low.

"There's nothing to worry about. It'll be fine," Henry soothed.

"But what if something goes wrong?"

"It won't."

"I hope so. I just can't wait until it's over," she replied, her voice anxious. They stopped talking when they saw me and resumed eating. Henry made faint grunts of appreciation as he ate. I pretended that I hadn't heard their conversation, much less Henry's enthusiasm for his breakfast. I had made a ruckus the night before, and now I was padding around in tattered pink bunny slippers. I didn't want to add "eavesdropper" to my list of bizarre behavior.

The rest of the morning went relatively quickly. After clearing the breakfast dishes, we made up the guests' beds and cleaned the bathrooms. I had time for a quick shower before helping Aunt Winnie with the dinner preparations. Due to my pitiful cooking skills, I was assigned the simple tasks of chopping the vegetables and herbs. Aunt Winnie handled the trickier items, like the Gorgonzola sauce for the filets, and the dessert—her specialty—chocolate ganache cake.

The faint headache I had had earlier was now threatening to become a full-blown migraine. I didn't need to look out the window to know that the weather must be bad; that's the only time I get these kinds of headaches. Even so, I was still surprised at the bleak intensity of the sky when I finally stole a moment and went out into the back garden. Dark, heavy clouds hung low in the air, blocking out all but the smallest amount of light. A storm was definitely on the horizon, I thought, as I pulled my coat tightly around me and headed across the yard.

The lawn stretched out ahead of me, a thin layer of ice covering the brown grass. To the right and left of me, enormous rosebushes, their tan branches now bare, formed a spiky border. In the distance, I could see the rough blue-green waters of Nantucket Sound churning and roiling underneath white hats of foam. Off to one side stood a majestic and immense maple tree, under which sat a tall bird feeder, a white metal table, a bench, and several tall-backed chairs. This arrangement may have made for a charming spot in the summer, but in the dead of winter, it was terribly forlorn. Walking closer, I saw Joan Anderson hunched in one of the chairs, staring out at the ocean with tears streaming down her face. Not wanting to intrude, I stepped back, snapping a branch. She raised her head at the sound and immediately wiped her face. "Are you okay?" I asked, before realizing the absurdity of my question. Of course she wasn't. She was sitting in the cold, alone, and crying. "I'm sorry," I continued. "I didn't mean to interrupt." I turned to leave.

"No, please. Don't go. I'm just being maudlin. Would you like to sit down?" She gestured to the bench.

I sat down awkwardly, not knowing what to say. Luckily, Joan was more in need of someone to talk to rather than someone to console her. "I don't know what came over me," she said. "I didn't intend to come out here and start sobbing like this. But after a few minutes, the tears just started."

"If it makes you feel any better, I was just thinking that the atmosphere was a little gloomy myself."

"Maybe so," she said with a half smile. "But being here again after so many years has brought back a lot of memories. I grew up near here, but everyone I knew has either died or moved away. That's what I did—I moved to New York and started Miss Baxter's Things of Yore. That's how I met Henry, actually. He'd just inherited his business from his uncle. He was selling and I was buying." She paused. "It's funny. I never thought I'd marry. I was quite prepared to live out my life alone. I wasn't some romantic waiting for my white knight, but Henry and I work well together." She nodded to confirm this thought. A second later, her face clouded over again. "The truth is, this time of year is always hard for me. My sister died a few weeks before Christmas." Tears welled up in her eyes. "We were so close. Our parents died when I was seventeen, you see, and . . . God, Vicky was so strong, even then. She was only a few years older than me, but she just stepped in and took over. I would have completely fallen apart if it hadn't been for her. She made sure I went to college and had everything I needed. I adored her. And then one night coming home, she . . . she had an accident and . . ." She broke off. Throughout her painful narrative, Joan angrily clenched and unclenched her hands. They now lay limp in her lap. "Sometimes I still can't believe she's gone."

I knew I had no words that could possibly comfort her, so I reached over and took her hand. I don't know how long we sat like that, but after a while Joan squeezed my hand and stood up. "Thank you for listening," she said, tucking a strand of red hair behind her ear. "I'd better go in now." She slowly made her way across the lawn back to the house.

I stayed outside, thinking about Joan's story and envying the closeness she'd shared with her sister. Ironically, my sister, Kit, also had a take-charge attitude regarding my life. But unlike Joan's situation, the trait did not foster closeness. In fact, it did just the opposite. I was wondering what this said about me when I was suddenly assailed by the acidic aroma of cigarette smoke. Turning in my seat, I poked my head around the large trunk to see who was there. Daniel was crossing the yard to where I sat.

"Bloody hell!" he said, jumping back when he saw me. "You scared the piss out of me! What are you doing sitting out here alone? It's beastly cold!"

He came over and sat down on the bench, casually throwing his arm on the seat behind me. My heart pounded like an adolescent schoolgirl's. Oh, God. Next my palms would probably begin to sweat.

"You smoke?" I asked stupidly.

He laughed. "You didn't know already? Poor Jackie must be slipping. I'm sure I told her just yesterday that I was ducking out for a quick fag."

I sputtered with laughter. "I think you're forgetting that has an entirely different meaning on this side of the pond."

Daniel paused, cocking his head at me. "Oh. Right. Well, that does explain Jackie's rather startled reaction." He shifted his gaze out to the roiling water. "This really is a lovely property. I can see why Gerald was so upset to lose out on it." He was quiet a moment. "So what *are* you doing out here alone?" he asked, dropping his voice to a conspiratorial whisper. "Are you hiding from that Peter bloke, or is it the cat?"

"Neither. I just came out to get some air. I have an awful headache."

"Sorry to hear that. You're still coming tonight, though, aren't you?"

"Of course."

"Here," he said, moving closer. "I can't stand to see a pretty girl in distress." He slid his hand up my back and kneaded the muscles in my neck. It was an odd sensation, relaxing and trying to restrain myself from lewd behavior all at the same time. After a minute, I became aware that the mood had changed slightly. I don't know if I leaned back into him or if he pulled me, but I suddenly found myself in his arms. "Hello," he said softly and leaned down toward me.

"Elizabeth?!"

You have got to be kidding, I thought, as Aunt Winnie's voice floated out across the yard. Daniel sat back, the mood broken. Aunt Winnie's voice called out again, "Elizabeth? Are you out here?"

I stood up and waved. "Over here."

"Oh, there you are. Can you help me for a moment?" She disappeared back into the house.

Hoping my face wasn't awash with disappointment, I said, "Duty calls. Thanks for the neck rub."

Daniel gave me a slow smile and I felt my insides liquefy in response. "Anytime," he said. "Maybe we can continue our conversation later? It's customary to start the New Year with a kiss in the States, too, isn't it?"

I think I said something clever, like "Hmmmggffh!" before I stumbled toward the house.

Around four, a black van pulled into the driveway. Emblazoned on the side, in large red letters, were the words JOIN US FOR DINNER . . . AND A MURDER. Clearly the entertainment had arrived. A young man with sandy-colored hair and round glasses alighted first. He introduced himself as Eric, and he seemed to be the leader of the small troupe. There were five of them in all, three men and two women. Eric quickly made the introductions. There was Tom, a muscular man with a shaved head, who appeared to be in his midforties, and Steven, a tall, almost painfully thin young man in his early twenties. The women were as different as night and day. Karen was a matronly looking brunette with a somber, serious face. Susie was almost as blond as she was buxom, and I seriously doubted if either attribute was God-given. After Aunt Winnie and I showed them their rooms, Eric went over the plan for the evening.

"Basically, we'll circulate among your real guests," Eric said, in a thick Southern drawl. "But we'll all be in character, so to speak. Tom and Karen are playing a married couple, as are Steven and Susie. I play an old school friend of Steven's. The basic premise is that both Karen and Steven suspect that Tom and Susie are having an affair. I play the concerned friend. Without giving too much away, various characters will appear to drink too much, flirt, and fight with one another. Ultimately, this will lead to the apparent death of one of them. At this point, the real guests will be asked to band together in an attempt to solve the crime and identify the so-called murderer. We've done this bit several times, and from start to finish it usually takes about two to three hours, so depending on when you want to start, we can be done in plenty of time for everyone to celebrate the New Year."

"I'd like it to end around eleven thirty," said Aunt Winnie. "That should give everyone time to enjoy themselves before ringing in the New Year. Our guests will probably start arriving around eight, so, let's plan to start your show around eight thirty. Dinner will be served in the dining room at nine."

"Sounds good," said Eric. "I look forward to it." Aunt Winnie smiled and excused herself.

"So"—I turned to Eric after Aunt Winnie had left—"do you guys perform these dinner theaters full-time or do you have other jobs?"

Eric laughed. "God, no. We'd all starve to death if this was our only income. No, this is just a part-time gig until we find real jobs or get discovered. Steve and I started the group about a year ago. We're in film school together. Steve met Karen in one of his acting classes and Tom is a retired cop I met at the gym. He's always wanted to be an actor."

"And Susie?"

"Steve met Susie at some party. At the time we were looking for another woman to round out the troupe, and she seemed a perfect fit for some of the glitzier characters."

"Does she attend film school with you, too?"

"Susie? No, she just wants to be in films. I don't think she necessarily wants to direct them."

Peter entered the room. "Hey, Cocoa Puff," he began. I glared at him. "Sorry." He smirked. "I mean *Elizabeth*. Can I get your help in the dining room?" Clenching my teeth into a semblance of a smile, I excused myself to Eric and exited the room in what I hoped was a dignified manner.

Once we were in the reception area, I swung around to face

Peter. My head was pounding, although it was hard to tell if it was from my headache or just sheer frustration. "Look," I said, "is it too much to ask that you stop calling me that name? In case you haven't noticed, I am no longer some sad little girl who is addicted to a stupid cereal."

His eyebrows pulled together. "What's the matter with you?" he said. "Don't tell me I interrupted another one of your conquests. Poor Daniel will be crushed."

As I had just met Eric, I took his comment as mockery. My jaw tightened in anger. "Seriously," I said, through gritted teeth, "don't you think we're a bit old for this?"

Peter peered down at me suspiciously. "What's the matter with your mouth?"

"I get lockjaw in cold weather," I said sarcastically.

"Really?"

My valiant effort for a devastating comeback resulted in one word: "Yeah!" Pithy, but still lame.

No doubt I'd think of the perfect comeback hours from now, when it would do me no earthly good. What did they call that? It was the French for "staircase wit." My mind drew yet another blank. Pathetic. I couldn't even think of the damn word. Maybe Mr. Collins had the right idea after all in writing down his little bons mots in advance.

Aunt Winnie came into the room. "Oh, good, Peter. You found her. Come on, you two. I need help getting the dining room ready."

Mentally composing acerbic comments for future use, I followed Aunt Winnie and Peter into the dining room. The man was simply impossible. None of this was doing much for my headache, and I forced myself to concentrate on what Aunt Winnie wanted me to do.

The long, narrow dining room ran front to back along the whole right side of the house. Aunt Winnie wanted to split the room into two sections, one for the tables and one for cocktails and dancing, so Peter and I moved the tables to one side. "I'd like there to be six at a table," she said, "but we're having seventeen guests total, so we'll need to put five at one of the tables."

I did a quick count in my head. "Um, Aunt Winnie? I think we only have sixteen guests."

"No, dear. It's seventeen. I have a little surprise for you tonight."

I looked questioningly at Peter, but he seemed equally in the dark. My stomach lurched. Aunt Winnie's surprises were famous—or perhaps infamous was the more appropriate word. I knew better than to try to cajole it out of her. She could keep a secret better than anyone else I knew. It was a trait I found quite vexing, actually.

Her announcement made, Aunt Winnie quickly changed the subject. "Elizabeth, you help me put on the tablecloths. Peter, would you mind making those wonderful napkins—you know, the ones that look like roses?" My face must have registered surprise because he blushed and mumbled, "It's a trick my mom taught me years ago."

Fascinated, I watched as he folded the heavily starched napkins into an intricate shape that did indeed resemble a rose. For the centerpieces, Aunt Winnie brought out a basket of white roses and some small silver bowls. "I saw this idea in Martha Stewart's magazine," she told me. Filling the bowls with water, we floated the flowers in them. "Now, all we have to do is sprinkle the tables with this silver confetti and we're done," she said.

"What do you want to do for the bar?" Peter asked.

"Let's use the sideboard," she said. "Elizabeth, help me move it to the front of the room. I think that will work just fine. Peter, I'd like you to act as bartender, if that's all right. Elizabeth, I'm leaving you in charge of the hors d'oeuvres tray." After completing all the last-minute tasks necessary for any party, we went to our rooms to get ourselves ready.

As I walked up the stairs, my foot hit something. Looking down, I saw it was a watch. I was reaching down to pick it up when Henry appeared at the top of the stairs. When she saw me holding the watch, an expression of relief crossed his face.

"Oh, good," he said, "you found it."

"Just this second. It was on the stairs," I said. As I neared him, I reached out my hand, the watch hanging facedown. On the back was an inscription. Without consciously meaning to, I read the looping words: "To Henry. All my love, V."

Raising my eyes to his, I saw that his face was flushed. Quickly taking the watch from me, he mumbled, "It was a gift. From, um, from my first wife."

"It's very nice."

A proud smile tugged at his lips. "Thank you. It *is* a handsome piece. Even Mrs. Dubois commented on it."

"Oh?"

"Yes. It is quite valuable to me," he said, before hurrying down the hall. I was left to wonder if his sentiment for the watch lay in its origin or Mrs. Dubois's praise.

After taking a shower and drying my hair, I unpacked my black sheath. It wasn't very fancy—far from it, actually—but it was the only decent dress I owned. My dark brown shoulder-length hair tends to get frizzy, so I put it up in a chignon. I don't generally wear much makeup, but inasmuch as it was New Year's Eve—and I'd be seeing Daniel—I made an exception. I studied my reflection in the mirror, wondering if I'd overdone it. I'd attempted to create a smoky effect with my eye shadow but was unsure if I'd merely produced a look that suggested malnutrition. After a few adjustments, I finally headed downstairs. Pausing on the landing, I looked out the window. Heavy, fat flakes of snow swirled and danced against a backdrop of white Christmas lights. The storm had finally arrived.

CHAPTER 4

What a swell party, a swell party,
a swellagant elegant party this is!

—COLE PORTER

As I WALKED across the foyer toward the dining room, I could hear Frank Sinatra and Bing Crosby singing "Well, Did You Evah?" It was one of Aunt Winnie's favorite songs by Cole Porter. Pausing in the doorway, I saw that Peter was dancing Aunt Winnie around the room, and doing it quite gracefully, I had to admit. They made a pretty picture against the room's backdrop of soft lights and ice-covered windows.

Aunt Winnie certainly hadn't pulled out any stops in dressing for the evening, I thought, as I watched her twirl and dip in Peter's arms. She was wearing a silver lamé top that was clearly intended to emphasize her ample cleavage. Her long black velvet skirt, which at first glance appeared demure, had an enormous slit up one side. I found myself thinking that Peter looked quite handsome, too, until I sternly reminded myself that all men look good in a tux. Especially expensive, well-tailored ones.

They hadn't noticed me yet, which explained why I was able to overhear their conversation. "Elizabeth's a lovely girl, Peter," Aunt Winnie said. "You should ask her out." Peter's next words floated across the room and smacked me squarely in the face. "I'm not in the mood to date a girl on the rebound, if it's all the same to you."

I must have made some sort of noise, because at that moment they both turned my way.

"Elizabeth!" said Aunt Winnie with a smile. "Look at you!" She crossed the room and hugged me. Studying her up close, I saw that she hadn't gone all out just with her clothes. Her makeup was also quite extraordinary; deep red lipstick, bright rouge, and silver eye shadow were all liberally applied. Her eyes even seemed greener than usual, and I suspected colored contacts. Any concerns I might have had about overdoing my makeup evaporated upon seeing her. Next to Aunt Winnie, I could pass for a visitor from the Amish country.

"You look beautiful, sweetheart!" she said. She turned back to Peter and in a loud voice demanded, "Doesn't she look beautiful?" Every inch of my face burned hot with embarrassment and anger. Sneaking a look at Peter, I saw that he seemed equally uncomfortable. In fact, he appeared to have been struck mute. Ignoring his lack of reply, Aunt Winnie grabbed me by the hand and dragged me across the floor.

"I know!" she said in chirpy voice. "You two dance! I think we have enough time before the guests start arriving."

For once Peter and I were in total agreement, and we both stumbled over ourselves in our excuses.

"Aunt Winnie, really, I think I should check on the hors d'oeuvres . . ."

"I probably should open the wine . . ."

"Nonsense!" she said firmly, pushing me into Peter's arms. "I can do all those things. Now, dance!"

Peter shrugged. "I think she wants us to dance."

"She might," I replied. "She's very hard to read sometimes."

We moved around the room, neither of us saying much. For the first time I was grateful that dance lessons at Mrs. Martin's School for Girls had been mandatory, because although my movements were mechanical, they were at least in step with Peter's. The silence between us was unbearable and I frantically struggled for something to say. He already thought that I was a girl passed over by other men; I didn't want him to think I was a lousy conversationalist as well. The trouble was, I couldn't think of a damn thing to say. Desperate, I was just about to ask him whether he'd read any good books lately, when he spoke.

"So, have you read any good books lately?"

I laughed.

"What's so funny?" he asked.

"I was about to ask you the same question."

"But?"

"I couldn't decide between that or, 'What's your sign?' "

He grimaced. "All right, fine. New question. What have you been up to for the past fifteen years?"

"Well, let's see," I said. "I finished school with a degree in English, which qualified me for either a low-paying secretarial job or an even lower-paying secretarial job."

"Is that what you do, then?"

I shook my head. "Not anymore. I work as a fact-checker for a local paper."

"Sounds interesting."

"It's not. What about you? What are you doing these days?"

"Mainly I've been working for my parents, helping them open hotels."

"Oh." My mind seemed to be working in slow motion. I could think of nothing besides my hurt pride. Around me Cole Porter's "Let's Do It, Let's Fall in Love" played. Suddenly Peter said, "I was surprised when Aunt Winnie told me that you were coming. I would have assumed that you'd have big plans for New Year's. But she said something about you and your boyfriend breaking up."

I glanced sharply at him. Was he deliberately trying to rub it in? His face was unreadable. "Yes," I said finally. "That's right. *I* did just end a relationship. Things were starting to get a bit too serious." Thankfully, my nose did not start growing with this last bit, but I couldn't stand the thought of him believing that I was some pathetic loser who'd come running to Aunt Winnie's for lack of a better offer. "And you?" I asked sweetly. "No one special in your life right now either, I take it?"

His expression grew cool and I regretted my nastiness. This was no way to start the weekend. But before I could apologize, he said, "Actually, there is someone—Maggie. But she couldn't make it this weekend. She's visiting family."

He abruptly stopped dancing and glanced at his watch. "Speaking of which, I should go and check in now," he said. "I promised to call before things got too busy here. Thanks for the dance, though." Releasing me, he turned and walked away. I was overcome by a sudden chill, and I rubbed my hands up and down my arms for warmth. I mentally rolled my eyes at his arrogance in bringing up his girlfriend. No doubt he wanted to make it clear that he was off the market. As if he needed to worry about that! Peter McGowan was the last man I'd ever run after. He probably had a closet stuffed full of argyle sweaters.

Unfortunately, the thought of argyle got me thinking about Mark. I wondered if he missed me or had tried to get in touch with me. More to give myself something to do other than stand alone in the middle of the dance floor, I decided to see if I had any messages. My cell phone was in my purse, which I had left in Aunt Winnie's office. I crossed the empty foyer and headed for it. Papered in a faded vintage rose pattern, the tiny room was sparsely furnished with only a desk, chair, and filing cabinet. This was fortunate because with all the clutter that Aunt Winnie had amassed, she couldn't possibly fit anything else in the room. I pushed aside some catalogs and files on the wooden chair, sat down, and retrieved my purse from underneath the desk. Flipping open my phone, I saw that I did indeed have three messages. My self-esteem rose a few notches as I entered my code to retrieve them. Maybe Mark *had* called me. I briefly entertained images of him pining away for me for the rest of his days while I pityingly sent him Christmas cards once in a while and encouraged him to get on with his life.

The messages, however, were not from Mark. One was from my mother, one was from Bridget, and the last was from Kit. She was calling to tell me that her party was starting at nine, "in case you change your mind." I scowled. Although I had repeatedly told her that I was going to Aunt Winnie's, she probably thought that I had made the whole thing up and was now huddled on my bed in the fetal position gorging myself on Ben & Jerry's. She was completely absurd. I hate Ben & Jerry's.

I deleted her message with an angry jab of a few buttons. I was debating calling her back when I heard the front door open. Voices floated in on a blast of cold air.

"This is a horrible night to be out. Really, Jackie, I don't know why I let you talk me into coming to this. I hate these things. They're so tiresome." It was a woman's voice. She spoke in a crisp, autocratic tone.

Next came Jackie's voice, all breathy and excited. "Oh, don't be that way, Linney. It'll be lots of fun. You'll see."

I exited the office. In the foyer stood Jackie and a woman I assumed was Linnet, mainly because I'd just overheard Jackie call her that. I'm clever that way. While the two women shared certain physical characteristics—they were both in their late seventies and of a similar height and build—they couldn't have been more different in their manner or dress. Linnet wore an extravagant fur coat over an elegant cream suit of cashmere. Jackie wore a serviceable black coat over a plain black dress of thick wool. Linnet's face was artfully, although heavily, made up. Jackie wore no makeup. Linnet's silver upsweep was, upon closer inspection, actually a wig, but the effect was still regal. Jackie, once again, was almost hidden underneath an enormous hat. This one was black silk with a large white velvet peony pinned to the upturned brim.

Jackie greeted me enthusiastically. "Hello, Elizabeth! We aren't late, are we? The snow slowed us up. It's really coming down now. Linnet was just saying how much she's looking forward to tonight." I ignored this little lie, as did Linnet. Jackie turned to her friend and continued, "Linnet, may I present Ms. Reynolds's niece, Ms. Elizabeth Parker?"

Linnet extended a perfectly manicured hand. "How do you do? Jackie's told me so much about you."

This I did not doubt. "It's very nice to meet you," I said. "I understand that you've recently moved to the area."

"Yes," replied Linnet. "I bought one of those cottages down by the beach." I had seen the houses she was referring to on the drive in yesterday. To refer to them as cottages was like calling Versailles a house in the country.

"Moving is always such a hassle," she continued. "But, of course, having Jackie with me has been a tremendous help."

"Have you two been friends long?" I asked.

Jackie opened her mouth to answer, but it was Linnet who spoke first. "Oh, my, yes. Jackie and I have known each other all our lives. We're actually distant cousins. My grandmother and Jackie's grandmother were second cousins or something like that. And we were roommates in college. We were inseparable back then. But after I got married, we lost touch."

"Linnet's husband passed away last year," said Jackie.

"Oh," I said. "I'm so sorry."

Linnet waved her hand slightly. "Thank you. But he's in a better place now," she said matter-of-factly. "That's actually how Jackie and I came to be reunited, as it were. When news of Marty's death was posted in our alma mater's newsletter, Jackie saw it and wrote me. Well, once we caught up with one another and compared notes on our lives, and I learned of Jackie's situation, I insisted that she come and live with me."

Jackie ducked her head a little. "Linnet's been very kind," she said softly.

Although Linnet waved her hand again, as if to dismiss Jackie's words, I noticed that she was smiling slightly. I felt a pang of sympathy for Jackie. I had known Linnet all of two minutes, but she had already managed to make it clear that Jackie owed her current improved situation to Linnet's own generosity. It struck me that while Linnet Westin might be generous to those in need, she also liked to be recognized for it. I wondered if it was difficult for Jackie to live with constant reminders of her benefactor's kindness.

Taking their coats, I led them into the dining room, where

Peter and Aunt Winnie stood talking with Joan and Henry. Henry preened proudly in his tux, mentioning often that he'd purchased it at one of Mrs. Dubois's favorite stores. Joan's bright red dress was very festive, but instead of adding color to her complexion, it had the opposite effect. She looked deathly pale. While Aunt Winnie made the introductions, I went to the kitchen to get the tray of hors d'oeuvres. I had just returned with it when Daniel arrived, looking like he'd stepped off the cover of *GQ* magazine. I deduced that the people with him were the Ramseys.

Gerald was a tall man who appeared to be in his early sixties. His thick mane of silver hair was meticulously brushed back from his face and his eyes were a cold, almost translucent shade of blue. I don't know if it was his solid build or direct, unblinking gaze, but he had a definite presence. And it wasn't a pleasant one. There was a ruthlessness in his expression reminiscent of creatures in the animal kingdom that eat their young. In fact, if it weren't for the young woman standing just behind him, who I could only assume was his daughter, Polly, I wouldn't have been surprised to find out that he had.

She was probably in her early twenties, but her plain gown with the Peter Pan collar made her seem younger. Her shoulder-length jet-black hair was pulled back in a tortoiseshell headband, further emphasizing her youthful appearance. The only discordant note was her eyes. Large and green, they slanted up like a cat's. Framed by delicately winged eyebrows, they hinted at an exotic and mature nature underneath the otherwise unremarkable and childlike façade.

Next to her stood a woman who, by virtue of the fact that she was both blond and tan, I took to be Gerald's wife, Lauren. With her heart-shaped face, large blue eyes, and faintly vacant expression, she reminded me of my first Barbie doll. Her pink silk dress was stunning in its simplicity—always an indication of expense. In fact, I suspected I could live off its cost for months. I felt a pang of jealousy. Here was the woman who purportedly held Daniel's interest. Any hope I had of her being nothing more than a nasty little freckled thing with money vanished.

Beside me, Linnet sniffed contemptuously. "What a pretty dress Lauren has on tonight, although I've always thought of pink as a young woman's color." A rather catty remark, considering Lauren couldn't be more than forty-five, but one I secretly enjoyed nevertheless.

Aunt Winnie rushed over to greet the newcomers. "Well, hello, Gerald, Happy New Year! Lauren, you look lovely! That's a gorgeous dress! And Polly, I'm so glad to see you, my dear."

"Winifred," said Gerald with a curt nod. Lauren and Polly each smiled a bit shyly and shifted uncomfortably.

Peter appeared with a tray of glasses filled with champagne. Following his cue, I picked up my tray of assorted hors d'oeuvres and followed.

"Who are you?" demanded Gerald of me as he reached for a crab cake.

"Gerald," said Aunt Winnie, "this is my grandniece, Elizabeth Parker. She's staying with me for the weekend."

"How do you do?" I inquired.

He ignored me and regarded the room with an appraising eye. "I see you've made some changes to the place since I was here last, Winifred."

"Yes," replied Aunt Winnie, turning to admire the room's blue-and-white motif. "Do you like it?"

"No."

Beside him, Lauren gasped slightly. "Gerry!" she said in a resigned tone. It was clear that she didn't expect her admonishment to have any effect on her husband's manners; instead she merely seemed to be letting us know that she didn't condone his behavior. There was a moment of awkward silence. Only Daniel watched the proceedings with unabashed amusement.

It took a second for Aunt Winnie to recover. She let out a loud laugh and said, "Oh, go pound sand, Gerald Ramsey! You're still sore that Mrs. Bruster sold this place to me and not to you. And if you hadn't been so rude to the woman, you might have had a chance of buying it. You've no one to blame but yourself!"

Gerald's blue eyes narrowed and for a moment I was sure that he was about to blast Aunt Winnie. To my surprise, however, he shrugged his broad shoulders. "Touché, Winifred. But this isn't over yet. Mark my words, one day this house will be mine." He picked up a glass of champagne and with a mock toast said, "By fair means or foul." He smiled as he said this, but even from where I stood, I could see that the smile didn't reach his eyes.

CHAPTER 5

There are different kinds of wrong.
The people sinned against are not always the best.

—IVY COMPTON-BURNETT

"I SWEAR TO God, Tom, if I find out that you're having an affair with Susic, I will kill you."

And with these words, shouted in the foyer by Karen, the show began.

We watched openmouthed as Karen stormed into the room and pulled up short, as if she was surprised to find us standing there. She wore a long gown of gray silk taffeta so voluminous that there could have been at least three prop guns hidden in its folds. A second later, Tom's large frame filled the doorway. His broad face appeared flushed and angry. A thin sheen of perspiration covered his face and head.

"Er, good evening," he said to all of us. "My name is Tom and this is my wife, Karen."

"Hello, everyone," she greeted us with an overbright smile.

I'm not sure how long we all stared at the two of them before I belatedly remembered that this was not a movie we were watching. We were supposed to interact with the actors as if they were actual guests. I returned their smiles and walked over with the tray of hors d'oeuvres.

"Good evening," I said. "Would you care for something to eat?"

"No, but I'll take a drink, if you've got one," replied Karen.

Peter heard her and came with his tray of champagne. Karen grabbed one of the glasses and took a long sip. Tom watched her anxiously. "Darling," he said, "don't you think that . . ."

But whatever Tom thought, it was lost in the flurried arrival of the second couple of the acting troupe, Susie and Steven. Well, I think Steven entered the room. The neckline of Susie's dress revealed so much cleavage that it blocked out all other visual stimuli. You didn't want to look, but you couldn't help it. And once you did look, it was difficult to see anything else. I sighed at the thought of my own neckline. My mother kindly describes my build as lithe, but the sad reality is that if I wore my bra backward, I'd probably get more cleavage from my shoulder blades.

"Well, hello, everyone," purred a woman's voice somewhere north of Susie's chest. "I hope we're not late?"

Aunt Winnie snapped back into her hostess mode and stepped forward to greet the newcomers. "Welcome, Susie. And hello, Steven. Hello, Eric. I didn't see you at first."

As I said, I don't think anyone had. But now that I did focus on them, I could see that Steven appeared very agitated. His thin frame was quivering, and his eyes kept darting back and forth between Tom and Susie, as if he were watching for some sign, some hint, that they were indeed lovers. Eric was also in character. His posture was rigid and tense, and he watched Steven with worried eyes.

As I circulated among the actors with my rapidly diminishing supply of food, I heard Steven say to Eric, "I can't take this anymore. I think I'm going crazy, man. I keep picturing them together."

Eric patted Steven's shoulder and said, "It's going to be all right, Steven. Just keep it together, buddy. I promise you that everything is going to be okay." Upon seeing me, Eric turned away.

I smiled as I roamed the room, listening in on the various conversations, happy that for once my penchant for eavesdropping was condoned. I looked around the room at the rest of Aunt Winnie's guests to see if they were also enjoying the show.

Jackie's clear laugh floated out. She looked like the proverbial kid in the candy store, smiling broadly as she eagerly watched and listened to the actors play their various parts, occasionally engaging one or two of them in conversation. Daniel also interacted with the actors. Well, actually with just one actor. He trailed Susie around the room like a besotted puppy. If nothing else, his behavior seemed to put to rest the rumor that he and Lauren were having an affair. He hadn't spent more than five minutes with her since they arrived. Of course, he hadn't spent more than five minutes with me, either, and I hadn't imagined our near kiss in the garden earlier.

As I surveyed the room, I found Peter staring at me. As soon as we made eye contact, he looked away. As he'd never looked at me before except to criticize, I immediately glanced down at my dress, half expecting to see various spills and stains. It was clean. I ran my tongue over my teeth, wondering if something large and green was stuck there. Again, nothing. I was reminding myself that Peter could find fault with me even on my best days when an elderly man entered the room. The newcomer was tall with a mass of white hair, a short trim beard, and glasses so thick they magnified his brown eyes to almost three times their actual size. He hesitated a moment, as if uncertain where he should go, before Aunt Winnie spotted him. "Randy!" she cried excitedly. She rushed over and enveloped him in a huge hug.

Randy? I looked over at Peter for an explanation, but as he seemed to be looking to me for one, I took the newcomer to be Aunt Winnie's surprise guest. Knowing her, he could be anyone from a voodoo doctor hired to perform a good-luck dance for the New Year, to her fiancé. Peter and I simultaneously crossed the room to where they stood.

Aunt Winnie glowed as she introduced us to Randy Whittaker. Apparently he was not a voodoo doctor. However, by the way Aunt Winnie was gazing at him, he might one day be her husband.

"Randy owns the best bookstore in town," she said. "That's where I met him."

"Well, to be perfectly accurate," said Randy, "we met in my back office after you burst in demanding to know why I was anti-Austen."

Aunt Winnie turned to me, her face alight with indignation. "Not one of her books was on the shelves. Can you believe it? Not one. Shocking oversight."

"And as I told you," he said, with a fond smile, "we had sold out and the shipment was on its way from the warehouse."

Aunt Winnie tossed her head. "I still say it's a shocking oversight. It's a good thing you've got charm on your side, Randy."

Randy laughed and adjusted his glasses. "I think I could say the same of you, Winifred. Now enough of Austen. Have I missed anything?" He surveyed the room.

"You can never have enough of Austen," Aunt Winnie retorted. "But no, you haven't missed much. As you can see, Gerald is here. Let's not have any fireworks, shall we?"

"Winifred, what do you take me for?" Randy replied indignantly.

"For a man who finds Gerald Ramsey as obnoxious as I do," she replied briskly. Turning to Peter and me, she said by way of explanation, "In addition to wanting to buy the inn, Gerald is in the midst of putting together a real estate deal for one of those large bookstore chains. You know, the kind that also sells coffee and T-shirts. Randy was looking into selling his business, but with news of this deal, no one wants to buy it anymore." Turning back to Randy, she linked her arm through his and said, "Now, I already filled you in on the performance; all you have to do is watch and listen. I'll introduce you to the actors." They walked away, leaving Peter and me alone. We stared blankly at each other.

"Well," I said.

"Well," he echoed.

Unless we were sniping at each other, it seemed we had nothing to say. "I guess I'd better circulate with these," I said finally, with a nod to my tray.

"And I should get back to the bar." He turned and walked hastily away.

I moved toward where Lauren and Gerald were standing. Although they stood close, they neither spoke nor even looked at each other. Gerald helped himself to several crab cakes, cheese puffs, and scallop-and-bacon spears from my tray, stacking them up in an absurd little pyramid on his cocktail napkin. Lauren eyed everything hungrily but politely refused.

Linnet was standing by herself, sipping champagne and watching the show unfold with a distant smile. I walked over to her. "Something to eat?"

She hesitated. "I really shouldn't. I'm trying to lose weight."

"Oh, but you can't diet on New Year's Eve. That's what tomorrow is for—lots of healthy resolutions and fresh beginnings. Besides, Aunt Winnie is a wonderful cook."

Linnet considered the tray again. "Well, I guess you're right. I suppose it is silly to start a dieting regimen today." She chose a crab cake and delicately popped it between her crimson-stained lips.

"You know," she continued, "when I was younger, I never had to worry about my weight. I was always the same size. But over the last couple of years, it's gotten harder and harder to keep the extra pounds off. I guess that's part of getting old." She reached for a cheese puff.

"Oh, I don't know about that," I responded. "I think it's hard for everyone, at any age."

She ate another cheese puff and nodded toward where Jackie stood talking to Lauren and Gerald. "Jackie doesn't seem to have any trouble," she said, with a trace of envy in her voice. "She's the same size as she was when we were in school." I remembered Aunt Winnie's observation that Jackie kept in shape by exercising; Linnet, however, attributed it to a different reason. With a faint sniff, she said, "Of course, given what her circumstances have been, I suppose it's not that surprising. After all, it's hard to overindulge when you're barely able to make ends meet."

The spitefulness of the remark took me by surprise and I struggled to keep my face neutral. Dear God. Why didn't she just stand on the nearest chair and shout out to the room, "If it weren't for *me,* Jackie Tanner would be living in a van down by the river"? Linnet kept talking. "Although it's hard to believe now, we used to look so much alike that people often mistook us for sisters."

"Where did you two go to school?" I asked, hoping to change the subject.

"Radcliffe. Jackie and I took drama together. We had this silly plan that after graduation we were going to move to Hollywood, where, of course, we'd instantly be discovered."

"What happened?"

"Well, I guess Marty, my late husband, happened. He was very good-looking back then and, of course, his family was as rich as Croesus. It made for a hard combination to resist. He was quite the ladies' man." She shook her head at the memory. "Actually, I think Jackie even dated him a few times, but once he and I met, well, that was that. It was a whirlwind romance. He proposed only three weeks after our first date. I remember Jackie was so upset, because that ruined our plans." She paused to eat another crab cake. "I doubt I would have gotten very far, anyway. My only talent was an ability to cry on command. Jackie, on the other hand, has always had a real talent for mimicry—more of a gift, really, than a talent. She was amazing." Linnet's voice held a tinge of regret; she immediately shook it away. "But, as I said, it was a silly idea. Neither of us had what you'd call the stuff of legends."

"What did Jackie end up doing?" I shifted the tray.

"Oh, she ended up taking a teaching job somewhere in Ohio. And Marty and I moved to Connecticut. Greenwich," she added after a brief pause. She was quiet for a moment, seemingly lost in her memories. "It's funny how things turn out," she said slowly, more to herself than to me. "I thought I would have such a perfect life with Marty. He came from a wonderful family. He was rich and handsome. But he was also the biggest lush I ever had the misfortune to meet."

"Oh," I said, taken aback at this blunt admission. "I'm sorry. That must have been very hard."

"It was. But I wasn't the first woman to marry an alcoholic. At least we had ample money so I never had to worry about losing the house. And, of course, I had my charity work to keep me busy. Thankfully, we weren't able to have children. At the time, it was quite distressing, but in hindsight I think it was a blessing."

I was thankful that Linnet's constant nibbling had emptied my tray, because it gave me a reason to excuse myself from the conversation. I had no idea what to say to her, not that it mattered. She struck me as the sort of person who talked a great deal but seldom required a response. She'd had a difficult marriage, but she didn't invite much sympathy. Maybe it was her lack of loyalty to people. By her own admission, she had tossed Jackie aside when they were younger, and from what she had told me about her husband, it sounded like once she realized he had a problem, she had pushed him aside, too. As I made my way across the room, I caught Peter staring at me again and I had a sudden immature urge to stick my tongue out at him. I restrained myself and continued to the kitchen.

On my way I saw Lauren. She stood with her back to me, talking on her cell phone. As I neared, I heard her say, "Okay, I'd better go. Happy New Year. I love you, baby."

With a soft click, she shut the phone and dropped it into her little purse. Seeing me, she pasted a bright smile on her face. "The party is going wonderfully, don't you think?"

"So far, so good," I agreed.

With a nod at my empty tray, she said, "Well, don't let me keep you." She hurried back to where Gerald stood. Of the many possibilities Lauren's conversation *did* suggest, I was secretly pleased that an affair with Daniel was not one of them. I continued on to the kitchen, my mood vastly improved.

After refilling the tray, I headed back to the dining room. As I passed the rear door that led to the garden, it opened and Joan and Polly walked in from the cold. My face must have shown my surprise because Joan quickly said, "Oh, hello, Elizabeth! My, it is really coming down out there! It's like a winter wonderland. Polly and I just couldn't resist—there's something about snow that brings out the kid in everyone, I guess."

As directed, I looked out the back window. The snow was indeed coming down heavily, transforming the backyard into a sea of white. I must be getting old, I thought. For unlike Joan and Polly, I had absolutely no desire to go stand in it. I was quite happy to enjoy the view from the comfort of the heated indoors.

Joan hurried back to Henry while Polly stayed with me, although she said nothing. Aunt Winnie laughed loudly at something and Polly said, "Your aunt seems like a lot of fun."

I looked over to where Aunt Winnie stood talking to Gerald and Lauren. "She is," I agreed with a smile.

Polly continued, "Sorry about my father's behavior earlier. He can be . . . overbearing at times."

That was one way of describing the man. I could think of several other terms, which while more fitting wouldn't be appropriate to share with his daughter. I snuck a glance at Polly. She was still staring at her father, her face an unreadable mask. Quite suddenly, an expression of pure hatred crossed her face. As quickly as it had come, it was gone, and the controlled mask was firmly back in place. It happened so fast that I wondered if I had imagined that look.

I felt for her. It must be hard to go through life with a father as obnoxious as Gerald Ramsey. I wondered if she often found herself apologizing for his rude behavior.

"I wouldn't worry about it," I said finally. "Aunt Winnie didn't seem upset."

"I'm glad. She seems like a nice lady. I hope she never sells this place."

That surprised me. "Oh, I don't think you have to worry about her selling anytime soon. She loves it too much."

"I hope so, but you don't know my father. When he wants something, he usually gets it." In a low voice, she added, "Just tell your aunt to be careful."

Before I could ask what she meant by that, Daniel walked up. "Well, here you are! Why are you two hiding in the corner?"

Polly smiled at him. From across the room, Gerald barked out, "Polly! Come here!"

Her smile instantly died and her checks grew red, but whether from shame or anger I couldn't tell. "Excuse me," she said quietly, and slowly walked to where Gerald stood.

Daniel watched her go, his lips pressed together in a thin, angry line. "That poor kid," he said finally. "He's a real prat." He absent-mindedly ate a cheese puff and surveyed the room. In one corner Linnet stood talking to Jackie. Daniel observed them quietly. With a nod to Linnet, he then said, "So, I take it that's the fine lady who single-handedly saved Ms. Tanner from a life of abject poverty?"

I glanced at him in some surprise, and he shrugged. "She made it pretty clear."

I shook my head, all the more sorry for Jackie. "Yes, that's Linnet. I guess they're old school friends. Apparently, when they were younger they were going to go off to Hollywood together."

Daniel ate another cheese puff. "Really?" He eyed them critically and then pronounced, "Well, they look like they once had the gams for it."

"What?" I sputtered with a laugh.

"Their legs. Being a connoisseur, I've found that there are really only two kinds of women's legs. Their ankles either curve in nicely from the calves or they don't. With the latter you get that tree-trunk appearance."

I knew the look he meant—that was a perfect description of my legs. A guy I once dated had cruelly referred to them as "cankles." I hoped he was dead now.

I shifted my weight uncomfortably and prayed he wouldn't look down. He did turn to me but thankfully he didn't look at my legs. Leaning in closer, he stared into my eyes and my heart beat a little faster. "You look quite lovely tonight, Elizabeth," he said.

Before I could respond, Susie walked by, and in the time it takes to say "fickle," his attention had transferred from me to her. "Save me a dance?" he said, before popping another cheese puff in his mouth and trailing after Susie. I had a sudden urge to hurl the heavy tray at his beautiful English head.

Making my rounds once again, I saw Tom raise his eyebrows at Susie. She, in turn, checked to see that Steven was looking the other way before nodding her head in affirmation. Glancing around to see if anyone else had noticed this exchange, I saw Karen, her face contorted with rage, glaring at Susie. When Karen noticed me watching her, she turned on her heel and marched toward the bar, where she accepted a drink from Peter and quickly downed it.

The grandfather clock in the front hall chimed. It was a quarter to nine and time to seat everyone for dinner. Aunt Winnie smoothly showed the guests to their assigned seats, while Peter and I went to the kitchen to load the plates.

"So," said Peter, as he tossed the baby arugula with the champagne vinaigrette, "do you have a guess as to who's going to be murdered?"

"My money is on Susie," I replied. "Although, if she gets shot in the chest, she's in grave danger of deflating."

Peter laughed and meowed at me. I studiously ignored him. Aunt Winnie joined us a minute later, and the three of us served the first course of salad with warm pears and walnuts, followed by the beef filets with Gorgonzola sauce.

Aunt Winnie had seated at least one of the actors at each table. Susie and Steven sat with Joan, Henry, Daniel, and Polly. Tom and

Karen sat with Aunt Winnie, Randy, and Peter. I was seated at a table with Lauren and Gerald, Linnet, Jackie, and Eric.

The purpose of this arrangement, of course, was for the guests to find out more about the murder. Unfortunately, Henry seemed to have missed this and monopolized the conversation at his table with rapturous tales of Mrs. Kristell Dubois's latest addition to her estate—an enormous outdoor fireplace. I heard Daniel politely ask if Mrs. Dubois was fond of s'mores. Beside him, Joan's face was awash with embarrassment and her none-too-subtle hints that he drop the matter went unheeded.

At our table, Eric talked freely and loudly about his friendship with Steven, dropping hints and making innuendos about fitting justice for infidelity in a marriage. Peering out at him from underneath her hat, Jackie peppered Eric with questions. As for Linnet, she occasionally added to the conversation, but it was hard to get an edge in with Jackie. Gerald paid more attention to his food than to us, and Lauren was so quiet she could pass for a mute. I tried several different conversation openers with her, but without much success. Books didn't interest her. She hadn't seen any of the movies I had seen. Even my question about politics was answered by Gerald, who flatly told me, "She votes Republican, like me."

Finally I said to her, "I really love your dress."

Bingo! She lit up. "Why, thank you!" she said. "When I saw it, I just fell in love with it. And you know what they say. Pink is the new black." There was a short pause during which she realized that I was wearing a black dress. "Well, I mean, black is very nice, too." I decided that perhaps it wasn't necessary for me to engage Lauren in conversation after all.

Soon everyone had finished dinner; coffee and dessert were served. In the interest of saving time, we had agreed that this course would not be served seated. Instead, we set up the coffee, cake, and plates on a side table for those who were interested.

Aunt Winnie increased the volume of the music, which she had lowered for dinner, and lost no time in grabbing Randy and heading for the dance floor. The two of them now dipped and twirled in perfect time with each other. Daniel and Polly were also dancing. Loudly announcing that he had no intention of dancing, Gerald watched them with a grim expression from our table. No doubt he considered the activity to be a damned tedious waste of an evening.

It wasn't only the volume of the music that had increased; the tension among the actors was now palpable. Karen appeared quite drunk. Steven was so upset he had developed a stutter. Tom was pretending that everything was fine, but whenever anyone spoke to him, he had trouble making eye contact. Eric stood very quietly by the bar, watching Steven. Only Susie seemed untouched by the tension. She laughed freely and flirted with all the men. But one thing was clear—something was about to happen.

And then it did. Without warning the room was pitched into inky blackness. An excited gasp went up from the guests. The "murder" was about to happen. Around me, several voices began talking at once. "Oh, it's starting!" "Ow, that's my foot!" "I can't see a thing." "This is asinine." (This last comment was uttered by Gerald, of course.) I listened for any subtle "clues," but there was nothing subtle about what happened next. I saw a flash of green and heard a pop. It was followed by a piercing scream. Someone fell heavily, sending dishes and glasses smashing to the ground in the process. I was just thinking that Aunt Winnie was going to be upset if her good china was broken all for the sake of the show, when I was roughly pushed aside and I heard a voice yell out, "For God's sake, get the lights." An icy finger slid down my spine—the panic I sensed around me seemed too real to be part of the show. I blindly stumbled for the door when the lights came back on. Blinking at the abrupt brilliance, I tried to get my bearings. The first face I saw was Eric's. That's when I knew that something was terribly wrong. His complexion was ashen and his eyes were wide with fear. No matter how good an actor he was, I could tell the horror on his face was real. I turned my head and saw why.

As Frank Sinatra's rendition of "It Had to Be You" blared around me, I stared down at the still body of Gerald Ramsey. He gazed uninterestedly back.

CHAPTER 6

The sooner every party breaks up, the better.

—JANE AUSTEN, *EMMA*

I DON'T KNOW how long we all stared at Gerald before Lauren's shrieks startled us out of our stupor. She ran to where Gerald lay on the floor and screamed his name and pushed at his shoulder, as if he had merely fallen asleep. Polly, on the other hand, stood motionless. Gazing at her father with an unblinking stare, she seemed rooted to the dance floor. Her face was so deathly pale, I thought she must be in shock. Daniel stood behind her and wrapped his arms around her shoulders, pulling her close.

Peter got to Gerald a split second after Lauren and began checking for the life signs we all feared weren't there. He pulled back Gerald's suit coat. Against the crisp white shirt, a crimson stain was spreading rapidly. He felt for a pulse and then slowly shook his head.

Without a word, Aunt Winnie ran from the room. I presumed that she was calling the police.

Tom, who only minutes before was playing the role of a philandering husband, spoke first. "We need to secure this room," he said with brisk authority. "No one touch anything." His cool and professional manner puzzled me until I belatedly remembered Eric mentioning that Tom was a retired police officer.

Daniel stepped forward. "What the hell are you people playing at?" He glared at the actors. "A man is dead because of you. How could you let this happen?"

Eric's jaw dropped open in shock. "Us?" he squeaked, his Adam's apple bobbing up and down like a cork. "We had nothing to do with this! We're actors doing a show. We don't even use guns!"

"Well, one of you blundered, then, because in case you haven't noticed, this man is dead!" Daniel retorted hotly.

Eric shook his head. "You don't understand, we don't use guns at all, real or prop. In our show, the victim is stabbed." Next to Eric, Susie adamantly nodded in agreement, her tawny hair falling over her shoulders. As if to corroborate Eric's statement, she held up a realistic-looking plastic knife. "When the lights came back on," she said, "I was supposed to be on the floor with this beside me."

A tiny part of my brain detached itself from the fact that I was standing ten feet from a dead man and silently crowed that I had correctly guessed Susie as the intended victim. Because of this, it took me a minute for the full meaning of Eric's words to sink in. Gerald Ramsey's death was no accident. He'd been murdered.

"Oh, my God!" gasped Joan, as she stared at Gerald's body. "But who would want to . . . ?" She sagged heavily into Henry, her question left unfinished, as she yanked her hand up to cover her mouth. Her eyes flew to Polly before she closed them as if in prayer. Jackie made a small noise. We all looked her way.

"Did you say something, Jackie?" asked Linnet. But Jackie slowly shook her head and turned away.

Linnet eyed Tom as if he were nothing more than an irksome insect. "I don't know who you think you are, but I am not going to stay in the same room with a dead man. A man who was apparently murdered, no less! This is absurd! Who are you to tell us what we can and cannot do?"

Tom listened calmly to Linnet's tirade but remained firm. He probably had had years of dealing with reluctant witnesses. "My name is Tom Cooper," he said. "I'm a retired police officer. I understand that this is difficult, but trust me, it's necessary."

Tom's reply had no effect on Linnet's ire. "Well, Mr. Cooper, I know my rights and you simply cannot keep me here against my will!" She marched to her seat where her purse lay. Whipping out her cell phone, she yanked off her clip-on earring, saying, "I'm calling my lawyer. I know my rights. Do you have any idea who I am?"

"All I know is that you're a potential suspect in a murder case," Tom replied. Linnet bristled as he continued unfazed. "No one is to leave this room. We must secure the scene and wait for the police."

Aunt Winnie returned. With a somber glance at Tom, she quietly said, "They're on their way."

Randy walked over to Linnet. "I realize that this is a horrible situation, Mrs. Westin," he said soothingly. "And that what you are being asked to do is quite extraordinary, but I really think we should do as he says. It will most likely make matters easier when the police do arrive. I am sure that your gracious tolerance of the situation will be appropriately acknowledged."

I wondered exactly how Randy thought the police were going to acknowledge Linnet's "gracious tolerance of the situation." I had an inkling that nothing short of a parade would assuage her monstrous ego. Linnet continued to glare at Tom, but Randy's words seemed to mollify her. She still watched the proceedings with an icy frown, her rigid posture radiating displeasure. However, she did put her cell phone back and replaced her clip-on. Jackie glanced anxiously at her friend but said nothing.

Aunt Winnie walked over to Lauren, standing mutely beside Gerald, and gently took her by the shoulders, easing her away from the body. Pulling Lauren to her, she guided her toward one of the chairs. After Lauren was seated, Aunt Winnie walked over to Polly, whispered something to her, drew her close, and led her to the chair next to Lauren. The rest of us stood awkwardly, eyeing one another suspiciously. The band of actors seemed especially ill at ease. No longer in character, they huddled together on one side of the room. As planned, there had been a murder tonight, but the premise had shifted. Now they were the spectators and we were the show.

I was struck by the resemblance of the scene to an Edward Gorey cartoon come to life—a room full of uneasy, elegantly dressed people, some standing, some sitting, and none of them making eye contact. And, of course, in the midst of this strange tableau, a dead body lay sprawled on the floor.

But this particular tableau is not a cartoon, I thought. It's real. And one of these elegantly dressed people just killed a man. A wave of dizziness overtook me and I sat down heavily on one of the chairs and stared at the floor.

Peter appeared beside me. "Are you all right?" he asked softly.

"Of course I'm not all right!" I shot back, my voice a strained whisper. "A man is dead! Murdered!" Nodding in Gerald's direction, I caught sight of his dead staring eyes and grimaced. A wave of nausea overtook me and I buried my head in my hands.

Peter walked over to the bar. Tom barked out at him, "What are you doing?"

Peter turned. Giving Tom a level look, he said evenly, "Elizabeth feels sick. I'm getting her a glass of water."

Tom nodded his approval.

"Does anybody else want anything?" Peter asked. Both Jackie and Linnet shook their heads, as did Joan and Henry. Lauren and Polly appeared not even to have heard the question.

Randy stepped forward. "I think Winifred could use something," he said. Aunt Winnie nodded gratefully.

"I could do with a spot of something, but it isn't a glass of bloody water," muttered Daniel, as he turned and rapidly walked to the bar. He poured three generous glasses of whiskey. He handed one to Lauren and one to Polly. The last one he drank himself in short order.

Peter poured the glass of water and came to hand it to me. "Here," he said. "Drink this."

I took the glass, but I didn't drink from it. I was quite sure that I was about to be spectacularly ill. Peter must have sensed this, too, for after a moment, he took the glass away. "Put your head between your knees," he ordered. "You look like you're about to pass out."

While I balked at his dictatorial tone, I was too dizzy to argue with him, and so I did as he said. Forcing the image of Gerald's lifeless face out of my head, I concentrated on slowly filling my lungs with air and letting it out just as slowly. I don't know how long I sat like that, but gradually my stomach felt less like it had been on a cheap roadside carnival ride. I sat back in my chair. Peter eyed me cautiously. "Better?"

"Yes," I said. "Sorry I snapped at you."

"Don't worry about it," he said simply. "Would you like the water now?"

I nodded, even though I really didn't. But it gave me something to do with my hands. When I was little and was scared or upset, I would count to myself. I don't know why, but I found the rote repetition of numbers soothing. I reverted to my old trick now as Peter and I sat with the body of Gerald Ramsey in Aunt Winnie's dining room.

Nobody said another word until 526 seconds later when we finally heard the sirens.

Desperate to get out of the room, I volunteered to open the door for the police. At the front door, I stood for a moment breathing in deeply the icy cold air and trying to settle my queasy stomach. The storm was in full swing now, and the lights from the ambulance and police cars made an eerie kaleidoscope of color in the swirling snow. Two paramedics pulled a gurney down from the ambulance and two policemen jumped from their cars. I motioned them in and quickly led them to the dining room. I pointed in Gerald's direction. "He's over here," I added unnecessarily.

The first police officer surveyed the room and announced, "I am Lieutenant Jansen." He was a tall man with a lanky build and a fleshy face.

Tom stepped forward. He introduced himself and succinctly provided Lieutenant Jansen with a brief report. Moving away, they spoke in terse whispers, leaving the rest of us trying to discern their seemingly coded speech.

Once briefed, Lieutenant Jansen moved to where Gerald lay. Kneeling beside the body, he asked, "Who is he?"

Peter answered, "Gerald Ramsey. He lives in town."

Lieutenant Jansen nodded. "I'm familiar with the name." He stared at Gerald's face a moment, then leaned back on his haunches. "Okay, what exactly happened?" he asked, as the first paramedic examined Gerald's body. The paramedic's name tag identified him as Todd. He had long black hair pulled back into a ponytail. A blurry tattoo of a peace sign peeked out occasionally from underneath his thin white shirt cuff as he performed his examination.

"I'm not really sure," replied Aunt Winnie. "It all happened so fast. We were waiting for the murder . . ."

Lieutenant Jansen jerked his head, staring at Aunt Winnie, and she realized how she sounded. Flustered, she tried to explain. "What

I mean is," she said quickly, "that this was a dinner theater party of sorts. Some of the guests are hired actors. They pretend to kill someone—one of *them.*" She pointed at the actors. "And then the rest of us were supposed to try to solve the mystery of who committed the murder."

I wondered if Lieutenant Jansen played much poker. If he did, I bet he won a lot. He gazed steadily at Aunt Winnie, giving no clue as to what he was thinking. He nodded for Aunt Winnie to continue.

She did. "Well, anyway, I turned the lights off as planned at about eleven o'clock. Once the lights were off, one of the actors was supposed to be murdered, but instead . . . we heard a gunshot and when the lights went back on . . . we saw Gerald."

During Aunt Winnie's narration, Lieutenant Jansen had pulled out a small notebook. He now rapidly scribbled into it. Todd, the paramedic, finished his brief exam of the body. "Gunshot wound to the chest," he said, stating what I thought was a fairly obvious fact.

"Did anyone touch or move the body?" Lieutenant Jansen asked.

Peter answered, "After the lights came on and I saw him on the floor, I ran over to see if . . . if he was alive." He paused. "I pulled back his suit coat and tried to find a pulse, but that's all."

"Anyone else?"

No one said anything, although we all looked at Lauren.

She was still sitting next to Polly at one of the tables. Polly was smoking mechanically, and I wondered if she was even aware of her actions. Lauren was sitting bolt upright, staring blankly in front of her. They had neither spoken to nor looked at each other since the gruesome discovery of Gerald's body. They were also completely dry-eyed. I found this a little sad but not very surprising given the kind of man Gerald Ramsey appeared to have been. Lauren's earlier hysteria had given way to a zombielike numbness, and I hadn't seen any reaction at all from Polly. In fact, they were so devoid of emotion that a stranger to the night's events would be hard-pressed to detect anything amiss in their manner. The only indication that something was wrong was Polly's hand. It shook slightly as she took a drag from her cigarette.

"Are you Mrs. Ramsey?" Lieutenant Jansen said, following our eyes.

At the sound of her name, Lauren swung vacant blue eyes in the lieutenant's direction, but I doubted that she'd heard anything else. Her expression was dazed and her eyes unfocused.

"Lauren!" said Polly sharply.

Lauren snapped back. "I'm sorry. What did you say?"

"Did you move or touch the body in any way, ma'am?"

"Move him? No. When the lights came back on I saw that Gerald was on the floor. I thought he might have had a heart attack. I ran over to him. And then Peter pulled back his coat and . . . and . . . I saw . . ." Her face crumpled and I thought she was going to cry. Instead, she gazed at Lieutenant Jansen with a lost expression.

"He was dead," she continued softly. "This all seems like a dream." She paused a moment and repeated, "Gerald. Dead," and shook her head as if she couldn't quite believe it. "He was so strong. I thought he'd live forever."

She lapsed back into silence. I thought her words odd. After all, it wasn't as if Gerald had suffered a heart attack—someone had shot him in the chest.

I looked at Polly to see how she was faring. She was staring at Lauren with a tired expression, but she said nothing. She silently turned her head away and took another long drag from her cigarette.

Lieutenant Jansen noted everything down. "We'll need to take statements from everyone individually. Is there somewhere private we can do that?" he asked Aunt Winnie. "We'll need to clear the room and look for evidence."

"Of course," Aunt Winnie answered. "You can use my office. It's off the foyer."

I doubted how productive Lieutenant Jansen's interviews would be if they were conducted in Aunt Winnie's tiny, messy office. I had a sudden image of Lieutenant Jansen's lanky frame squashed and half hidden behind a desk piled high with catalogs and papers, trying to carry out a serious interview with a suspect who, for lack of space, was forced to stand pressed up against a wall papered in faded roses.

I was about to suggest that the reading room might be more comfortable when a hissing sound from the corner distracted me.

It was Lady Catherine. She was standing next to her pillow bed with a particularly peevish expression on her feline face. In the center of her bed, and the apparent reason for her displeasure, lay a gun. It had a curved wooden handle and was so small that at first glance it looked like a toy, especially as it lay nestled among Lady Catherine's embroidered pillows. But this was no toy. It was a Derringer, and unless I was very much mistaken, it was the gun that had killed Gerald Ramsey. Next to it lay a crumpled white glove.

"Well, well," said Lieutenant Jansen with a grim smile. "Look what the cat dragged in."

Almost as if on cue, the grandfather clock in the foyer chimed midnight.

Happy New Year.

CHAPTER 7

He had the sort of face that makes you realize
God does have a sense of humor.

—BILL BRYSON

IT WAS ALMOST four in the morning when I finally crawled into bed. Granted, I'd been up that late before on New Year's Eve, but then it had been the result of an unfortunate combination of tequila and karaoke. I promptly swore off karaoke the next afternoon. This time my late night was due to relentless questioning by a humorless detective. All things considered, I preferred the tequila/karaoke debacle, even with all its nasty aftereffects.

The detective who'd been put in charge of the case was a burly man by the name of Stewart. As far as I could tell, he had no first name. He was about forty years old, with thick black hair, cropped short. His hazel eyes hinted at a sense of humor and were framed by the thickest lashes I'd ever seen wasted on a man. But after spending less than five minutes with him, I found myself mentally humming the Eagles' hit "Lyin' Eyes."

I was glad Aunt Winnie had agreed to my suggestion that the reading room, rather than her cramped office, be used for the questioning. But even settled in the relative comfort of an overstuffed yellow chair, the interview process with Detective Stewart was a painful one.

He had seated himself in the only hard-backed chair in the room, no doubt to lend an air of authority to his questioning. I suppose he felt it would be difficult to intimidate his subjects while being half swallowed by a gaily patterned club chair. But after my seemingly endless interview with him, I realized the man would be daunting even if lounging on a pool raft with an umbrella drink in his hand.

After asking standard questions such as my name, age, and address in a raspy voice reminiscent of the chain-smoking aunts on *The Simpsons,* he launched into the heart of his interrogation.

"Where were you when the lights went out?"

I refrained from asking if that was the title of a song and obediently answered, "I was standing near the sideboard, opposite the door."

"Right. And where was Mr. Ramsey in relation to you?"

"He was still sitting at the dinner table. It was in front of me, to my right."

"What was he doing?"

He'd been glaring at Daniel or Polly or both of them, but I didn't say that. Instead I said, "He was watching his daughter on the dance floor."

"I see. And how was his demeanor?"

"He didn't seem pleased."

Detective Stewart looked up from his notes. "Really? Any idea why?"

I could think of at least eight reasons off the top of my head, but somehow it didn't seem right to assign motives to a dead man. I shrugged. "Not really."

Detective Stewart didn't respond. Instead, he stared at me. I wish I could say my courage rises with every attempt to intimidate me, but I can't. Instead, my reaction is Pavlovian: my palms begin to sweat and all the moisture evaporates from my mouth. In fact, his piercing gaze produced such a pronounced reaction in me that I briefly wondered if it was a skill taught at the police academy. If Detective Stewart noticed my reaction, he gave no indication. He merely noted my answer and moved on to the next question.

"Who else was near him?"

I tried to remember. "No one, really," I said. "Everyone else was milling about the room. Mr. Ramsey was the only one still sitting."

"Okay. And then the lights went out. Did you know that your aunt was going to turn off the lights?"

"No, I didn't. She told us afterward that she was supposed to do it for the show, but I didn't know that in advance."

"I see. Did anyone else?"

"I don't know. I mean, the actors must have been aware. But . . ." I thought about it. While I hadn't known that the lights were going to go out, I wasn't surprised when they did. Why? I was struggling to figure out why when it came to me: Aunt Winnie's invitation.

"Ms. Parker?" Detective Stewart prompted.

"I was just remembering the invitation for this party. It said something about 'screams in the dark.' I was wondering why I wasn't surprised about the lights at the time. It must have been because of the invitation."

"I see. Can I get a copy of that invitation?"

"Yes. My aunt kept an extra one."

"Good. Okay. Now, what happened after the lights went out?"

"Well, at first I think everyone thought it was part of the show. I mean there was no sense that anything was wrong. I saw a flash of green, then I heard a gunshot, and someone screamed—"

Detective Stewart interrupted, "A man or a woman?"

I considered the question. "It was a woman," I said finally.

His pen scribbled. "Thank you. I'm sorry. You said you saw a flash of green?"

"Yes. I guess it was the gun going off." But that didn't make sense. I had seen the flash *before* I heard the shot.

"And then what happened?" he prompted.

"Well, there's really not much else. I heard the plates and glasses shattering. I guess that's when I first thought that something seemed odd. I mean, I doubt if these actors usually break the hostess's good china."

He nodded to his notebook. "Anything else?"

"Someone pushed past me. And then the lights went back on. I saw Eric's face—he's one of the actors—and that's when I really knew that something was wrong. He looked horrified."

"Do you know who pushed you?"

"No. I just assumed it was someone moving around in the room."

"From what direction did he come?"

"He ran toward me."

He noted all this down. By this point, I was nauseous and more than a little panicky. The last time I had been interviewed by a policeman, I was sixteen and had been pulled over for speeding. The officer's name was Ed Tighe and he couldn't have been more than twenty-five. In the end, he had let me off with a warning, but I had been so shaken from the encounter that when I got home, I promptly threw up.

Detective Stewart was about a million miles away from Officer Tighe. Plus, he had that scary stare thing on his side. "What exactly was your relationship with the deceased?"

"I had no relationship with him," I replied. "I'd just met him this evening. I served him some hors d'oeuvres."

Detective Stewart studied me for a long time after I said this, as if he were debating the veracity of my statement. Finally, he wrote something in his little battered black notebook. No doubt something like, "Suspect is unstable and unreliable." I was now officially nervous. Unfortunately, when I get nervous I tend to get "chatty," which explains why I added, "He seemed particularly fond of the crab cakes."

Detective Stewart frowned. After a long pause he said, "Are you trying to be flip, Ms. Parker?"

"No," I mumbled, embarrassed.

"All right. How did Mr. Ramsey seem to you tonight?"

"Well, having never met him before, I really couldn't say."

"I understand that, but why don't you just give me your general impression of his behavior this evening."

As I'd been raised a strict Catholic, it had been ingrained in me not to speak ill of the dead. My personal view was that Gerald Ramsey was a self-important, controlling bastard, but I opted for a more sedate version. "He seemed to be enjoying himself."

My evasion did not go unnoticed. Detective Stewart leaned as far back as the wooden chair would allow. Raising his left eyebrow slightly, he said, "Come now, Ms. Parker. This isn't a cocktail party where it isn't polite to gossip." Clearly he and I went to completely different kinds of cocktail parties. "This is a murder investigation," he continued, as if addressing a particularly slow child. "I need absolute honesty, not polite double-talk. Now, if you can't do that, we can continue this conversation at another time and in another place."

I was relieved that he hadn't said "downtown." If he had, my strained nerves would surely have given way to a fit of giggles. I had seen "downtown" on my ride in yesterday. It consisted of four antiques stores, three gourmet bakeries, two garden centers, and more boutiques than you could shake a credit card at. It certainly wasn't the kind of atmosphere that inspired fear, unless maybe you were a recovering shopaholic.

Nevertheless, something about his tone got under my skin. I sat up a bit straighter and looked him directly in the eye. "Fine, you want my opinion of the man? I'll tell you. He struck me as a controlling, disagreeable, pompous ass. I don't know what he was like on the other nights of his life, but that's how he was on his last."

For a second, I thought he was going to laugh. His eyes glittered and his mouth twitched a little. But he merely said, "I see. You didn't like him. That's interesting." Crap, now what had I done? I tried to undo the damage. "No, Detective Stewart, I didn't like him. But if you're insinuating that I killed a man because I didn't like him, may I just add that there are a lot of people I don't particularly like. My boss, for one. She thinks running her clothes to the dry cleaners is part of my job description. I'm also not particularly fond of the checkout clerk who routinely comments on my purchases. And don't get me started about my mother's boyfriend. But I think you'll find, Detective Stewart, that I didn't kill any of them."

Detective Stewart's eyebrows rose so high they were in danger of disappearing into his hairline. "Are you always this angry, Ms. Parker?"

I sighed. "No. I think I'm usually a very nice person. But it's been a stressful night."

"I can understand that," he said. "And I'm sorry to add to your apparently *considerable* stress level, but we do need to get as much information about what happened here tonight as we can. Let's try this again."

He read something in his notebook and said, "Why don't we skip over Mr. Ramsey for now, other than to note that he was not to your liking." I searched his face for any traces of irony but found none. "Who did he talk to?"

I closed my eyes, trying to remember. "When he first arrived, he was with his wife, daughter, and their friend, Daniel Simms," I replied. "But they weren't really talking to each other. Mr. Ramsey did all the talking." I vividly remember what happened next: Gerald had all but threatened Aunt Winnie that he would force her to sell him the inn. Gerald's words hadn't bothered Aunt Winnie in the least. She wasn't afraid of bullies and she wouldn't have lost a minute's sleep over his threat. But I knew Aunt Winnie and the police didn't. To an outsider, their exchange about the house could look incriminating. I had to make sure that Detective Stewart didn't get the wrong idea about Aunt Winnie.

"He commented on the changes that my aunt had made to the inn since she'd purchased it," I continued. "From what he said, I gathered that when this place went on the market, Mr. Ramsey was interested in buying it, but the owner took a liking to my aunt instead. Mr. Ramsey indicated that he was still interested in owning the place and was hoping to convince my aunt to sell it to him." I remembered what Aunt Winnie had said about Gerald's influence with the zoning board and I could still hear Gerald's "by fair means or foul" threat. "He was, in my opinion, somewhat rude about the whole thing, but my aunt just laughed it off." There. That should downplay the exchange on the off chance that any of the other guests had repeated Gerald's exact words.

Detective Stewart thumbed through his notebook, apparently in search of something. Finding it, he tapped his blunt forefinger against the page and said, "I have here that Mr. Ramsey was using his influence with the zoning board to put your aunt out of business and threatened your aunt regarding the inn."

Shit. I had little doubt who would have repeated that bit of information to the police and I silently cursed Jackie. "Threatened?" I said, with what I hoped was an authentic tone of disbelief. "Mr. Ramsey was, I suppose, confident in his skills as a persuader, but he clearly didn't know my aunt. She loves this place."

Even before he continued, I knew I had phrased that badly, but still, the starkness of his next words took me by surprise. "Enough to kill for it?"

"No!" I said, scrambling to undo the damage. "You've got it all wrong." My mouth went dry and my heart hammered in my chest. The police couldn't suspect Aunt Winnie. It was absurd! "My aunt is the sweetest woman I know! As a kid, she wouldn't even let me kill spiders in her house. Yes, she loves this inn, but she's not insane. And besides, she's not the kind of woman to let herself be pushed around by someone like Mr. Ramsey. She can take care of herself." I realized I was shouting and struggled to compose myself.

Detective Stewart said nothing but raised his left eyebrow again, a trick I found increasingly irritating. "So, by your account," he said slowly, "your aunt, who was being bullied by the deceased, could have had nothing to do with this, despite the fact that the murder took place in her home after she turned out the lights? In short—according to you—she is a harmless woman, incapable of violence."

"Yes," I said emphatically, even as some far-flung memory swam to the surface of my consciousness. Hadn't there been a terrible altercation between Aunt Winnie and a friend's husband long ago? As the details came back to me, I inwardly blanched. But surely the police here couldn't know about that, could they? And besides, that had been a completely different situation. In that case, Aunt Winnie's actions had been justified—almost noble, in fact. But to someone of limited imagination—I sized up Detective Stewart and sighed—it could look damning. I resolved to say nothing of the incident.

"Besides," I continued in a calmer voice, "how do you even know that Gerald was the intended victim? I mean, it was pitch-dark in the room. Any one of us could have been shot."

"We considered that possibility, Ms. Parker. However, there is no question that Mr. Ramsey was the intended victim. We found a piece of reflective tape, the kind that glows in the dark, on Mr. Ramsey's suit coat. That was probably the green flash you saw. It is our theory that the murderer put the tape on Mr. Ramsey to ensure that he, or *she,* wouldn't have any trouble hitting the target once the lights went out. Derringers generally hold only one or two shots. Our killer couldn't risk wasting bullets."

"Then you believe that one of the guests did this? There's a door to the outside in the dining room. Someone could have opened the door, shot Gerald, and then run off."

"Yes. Funny enough, but we actually came up with that possibility on our own, Ms. Parker. However, unless you are suggesting our murderer can fly, I don't think that theory works. While there are footprints in the snow just outside the door, there are no tracks leading away from the house. Furthermore, the footprints outside the door were not fresh. A significant amount of snow had fallen on top of them. So much so that it seems unlikely that an intruder made them at the time in question. Did you happen to see anyone go outside during the evening?" he asked.

"Yes, actually. Joan Anderson and Polly Ramsey went outside."

"Do you know about what time that might have been?"

I tried to remember. "Maybe around eight-thirty? I'm really not sure. I know I was still passing around the hors d'oeuvres. I had just refilled my tray in the kitchen and was returning to the dining room when they came back inside."

Detective Stewart noted something down before he continued. "Do you know what they were doing out there?"

"They said they were looking at the snow."

The eyebrow went up again. "Looking out the window wasn't sufficient?"

It was an interesting point. I had been too busy making my rounds at the time, but now that I thought about it, it was strange. I don't care how much of a kid you are at heart: adult women in evening gowns generally do not willingly go out in the middle of a snowstorm unless their car has broken down or they've partaken too much of the holiday spirit. As far as I could tell, neither Joan nor Polly had had too much to drink.

One of the many uniformed officers who had descended on the inn quietly walked into the room. Avoiding my eyes, he went straight to Detective Stewart, leaned in close, and whispered in his ear. Detective Stewart whispered back and they both glanced at me. I tried to radiate innocence and stared at the contents of the evidence box while they continued their conversation. In one sealed bag lay the gun. In another, lay the unisex, right-handed glove worn by the killer. Hearing a noise in the foyer, I saw the medical examiner putting on his coat to leave. Behind him, two officers rolled the gurney bearing the body of Gerald Ramsey out of the dining room and toward the door. The words from Aunt Winnie's invitation came back to me: "Many will come, but one won't be going home." I felt sick.

The officer finally left and Detective Stewart shifted his attention back to me. "Sorry about the interruption. Let's see, where were we?" He contemplated his notebook. "Oh, yes. How did Miss Ramsey act around her father?"

I thought of how Polly and I had stood talking after she had come back inside. When Gerald called her over like an errant dog, there was no mistaking the look of hate on her face. But I felt funny about telling the detective what I'd seen. I was sure that most people who encountered Gerald Ramsey had, at one point or another, made a similar face. It seemed unfair to cast Polly in a guilty light over what I considered an honest and justified emotion. But, I reminded myself, someone in that room tonight had shot Gerald. I knew it wasn't me and I knew it wasn't Aunt Winnie. My main goal was to convince the police of that. As for the others—well, I'd just have to tell what I knew and let the police sort out the rest.

Feeling like a parrot reciting my lines, I dutifully told Detective Stewart that I thought Polly resented her father's dictatorial nature and that while I thought Lauren was firmly under Gerald's control, she seemed unhappy. I did not, however, repeat Jackie's unfounded assertion that she suspected Lauren of having an affair with Daniel. I told myself that it was because I didn't want to spread vicious rumors, but I wouldn't have wanted to be hooked up to a lie detector when I made that statement. The simple fact was, right or wrong, I liked Daniel.

I had little information about Joan and Henry or Jackie and Linnet. I had even less about the acting troupe, unless augmentation was a crime. As for Peter, I could have told the detective stories that would have set his hair on end and no doubt resulted in Peter's immediate incarceration, but as they had nothing to do with the night's events, I restrained myself. However, Detective Stewart did seem oddly interested in the fact that Peter's parents were in the hotel business.

After an eternity of pregnant pauses, raised eyebrows, and seemingly random scribbling into his ever-present notebook, Detective Stewart stood up. "Well, thank you very much for your cooperation,

Ms. Parker. I think I have everything I need for tonight. You can go now. But if you think of anything, please call me." He pushed a small white card at me. I took it and stared at the name on it. "Your first name is Aloysius?" I blurted out impolitically.

He reddened a bit. "Yes."

I was about to ask if he'd really been named for Sebastian's bear in *Brideshead Revisited,* but the question died on my lips under his withering expression. It was clear that the subject was off-limits.

I stood up awkwardly, my legs stiff, while I struggled to comprehend that the burly, gruff man standing before me could have been named for an effeminate man's bear companion. As Alice had said when she fell through the rabbit hole, "Things are getting curiouser and curiouser."

As I turned to leave the room, I caught sight of myself in the heavy gilded mirror by the door. My eyes were bloodshot, my skin was blotchy, and my chignon had long ago come undone, leaving my hair hanging in a bedraggled mess around my face. The last time I had looked this bad at the end of an evening, I'd had a hell of a better time to show for it.

I was at the door when Detective Stewart spoke. "Oh, and one more thing, Ms. Parker."

I sighed. The man clearly had watched too many episodes of *Columbo* at an impressionable age. I wearily turned back.

His lips stretched and twisted into an unnatural position, and it took me a minute to realize that he was actually trying to smile. "I'd prefer it if you didn't leave town for the next couple of days."

I didn't bother asking why. I was pretty sure it wasn't because he wanted to ask me out to dinner.

CHAPTER 8

The average, healthy, well-adjusted adult gets up at seven-thirty in the morning feeling just plain terrible.

—JEAN KERR

IN MY DREAM, I was standing on the driveway outside the inn. In front of me, a large Mack truck was slowly and purposefully backing down on me. I tried to move out of its path, but I was frozen to the spot. The mechanical beeping of the truck grew louder and louder and I frantically screamed at the driver to stop. Finally, he stuck his head out the window. It was none other than Detective Stewart. Instead of stopping, he merely grinned at me and increased his speed. I awoke just as the truck touched me, then looked dazedly around my room and slammed my hand down on the beeping alarm clock.

My brain was fuzzy with sleep and it took me a minute or two to remember the previous night's events and the reason I had set my alarm for such an absurdly early hour. But then I recalled Gerald Ramsey's dead, staring eyes and everything came rushing back. Throwing on jeans and a sweatshirt, I hurried down to the kitchen. I had hoped to get a head start on the breakfast for Aunt Winnie, but she was already busily puttering about the kitchen when I arrived.

"What are you doing up so early?" she asked. "Coffee's over there if you want any." She gestured to the counter.

"I wanted to get the breakfast ready for you," I said, pouring myself a cup of the aromatic brew. Adding a generous splash of cream and two heaping spoonfuls of sugar, I took a restorative sip. Leaning against the counter, I focused on the soothing warmth of the kitchen. One would be hard-pressed to maintain a bleak outlook in this room; the brightly patterned red toile alone could banish the darkest of fears.

Aunt Winnie was stirring something in a large red pot. I glanced curiously around the kitchen. There were quite a few pans out and, now that I noticed it, several competing smells. I could identify at least one.

"Why are you making lasagna for breakfast?" I asked.

Aunt Winnie shot me a bemused look before replying patiently, "Drink your coffee, dear. We're having cranberry muffins for breakfast. I'm making the lasagna, a stew, and some other odds and ends to take to Lauren and Polly. They're in for a rough time of it. I doubt they'll be up for cooking much. I thought I'd take everything over later this morning."

"That's nice of you," I replied, stifling a yawn. Lady Catherine perched on one of the chairs at the table, eyeing me with an expression that could only be described as disdainful. I was about to shove her off the chair when I decided to try a different tack. Maybe it was because of the murder or the New Year, but I suddenly felt an urge to befriend Lady Catherine. I was a nice person. Why shouldn't she like me? I slowly stretched out my hand to her and clucked my tongue lightly. She did not move. I reached up and gently rubbed behind her left ear. She still did not move. A sense of accomplishment overcame me. All she really needed was some kindness and I had shown her that. I had won her over with my . . . with a sudden movement she dug her claws deep into my wrist. Letting out a howl of pain, I jumped back, spilling my coffee in the process. Lady Catherine shot me a smug glance of satisfaction and bounded away. As I grabbed a napkin to blot the blood, I remembered again why I hate cats.

I cleaned up my mess and poured myself another cup. After donning an apron—made of red toile, naturally—I helped Aunt Winnie prepare the food. I wondered if she was aware of Detective Stewart's suspicions. I didn't want to upset her, but at the same time I didn't think it fair to keep her in the dark. I surreptitiously studied her, trying to gauge how badly the murder had affected her. Other than a drastic wardrobe change, prompted no doubt by the previous night's tragedy—she was wearing an ultraconservative black cashmere sweater and gray flannel trousers—she looked pretty much as she always did. Her bright red curls were firmly in place, and her face showed no obvious ill effects from last night's ordeal. But a closer inspection revealed her to be quite pale underneath her blush, with worried eyes and . . .

"Elizabeth!" she barked suddenly. I jumped and spilled my coffee. Again.

"What?" I said, flustered. Grabbing a dish towel, I mopped my sweatshirt.

"Stop staring at me like that! It's incredibly unnerving and, frankly, my nerves have had just about all they can take!"

"I'm sorry, Aunt Winnie," I said ruefully. "I'm just worried about you. Last night was awful. I know this must be terribly stressful for you."

"Not as stressful as your staring," she muttered, adding, "I'm sorry, dear. I know you mean well. And I am fine. Really."

I made no reply. I tried to raise one eyebrow the way Detective Stewart did when he heard something that didn't ring quite true. From Aunt Winnie's perplexed expression, I had a feeling it wasn't a talent I possessed. But my continued silence prompted her to amend her previous statement.

Letting out a sigh, she added, "Well, I'm as fine as I can be after a man has been murdered in my house." She gripped the edge of the sink and her shoulders hunched. "The whole thing is too unbelievable! Although I suppose if you'd asked me to name the one guest most likely to be murdered, I would have picked Gerald. He wasn't very likable, as I'm sure you saw. But as odious as the man was, he didn't deserve to die in that manner."

The oven timer rang, and I walked over to turn it off. "So who do you think might have done it?" I asked, as I pulled the tray of twenty-four neat cranberry muffins out of the oven.

"I've been trying to puzzle that one out myself," she said, as she added tiny carrots and onions to the stew. "I think we can rule out the actors, unless it turns out that one of them is Gerald's illegitimate child who has secretly been planning to avenge his mother's ill treatment at Gerald's hands."

"Sounds like something out of a bad novel."

"Oh, I agree. It's quite fantastic. But I do think we can safely rule out the actors. Although when you really think about it, most of the people here last night were apparent strangers to Gerald. Joan and Henry live in New York and Jackie and Linnet just moved here. Logically, the murderer has to be someone who was close to Gerald. And, unfortunately, that means it's probably Lauren, Polly, or Daniel."

Daniel! I had forgotten about him. If the rumors about him and Lauren were true, he had an excellent motive for doing away with Gerald. He'd get the girl and the money. I realized Aunt Winnie was watching me carefully. "Are you okay?" she asked gently. "I know you like him."

I blushed. As I said, my mother always warned me to never play poker. "I'm fine." I resolutely popped the muffins out of the tray and onto a blue ceramic platter. "Although I must admit, it threw me when Detective Stewart asked me not to leave town." Attempting to make light of the situation, I added, "And as he didn't try to tempt me by promising a ride in the barouche box, I don't think it was a compliment."

Aunt Winnie only responded with a grim smile.

"My only concern," I continued, "is that the police find out the truth. But no matter who it turns out to be, it won't be pleasant."

"I agree," said Aunt Winnie. "And this must be cleared up as soon as possible. Gerald Ramsey was a disagreeable—maybe even horrible—man, but he did not deserve to be shot down like a dog. I'm not going to lie and say I'm going to miss the man. In fact, I suspect that several lives will be all the happier because of his passing. But the sooner his murderer is discovered, the sooner the rest of us can get on with our lives."

Realization dawned. "Is that why the sudden urge to cook for Lauren and Polly?" I asked. "Are you hoping to learn something from them when you drop off all this food?"

Aunt Winnie shrugged but did not deny the charge. "I do want to help them out. I'm not that coldhearted. I'm truly fond of them both. If they had nothing to do with this, then they must be in hell this morning. But if they did have something to do with it . . . well, let's just say I'm more than a little curious to see how they are coping. I don't think either of them had a particularly happy life with Gerald."

"Aunt Winnie! What are you saying? Do you honestly believe that by taking up all this food you're going to hear one of them slip and admit that she shot Gerald? That's crazy!"

"Don't be absurd! I'm not expecting a confession. I just want to see for myself how they're doing."

I had seen that dogged expression on her face before, and I knew that it was no use trying to convince her otherwise. "Fine," I said reluctantly, "but I'm going with you. I'm not letting you play detective by yourself. It's too dangerous. You could get hurt."

"Someone already did get hurt. And in my dining room!" she said, as if the killer owed her a separate apology for that. She took out her frustration on the stew, stirring it vigorously with her wooden spoon. "I only want to talk to them. It's probably a long shot, but I'll do anything that might speed up the investigation. Because, let's face it, we don't know if this murder is an isolated event or the work of a deranged killer. Everyone assumes that it must be solely directed at Gerald because he was so odious. But until they catch whoever did this, we just don't know."

Her words had a chilling effect. The same thoughts had been lurking in my head, but to hear them spoken out loud gave them a frightening reality.

"And besides," she added, trying to lighten the mood, "until the killer is found, people may drive by and gawk at Longbourn, but no one will want to stay here. I've worked too hard on this place to let it slip away now. I wasn't going to let Gerald Ramsey take Longbourn from me when he was alive. I'm sure as hell not going to lose it now that he's dead."

I was glad Detective Stewart wasn't here to see the combination of Aunt Winnie's words and the steely determination in her eyes. He might get terrible ideas.

Leaving Aunt Winnie to finish up in the kitchen, I headed for the reading room to set up the breakfast items. Even if the police hadn't sealed off the dining room, I doubted if anyone would want to eat breakfast, or any other meal, there anytime soon.

The room was as I had left it last night—the chairs and tables still set up for an interrogation. Maybe because of the stressful exchange I had had there with Detective Stewart, the whole ambience of the room seemed to have changed. It was no longer the cheerful retreat it had been two days ago. Instead it struck me as a cold and uneasy place. A chill seemed to permeate the room, although whether this was due to the temperature outside or the events of last night I didn't know. Nevertheless, I lit a fire in the fireplace. A few minutes later, pale orange and yellow flames leaped and crackled in the hearth. I quickly pushed the furniture back into its original position and set up the breakfast dishes. But as I surveyed the results of my work, I realized that it wasn't just the position of the chairs that had altered the mood of the room. It was as Aunt Winnie had said. A murder had taken place at Longbourn. And until the murderer was caught, it was going to change the way people felt about the inn.

Stepping out into the foyer, I saw that Lady Catherine had taken up her usual position on the green brocade chair, her blue eyes languidly surveying the room. In them, the pulsating lights from the Christmas tree were reflected. That effect, combined with her already peevish expression, made the ambience of the reading room seem downright cozy.

Lady Catherine heard the footfalls on the stairs before I did. Following her laserlike stare, I saw Peter coming down. He was wearing a blue button-down shirt and faded jeans. His thick brown hair was slightly damp where it curled around his neck. In short, he looked well rested and showered—two adjectives that most certainly did not describe me. Staring at me with some surprise, he asked, "What are you doing up so early?" He pointed to my feet and added, "No bunny slippers this morning?"

"I got up early to help Aunt Winnie with the breakfast," I replied curtly, putting extra emphasis on the word *help* and ignoring his second question altogether.

Peter coughed. "If you are insinuating that I am a lazy ingrate because I did not help with the breakfast, may I direct your attention to the driveway. The *freshly shoveled* driveway. Actually, a better description might be the *freshly shoveled, ridiculously long, heart-attack-inducing* driveway."

As directed, I looked out the window to see a freshly shoveled driveway. And now that I noticed it, it was ridiculously long. Feeling petty and foolish, I turned back to apologize but Peter held up his hand to stop me. "And may I just add," he continued, "that the reason I was surprised to see you up so early is that I know that you were up late with that detective. Aunt Winnie and I were hoping that you'd sleep in a bit. She mentioned that when you don't get enough sleep, you have a tendency to get . . . cranky." He paused to cock his eyebrow at me. "Seriously, though, how did your interview with the detective go?"

"Not very well," I mumbled, remembering my various outbursts.

"I had a feeling," Peter replied dryly. Turning to him for an explanation, he went on. "He was here this morning. He asked me a few questions about you. He said you were a spitfire." Peter paused and folded his arms across his chest. "I don't think he meant it as a compliment."

"I can assure you he didn't." I was embarrassed that my temper had once again gotten the better of me. "He asked me not to leave town."

"Well, don't let that get you down," said Peter. "He asked the same of me."

The rest of what Detective Stewart said came back to me as well, especially his suspicions about Aunt Winnie. "Peter," I said impulsively, "I think that the police suspect Aunt Winnie."

His dark brows knitted together in concern. "Really? Why?"

"Because of some things Detective Stewart said to me last night. Apparently, someone told him that Gerald still wanted to buy the inn and that he was harassing her through the zoning board. And now Detective Stewart has it in his head that Gerald actually threatened Aunt Winnie. It looks bad for her—after all, she was the one who turned off the lights. And what if they find out about that time with her friend's husband? If you didn't know the whole story . . ." I began.

". . . it could look pretty bad," Peter finished. He thought for a moment. "So you think the police suspect Aunt Winnie of killing Gerald just so she can keep the inn?"

"Something like that. Do you think I should tell her?"

Confusion registered in Peter's brown eyes. "I don't understand. Why wouldn't you tell her?"

Last night, I could have listed at least eight reasons why I shouldn't tell her the police's suspicions. In the light of day, after a cup of hot coffee, I couldn't think of a single one.

"You're right," I finally said. "I'll tell her. There's no reason not to."

"She's a smart woman, Elizabeth. I'm sure she can handle the likes of Detective Stewart."

"I know. I guess I wasn't thinking clearly." I smiled at him. "Thanks, Peter. I've got to run and take a shower. See you later."

"Right," said Peter. "I'll go see if Winnie needs any help."

As I walked up the staircase, I was sure that Peter was right. There was nothing to worry about. Aunt Winnie was a smart, strong woman. More important, I assured myself, she was innocent. I turned back to Peter. He was staring out into space, his shoulders hunched and his expression a mass of worry. My good feeling went right out the window.

CHAPTER 9

We're all in this alone.

—LILY TOMLIN

I WAS SURPRISED to see all the guests file dutifully into the reading room for breakfast, until I realized that no one wanted to be left alone in a bedroom. With a murderer on the loose, there was something to be said for that old adage about safety in numbers.

Joan and Henry sat woodenly together on the yellow couch. They neither spoke nor ate. Joan's eyes were red and swollen behind her glasses, and Henry's round face appeared to have aged ten years overnight. My good-morning greeting received only a muttered response and they both had trouble making eye contact with me.

As they had last night, the actors huddled together, clearly more comfortable with one another than anyone else. Standing as one body by the fireplace, they whispered among themselves and warily eyed the rest of us. I couldn't blame them, but it still made me feel rotten.

The only one entering the room who didn't seem affected was Daniel. He looked gorgeous. Wearing a blue wool sweater and faded jeans, he strode into the room and issued a general greeting that managed to convey a respectful acknowledgment of last night's tragedy as well as a sense of unity. Unlike my earlier greeting, which had been essentially ignored, his was appreciated by everyone. Joan even smiled at him.

After pouring himself a cup of coffee, Daniel crossed the room to where I was sitting on the window seat and squeezed in next to me. He was so close that I could smell his spicy aftershave.

"Hello," he said quietly. "How are you getting on?"

"You mean aside from seeing a man murdered, apparently by someone who is a guest here, and being informed by the police that I am not allowed to leave town?"

Daniel smiled. "Right, aside from all that."

"Oh, well, other than *that,*" I said with mock cheerfulness, "I'm doing just super, thanks. And yourself?"

He matched my tone. "Never better. Never better. In fact," his whisper was conspiratorial, "I'm having such a brilliant time that I've decided to extend my visit by a few days."

"Detective Stewart asked you to stay on, too, I take it."

"In a word, yes. Apparently, the police have taken it into their heads that Lauren and I are more than friends."

"Really?"

"I see from your expression that you already heard that," he continued matter-of-factly. "And I have little doubt where that tidbit of misinformation came from." He took a sip of coffee. When he spoke again, the teasing tone was gone. Anger now laced his words. "Miss Tanner would do well to take care. One day she may find herself on the receiving end of a slander suit—or worse."

I agreed with him. Jackie wasn't going to make many friends in town if she merrily continued to spread gossip about everyone. She'd managed to get Aunt Winnie unwanted scrutiny by the police and now she'd done the same for Daniel. I could well understand the anger behind his words.

Daniel stared at the snapping fire for several moments. Finally, he shifted his attention back to me, a suggestive smile on his lips.

"So, you are staying on as well," he said. He glanced out the window at the trees bent and bowed under the weight of the snow. "Terrible snowstorm last night," he continued, picking up the teasing tone again. "Better to stay in and keep warm." His blue eyes locked on mine. "Any ideas on how we can stay warm? Indoors?"

"Roast marshmallows?" I was trying to appear calm and composed. I knew that his sexual banter wasn't serious—the man flirted as naturally as he breathed—but I could feel my face flush and I knew that my cheeks must be bright red. My upper lip began to twitch, another of my attractive manifestations of nervousness.

Daniel shook his head. "Gave up sweets for the New Year. Any other ideas?"

I knew that one of two things was going to happen. I was either going to fling myself into his arms, yelling something idiotic like, "Shag me!" or I was going to have a hideous breakout of nerve-induced hives. Either way, I was seconds away from making a complete ass of myself.

For once the Fates smiled upon me and I was saved. Aunt Winnie entered the room and said loudly, "Everyone, if I could have your attention, please. Detective Stewart is here and he's asked to speak with all of us for a moment."

Detective Stewart appeared in the doorway. He'd been up as late as I had, if not later. Yet there was no sign of exhaustion on his face. I took this as yet another sign that the man was inhuman. He threw his head back and straightened his shoulders. His hands were shoved deep into his thick overcoat's pockets. His entire stance was suggestive of a man ready for a battle. The tension level in the room instantly jumped several notches.

"Good morning," he said in his raspy voice. Either the man smoked three packs of cigarettes a day or he had affected the voice for purposes of intimidation. There was simply no way that the terrible sounds emitting from his throat could have been God-given. He deliberately surveyed the room, pausing when he got to me. Almost imperceptibly, he inclined his head and nodded before turning back to the others.

Henry unfolded his bulky frame from the couch and stood up. Raking a hand through his hair, he said in a voice shaking with indignation, "Look here. I want to know why my wife and I have to stay here. We've nothing to do with this . . . this . . . sordid business. Neither of us even knows anybody in this town. I have to leave. I have a very important meeting tomorrow with . . ."

"Mrs. Kristell Dubois," Daniel and I both muttered under our breath.

". . . Mrs. Kristell Dubois," Henry intoned gravely. "If you do not know that good lady, let me tell you that she will be seriously displeased if I am not able to meet with her. She is an exceedingly busy woman and—"

Detective Stewart raised one of his large hands and like a puppet Henry fell silent. Jamming his hands into the pockets of his charcoal-gray slacks, Henry stared sullenly at the ground and jangled his coins. Detective Stewart's face stretched to accommodate a thin smile. "I know that you all want to leave," he said. "However, in the interests of the case, I have to ask that you be patient. Those of you who are from out of town will have to stay on here a few more days. But those of you who are local"—he nodded to the acting troupe—"can return to their homes, with the understanding that you are not to leave town." A gasp of relief escaped from the actors, followed by a frustrated one from the rest of us.

Next to me, Daniel stood up, upsetting his coffee in the process. "I say!" he said, his handsome face pulled into a scowl. "That is simply not fair. Why do I have to remain here?" Buoyed by Daniel's outburst, Henry joined him in angry protest. I remained silent. Even if Detective Stewart had told me that I could go, I wouldn't have. Not now. I was going to stay with Aunt Winnie until the murderer was caught and I knew she was safe. Henry and Daniel badgered Detective Stewart about their rights, previous commitments, and whatever else they could throw at him. Their pleas had no effect on him; in fact, if anything, they seemed only to gratify him. What had begun as a thin smile of amusement now bordered on a full-out grin.

While they continued to argue back and forth, I studied the actors. They were watching the proceedings with all the intensity of spectators at a Wimbledon finals. Across the room, Peter sat quietly, frowning at his cup of coffee. He had not argued with Detective Stewart's decree either, and I suspected that he felt as I did. He would not leave until Aunt Winnie was out of danger.

Detective Stewart raised his voice. "Enough! You can file a complaint if you like, but right now I am in charge of this case, and my decision stands. I can make this easy or hard. It's entirely up to you."

Both Henry and Daniel fell silent. Detective Stewart contemplated them with undisguised scorn. The actors took advantage of the lull to make their escape, no doubt afraid Detective Stewart might change his mind. They rose as one body and sidled out the door, like some weird human crab.

Detective Stewart and Aunt Winnie followed them out into the foyer. Detective Stewart told the actors that he would be in touch with them. He ensured that he had accurate phone numbers and addresses, while Aunt Winnie apologized for the inconvenience. The rest of us sat silently, lost in our own thoughts. To be honest, I had never really suspected any of the actors of the murder. But, with their exit, the range of possible suspects had been obviously and drastically narrowed. It made for a very uncomfortable atmosphere.

Perhaps because of this, Joan and Henry abruptly left the room. Daniel forgot his flirtation with me and departed as well. Only Peter and I remained.

"Well, at least they'll have a nice, freshly shoveled driveway to peel out of when they leave."

Peter's head jerked up at the sound of my voice, but he didn't respond. I don't think he'd heard me at all. He stood up, placed his coffee cup on the low table in front of him, and walked out of the room.

I felt like the girl in the commercial who is unwittingly driving everyone away with her terrible breath. I surveyed the empty room, littered with breakfast dishes and coffee cups. "That's okay," I yelled at Peter's retreating form. "I'll get all this."

My sarcasm was met with silence.

When I got back to my room, my cell phone was ringing. It was Bridget.

"Elizabeth!" she yelled happily when I answered and I knew why she was calling. Colin had proposed. I didn't want to burst her bubble by beating her to her own announcement, or worse, telling her what had happened here.

"Hey, Bridge," I said, keeping my voice neutral. "Happy New Year. What's up?"

There was a split second of silence before she said, "You know, don't you? Damn it!" I heard her pull the phone away and yell, "Colin, you told Elizabeth, didn't you?" I heard Colin's muffled response and she came back on the line. "Oh, well, no matter. Isn't it fantastic? I'm so excited! I wish everyone could be this happy!"

I smiled. I was glad that at least someone had had a nice New Year. "I'm really happy for you, Bridge," I said. "How did he do it?" I cradled the phone to my ear and closed my eyes. Her voice was the closest thing I'd had to normalcy since arriving here.

"Over dinner," she replied. "He pushed this little black velvet box onto the table. As soon as I saw it, I started crying. I was just about to scream, 'Yes, I will marry you!' when I had an awful thought—what if the box had a pair of earrings in it and not a ring? But thankfully it was a ring. Oh, Elizabeth! I can't wait to show you. It's absolutely gorgeous!"

She was right. It *was* a gorgeous ring. I had helped Colin pick it out two months ago, and trying to keep that secret had nearly killed me.

"You'll be my maid of honor, right?"

"Of course I will! Just promise me that you won't make me wear some god-awful dress with a bow on the butt."

"Don't be absurd. You know me. I want to keep this very casual. What do you think about us getting married on a beach somewhere?"

"I think your mother would slit her wrists," I said honestly. Bridget's free-spirited ways were a constant source of frustration to her mother. Mrs. Matthews was aghast at Bridget's spiky hair, which veered from bright red to magenta or purple—a bit like Aunt Winnie's. And Bridget's clothes had a tendency to render the normally loquacious Mrs. Matthews mute. A wedding on the beach would no doubt push her over the edge.

"You're probably right." Bridget sighed. "But I'll be damned if

I'm going to wear some ridiculous dress that makes me look like a giant meringue."

I heard Colin's voice in the background and Bridget yelled, "That's not funny, Colin!"

She got back on the line. "So, how are you? How was your New Year's?"

My stomach sank. Caught up in Bridget's excitement, I had almost forgotten about Gerald. Almost.

"Well, it was a bit more exciting than anyone had planned for," I said, attempting to downplay the seriousness of the situation. It might have been more believable had my voice not caught.

"Elizabeth? What's happened? Isn't the inn doing well? Is Aunt Winnie okay? Are you okay?"

"She's fine. I'm fine," I said, focusing on not crying. "It's just, well, well, a man was actually murdered during the dinner show."

"Holy shit!"

"Yeah, that about sums it up."

"Are you kidding me?"

"Afraid not." I took a deep breath. This was ridiculous. I had to pull myself together. There was no reason for me to fall apart over Gerald Ramsey's death. After all, it wasn't as if he was someone I knew, or even wanted to know, for that matter. I refused to listen to the more emotional side of my brain, which told me that Gerald's odious personality wasn't the problem. It was the memory of his blank stare. I quickly told Bridget the rest, from the cliché-like shot in the dark to Detective Stewart and his intimidating eyebrow.

"What a nightmare!" Bridget said when I was done. "How's Aunt Winnie?"

In the background I could hear Colin peppering Bridget with

questions. "Colin," she barked at him, "would you please shut up for half a minute! I can't hear Elizabeth with you yelling at me! I'll tell you in a second!"

"She's as good as can be expected," I said. "Actually, I think she's doing better than the rest of us."

"Well, that's good. I'd be more worried if she were a mess. When are you coming home?"

"I'm not sure. The police have asked me to stay for a few more days until this is all cleared up."

"But why? I don't understand. Why do you have to stay? They can't possibly think that you had anything to do with this!"

"I don't know what they think," I said wearily.

The sounds of a struggle floated over the phone line. Bridget yelled out angrily, "Colin, knock it off! Hey! What the hell are you doing? Give me back the phone!" The next voice I heard was Colin's.

"Elizabeth!" he said abruptly. "What's going on? Are you okay?"

At the sound of the concern in his voice, my eyes welled up, but I held the tears in check. "I'm fine, Colin, really. One of the guests died last night—well, he was murdered, and the police are still trying to figure out what happened."

"Jesus," he said. "Do you want us to come up? We could be there in a couple of hours." I heard Bridget yell something.

"No! Please, Colin, don't do that. I'm fine, really." I added quickly, "I'm sure that I'll be home in a day or so. Besides, I think the fewer people trampling around here, the better it will be for the investigation and for Aunt Winnie."

He hesitated. "Okay, if you're certain. But make sure you keep us posted."

"I will," I said. "I promise. Now go enjoy being engaged. Give Bridget a big hug for me. Don't worry, Colin. I'll see you soon. I'm perfectly fine."

He hung up and I congratulated myself. Apparently, I was finally getting better at hiding the truth from people.

CHAPTER 10

That would be a good thing for them to cut on my tombstone:
Wherever she went, including here, it was
against her better judgment.

—DOROTHY PARKER

ALTHOUGH SHE WASN'T expected to provide lunch, it being a B and B, not a B and B and L, Aunt Winnie nevertheless put out a tureen of clam chowder and some chicken sandwiches for the guests. It was a bit like leaving cookies out for Santa. You never saw anything eaten, but soon there was only an empty tray with a few crumbs. Not that I was complaining. I wasn't keen on sitting in a room and watching other people not make eye contact with me.

My conversation with Bridget and Colin reminded me that I had other phone calls to make. I would have to call my mother, sister, and boss to let them know what had happened. Unfortunately, my mother wasn't home and I ended up speaking with George. He oozed concern for my safety—a sentiment that would have been more believable had he bothered to turn down the football game blaring in the background. My phone call to Kit was no more enjoyable. For five minutes she screamed incoherently about how this news affected her stress, which apparently had reached its zenith over the weekend. I didn't bother to point out that had her stress indeed reached its zenith (her words), then my news could not have possibly added to it. She then proclaimed that had I joined her for New Year's Eve "none of this would have happened" and asked if I had "even the slightest idea" of what this was doing to her blood pressure. It was on the tip of my tongue to ask how my presence at a hot tub party could have prevented a murder, but I restrained myself. As for her query about her stress and blood pressure, I refrained from calling them my old friends, having heard them mentioned with consideration for twenty years at least. She wouldn't have caught the reference anyway and I saw no reason to waste a perfectly good line.

The only call I enjoyed was the one to my boss, Cheryl. As I had anticipated, she ranted and raved once she understood that I would be out of the office for the next several days. She demanded to know who was in charge of the case and I happily obliged her by giving her Detective Stewart's direct line. I hoped she would call him; they deserved each other.

By midafternoon, Aunt Winnie and I had packed the food for Lauren and Polly and were on our way to their house, with the car radio blasting. When Aunt Winnie is stressed she likes to listen to country music. She says the songs are so depressing that they make her feel better in comparison. So as we drove along in her light blue '68 Mercedes, I stared out the window, trying to ignore both the blaring music and her horrible attempts to sing along. Finally, it was too much for me and I reached over and turned the volume down. "What are you doing?" she asked.

"Do you know what happens when you play country music backward?" I replied conversationally. Without waiting for her to answer, I continued. "You get your job back, your wife comes home, your dog comes back to life, you sober up . . ."

"You know, some people consider country music an art form," she countered.

"Some people feel the same way about body piercing."

"Are you saying you prefer body piercing to country music?"

I pretended to consider the question. "Would you be singing the country music?"

She laughed. "Oh, never mind. We're here." Before us was a massive colonial situated a couple of hundred yards from the beach. Dusk was starting to settle by the time we pulled into the driveway, and the trees out front blazed with thousands upon thousands of tiny white lights. It was beautiful, to be sure, but in all honesty, I preferred the simple charm of Longbourn.

A somber-looking woman of indeterminate age answered the door. She briskly introduced herself as Mrs. Jenkins. She had an intelligent face, fine brown hair pulled back into a tidy bun, and neat, serviceable clothes. This, combined with her aura of cool efficiency, made her subsequent announcement that she was the Ramseys' housekeeper superfluous. In fact, so perfectly did she fit that part I wondered briefly if she was from central casting. I didn't think people like Mrs. Jenkins existed outside of Agatha Christie novels.

Explaining that Lauren was on the phone, Mrs. Jenkins graciously took our wicker baskets of food and led us to wait in the sitting room. I was curious to see what an actual sitting room looked like, having only read about them in books that boasted characters like Mrs. Jenkins. Sadly, the room held only standard doors, not the French-window variety that Agatha Christie's characters were forever popping in and out of. I felt cheated.

The room was a curious blend of both Gerald's and Lauren's personalities. The formal atmosphere, with its brocade fabrics in red and cream and Queen Anne furniture, was clearly Gerald's choosing. The collection of ceramic pug dogs with giant faux-sapphire eyes, however, was just as obviously Lauren's contribution.

The rest of my inventory was cut short by the discovery that Aunt Winnie and I were not alone. At the far end of the room stood Daniel and Polly, their heads bent close together. Upon seeing us, they pulled apart with startled expressions. Daniel recovered first and crossed the room to Aunt Winnie and me.

"We're sorry to interrupt," began Aunt Winnie. "We were just bringing some food over for Lauren and Polly."

"That's very kind of you," said Daniel. "But please, don't apologize. It's always a pleasure to see you, Ms. Reynolds, and of course you, too, Elizabeth."

The wink that accompanied this aside to me happened so fast I wondered if I had imagined it. By now Polly had joined us. Her hair was pulled back with her signature tortoiseshell headband and she wore another shapeless dress, this one of dark blue corduroy. She looked terrible. Her face was pale and drawn, and there were dark circles under her eyes. "Lauren is on the phone," she said, "but I'm sure she'll be off any minute. I know she'll want to thank you."

"How is she doing?" I asked.

Polly shrugged and glanced at Daniel before answering. "She's doing all right, I guess," she said, "as well as can be expected. With Lauren you never really know."

Daniel opened his mouth as if he was about to say something, but Aunt Winnie spoke first.

"And how about you, dear?" she asked kindly. "How are you doing?"

Polly's lower lip twitched and she took a steadying breath before answering. Daniel watched her intently.

"I'm okay," she said, giving us a humorless smile. "I'm not going to pretend that my father and I got along particularly well, or that I was overly fond of him. But . . . he was my father."

I wasn't sure what to make of Polly's answer. Granted, I had found Gerald Ramsey to be a singularly disagreeable man, but he wasn't my father. It was another thing altogether for his own daughter to react this coolly to his death. But then again, she was his daughter. Maybe she was more like him than anyone realized. That said, the line "sharper than a serpent's tooth" still sprang to mind.

Aunt Winnie tilted her head to one side and said quietly, "I think that with all things considered, you're holding up just fine, dear."

Something unspoken passed between them and Polly's eyes welled with unshed tears. The door suddenly swung open, breaking the mood. Mrs. Jenkins entered. Beyond her right shoulder was a bright red hat covered in tiny white flowers that bobbed furiously up and down. Mrs. Jenkins's announcement was unnecessary. Miss Jackie Tanner had arrived.

She instantly swooped down on Polly. "Oh, you poor, poor child!" she gushed as she enveloped Polly in a tight hug. Polly's startled face hovered above the mass of white flowers before she deftly removed herself from Jackie's grip. Jackie appeared not to notice the maneuver.

"What an awful thing for you to go through," Jackie said in a tone that belied her words. Having a close relative murdered not ten feet from her was probably Jackie's idea of high drama. "If there is anything I can do to help," she continued, "just let me know. And don't you worry. I know that the police will find out who did this terrible, terrible thing. Tell me, dear, have they given you any idea as to which one of us they think killed your father?"

Jackie's words hit like a bucket of cold water. There was a startled pause, a lot of rapid blinking, and, for some reason, slightly better posture. Only Jackie seemed unaffected. She gazed expectantly at Polly, calmly waiting for a response.

Polly gaped at Jackie before glancing at the rest of us for help. None came, and I realized that while we all might abhor Jackie's tactics, we nevertheless were eager to hear what they produced.

However, if Polly knew anything, she wasn't telling. She merely shook her head and said, "I don't know any more than you do. Detective Stewart has asked Lauren and me to stay in town for a few more days, but other than that, he hasn't told me anything."

"I heard that there's no chance it was a mistake," said Jackie.

"What do you mean?" asked Daniel, his voice hard-edged.

Jackie turned to him, her eyes big with excitement. "Well, from what I understand, the police found reflective tape on Gerald. They think the killer must have put it on him sometime during the evening, to be sure the bullet found its mark."

Polly let out a little gasp. This had gone too far for me. "Ms. Tanner!" I said firmly. At the same moment Aunt Winnie snapped, "Jackie! Really!"

I continued, "I don't think this is an appropriate conversation to be having right now."

Jackie's brow furrowed underneath the shadowy brim of her hat. "Why?" she asked, with the simplicity of a small child.

My mind went blank. She was too unbelievable for words. I tried without success to explain why I thought a conversation in front of Polly about the details of her father's murder was in bad taste. Thankfully, my incoherent sputtering was interrupted by the arrival of Lauren.

She looked amazing. She floated rather than walked into the room. Her long blond hair hung in a simple ponytail, giving her a youthful and somehow innocent appearance. Her skin glowed and her eyes appeared almost luminous. My first thought was that death became her—the death of her husband, that is. I snuck a peek at Daniel to gauge his reaction. His blue eyes watched her with what seemed a mix of open admiration and bemusement.

She glided toward our little group. She was holding a dog in her arms, clearly the inspiration for the ceramic collection. The dog eyed us with such an expression of enthusiastic desire that I found myself almost missing Lady Catherine's icy disdain.

"I am so sorry to keep you waiting," Lauren said. "Mrs. Jenkins tells me that you brought us some food," she continued, addressing Aunt Winnie. "Thank you. That was very thoughtful of you."

"It's the least we can do," Aunt Winnie replied.

Lauren smiled again but said nothing. Her message was clear. Thank you for the food, now please leave. I didn't fault her. Only a ghoul would expect a wife to entertain guests mere hours after her husband had been murdered.

"What a lovely room you have here," said Jackie, settling herself comfortably into one of the chairs. "You have such nice things," she wistfully continued, delicately touching one of the hideous ceramic pugs.

Even Daniel's composure was shaken at this audacious display. For the first time since I'd met him, he was speechless. It was Polly who spoke. "Thank you, Miss Tanner. Why don't I have Mrs. Jenkins bring in some tea?"

"That's very kind of you, Polly," said Aunt Winnie, "but Elizabeth and I should go—"

"Oh, please stay," Polly implored Aunt Winnie and me. "I insist." I don't think she wanted to deal with Jackie alone. I can't say that I blamed her.

"Well, just for a little while," replied Aunt Winnie. We both sat down.

"Thank you," said Polly, with a grateful expression. "I'll go and tell Mrs. Jenkins. I'll only be a minute."

From Lauren's arms, the dog now gave an impatient bark. "Does my sweetums want down?" she crooned, lowering the dog to the floor. "Now play nice with our guests, Denny." She smiled at us and added apologetically, "He gets a bit wound up with strangers."

Super. I was stuck in a room with a hyper dog by the name of Denny, no less. More and more I felt as if this whole weekend was a terrible joke in awful taste and someone from *Candid Camera* was minutes away from popping out and admitting to the prank. But no one emerged from a hidden doorway to call an end to the gag. Instead, it got worse. Mere seconds after leaving Lauren's arms, Denny hurled his body at my leg. With a low grunt of satisfaction, he wrapped one fat paw around my calf and then the other. Seconds later, he latched on and was furiously humping away, his pink tongue lolling out the side of his mouth and his eyes rolling back into his furry little head. Before I was the recipient of some premature pugalation, I jerked my leg, sending him flying flat on his back. Apparently Denny liked the rough stuff, because seconds later we were eye to eye, literally. He planted himself on my lap, his squashed face not two inches from mine, panting heavily. He appeared in no hurry to move.

"What a sweet little doggie," Jackie said.

Daniel was overcome with a violent coughing fit that I was sure was designed to mask uncontrollable laughter. I glared at him from over the top of Denny's furry head.

"I hope you don't mind, Elizabeth," said Lauren. Mind? Mind what? That the family dog was trying to molest me?

"Not at all," I mumbled. "It's just that I usually get dinner and a movie first." Daniel's coughing grew louder.

"Denny hasn't been himself today," Lauren continued. "I think he senses the stress. There's so much to arrange. I've been on the phone all morning. But at least I was able to get through to Jamie."

"Jamie?" repeated Jackie, instantly on the alert for new information. "Who's that?"

Clearly regretting her words, Lauren's answer came a half beat slow. "Jamie is my son," she said. She eyed Jackie distastefully, no doubt anticipating that this information would be all over town by nightfall.

"Why, I didn't know you and Gerald had a son," exclaimed Jackie. Polly had returned in time to hear Jackie's words. She looked aghast.

"We don't," replied Lauren testily. "Jamie is my son from my previous marriage."

"Oh, I see," said Jackie. "How old is he?"

"He's fourteen," Lauren said briskly. She smoothed nonexistent wrinkles on her sleeve.

"Such a wonderful age," Jackie said, oblivious to the fact that Lauren seemed not to share her enthusiasm for the conversation. "Does he live with his father, then?"

"No."

"Really?" The little white flowers quivered like radar picking up a signal.

Lauren made no further comment, and Daniel said curtly, "Jamie has special needs. He lives in South Carolina."

Jackie's mouth made a silent O, but thankfully she said no more. If she was aware of Lauren's animosity, she was doing an excellent job of hiding it. Mrs. Jenkins entered with the tea tray and the rest of us busied ourselves with pouring and trying to make small talk.

"Miserable day out," said Daniel.

"Yes," said Aunt Winnie. "They're calling for more snow, I believe."

"Yes, I heard that, too," I said to Denny's nose. I debated shoving him off me but decided I'd rather have him sitting on my lap than molesting my leg.

"Downtown was a complete mess," said Polly, as she picked up the silver teapot. "The streets are treacherous. I'm supposed to visit Harriet up in Brighton later this week, but unless the roads improve, I'll have to cancel."

"You went downtown?" asked Lauren. "I didn't know that. When?"

Polly concentrated on filling Jackie's cup before answering. "I thought I told you. I was sure that I did. I went this morning. I needed cigarettes." She handed Jackie her cup.

"Speaking of which," said Daniel, "I'm out. Can I pinch one from you?"

"Oh," said Polly, "that's right. I forgot. I should have picked some up for you."

"Could you two please not smoke in here?" said Lauren, with a sigh. "You know it triggers my migraines."

Jackie abruptly set down her teacup, spilling the contents in the process. "Oh, dear," she said as she tried to mop it up with her napkin, "what a klutz I am. I'm always making a mess of things. Only this morning, I broke one of Linnet's china figurines. I don't know how she puts up with me. I really am sorry, Lauren. I hope I haven't ruined your lovely chair." Jackie's face was pinched and worried underneath her hat.

"It's fine," said Lauren stiffly. "Please, don't worry about it."

But the incident seemed to prey on Jackie's mind and she was silent for the rest of the visit. As I watched her over the top of Denny's immovable head, I felt a surge of sympathy for her. After all, she was a lonely old woman whose only excitement seemed gleaned from the lives of others. Still, I was grateful for her silence. For, in the words of Jane Austen, I was quite sure that it would pass. And, no doubt, more quickly than it should.

When the tea was finished, Aunt Winnie and I made our excuses to leave. They were readily accepted. Even Jackie was ready to go. After extricating myself from Denny, I went out into the foyer to see about our coats.

On the hall table lay a stack of mail. On the top was a large envelope from the State Department. It was addressed to Polly. I laid my hand on it, my fingers feeling the definite outline of a passport. It would seem that Polly was going to Oxford after all. The question was, did she make that decision despite Gerald's protestations or because she knew they wouldn't be an issue?

I had just stepped back from the table when Daniel appeared behind me. "It was good of you to come, Elizabeth," he said into my ear.

"Well, we wanted to see if there was anything we could do."

"I see." He turned me to face him. With an impish smile, he took my hands in his. I willed them to neither sweat nor tremble. "And have you done everything you can do?" His face was so close to mine that I could see the faint laugh lines intertwined around his blue eyes.

I knew I was blushing, but I refused to let him turn me into a blithering idiot. "Daniel," I said, "it's been a long couple of days. I'm really tired and I'm not up for innuendos right now."

"I couldn't agree more," he said. "I've wanted to do this from the first moment I saw you. New Year's resolutions and all that." He bent down and kissed me.

He had just stepped back when Mrs. Jenkins appeared with our coats. Or maybe she appeared once he stepped back. I didn't know and I didn't care. I took my coat without interest. I was already quite warm.

Lauren, Polly, Jackie, and Aunt Winnie joined us in the foyer. We all said goodbye and walked outside. Jackie was still very quiet.

"Are you all right, Jackie?" asked Aunt Winnie, pulling her coat tightly around her.

"What?" Jackie answered distractedly. "Oh, yes. Yes, I'm fine. I just have a sudden headache, that's all. Something doesn't make sense. I need to sort it all out. I know the answer is there, I just can't puzzle it out."

Aunt Winnie and I waited politely for an cxplanation, but none was forthcoming. Instead, Jackie smiled at us and merely said, "Good afternoon, ladies. I will see you soon."

Jackie's car was a burgundy '93 Oldsmobile Cutlass. Slapped over a dent on the back fender was a bumper sticker that read I BRAKE FOR PEOPLE. Once inside, Jackie gave us a little wave and slammed the door shut.

And with that, she left.

CHAPTER 11

General notions are generally wrong.

—LADY MARY WORTLEY MONTAGU

"WELL, THAT WAS . . . interesting," I said to Aunt Winnie once we were inside her car.

"Which part?" she replied as she gunned the engine and sped down the driveway. I gripped the door handle. Aunt Winnie likes to drive fast. She says it makes her feel young again. Unfortunately, it has the opposite effect on me. Death never feels so close.

"All of it," I said. "Remind me not to pay house calls with you anymore."

"Oh, come on! I thought you and Denny made a charming couple."

"You're not nearly as funny as you think you are," I said. The car careened out onto the main road. "Did I miss something?" I asked, craning my neck over my shoulder to peer behind us. "Is someone chasing us?"

Aunt Winnie laughed. "Don't be such a worrywart! You need to live a little."

"That's what I'm trying to do," I muttered, closing my eyes tightly as she sped up for the yellow light.

Health experts recommend elevating your pulse rate to achieve cardio fitness. By the time we skidded to a stop in the inn's driveway, mine was so elevated I was sure I didn't have to bother with any additional exercise for the day. Maybe even for the entire week.

My legs were shaky from continually slamming on an imaginary brake and I walked unsteadily to the front door. Stumbling into the foyer, I met Peter emerging from the back office.

"Hello," he said. "How was your visit?"

"Elizabeth made a new friend," said Aunt Winnie. "His name is Denny."

"You know," I said pleasantly, "I'm not above striking defenseless old women."

"Really?" Aunt Winnie countered with a wink. "Let me know if you find one."

Peter, who had been listening to us with an increasingly puzzled expression, now interrupted. "Right," he said. "Can I interest either of you in a cocktail? The Andersons have gone into town for dinner and Daniel is dining with Mrs. Ramsey. We are, for the first time this weekend, alone. I vote we put our heads together and see what we can come up with about Gerald's murder. The sooner the murderer is found, the better for all of us."

"Agreed," said Aunt Winnie. "Would you mind, though, if I invite Randy? I haven't had much chance to see him lately, and I trust him."

"Not at all," said Peter. "I'll get started on the drinks."

"Thanks. I'll just be a moment," said Aunt Winnie, as she went into the office. "Oh, Peter, make mine a gin and tonic. Strong."

"And for you?" Peter said to me.

"The same, please. I'll go see if I can rummage up some cheese and crackers."

In the kitchen I cut up cheese and salami. Placing them on a tray, I added some crackers and a small bowl of olives. I was returning with the tray when Aunt Winnie came out of the office. "Randy is on his way," she said. "I invited him to stay for dinner, too."

"You really like him, don't you?" I said.

"I think that I do. He's a very nice man." With a smile, she quoted, " 'He is also handsome, which a man ought likewise to be, if he possibly can.' "

I laughed and quoted back, " 'Well, I give you leave to like him. You have liked many a stupider person.' "

In the reading room, I settled into my chair, taking in the calming atmosphere of the room. For the first time today, I felt relaxed—almost at home. I smiled, thinking how my attachment to Longbourn seemed to increase daily. I thought about my apartment back in Virginia with its temperamental heating/cooling system and utter absence of architectural style. Now that Bridget was engaged, I would have to start thinking about getting a new roommate next year. Idly, I wondered about moving to the Cape instead. Maybe I could find a job here and help Aunt Winnie with the inn.

Peter entered with the drinks and I took mine gratefully. After everyone had settled into their chairs, Peter asked, "So, did you learn anything interesting at the Ramseys'? I'm assuming that's why the two of you went there. Although I admit that showing up laden with baskets of homemade food was a nice touch."

"Don't look at me," I said, raising my hands. "I was just following orders."

Aunt Winnie gave Peter a level look over the rim of her crystal glass. "Aren't you a little young to be so cynical?"

"I'm not cynical. I just know you. You're not going to deny it, are you?"

"Of course not. But I'm still reserving the right to call you cynical."

"Duly noted," Peter said with a wave of his hand. "Did you learn anything?"

"Well, no one was suddenly overcome with remorse and confessed, if that's what you mean," I said. Outside the sun had long ago set and long shadows now spread into the room. I got up and started a fire in the fireplace.

"Don't be such a smart-ass," said Aunt Winnie. "We learned about Jamie."

"Who's Jamie?" Peter asked, as he helped himself to a cracker and a piece of cheese from the tray.

"He's Lauren's son from a previous marriage," said Aunt Winnie. "Apparently, he has special needs and lives in some sort of home in South Carolina."

"What does that prove?" asked Peter.

"It doesn't necessarily prove anything," she said. "I just think it's interesting, that's all. Don't you think it's strange that the boy isn't living with his mother? Even if he needs to be in some sort of supervised community, you'd think she'd live closer."

"You think that Gerald didn't want anything to do with Jamie and had him shipped away?" I gave the burning logs a thoughtful shove with the poker.

"Would you really be surprised if that were the case?"

"Oh, I'm not arguing with you," I said. "It sounds exactly like something Gerald would do. But then again, Lauren doesn't strike me as the most maternal of women. She may have preferred having her son live far away."

Aunt Winnie nodded.

"Oh! I almost forgot. Polly got a passport!" I said, quickly explaining my find.

"Why didn't you tell me?" asked Aunt Winnie.

"Your driving must have scared the memory out of me," I replied, although I knew that wasn't the reason. Daniel's kiss was the reason. I hoped I wasn't blushing.

The doorbell chimed. "That's Randy," said Aunt Winnie, jumping up.

"And who's Denny?" Peter called after her.

Aunt Winnie let out a snort of laughter as she went to answer the door, leaving me to explain my attractiveness to a spoiled pug.

"Don't be too hard on the dog," Peter said, laughing when I had finished. "Maybe he's just cuckoo for Cocoa—"

I swung the poker menacingly at him. "If you finish that sentence, you will regret it! Why your parents ever encouraged you to talk, I'll never understand."

"Touchy, touchy," Peter muttered, as Aunt Winnie returned to the room with Randy. He was wearing a rumpled brown cashmere sweater and tan slacks. Behind his glasses, his magnified brown eyes resembled fish swimming in a tank. He smiled at Peter and me, and said, "I understand from Winifred that the three of you are playing amateur sleuth. Have you discovered the culprit?"

"Don't answer him," instructed Aunt Winnie. "He's making fun of us."

Randy laughed. "I am not."

"You just called me Miss Marple in the foyer."

"I meant it as a compliment."

"Liar. And anyway, I'd prefer to be compared to Amelia Peabody."

Randy lowered the top half of his body into a mock bow. "Whatever you say, *Amelia*."

Aunt Winnie was a die-hard fan of Elizabeth Peters's Egyptian mysteries featuring the indomitable sleuth Amelia Peabody. So was

I, for that matter. We tended to look with horror on those who did not share our admiration.

"Well, regardless of who we fancy ourselves to be," said Peter, "I think we have to be serious about the fact that one of the guests here murdered Gerald Ramsey. And, if the police are right, this was no spur-of-the-moment crime of passion. It was a well-thought-out and deliberate murder."

"I agree," said Randy, taking a seat next to Aunt Winnie on the couch. "And until the police find the killer, I fear that there may be more trouble." He glanced meaningfully at Peter and me.

I knew he was alluding to Aunt Winnie. He must have also caught wind of Detective Stewart's suspicions.

"If you are referring to the police's ideas about me," said Aunt Winnie, pushing her bright red curls back in an angry gesture, "I do wish you would just say so. I dislike being talked of as if I'm some doddering old fool."

"Nobody said you were a fool!" I said.

"Or doddering!" Peter chimed in.

"They didn't have to." Pointing at me, she continued. "You've been staring at me all day like I was an egg about to crack. And you," she said, addressing Peter, "you've been treating me with kid gloves and making furtive phone calls when you think I'm not around!"

Peter squirmed in his chair but did not deny the charge. I wondered whom he had been calling.

Aunt Winnie continued. "I am quite aware that Detective Stewart thinks that Gerald's determination to buy me out of this inn may have been why he died." She added, "The man's a dammed idiot. Unfortunately, he knows about what happened with Marion."

As soon as she said that, my stomach sank. It was exactly as I had feared. The police knew.

Randy looked from Aunt Winnie to me and then to Peter for clarification. "Who's Marion?" he finally asked.

Aunt Winnie sighed. "Marion is one of my oldest friends. I've known her since I was sixteen. Years ago she married a man by the name of Danny Baker. Well, Danny was a big hulking jerk, but Marion fell for him." Aunt Winnie shook her head sadly. "No matter how boorish or obnoxious Danny was, Marion would stand up for him and say he was just misunderstood. Because she seemed to love him so much, I tried to keep my mouth shut. But then Marion started showing up with bruises. She always had an excuse—she fell or tripped or some sort of other silly story. I became suspicious, of course, but Marion never said a word against Danny. I tried to do what I could, but she was completely under his spell. Then one day, I'll never forget it, Marion showed up at my house sobbing hysterically. It was awful. She was a mere slip of a thing and Danny had beaten her within an inch of her life. One of her eyes was swollen shut, her lip was split, and her jaw was purple and raw. But that wasn't even the worst of it. In her arms was her beloved little dog, Pixie. He was dead. Danny had apparently flown into a rage because the dog had gotten into the trash can. Danny had snapped his neck."

Aunt Winnie fell silent at her memory of the broken dog's limp body. "Marion had tried to protect the dog, so Danny went after her as well. Seeing Danny kill Pixie made Marion finally realize what a monster Danny was. She had come to me to ask for help in getting her things out of the house while Danny was at work. Of course, I said yes. As far as I was concerned her life was in danger." Aunt Winnie's eyes flickered uneasily in Randy's direction before continuing. "We were getting ready to leave when Danny returned home, drunk. When he realized that Marion was leaving him, he flew into a rage. And that's when I pulled out my gun. Danny was a rather large man and I wasn't taking any chances."

There was a sharp intake of breath from Randy. "You had a gun?"

"Yes. As I said, it was a long time ago, and I thought I needed it for protection." She added defensively, "I took the recommended classes and was very careful with it!"

"I'm not judging you," said Randy. "I'm just surprised."

"Well," Aunt Winnie continued with a shrug, "once Danny saw the gun, he calmed down. I explained that Marion was leaving and that he had better not try anything. I thought he was going to let us leave, but at the last minute he lunged at me and I . . . fired."

"Jesus!" said Randy. "Did you kill him?"

"Of course not!" Aunt Winnie snapped. "I'm an excellent shot! I nicked him on the leg so he couldn't chase us. I knew what I was doing. Trust me, if I'd wanted to kill him, he'd be dead."

Her words hung in the air. No one said anything.

"Which is why, I suppose," she finally continued, "that things might look a little dark against me now. I have a record. I was charged with assault with a deadly weapon, attempted murder, and about six other things I've forgotten. Of course, they dropped them once they learned what had actually happened, but the fact remains that the police know that I know how to use a gun, I'm a very good shot, and I don't put up with bastards."

"But that was a completely different situation," I said. "You were defending yourself. Your life was in danger."

"Yes, but our local detective seems to be channeling the intellectual prowess of Inspector Clouseau. He's looking at that incident and coming away with a very different impression. Therefore, I've resolved that I must find out who the killer is. I want whoever did this caught and put away, and soon. I have to clear my name so people will feel comfortable staying at Longbourn. In short, I want my life back."

"You're right," said Randy, extending his hand to her. "And I'll do anything to help."

"I know you will." Taking his hand, she smiled softly at him.

"And so will Elizabeth and I," said Peter. "We're a part of this team, too."

It was odd to hear Peter speak of us as a team. But this whole weekend had been one odd experience after another. Then Peter suggested we move to the kitchen to discuss what we knew while he cooked us dinner, and I was forced to add yet another odd experience to my list.

An hour and a half later, we were still in the kitchen drinking coffee after finishing remarkably good chicken Marsala. The aroma of sautéed mushrooms mingled with chicken and wine still hung in the air. I stirred some sugar into my coffee.

"Thank you again for dinner, Peter," said Aunt Winnie. "It was very good."

"My pleasure," he replied. "I was just lucky that you happened to have all the ingredients for the one meal I can make."

"Speaking of which, I think I'd better restock," said Aunt Winnie. "I'm not sure how long Detective Stewart is going to keep everyone here, but however long, I'm going to have to feed them. I'd better make a run into town tomorrow."

"I'll do that for you, Aunt Winnie," I said.

"I'll go with you," said Peter. I looked at him in surprise, but he ignored me. "Now, for everyone's ideas about the murder," he continued. "Does anyone have a favorite suspect they'd like to share with the group?" He smiled as he said this, but his tone was grim.

Lauren was my bet. Could she have ever loved Gerald? They were such complete opposites—and not in the charming way that some people say "attract"—that I found myself agreeing with the local gossip: she must have married him for his money. Plus there was her phone call on the night of the murder. In addition, her behavior and appearance today were about as far as you could get from a grieving widow. Emotionally cool was a better description. I said as much.

"You may be right," said Aunt Winnie thoughtfully. "But then again, if Lauren did have something to do with it, wouldn't it make more sense for her to appear distraught?"

"And, as much as you may personally want to, you can't condemn her simply because she's a beautiful woman," said Peter.

"I'll admit that you both have a point," said Randy. "But Lauren is not, shall we say, the cleverest of women. It may not have occurred to her that she should wear black and cry a lot."

"Which is only another point in Lauren's defense," said Peter. "She just doesn't strike me as clever enough to pull something like this off."

Aunt Winnie nodded in agreement.

Randy looked unconvinced. "Perhaps, but there's something else." He paused. "I feel funny telling you this, like I'm breaking a kind of trust, but Lauren was in my store a few weeks ago. She bought several books dealing with legal contracts—prenuptial agreements, to be specific."

"Really?" said Aunt Winnie. "That is interesting. If Lauren wanted out of the marriage but was bound by an ironclad prenup, then she had an excellent motive for killing Gerald."

"I would have thought just living with Gerald was motive enough," I added.

"I agree with you there," said Peter. "The question becomes, then, whether Lauren wanted out because Gerald was so odious or because someone else was so attractive."

For some unknown reason, they all looked at me. Well, not for some unknown reason. I knew damn well why they were all looking at me: Daniel. I refused to let them get to me.

"You're blushing, dear," Aunt Winnie said mildly, as she sipped her coffee. Peter rolled his eyes in disgust.

I ignored them both. "Well, how do we go about finding out whether Lauren was considering divorcing Gerald?"

"My niece works in a law office in town," said Randy. "The paralegals are all very chummy. She might be able to help us."

"Isn't that privileged information?" asked Peter.

"Probably," said Randy, as he thoughtfully stroked his white beard, "but it's still worth checking into."

"What about Polly?" I asked.

"What about her?" said Peter. "You think she might know if Lauren was planning to divorce Gerald?"

"No. I mean what about the possibility that Polly killed Gerald? Maybe she was sick of his controlling ways and wanted her freedom. By all accounts, Gerald wasn't going to let her go to Oxford for the graduate program, yet she still applied for a passport. Why?"

"I think there's another possibility that we're overlooking," said Peter. "Daniel. It's all over town that he and Lauren were carrying on. He might have killed Gerald hoping to get Lauren and the money."

"I know that's the rumor," I said, "but I haven't seen anything that would suggest that they're more than friends." I quickly told them about Lauren's phone call the night of the murder. "And, if Lauren is having an affair, then that phone call I overheard points to someone other than Daniel. And in any case," I added in a rush, "some of Daniel's behavior suggests that he's not interested in her at all." I busied myself by pouring more coffee.

"I've no doubt that you haven't seen anything between them," said Peter. "In fact, I think it's far more likely that they would pretend to be just friends, or even to be interested in someone else."

His words felt like a physical slap and my face blazed. "Are you suggesting that the only reason Daniel might show interest in me is so that I can serve as his cover?" I asked angrily.

"I think you're being foolish if you haven't considered that possibility," Peter retorted. "How long have you known him, anyway? A day and a half? Haven't you wondered yourself why he's giving you such a hard sell?"

"Well, according to you, the idea that he should actually find me attractive and interesting is absurd. Apparently it's easier for you to believe that he's using me."

"That's not what I meant!" Peter said.

"The hell it wasn't!"

Aunt Winnie interrupted us. "Stop it, both of you!" she said sternly. "If we're going to find out who killed Gerald, we have got to stick together. I need you both to help me. Remember, we're a team."

"I'm sorry, Elizabeth," Peter said. "I didn't mean it the way you thought. Aunt Winnie's right, we are a team." I was about to reluctantly accept his apology when he ruined it by adding, "And after all, as my lacrosse coach used to say, 'There's no I in T-E-A-M.' "

I stared at him. Somewhere a village was missing its idiot. And I was going to spend tomorrow shopping with him.

After Randy left, Peter and I persuaded Aunt Winnie to go to bed early. She didn't put up much of an argument, which told me that she was far more tired than she was admitting. Peter and I cleaned up the kitchen and prepped tomorrow's breakfast. If he sensed that I was still upset with him, he didn't let on.

Peter had just gone up to bed when I heard the noise. It was coming from the dining room. This time, however, I wasn't going to let Lady Catherine get the better of me. I marched into the room, flipped on the lights, and said in a loud, confident voice, "All right, you sly wench, get out!"

I don't know who was more surprised—me or Joan Anderson.

She was standing motionless by the back door of the room, dressed in a dark sweater and slacks. Her red hair stood out around her head like a flaming halo. In her hand was a flashlight. Neither of us spoke for what seemed an eternity, although it was actually only a few seconds.

"Oh, Elizabeth, you scared me!" she said in a rush. Her hand went to her neck in a reflexive gesture. Was she kidding? I had scared her? My heart felt like it was about to leap out of my chest. "I hope I haven't done anything wrong," she continued. "I snuck outside for a cigarette."

"A cigarette?" I repeated stupidly.

"Yes. I hope that's okay. I didn't want to smoke inside. I know I should probably quit, but . . ." She let the sentence hang unfinished in the air.

"I still don't understand," I said slowly.

Joan twisted the flashlight in her hands, so hard her knuckles showed starkly white. I doubt she was even aware she was doing it. "Well, to be honest, Henry would kill me if he knew I was still smoking. He thinks I quit. I snuck down here after he went to sleep. I'm sorry I startled you. I didn't mean to." Again, her hand strayed to her neck.

"But why are all the lights off?" I asked.

"Given what happened here last night, I guess I didn't want anyone to see me in here," she said. "I thought it might look bad." She let out a small, nervous laugh. "But, of course, I see now that this looks even worse."

She walked toward me and I took an involuntary step back. She was still clutching the flashlight in her hand, one of those large, heavy models that would do a very neat job of bashing in someone's head. She noticed my movement and stopped short.

I didn't say anything. She continued to stare at me and twist the flashlight. There seemed nothing more to say, so she finally said good night and moved toward the door. When she reached the doorway, she turned around. For a second I thought she was going to say something more. She didn't. She scanned the room, gave me a slight smile, and turned to go. As she scurried across the foyer, I saw her hand unconsciously reach up to her bare neck again, seeking comfort from something that was not there.

CHAPTER 12

It's when you're safe at home that you wish you were having an adventure. When you're having an adventure, you wish you were safe at home.

—THORNTON WILDER

LAZY BEAMS OF sunlight bathed my room in soft orange. Rolling over, I buried myself deeper into the warmth of the covers, savoring the brief seconds of blissful ignorance that precede full waking. But all too soon the madness of the last few days tumbled back. One memory in particular promoted a low groan: I was spending the morning with Peter.

Downstairs, I found Peter and Aunt Winnie huddled together in the kitchen. Jumping apart when they saw me, Aunt Winnie sang out a cheery, "Good morning, sweetie!" in a voice that I had long ago learned to associate with trouble. Lady Catherine was also in attendance. With her tail lazily switching back and forth, she watched me. From the inscrutable expression on her peevish face, it was hard to tell whether she was merely waiting for food or silently mocking me. With cats, you never can tell.

"What are you up to?" I asked without preamble.

Aunt Winnie shot Peter a warning glance before answering. "Would you like some coffee, dear?" she asked.

"Please," I said, but did not relent. "What are you up to?"

Aunt Winnie opened her green eyes very wide in an attempt to appear innocent. She failed miserably. "Why, nothing at all," she said in the chipper voice reserved for small children or the criminally insane. "You're imagining things. You know how you are in the morning." She poured coffee into a bright green mug that boldly proclaimed I ♥ VEGAS! and held it out to me. "Here, have some coffee."

I looked at her and then at Peter, who seemed very interested in the floor.

"I'm not imagining things," I muttered, before taking the coffee from her. I knew there was no use arguing. I would just have to brace myself for whatever it was that she was scheming. Besides, I thought as I sipped the hot coffee, Aunt Winnie looked tired. There were dark circles under her eyes and her cheeks were pale beneath her pink rouge. The stress and worry of the past few days were taking their toll on her.

"I was just going over my shopping list with Peter," she continued smoothly. "I can't thank you both enough for doing this for me."

"Don't be silly. Elizabeth and I are here to help," said Peter. I suppressed an urge to throw my Vegas-loving mug at him. I wasn't sure when he and I had become this big buddy team, but I found it irritating. The memory of our exchange over Daniel last night prompted another one—my encounter with Joan.

"I almost forgot," I said. "Guess who I found prowling around the dining room last night?"

"Who?" said Aunt Winnie.

"Daniel?" said Peter.

My hand itched to launch my cup at his head, but I restrained myself.

"Joan Anderson," I said, ignoring Peter.

"Really?" said Aunt Winnie. "What was she doing?"

"She said she'd been outside in the garden having a cigarette."

"Well, that doesn't sound too strange," Peter said.

"She was sneaking around in the dark with a flashlight," I added.

"Oh. Well, yes, that is a little strange," he amended. "What do you think she was really doing?"

"I don't know. She was upset about something. There's more to it than she's telling."

"So you think she was lying about having a cigarette?" asked Aunt Winnie.

"I do," I said. "I don't know why, but I think there's something she's not telling us, or the police. Remember, she and Polly were outside together before the murder. They said they were looking at the snow, but as Detective Stewart pointed out, women generally don't go outside in freezing weather wearing evening gowns."

Aunt Winnie looked thoughtful. "I'll see what I can find out from her today."

"I'll help," I said.

"No," she said firmly. "I need you to help Peter with the shopping. And speaking of which, you had better get ready, Elizabeth. Everything will be picked over unless you hurry."

I looked down at my jeans and sweatshirt. "But I am ready," I said.

Aunt Winnie cast a disparaging glance at my outfit. "You're going into town, dear, not fishing. Trust me, you two are going to be scrutinized within an inch of your lives. We already have one black mark against us in that Gerald was murdered here. Let's not add 'slovenly appearance' to our list of sins." Her tone was light, but she wasn't kidding about the message.

I felt my face flush and was about to tell her that I couldn't care less what the locals thought of my appearance, when I caught sight of Peter's face. Without another word, I turned and stormed out of the kitchen. I was so furious that I stalked by Daniel on the landing without so much as a hello. I thought I heard him call to me, but I kept walking. In my room, I angrily tore off my jeans and sweatshirt. But looking down at the ratty heap of clothes on the floor, I realized that Aunt Winnie was right. Peter and I would be the objects of study and gossip. How we looked, what we said, and what we did *would* be discussed. I owed it to Aunt Winnie to make as good an impression as possible. If the tide of public opinion turned against her, her business would assuredly fail.

After a quick shower, I pulled on cream-colored corduroy pants, a white oxford shirt, and a turquoise V-neck sweater—my one remaining decent outfit. If I was going to stay a few more days, I would either have to buy more clothes or do laundry. Buying more clothes won. I studied my reflection in the mirror and decided to pull my hair back into a loose French twist. I found my makeup bag and carefully applied powder, blush, eyeliner, mascara, and tinted lip gloss. Upon closer inspection, I decided to add a little concealer under my eyes and made a mental note to get tea bags and a cucumber at the store. While I assured myself that I was making this extra effort for Aunt Winnie's sake, truth be told, I was remembering Peter's smirk and his bland assumption last night that Daniel was only using me as a cover.

Surveying the result, I had to admit that I looked nice. No amount of makeup was going to turn me into a striking beauty, but at least I could hold my head up in town and, just as important, with Peter.

There was a knock at the door and Aunt Winnie stuck in her head. Turning her way, I struck a pose. "There. Will I disgrace you?"

She laughed. "You look very pretty. Thank you. I gave Peter the list and the money. It should cover everything."

"Well, I'll chip in some," I said.

"Don't be silly. Now get going. I think Peter is already downstairs."

I headed down the stairs. Daniel, still in the hall, gave a low whistle when he saw me and I felt my face grow warm.

"Hello, Daniel," I said.

"Hello, yourself." He smiled and walked toward me with a definite glint in his eye just as Peter rounded the corner.

"Elizabeth!" Peter called out, exasperated. "Are you ready yet? We need to get going!" He stopped short when he saw Daniel. "Oh," he said briskly. "Morning, Daniel. I didn't see you." He turned back to me, suddenly all smiles. "We really should get going, Elizabeth." His voice sounded peculiar, and with a jolt I realized he was trying to sound friendly.

"I am ready," I said. "Let me just get my coat."

"I've already got it." Peter thrust it toward me. I started to take it from him when he suddenly changed his mind and tried to help me into it. A small wrestling match ensued as we both tried to put my coat on me.

"You two have a big day planned?" Daniel asked in an amused voice.

I opened my mouth to respond but Peter answered instead. "Oh, nothing too special. Just the usual."

Before I could ask Peter what was "usual" about us going shopping, he pressed his hand firmly against the small of my back and propelled me toward the door. Feeling like I had been dropped in *medias res* into a play where I didn't know my lines, let alone what the other actors were doing, I reluctantly allowed myself to be led away.

"See you later, Daniel," I said.

"I'll be here," he answered.

"Goodbye, Daniel," Peter called over his shoulder. I glanced back. Daniel watched our exit, a puzzled expression on his face.

Outside, I turned to Peter and said, "Just what the hell was that all about?"

"Shut up," he said through a fake smile. "He's still watching us."

"Who is?" I asked, bewildered.

"Daniel, of course."

At the side of his black Jeep, he opened the door and pushed me in. I waited until he had climbed into the driver's seat before I continued. "Why are we putting on a show for Daniel?"

"I want to throw him off his guard a little" was Peter's cryptic reply. My additional questions were met with similar nonresponses. After a few minutes, I gave up and stared out the window in frustrated silence. Long stretches of flat sand dotted with empty lifeguard chairs gave way to sandy dunes and faded gray cottages. A sign in front of a washed-out red general store promised to see us in the summer.

"I thought we would go to the grocery first," Peter said, breaking the silence as he maneuvered the car into town.

"That's fine with me. I assume you have the list?"

"Got it right here." He patted the pocket of his coat. He deftly parked in a spot on Main Street and we got out. The temperature had dropped during the night and the wind had picked up. I pulled my coat tightly around me. "Which way?"

"Follow me," he said, making his way quickly down the street. In spite of the blustery weather, the streets were alive with activity. Aunt Winnie had been right: Peter and I were not going unnoticed. While no one stopped and outwardly gawked, a fair number of heads turned our way. I was surprised that we had been spotted so easily until I remembered that this was a small town and Peter was probably already known by most of the inhabitants. We crunched down the snow-covered, tree-lined street, passing several clapboard buildings in various shades of white and pale yellow. Most were still decked out in their Christmas decorations. Finally, we came to a freshly painted white building sporting a wooden sign in the window that simply read PRITCHARD'S. It was a small, well-stocked grocery store. Several of the customers noted our entrance, and not for the first time that morning I was glad that I had followed Aunt Winnie's advice.

As Peter and I bagged shiny red apples that looked as if they had been buffed within an inch of their lives, a heavyset woman with a pinched mouth and small, shrewd eyes spotted Peter. She bore down on him with predatory intent.

"Why, Peter!" Her tone was overly familiar. "I thought that was you! Happy New Year!"

At the sound of her voice, Peter stiffened. He turned to face her. "Hello, Mrs. Pritchard. How are you today?"

"Well, *I'm* fine, of course. The real question is, how are *you*? It sounds like I missed *quite* a time at Ms. Reynolds's New Year's party." In a conspiratorial tone, she added, "Are the stories I'm hearing true?"

"I don't know," Peter said evenly. "What stories have you been hearing?"

"Well," said Mrs. Pritchard, eagerly leaning her massive frame closer to Peter, "from what I hear, Mr. Ramsey threatened Ms. Reynolds—told her that he would force her to sell him the inn come hell or high water—and she shot him right through the heart! I know she's an old friend of yours, Peter, but I've always said that there is something odd about that woman, if you know what I mean. For one thing, she drives through this town in that car of hers like a raving lunatic." My hand constricted around the apple I was holding and I fantasized lobbing it at her head. Peter must have sensed this because he discreetly took the apple from me and silently added it to the others in the bag.

"Well, you can take it from me, Mrs. Pritchard," he said calmly. "Ms. Reynolds was not threatened by Mr. Ramsey, nor did she shoot him. The police are still investigating the matter."

Mrs. Pritchard's fleshy face fell in disappointment. "Oh, well, I suppose there's no dearth of people who wanted to get rid of that old buzzard. He made his daughter's life a sheer hell, I can tell you. I heard he wouldn't even let her move out and live on her own. Said it wasn't proper for a single girl to live alone or some such nonsense. And then there's that wife of his." With a crude twist of her mouth, her eyes flashed knowingly at Peter. My stomach roiled in disgust. "I heard that she'd had enough of His Nibs and wanted out. And from what I hear, she has someone waiting in the wings, if you know what I mean."

I must have made a noise, because her birdlike eyes homed in on me. "And who is this?" she asked. "Your girlfriend?"

"This is Elizabeth Parker," Peter said. "She's Ms. Reynolds's grandniece." A normal person would have been embarrassed, but not Mrs. Pritchard. She merely stared at me more openly, as if I were a specimen under glass.

"Really?" She studied me from head to toe. "I've heard about you." Her expression indicated she found the inventory lacking. "You're not at all how I pictured you."

"Oh?" I said politely. "That's funny. You're just how I pictured you, Mrs. Pritchard."

She blinked. Twice. Before she could respond, a smallish man poked his head out of the back room and called to her.

"Doris!" he yelled in a thin reedy voice. "Can you come here a moment? I can't find the green beans." He was as thin as she was heavy. They were Jack Sprat and his wife come to life.

"Helpless man," Mrs. Pritchard muttered before excusing herself. "Alfred, they're right next to the canned tomatoes!" she yelled, stalking toward the back room.

"She's a real charmer," I said, watching her wide retreating back.

"I think every town must have a Doris Pritchard," Peter said in a resigned voice.

"Maybe so. But she manages to make Jackie seem innocuous."

Hoping to avoid another encounter with Doris, we quickly loaded the cart with the remaining items on the list. We were just nearing the checkout line when she descended on us again. With her was a pale, anemic-looking girl. Peter saw them first. "Oh, God," he moaned under his breath as they approached.

"Oh, there you are!" said Mrs. Pritchard. "I was hoping I would catch you! I was just thinking that there's no call for you two to lug all this stuff back to the inn. My daughter will be happy to deliver it for you. I'm sure you remember Jessie, don't you, Peter?"

She thrust the girl forward. Jessie was an unfortunate mix of her mother's birdlike features and her father's scrawny build. She peered eagerly out at Peter from behind a lock of limp mousy brown hair with an expression that had nothing to do with a desire to deliver groceries.

"Hello, Peter," she simpered.

Peter appeared to have lost his voice. I had lost my patience.

"Thank you very much, Mrs. Pritchard," I said, forcing a jolly smile on my face. "But we can't take you up on your offer."

"But why ever not?" said Mrs. Pritchard. "I'm sure you have other errands to run today."

"True," I said. "But the police have asked us to keep outside traffic to a bare minimum until they've finished their investigation. Emergencies only." It was certainly a bold-faced lie, and expressly against my New Year's resolutions, but there was no way I was going to let that woman or her daughter within ten feet of Aunt Winnie or the inn.

Mrs. Pritchard raised her eyebrows questioningly at Peter. He said nothing. I gave him a small nudge. What was wrong with him? "Um, yes," he said finally. "That's right. Police orders."

Jessie, looking like a child whose favorite toy had just been snatched away, shrugged her bony shoulders. "Well, if you ever need me—for anything—give me a call," she said to Peter.

I linked my arm through Peter's and smiled at her. "Well, thank you, Jessie, that's very kind of you. Peter and I will do just that."

The girl peered uncertainly at me and then back at Peter before moving away. Mrs. Pritchard turned to me, her small eyes cold and appraising. "How long are you staying in town, dear?"

"I really haven't decided yet." I smiled coyly at Peter. "It all depends."

Mrs. Pritchard bared her undersized teeth in a semblance of a smile. It wasn't pretty. "Very well, then," she said with exaggerated sweetness. "We'll just have to wait and see."

"Yes," I replied just as sweetly, "we will."

Gathering up our purchases, we said our goodbyes, fake smiles all around, and lugged everything out to Peter's car.

"What got into you back there?" he asked.

"Nothing," I said, surprised at the annoyance in his voice. "I was only trying to help you escape the clutches of that pubescent anemic vamp."

"Who? Jessie?" he said. "Don't be silly. She's just a kid. I can handle her."

"You didn't seem to be handling anything, actually," I said. "God help Maggie if that's how you ward off unwanted attention."

Peter's dark brows pulled together and he took his time answering. "Maggie isn't the jealous type," he said. "We have a solid relationship. She's very understanding."

"Well, she'd have to be, wouldn't she?" I said, before adding, "Look, I'm sure she's just wonderful and you two are love's ideal together. But my point back there," I said crossly, jerking my thumb in the direction of Pritchard's, "is that I'm not going to let that woman or her daughter anywhere near Longbourn just so they can snoop around and spread nasty rumors about Aunt Winnie. Don't you see that more has been lost here than a life? Aunt Winnie's reputation is also in danger. Let the Doris Pritchards of the town gloat at us from a distance and be happy with that."

"I agree with you there," he said. "But haven't you ever heard the expression 'You can catch more flies with honey than vinegar'?"

"That's the most ridiculous expression!" I snapped angrily back at him. "Who wants flies anyway?"

Peter paused and burst out laughing. After a minute, he said, "Come on, we've got two more stops to make. Just try not to start a rumble or anything, will you? I don't think I've got enough bail money on me."

I consoled myself with the knowledge that I had to put up with Peter for only a few days. Somewhere out there was a poor girl named Maggie who surely had it far worse.

CHAPTER 13

Human nature is so well disposed towards those who are in interesting situations, that a young person who either marries or dies is sure of being kindly spoken of.

—JANE AUSTEN, *EMMA*

OUR NEXT STOP was the Flowering Teapot, a combination tea shop and bakery. It smelled of cinnamon, apple, and pumpkin. One side of the small room was clearly designated for tea service, where several small round tables draped in crisp white linen serenely awaited customers. The other side was dominated by a long glass case filled with every kind of tempting pastry and baked goods. Blue Wedgwood china plates, in various shapes and sizes, covered the back wall.

The shop was empty save for the two sisters who ran it. Both appeared to be in their late sixties. One was blond, the other brunette; otherwise they appeared identical. They reminded me of the tea cakes they sold—delicate, plump, and lightly powdered. Greeting Peter warmly, they leaned across the wooden top of the pastry case, their round faces expectant.

"Peter! How are you?" said the brunette.

"How is Winifred?" said the blonde.

"You could have knocked me over with a feather when I heard the news," said the brunette in quick succession.

"Not to sound ghoulish, but I wish we had gone . . ." began the blonde.

". . . but we had already promised to go to our niece's," finished the brunette.

"She always hosts the New Year's dinner . . ." said the blonde.

". . . such a wonderful time, really," said the brunette.

"Of course, it must have been simply terrible for *you,*" said the blonde.

"Awful," agreed the brunette. "So, how *is* Winifred doing?"

"Aunt Winnie is fine," replied Peter. "She sent me here to place an order for 'the usual.'" He smiled at them and added, "I assume you know what that means?"

"We do indeed," said the blonde. She quickly recited the list. "Two loaves of lemon bread and pumpkin spice bread each, three dozen raspberry tarts, four dozen almond shortbread cookies, and one blueberry crumb cake."

"Winifred is one of our best customers," added the brunette. Both women glanced curiously at me. Peter turned my way and said, "Ladies, this is Elizabeth Parker, Ms. Reynolds's grandniece."

They both smiled at me. "Hello, Elizabeth," said the blonde. "I'm Lily."

"And I'm Pansy," said the brunette.

"Our mother had a thing for flowers," said Lily.

"Her name was Rose," added Pansy. "This used to be her shop."

"But now it's ours," Lily finished quickly.

"It's lovely," I said, feeling a bit dizzy at their rapid back-and-forth manner of speaking. "And everything smells wonderful."

"Oh, that would be the pumpkin spice bread," said Lily.

"It's fresh out of the oven," said Pansy.

"Let me get you a piece," said Lily.

"Oh, thank you," I began, "but you don't have to—"

"But I insist," said Lily, disappearing into the kitchen.

"I'll get you some tea," said Pansy. "It's terribly cold out there today." In a flash, she had disappeared as well. As unnerving as their constant conversation was, the abrupt absence of it produced a similar sensation—I felt oddly disoriented.

"My head is spinning," I whispered to Peter.

He chuckled. "I know. They take a little getting used to, but they are two of the nicest women you'll ever meet. And they're the best bakers on the Cape."

Lily returned with a plate piled high with thick slices of warm pumpkin spice bread. "Pansy should have your tea ready in just a second," she said, leading us to one of the empty tables. "Please have a seat."

"Thank you." Peter took a large piece of bread and popped it into his mouth.

We sat down as Pansy returned with our tea. She quickly filled four blue teacups and the two sisters sat down with us. "Now tell us everything," commanded Pansy.

"Yes," said Lily. "Don't leave anything out. Lemon in your tea?" she asked me.

I nodded yes to Lily, while between bites of bread Peter told the sisters what had happened. They listened in enthralled silence.

"Well," said Lily, "it's just too amazing for words. Gerald Ramsey. Murdered."

"Although if you were going to murder someone in this town . . ." began Pansy.

". . . it would be him," finished Lily.

"I remember Violet used to babysit him," said Pansy.

"Our older sister," Lily said as an aside to Peter and me.

"She used to dread having to go to his house," Pansy said.

"Said he was a horrid little beast of a boy," said Lily.

"Turned into a horrid beast of a man, if you ask me," said Pansy.

"Not too surprising, really," said Lily. "Rotten children usually do turn into rotten adults."

At this damnation of horrible children, I snuck a look at Peter, but the remark was lost on him. He sat unaffected, happily eating his bread.

"Still, he managed to con a lot of people into thinking otherwise," said Lily with a knowing tilt of her head.

"Especially the women," said Pansy, returning the nod.

"Do you mean Mrs. Ramsey?" I asked, feeling that if I didn't break into the conversation, I was going to get whiplash.

"Well, that depends on which Mrs. Ramsey you mean," Lily said.

"How many have there been?" I asked, surprised.

"Three," said Pansy.

"That we know of," amended Lily.

"But it was the first one . . ." began Pansy.

"Polly's mother," said Lily.

". . . that I felt the sorriest for," finished Pansy.

"What was she like?" I asked. Peter continued to munch his bread.

"She was a pretty little thing," said Lily.

"She had the loveliest auburn hair," added Pansy.

"What was her name again?" Lily asked.

"Tory," replied Pansy. "She died so young."

"What happened?" I asked.

"Car accident," said Lily. "Although at the time there was talk that it wasn't completely an accident." Pansy had just taken a bite of the bread and so could only nod her head in agreement. "I was away at school when it happened," Lily continued. "But I do remember Mother saying that Tory's car had run off the road and the police were investigating reports that another car was seen speeding away from the area. Then it came out that Tory had been seeing someone else—but really, considering what Gerald was like, who could blame her? Anyway, Gerald behaved very oddly afterward. He got rid of practically everything that had belonged to her. Some people thought that he might have had something to do with it, but in the end nothing ever came of it. Poor Polly was only about four or five at the time."

"I saw someone just the other day who reminded me of her," said Pansy.

"Was it Polly?" I asked.

"Oh, no," said Pansy quickly. "Polly is her father's daughter. At least in looks. I don't know what she's like in person. Keeps to herself a lot. Can't have had an easy life."

"I remember her as a little girl," said Lily. "Never saw a more determined child. Do you remember the time she wanted that bicycle from Fred Johnson's toy shop?" she asked Pansy.

"Oh, that's right!" said Pansy. Turning back to me and glancing at Peter, who was still stuffing his face with the pumpkin spice bread, she explained, "She couldn't have been more than seven. There was this bright yellow bicycle in the front window of the toy store, one of those banana bikes. I remember it had a long purple fringe on the handlebars. Well, anyway, every little girl in town wanted that bike, including Polly. But Gerald said no. I forget why, probably just to be mean, but he flat-out refused. Now another girl might have thrown a tantrum or pouted, but not Polly. Instead, she talked Fred Johnson into holding a jump-roping contest. He would get the publicity and the winner would get the bike."

"She outjumped everyone and got that bike," said Lily.

"But wasn't there some sort of incident with her friend?" asked Pansy.

"Yes, I'd forgotten," said Lily. "That little girl—now what was her name?—Mary. That's it, Mary King. Well, she and this Mary were playing tag the day before the contest—Mary was a pretty good jump roper, too. Anyway, Mary fell and twisted her ankle or something. She couldn't jump in the contest. I remember at the time that some people said Polly had pushed her down on purpose."

"I don't believe that," said Lily.

"Well, maybe so," said Pansy, "but they weren't friends after that."

"Gerald remarried right around then," said Lily. "He said he thought that Polly was turning into a tomboy and needed a woman's influence."

"Well, he certainly married an influence," said Pansy. "Pamela was a real witch. Gerald found out that she was stealing money from him or something like that. He got rid of her in short order."

"And now there's Lauren," said Lily. Again the sisters exchanged knowing looks.

"What's she like?" I asked.

Pansy leaned across the table and lowered her voice. "Well . . ."

I eagerly leaned in, but the bell above the door sounded, announcing customers. Pansy jumped up from the table and went to wait on them.

Peter popped the last piece of bread in his mouth and stared sadly at the empty plate. "We probably should get going," he said.

"I'll just go and wrap up your order," said Lily.

Minutes later, we collected three large white boxes, each wrapped with a blue bow covered with small white teapots. Customers streamed into the shop now for their afternoon tea and Pansy whispered to me to come back later so we could finish our conversation. Peter and I said our goodbyes and thanks, and stepped out again into the freezing air.

"That was informative," I said to Peter.

"Yeah. I didn't know that Gerald had been married three times. Do you think his ex-wife could have something to do with his murder?"

"I don't know. Really, there are so many people who might have wanted him dead. It's a bit overwhelming." The wind picked up. "What's next?" I asked Peter, trying to shield my body from the wind with the box of pastries. Next door was a clothing shop, with several outfits on display in the window. I wistfully eyed them and the heated interior.

"Butcher," he replied. I stared longingly in the window. He read the shop's sign and then turned back at me. "You're not going to make me go in there, are you?"

"Well, I do need to get a few things . . ."

Peter sighed and shook his head. "I've never met a woman who didn't."

"That's not fair!" I said. "I only packed for one weekend. Who knows how long I'm going to be staying!"

"Uhh-uh," Peter said to the sky.

"Whatever," I said. "I'm going in. Are you coming?"

"No offense, but I'd rather go to the butcher."

"Coward. Don't you go shopping with Maggie?"

"Maggie isn't into material goods," Peter said loftily.

"Then Maggie doesn't know what she's missing," I retorted, handing him the box. "I'll meet you here in an hour."

Inside the store was quiet—that serene, tranquil quiet that permeates shops with expensive clothes. The salesclerk smiled vaguely in my direction as I wandered around the store. Forcing myself to keep a casual face, I peeked at some of the price tags. Dear God! Did they mark up the prices while they were drunk? Still, there were several outfits that I would give my eyeteeth for—or at least the better part of the contents of my checking account. I made some quick mental calculations. It seemed unlikely that I would be taking that ski trip to Vermont with Mark next month, which meant that I had a fair chunk of change to play with.

Assuring myself that it was healthy to splurge on oneself occasionally, I gathered up several outfits and headed toward the dressing rooms. The salesclerk, seeing that I was a serious customer, abruptly changed her attitude and now fawned over me. Her name tag indicated her name was Brooke. She was a tall, leggy girl in her early twenties, with long, straight brown hair. While I was predisposed to dislike her based on those facts alone, she actually proved to be very helpful. While she put together several outfits for me, we chatted politely until she discovered that I was staying at Longbourn.

"Oh, my God!" she yelped. "But that was where Mr. Ramsey was killed!"

"Yes." I paused. "Did you know him?"

"I did! His daughter, Polly, and I are friends. How is she? I've been trying to get in touch with her all day."

Not knowing if Brooke was really a friend or a gossip, I merely said, "She's holding up okay."

"Well, if you see her, please let her know that I'm thinking of her. We've been friends for years." She added, "This must be such a nightmare for her. I just wish she had come away with us like we originally planned."

"You were going away?" I asked.

"Yes," said Brooke as she handed me a bright pink cashmere sweater. "Every year a bunch of us go to my parents' ski house for New Year's. Polly usually can't wait to go—her dad is . . . was unbelievably strict. She didn't get out much. He wouldn't even let her do that graduate program at Oxford. She was furious about that. I can't remember ever seeing her so mad. I thought she would have been dying to get away from him, even if it was only for a weekend, but Polly backed out."

She handed me a green brocade skirt. "These look nice together. Especially with your coloring."

"Why did Polly back out?" I asked, taking the clothes.

"She didn't say. She just said that something had come up and she wasn't going to be able to make it after all." Brooke added a pink silk scarf to the outfit and shook her head. "I bet she wishes she'd gone with us now."

I wondered if that was true. I thought of what I knew of Polly—a determined young woman, by all accounts miserable living with her father. Now her father was gone and she was free to live her life without his interference. Brooke was dead-on with her fashion sense, but was she as perceptive about Polly?

One hour and several hundred dollars later, I left the store. Peter was just walking up the street toward me.

"I'm hungry," he said by way of a greeting.

"I don't see how you can possibly be hungry after eating all that bread."

"Well, I am. Do you want to get something? I know a place that makes the best clam chowder on the Cape."

"Is there anyplace on the Cape that *doesn't* claim to make the best clam chowder?"

"You have a point," he acknowledged with a tip of his head. "But this place actually *does* have the best. Are you interested?"

I was. I had only nibbled at my cranberry muffin at breakfast and Peter had eaten all the bread at the Teapot. It was now late afternoon and I was starving.

We put our bags in the Jeep and Peter drove us to the Captain's Knot, a restaurant overlooking the harbor—a description that sounds much nicer than the reality. Since the temperature was well below freezing, we had no qualms about leaving the groceries in the car, as we hurried into the tavernlike restaurant. A few locals sat at the worn mahogany bar, sipping from large mugs of beer and watching football on the overhead television. To the right, several tables had a view of the water. The hostess waved to us to take our pick and we chose a table next to the large window.

As we sat down, an awkward silence descended between us. I busied myself by studying the laminated map that covered the tabletop. Peter stared out the window. Outside, a horn sounded and I turned in my chair. A large white ferry was slowly maneuvering its way out of the harbor. The wind slapped at the boat's flags and at the few people who had decided to brave the cold and stand on the top deck. Proud of their hardiness, they waved manically to anyone who looked their way.

"There goes the ferry to Nantucket," said Peter.

"Cool," I said. Cool? What was I, twelve? Why did I turn into such an idiot when I was around him?

"Do you remember that time we went with Aunt Winnie?" he asked.

How could I forget? He had terrorized me during the entire journey with horrible tales of children being swept up by sudden gusts of wind and tossed overboard. I think he may even have swiped my chocolate doughnut, too.

"I remember," I muttered. "It was two years before I could get on a boat again without clinging to the rails."

"Now that you mention it, I do remember you looking a bit green around the gills. A green Cocoa Puff," he said and laughed. As he chuckled gleefully in fond memory of my nautical misery, all the pent-up embarrassment and frustration I'd suffered at his hands as an insecure, overweight kid boiled over.

"Look," I hissed at him. "Do you think you could drop that stupid nickname? In case it has escaped your notice, I'm not some dopey kid anymore. I've changed. I'm a grown woman. However, you appear to be the same misogynist who delighted in making me feel like a moron, so you can take me back to Longbourn right now. I don't need you to make me feel like a moron. My skills at *that* outrank yours any day."

Peter's face was a caricature of surprise. "I don't think you're an idiot, Elizabeth," he said finally. "I know I teased you a lot when we were kids, but I always liked you. If I hadn't, I would have ignored you. To be honest, I always thought you were a pretty good sport."

I couldn't believe this. "You liked me? You called me names and locked me in the basement! Who does that to someone he likes?"

He shrugged. "Most fourteen-year-old boys, I think. And while we're on the subject, I recall certain names being flung my way and, on one occasion, finding something wet and slimy moving around in my bed." I stared at him dumbfounded. That's how he remembered things, with me as a willing adversary rather than a hapless victim? In my memories, I had cast myself in the role of a young Jane Eyre—plain and unhappy. Rather than her counterpart, the moody Mr. Rochester, I had pegged Peter as a more sinister version of Simon from *Lord of the Flies*. Had I been wrong?

He reached across the table and gently took my hand. Giving it a squeeze, he said quietly, "Elizabeth? I'm sorry if I was horrible. For what it's worth, I was pretty miserable that summer, too. My parents were off in Europe and I had to stay behind. Aunt Winnie was great, but she wasn't family. If I remember correctly, you were this smart-alecky kid who walked around with her nose in a book most of the time. You thought I was a creep."

"That's because you *were* a creep."

"Yeah, well, when you're fourteen you're insecure enough. You don't need someone else pointing out your failings."

I was speechless. Luckily, the waitress arrived to take our order or I would have continued to gape at him like one of the fish offered on the daily specials.

After ordering the obligatory cup of clam chowder, I opted for fried clams. Peter ordered a steak sandwich. I idly played with the blue-and-white sugar packets in their little stand and struggled to reconcile the memory of the unrelenting nemesis of my youth with this new version of Peter as just a goofy, although utterly obnoxious, kid.

He raised his water glass. "Friends?" he asked, by way of a toast. I hesitated a long moment but finally gave in. Raising my glass to his, and meeting his warm brown eyes, I reminded myself that with a murderer on the loose I needed all the friends I could get.

The awkwardness slowly faded and we started to chat like old friends. He told me that he was following in his parents' footsteps and getting involved in their hotel business. He was in the process of getting his MBA and after that he was going to take over one of his parents' hotels. I told him about my goal of becoming a writer and of my frustration at being limited to just fact-checking other people's stories. Before I knew it, two hours slipped by; the sun was sinking onto the horizon, sending red bands of light across the water, and our waitress was hovering impatiently with the check.

Peter relieved the woman of the bill. "This is on me."

"Oh, but you don't have to do that," I said.

"No, I insist. Consider it restitution for the bad behavior of my youth."

I laughed. "Oh, no. If this is an attempt at restitution, it's just a drop in the bucket."

"I was afraid of that," he said with mock seriousness. "Well then, by your calculations, how many lunches will it take to clear my name?"

I pretended to consider the question before answering, "At least eight thousand six hundred and forty-two."

"Seems a fair trade," he said with a smile. Peter could be very charming when he wanted to be. I tried to ignore the cynical part of me that questioned *why* he was suddenly being charming to me.

CHAPTER 14

You are too sensible a girl . . . to fall in love merely because you are warned against it.

—JANE AUSTEN, *PRIDE AND PREJUDICE*

BY THE TIME Peter and I got back to the inn, the sun had set. All around us, houses blazed with Christmas lights. The inn was conspicuously dark. I knew the gesture was meant to convey respect for Gerald and his family, but in the midst of so many other cheerful displays, the absence of lights created a different kind of tribute, one of darkness and gloom.

Inside, Daniel was sitting in the reading room. He immediately stood up and came over.

"Here, let me get these for you," he said, taking the grocery bags from my arms. Looking them over, he added, "I hope all this food doesn't mean that you already have plans for dinner?"

"Why, I, um . . ." I began, unsure how to answer.

"Because I was hoping I could convince you to join me," he continued. "I know a place that makes great clam chowder."

I stifled a laugh and glanced at Peter, but he wasn't looking at me. He was staring at Daniel with a bland expression. It was a look I had seen often that summer years ago, usually right before an attack was launched on my person. The hairs on my neck stood up in a long-forgotten salute. The feeling only increased when Peter asked in a disinterested voice, "You're not dining with Mrs. Ramsey this evening?"

"No," Daniel said simply.

"Oh," said Peter. "I see."

Daniel must have caught the faint disapproval that these words carried because he hesitated and added, "People have visited and interviewed Lauren and Polly nonstop for the past two days. What they want now is a little privacy. They should absorb this without an audience."

Peter said nothing. Perhaps driven by his silence, Daniel continued, "Sometimes monstrous things happen to monstrous people," he said slowly, choosing his words with care. "But when that monstrous thing is a murder, well, it may force one to hide true feelings. Just because you dislike someone doesn't mean you murdered him. But let's not be naïve, it does give you a motive. And that's what the police are looking for. Motive."

"I think I know what you mean," said Peter. "When you know you're being scrutinized, you act accordingly. You play a role."

"Exactly," said Daniel.

I thought of what I had seen of Lauren's behavior yesterday. If that had been a toned-down version of her true emotions, then she must be dancing a jig in private. "No offense," I said gingerly to Daniel. "I know Lauren is your friend, but if she's trying to downplay her true feelings, she's not doing a very convincing job of it."

Daniel turned to me with a shake of his head. "I didn't say I was talking about Lauren."

His words took me by surprise. Although Polly had professed that she hadn't cared much for her father, she nevertheless seemed genuinely upset. If not because he died, at least at how he died. Had that been an act?

"Well, all the same," said Peter, "I expect that Lauren appreciates your role in this."

Daniel eyed Peter with a puzzled expression. "My role?"

"Of a good friend," Peter explained. "It must mean a lot to her knowing she has you on her side."

Daniel's eyes narrowed slightly. He seemed to sense that Peter's words held another meaning. Of course they *did,* but that meaning was meant for me.

"Well, I'll leave you two to discuss dinner," said Peter. His attack completed, he took his bags to the kitchen.

"Did I miss something?" Daniel asked. Traces of a faint scowl lined his face, as he watched Peter's retreating form.

"Oh, who knows," I answered. "Just ignore him." Changing the subject, I asked, "You mentioned dinner?"

Forcing his face into a more pleasant expression, Daniel turned to me. "Yes." He smiled. "Dinner. How's eight o'clock sound?"

"Perfect. Just let me check first that Aunt Winnie doesn't need me."

"Of course," said Daniel, following me into the kitchen.

Daniel helped Peter and me put away the groceries. Thankfully, nothing more was said about acting or roles. In fact, not much of anything was said, as Peter had apparently gone mute. Once the groceries were put away, I went to Aunt Winnie's room.

"Come in," she called out in answer to my knock.

I found her at her desk, scribbling away in a tattered notebook.

"What are you doing?"

She held up her hand, signaling me to wait while she finished.

I plopped down on the bed next to Lady Catherine, who displayed her displeasure at my proximity by flicking her tail at me in a suspiciously vulgar gesture. Ignoring her, I sank back into the bed's thick pillows and studied the room. Years ago, I read that a person's bedroom is the best indicator of his or her personality. I had laughed because at the time I was sleeping in a depressing space with colorless walls, battered furniture, and mismatched sheets, though in hindsight that was an accurate reflection of my life then. Looking around me, I realized that this room did mirror Aunt Winnie's personality, which was probably why I liked it so much. The walls were painted a tangy shade of sage green. The curtains were a jumbled mix of soft tangerine, crisp rose, and lime green. The furniture was simple, except for the headboard, which was an enormous wrought-iron structure that looped and intertwined halfway up the wall. Piles of books, some stacked, others just strewn about, covered every available surface. The whole effect was just like Aunt Winnie—colorful, energetic, and unconventional.

After a few minutes, she put down her pen with a satisfied air. "There," she said, stretching her arms out in front of her. "Done."

"What are you doing?"

"I decided to write down everything we know about the murder and the suspects," she said. "I know it sounds silly, but if I can just get everything organized on paper, something important might jump out at me."

"It doesn't sound silly," I said. "I think it's a good idea. What do you have so far?"

She handed me the notebook. In her familiar sprawling handwriting, I read:

> GERALD RAMSEY: early 60s. Wealthy. First wife died. Has one daughter, Polly, from that marriage. Married to Lauren for a few years. Disliked by most who knew him. Wanted to buy Longbourn—was that his reason for coming to New Year's

party? Reflective tape found on body suggests that his death was no random act of violence.

LAUREN RAMSEY: mid-40s. Married to Gerald. Has one child, Jamie, from previous marriage. Jamie lives in South Carolina—has special needs. Rumored to be unhappy in marriage and possibly seeking divorce. Could have been worried about prenuptial agreement. Overheard on phone New Year's Eve with someone—lover? Is close with friend Daniel Simms—but how close?

Motive: Freedom? Money?

POLLY RAMSEY: early 20s. Single. Lives at home with Gerald and Lauren. Does not seem happy. Does not seem particularly close to Lauren. Resented her father's control over her life but did not leave. Why? Was she too fond of the money? Applied for passport even though Gerald purportedly refused to let her attend Oxford.

Motive: Freedom? Money?

DANIEL SIMMS: late 30s. Single. Visiting Lauren Ramsey—they are old friends (?).

Motive: Help Lauren out of unhappy marriage? Wants to marry Lauren himself?

JACKIE TANNER: mid-70s. Single. Recently moved to Cape with old friend Linnet Westin. Lives with her as a kind of companion. No known connection between her and Gerald. Terrible gossip—seems to know a lot about the purported relationship between Daniel and Lauren. What led to her dire straits?

Motive: none known

LINNET WESTIN: mid-70s. Widowed. Wealthy. Recently moved to Cape. Lives with old friend Jackie. Not very likable but no known connection to Gerald. Check into her husband's past (Martin Westin)—maybe he had a connection.

Motive: none known

JOAN ANDERSON: mid-50s. Married to Henry Anderson. Visiting from New York. Claims not to know anyone here. Out with Polly in the snow on night of murder—why? Found in dining room after the murder. Claims to have been outside smoking to hide habit from Henry.

Motive: none known

HENRY ANDERSON: late 50s. Married to Joan. Second marriage. First wife died. Visiting from New York.

Motive: none known.

I handed the list back to her. "Very good," I said with a nod. "I learned a few more things today that might be of significance." I quickly told her that Gerald had been married not twice but three times, that his first wife had been having an affair when she died, and that Polly usually went out of town with friends for the New Year but this year she had canceled at the last minute.

"That is interesting," Aunt Winnie said, as she added those facts to the list. "Did Lily and Pansy say anything specific about Gerald's second wife?"

"Not really. After his first wife, Tory, died, Gerald acted oddly—he abruptly got rid of all her belongings. He married his second wife, Pamela, shortly after in the hopes of using a woman's influence to rein in Polly." I told Aunt Winnie the story about the bicycle and Polly's determination to have it.

"From what Lily and Pansy said," I continued, "Pamela wasn't very nice, and Gerald got rid of her pretty quickly."

"Slow down," said Aunt Winnie as she frantically scribbled on the list. "Okay, so there could be an ex–Mrs. Ramsey out there with a bit of a grudge?"

"It's something to consider," I said. "So, what did you learn today? Did you get a chance to talk to Joan?"

"I did, but I didn't learn anything new. She told me the same story she had told you, but I see what you mean. She is holding something back. I just can't tell what."

Aunt Winnie chewed on the end of the pen as she reread her list. A slight nagging started at the back of my head. I was missing something. "Let me see that list again." I reached out my hand. Aunt Winnie handed it to me and I reread the information on Joan. A memory swirled and settled. "The phone call!"

"What phone call?"

"The first night I got here, Joan was just coming out of your office. Do you remember?" Aunt Winnie nodded uncomprehendingly. "She said that her cell phone was dead or something and that she had used the phone in your office to make a local call."

"So?"

I tapped the list. "According to Joan's statement to the police, she doesn't know anyone here. So who was she calling?"

Aunt Winnie leaned forward and eagerly took the list from me. Over her purple-framed glasses she scanned it again. "You're right. And she couldn't have made a long-distance call on that phone. I have it set up for local calls only." She pursed her lips. "Looks like this requires another chat with Mrs. Anderson." She pushed the list away with a frown.

"What's wrong?" I asked. "We've found something else."

"I'll admit it's a start." She sighed. "But we have so little to go on. We need more. Jackie and Linnet have invited us to lunch tomorrow. I can't see what they have to do with this, but if nothing else, Jackie might know something. She seems to know a lot about everything else."

"Sounds good." Adopting a casual tone, I added, "I may be in a position to find out a bit more tonight. Daniel has invited me out to dinner."

She gazed at me over the rims of her glasses. "I see" was all she said.

"What?" I said, still trying to act casual. It might have been more believable if I'd been able to make eye contact.

"Just be careful, dear. Daniel may really like you. That kiss he planted on you yesterday would certainly indicate that he does." I felt my cheeks burn hot. I didn't realize she had seen that. "But we don't know a lot about him," she continued. "And he does have a motive for killing Gerald." She tapped her list. "Even if he's not romantically involved with Lauren, he may have tried to help her out of a horrible marriage."

I was quiet. A small part of my brain understood what she was saying, but the larger part was hurt. It was as if Aunt Winnie and Peter still saw me as an unattractive and gauche ten-year-old.

"Elizabeth?" said Aunt Winnie gently.

"I just don't understand why everyone's first assumption is that Daniel is using me."

"I never said it was my first assumption, Elizabeth," Aunt Winnie said sternly. "But a man was murdered in this house not two nights ago by someone who is still on the loose. That means everyone is a suspect and should be treated as such. Daniel may very well like you. But he might also be using you. I know that's hard to hear, but I'd be horribly remiss if I didn't make sure that you understood that. Do you understand?"

"I do." Even as I said it, I knew it was only partly true. On some childish level I was angry and wanted to prove her—and Peter—wrong.

Aunt Winnie gave me a searching look before changing the subject. "Very well, then," she said. "Go out with Daniel tonight—see if you can find anything out. And tomorrow we'll go to Linnet's and Jackie's. I've no doubt Jackie will have much to tell us," she added wearily.

I gave a small laugh, trying to restore the early friendly atmosphere. "Yes," I said, "but just how much of it is truth and how much is rank speculation is yet to be seen." I stood up to leave. "Are you sure you don't need me for anything else tonight?"

"No," said Aunt Winnie. "If I want anything, Peter can help me. Go and have a good time."

I kissed her good night and turned to leave.

"Elizabeth?" she said.

I turned.

"Be careful."

I nodded and shut the door behind me.

The restaurant that Daniel took me to had originally been a private residence but had been renovated to accommodate five separately themed dining areas on the main level. Our table was in the garden room, which was a study in brightly colored floral prints and hand-painted French antiques.

We quickly got through the awkward first-date chatter—childhood memories, school experiences, and job histories—and fell into an easy rapport. Leaning over to pour me a glass of wine, Daniel said, "So tell me again how you used to draw pictures of naked men."

"It wasn't like that." I laughed. "It was for art class. You know, sketching the human form and all that."

"The buck-naked human form, you mean. Bit pervy, if you ask me. But don't get me wrong, I like pervy."

"Didn't you ever take art class in school?" I said in an attempt to regain control of the conversation.

"Sure. We covered all the basics—crayon, finger paints. I just don't recall the naked people. To be honest, I feel a bit cheated."

"I'm sure you'll survive," I said, sipping my wine.

"I suppose," he said. "So I take it that you decided to nix a career as an artist?"

"Yes. Unfortunately, my sketches looked as if they'd been done by someone more comfortable with finger painting. And how about you? How did you land in investment banking?"

"I like money," he said frankly. "I never seemed to have a knack for my own, mind you, but I knew a lot of people who had loads of it. Those contacts made me a perfect fit for the firm. That's actually how I met Lauren. She was a client."

"Really?" I said, trying not to sound too interested. "I didn't know Lauren had lived in England."

"Well, it was a long time ago. She came over to do some modeling. It never really took off, but she did. She became quite popular with a certain set. That's how she met her first husband. He was a mate of mine."

"What happened?"

"Well, James was a bit of a bounder. He made a beeline for Lauren the first moment he saw her. They had a great time together for a while, but then Lauren found out she was pregnant. She was happy about it. I think she had the naïve idea that James would settle down into domestic bliss with her and the baby, but that just wasn't in James's nature. He married her, of course, but once the baby was born he quietly divorced her."

"That's terrible," I said, aghast.

"Yes. His family made sure she received a decent settlement, and then they basically washed their hands of her and Jamie."

"Did they know that Jamie had . . . ?" I faltered.

"Problems?" Daniel finished for me. "No. Jamie's fine. His only real problem is that he's a delinquent."

"But you said . . ."

"I know," said Daniel with a small smile. "That he has 'special needs.' I only said that to throw Jackie off the scent. Lauren has a hard enough time without word getting out about Jamie. He's not a bad kid, actually, most of the time. What he really needs is a swift kick in the ass. Or a dad."

"Doesn't his father have any contact with him?"

"No. James died in a car accident a few years back. But he wasn't much of a father even before that."

"What about James's parents?"

"Clive and Anne?" He scoffed. "They've never even seen Jamie. I think they convinced themselves that Jamie wasn't James's son to begin with."

"How sad," I said. "Poor Lauren."

"Yes," agreed Daniel. "It hasn't been easy for her. I made sure that she invested her money wisely, but it was still a struggle for her."

"And then Gerald came along."

Daniel nodded. "And then Gerald came along," he repeated. "I think she did care for him at first. Gerald could be charming when it suited him, and Lauren's instincts with men aren't exactly what you'd call razor sharp. By the time she realized what a bastard he really was, it was too late. But she was determined to stick it out for Jamie's sake. She'd do anything for that boy—she completely dotes on him. With Gerald's money, she was able to get Jamie into one of those treatment centers for wayward boys. And she's convinced that he's making progress."

"I gather Gerald would never have considered moving so she could be closer to Jamie."

"Are you kidding?" Daniel scoffed. "He'd never have left here. He was too intent on buying up all the land he could—like your aunt's inn. He was incandescent with rage at losing that place."

"So I gather," I said. "And now he's dead."

"And now he's dead." Daniel nodded. In a solemn voice he recited from Sir Walter Scott, " 'The wretch, concentred all in self, living, shall forfeit fair renown. And doubly dying, shall go down to the vile dust from whence he sprung, unwept, unhonour'd and unsung.' " After a brief pause, he added, "More wine?"

By the time we pulled into the inn's driveway, I was feeling rather floaty. It might have been the wine, or it might have been the way Daniel kept looking at me. I really didn't care what the reason was—I just didn't want it to end. Turning off the ignition, Daniel turned in his seat to face me.

"Thank you again for asking me to dinner, Daniel."

"No, thank you." He leaned in close to me. Cupping my face in his hand, he stroked my cheek lightly with his thumb. My heart jerked into a pounding rhythm. "You've done me quite a service. This is something I could get used to," he said softly, before kissing me.

I returned his kiss, but part of me blanched at his words. How had I been a service? Peter's and Aunt Winnie's intimations reverberated in my head. Was that the reason behind tonight—to fortify his "just friends" story with Lauren? Putting my hand on his chest, I lightly pushed him away.

"Elizabeth? What's wrong?"

"I don't know. Something you just said. What do you mean, I did you a service tonight?"

"By going to dinner with me," he said. "I enjoyed your company. I think we go well together. I like the idea of being with you. Why? What did you think I meant?"

I couldn't ask for a nicer answer, but something deep inside me wasn't buying it. After all, we didn't know each other that well. A few flirtatious conversations and one dinner generally didn't provoke such a serious reaction in men like Daniel—at least not with women like me.

"I don't know," I said. He leaned toward me. "Wait." I put my hand on his chest again. "Daniel," I said slowly, unsure how to phrase my question, "I don't know how to ask you this, but are you and Lauren . . . ?"

He immediately stopped trying to kiss me. "Are Lauren and I what?" he asked, with an edge to his voice.

Blushing, I averted my face from him. "More than friends," I said, my voice small. I hated having to ask, but I had to know.

Daniel leaned back, his eyes dark with annoyance. "Why would I be here with you if that were the case?"

"I don't know. It's just that there's been a lot of speculation about you and Lauren, especially since Gerald was murdered. Everything is moving so fast. We don't know each other very well, and I . . . well, I . . ."

"I realize that we don't know each other very well," he said, "but I thought that was the point of dinner—to get to know each other better."

My face burned with embarrassment. "I know, but . . ." I began lamely.

"Is that why you went out to dinner with me tonight? To see what you could find out about me? About Lauren?"

"No! But just now, I wondered."

"You suddenly wondered if Lauren and I are more than friends." He frowned. "And if we are, what would be the point of my seeing you? To throw off suspicion about my relationship with Lauren?"

"Something like that." Hearing it voiced out loud rendered the whole thing silly and melodramatic, but nevertheless I noticed that he hadn't answered my question.

Daniel reached into his jacket pocket and took out a cigarette. As he lit it, I noticed that his fingers shook slightly. He inhaled deeply before continuing. I watched the smoke curling out into long, wispy tendrils. "I like you, Elizabeth," he finally said slowly, choosing his words with care, "but this isn't a good way to start a relationship—with suspicions and insecurities."

"I'm sorry, Daniel." I lowered my voice. "I didn't mean to offend you. Everything has been so crazy the past couple of days. I can't tell which end is up anymore. The police think that Aunt Winnie might have had something to do with Gerald's murder, and I can't let them think that."

"So what are you doing? Playing girl detective to get her off the hook?"

His words stung. "I'm trying to find out what I can. And if it helps Aunt Winnie, then all the better. There's a lot going on here that doesn't make sense. I'm just trying to make sense of it."

"What doesn't make sense?" he asked sharply.

I opened my mouth to answer but realized there was nothing I could tell him. Daniel watched me closely, and I suddenly was aware of what a stupid position I had put myself in. I was alone in a car, in the dark, with a man I really didn't know, who had an excellent reason for killing Gerald Ramsey. I inched backward toward the door. Daniel saw the movement and frowned. "What doesn't make sense?" he repeated.

"I'd really rather not say," I said. "I think we probably should go inside."

"I agree. But before we do, I think I should tell you—if you're trying to play sleuth here—stay away from Lauren and Polly. They had nothing to do with Gerald's murder. And I will not let them be dragged through the mud just so you can divert attention from your aunt."

"That's not what I'm doing!"

"The hell it isn't," he said, yanking his key out of the ignition. He glared at me, his pupils cold black dots. The inside of the car seemed to shrink. What had minutes ago been a cozy atmosphere was now decidedly claustrophobic. He leaned toward me and said in a low voice, "Leave Lauren and Polly alone."

I was too startled to answer. His blue eyes watched me with a guarded expression. Rolling down the window, he threw out his cigarette butt. A blast of cold air rushed in, but its chill was nothing compared to the arctic atmosphere between us. He took a deep breath and forced a smile back onto his face. "What are we doing here, anyway?" he said. "Arguing about nothing. All I'm saying is that Lauren and Polly are my friends, and I don't want to see them hurt. Just as you don't want to see your aunt hurt. And to be honest, I'm worried about you."

"About me? But why?"

He shrugged slightly. "Call it a gut feeling. A man was murdered here, after all. If word gets out that you're poking around, you could be in danger. You know what they say about curiosity killing the cat." He tipped my chin up with his fingers as he said this. "Just be careful, okay?"

I could only nod my head in agreement.

Once inside, he bade me a chaste good night in the foyer. As he disappeared up the stairs, I wondered about his bringing up curiosity killing the cat. Was it a well-intended warning or a veiled threat? The thought of cats made me think of Lady Catherine and the dining room. Every night since I'd arrived, it had been the scene of one kind of nocturnal event or another. I wandered over to see if tonight would be any different. Cautiously peeking into the dark room, I was relieved to find it empty. Just as I turned around to go upstairs, a puff of cold air brushed my face. I peered toward the back of the room. Was the door to the garden open?

Quietly, I crept across the room to the door. It was indeed open a crack. I peered out into the backyard. It was dark and still. Thinking that the door had been left open by mistake, I reached out my hand to pull it shut. As I did, the small red ember of a cigarette cut the darkness outside.

My breath caught in my throat. Who was out there? I was debating calling out when the clouds shifted, releasing a bright beam of moonlight onto the form of Henry Anderson.

He was sitting on the bench, seemingly lost in thought and staring intently at his feet. He stood up and flicked the cigarette out into the snow, the ember arcing a fiery red against the black sky. Joan had told me that Henry hated smoking and that's why she'd been forced to sneak her cigarettes. Yet here was Henry smoking away. Clearly, someone was lying, but who? Henry stood for several minutes with his back to me. What was he doing? Could he be hiding something? Finally, he turned around and rapidly made his way toward the house.

I had just hidden myself in Aunt Winnie's office when he quietly slunk into the foyer. Pressed against the backside of the door, I watched through the crack as he slowly climbed upstairs.

I heard his door upstairs softly open and shut, but I forced myself to count to one hundred before leaving the office. I ran through the dining room and out the back door. The snow crunched under my feet as I crossed the yard. When I reached the bench where he'd sat, I looked around, for what I don't know. Then I saw the bird feeder. Could he have hidden something in it? I stuck my hand through the opening and felt around. My fingers touched something hard and round, and my heart began to pound with excitement. Grasping the item, I yanked it free from the bird feeder. I held my breath as I opened my hand. I was holding a cluster of acorns. With a snort of disgust, I threw the nuts to the ground. What the hell was the matter with me? I was turning into Catherine Morland in *Northanger Abbey,* seeing intrigue and deception at every turn. Who the hell would hide something in a bird feeder, anyway? Embarrassed, I walked back to the inn with my head low.

I was just nearing the door when a glint of silver, half buried in the snow, caught my eye. I picked it up.

It was a simple silver pendant. I flipped it over. On the back were three initials. V.A.B.

Who the hell was V.A.B.?

CHAPTER 15

Some people develop eye strain looking for trouble.

—ANONYMOUS

I DON'T KNOW how long I stood there, staring at the necklace. Eventually I realized that my fingers were numb with cold and I was shivering. Behind me a twig snapped. Whirling around, I searched the inky darkness. I couldn't see anything, but I felt the vulnerability of my position. My skin prickled with the uneasy sensation that I was being watched from behind one of the windows that ran along the back of the inn. With my heart pounding in my ears, I glanced up at the dark casements and ran for the house. My stumbling footsteps on the ice-covered snow sounded like rapid gunfire.

Back inside the dining room, I fumbled with the latch. When I finally secured it, I sagged against the wall. Rubbing my hands together for warmth, I wondered if the necklace could be a clue to Gerald's murder. The initials didn't belong to anyone staying at the inn—that is, if the owner was under her real name.

I crept up the stairs, desperate not to make any noise. Turning the corner, I was surprised to see a line of light spilling out from under Peter's door. Wondering why he was up at this hour, I moved toward his room and gave the door a light tap with my knuckle. Almost instantly it was flung open. Shock registered on Peter's face when he saw me. "Elizabeth!" he said. "I didn't hear you get back. What's going on?"

"Can I come in?" I whispered, glancing behind me down the dark hallway.

"Of course." He stepped aside. "Is everything okay? Did Daniel do something?"

"No, Daniel didn't do anything," I snapped, pushing past him into the room.

"Then what's going on?" he asked. Surveying the room, I saw that the bed was still made; there weren't even indentations in its brightly colored patchwork quilt. An open book lay on the seat of a rocking chair by the floor lamp. I looked at Peter. He was wearing the same jeans and sweater he had had on earlier.

"What are you still doing up?" I asked, suddenly suspicious.

"Nothing," he mumbled. "I . . . couldn't sleep, so I was reading." He had obvious trouble meeting my eyes.

I stared at him. "In a chair? Fully dressed? Across the room from the bed?"

"Um . . . yeah," Peter said feebly.

Realization dawned. "Oh, my God! Were you waiting up for me?"

He still refused to meet my eyes. Stuffing his thumb into his belt loop, he mumbled, "Something like that."

"Are you kidding me? Why?"

Peter closed his eyes and ground his teeth before answering. "Because I was worried, all right? I know you like Daniel, but I don't. I don't trust him. Aunt Winnie wanted to do it herself, but I talked her out of it. She's tired enough as it is."

I didn't say anything. I was torn between hugging him and throwing something at him.

"Well, you needn't have bothered," I said after a minute. "I'm fine."

"Then what's going on? Why are you here?"

I pulled the necklace out of my pocket and told him what had happened. I did, however, gloss over the part where I frisked the bird feeder.

Peter perched on the edge of the bed. "What do you think it means?"

"I don't know." I took a seat in the rocking chair. "Whose necklace could it be? I don't see how this connects to Gerald's murder, but it's got to."

"It might. I think you should tell Detective Stewart."

"Oh, I will," I said. "I can't wait to point him to a clue that has nothing to do with Aunt Winnie." I pushed back in the rocking chair. The resulting creak from the wood sounded like a supernatural shriek. I stopped moving.

"Do you want me to drive you to the police station tomorrow?"

"No, that's okay. I'll call him first. Besides, I can't go right away. Linnet has invited Aunt Winnie and me to lunch tomorrow."

"I know. Aunt Winnie told me. I didn't think she was particularly close to Linnet. What's the reason for the visit?"

"Officially, it's just a social visit, but of course that's only a pretense. I imagine that Linnet extended the invitation to appease Jackie's curiosity. Jackie probably thinks that we're a source of information about the investigation." I smiled. "The irony, of course, is that that's precisely why Aunt Winnie and I are going—to see what we can learn from Jackie."

"What makes you think she knows anything?" He stretched his long frame back onto the bed. Raising himself onto his elbows, he stared straight into my eyes. If it had been anyone other than Peter, I would have thought he was trying to flirt with me.

"Well, you have to admit that she has a special knack for gossip," I said. "I don't know how she does it, but she's managed to uncover an awful lot about everything that's going on in this town since she's arrived. And there's something else. When we were leaving Lauren's the other day, she seemed upset by something." I sighed and rested my head against the back of the chair. "I know it's a long shot, but if Jackie knows something that might help Aunt Winnie, then I'll have lunch with her every day of the week until the murderer is caught."

Peter nodded and tried to suppress a yawn. I stood up. "All right. I'm going to bed. Which," I added dryly, "means you can, too."

"Wait, you didn't tell me what happened with Daniel." Peter scrambled into an upright position. "Did you find out anything about his relationship with Lauren? What did he say?"

I gritted my teeth and opened the door. "He said lots. But if I repeated it, it would only make you blush."

Peter scoffed. "The inane mutterings of some poncey Englishman might make me laugh, but I seriously doubt they would make me blush."

I was tired of sparring with him. I was tired, period. Without another word, I shut the door behind me and walked down the hall to my room.

Before I went down to start breakfast the next morning, I called Detective Stewart from my room. Sitting in the wingback chair, I nervously traced the floral patterns of the fabric with my forefinger and practiced what I was going to say. But as soon as I heard his gravelly voice on the line, my mind went blank. Instead of a concise description of last night's events, I blurted out, "This is Elizabeth Parker. I found a necklace."

There was a pause on the other end. "Hello, Ms. Parker," he finally said. "And this concerns me how, exactly?"

I took a deep breath. "I'm sorry. I think it may have something to do with the murder." I rose from my chair and walked around the room. The floor's wood planks were cold under my bare feet, but the pacing helped my nerves.

"I see," he said noncommittally. "Would you like to come down to the station to discuss it? I could meet you here around noon."

I thought of the luncheon with Linnet and Jackie. I couldn't risk missing it on the off chance that Jackie did know something. "I can't meet you then," I said. "How about later this afternoon? Will you be in your office then?"

"Let me see." The sound of papers shuffling as he flipped through his calendar floated over the line. "I'm going to be out of the office most of the afternoon. Why don't I meet you at the inn around four o'clock?"

"No. Not here. How about at the Flowering Teapot? Can you meet me there at four o'clock?"

"Yes," he said reluctantly. "But what is this about, Ms. Parker?"

"Last night, I found a necklace outside. It looks expensive. It was half buried in the snow. It's engraved with the initials V.A.B. No one at the party has those initials."

Detective Stewart coughed, or maybe he was just trying not to laugh. "Just because it doesn't have one of the guest's initials on it doesn't mean it doesn't belong to any of them. People inherit engraved jewelry and silverware all the time."

"Then why has no one come forward to say it's been lost?"

He did what sounded like deep-breathing exercises. Finally, he said, "What were the initials on the necklace again?"

"V.A.B.," I said quickly, hope rising in my chest. "So you'll check it out?"

"I'll check it out."

Relief swept over me. "Thank you. In the meantime, what should I do with the necklace?" My bare feet had had enough of the cold floorboards. I moved my pacing to the warm braided rug.

"Where is it now?"

"With me," I said, reaching up and fingering the delicate pendant, which now hung around my neck. My voice dropped a notch. "Why, what do you think I should do with it? Hide it?"

"Nothing as dramatic as that, although I would avoid wearing it, of course." I instantly dropped the pendant, wondering if the man could somehow see through the phone. "Just bring it with you this afternoon," he continued. Through the phone line, I heard a gruff voice suddenly boom out, "Hey, Al, we got something on that tape."

Detective Stewart said, "Hold on a sec, Paul. Ms. Parker? I'm going to have to put you on hold for a moment." I heard a click, but I was not on hold. I could still hear everything being said. Detective Stewart spoke first. "What did you find, Paul?"

"The tape we found in Ms. Reynolds's office is definitely a match to the tape found on the body." Paul's voice was hard to hear; he sounded far away from the phone. I pressed the receiver into my ear. "Do you want me to get a warrant for her arrest?"

The room spun. I clutched one of the bedposts for support and almost missed Detective Stewart's response. "No, not yet," he said. "I want to dig around a little more."

The faceless Paul was evidently displeased with this. "Jesus Christ, Al! What the hell are you waiting for? We found the tape in her office! We know that Gerald was trying to push her out of her inn and we know that she's got an assault record! She admitted that she turned off the lights. What more do we need?" Paul may have been far away from the phone, but he was now yelling so loudly that it was easy to hear his every word.

"I understand your frustration, Paul," said Detective Stewart, "but I don't want to rush to an arrest until I'm sure."

"What else do you need? Her bloody footsteps leading to the body? A signed confession? If we don't get this resolved soon there's going to be hell to pay."

"Don't you think I know that?" snapped Detective Stewart. "The mayor's been calling me every hour for an update."

"Then do yourself a favor and arrest Ms. Reynolds." A door slammed. Detective Stewart angrily drummed his fingers on his desk next to the receiver. It sounded like a stampede of horses. After a long pause, there was a click and he got back on the line, seeming not to realize that I'd never been off.

"Ms. Parker?"

I took a deep breath. "My aunt did not kill Gerald Ramsey, Detective Stewart. I don't care what evidence you have. You're wrong."

"What are you talking about?" His tone was angry.

So was mine. "If you found reflective tape in my aunt's office," I said, "then someone is trying to frame her."

"Were you eavesdropping?" he exploded. "This is police business and you have no right—"

I cut him off. "It's not my fault that you didn't put me on hold!"

"You should have hung up as soon as you realized what had happened!"

"You can't be serious."

He swore. I ignored him and continued. "You're wrong, Detective Stewart. My aunt is innocent."

He sighed and said, "For your sake, Ms. Parker, I hope I am

wrong. I'll see you at four o'clock." It was the unexpected kindness in his voice that really scared me.

Numbly, I went downstairs to start breakfast. I let my hand slide down the wide banister, taking comfort in the feel of the smooth wood against my skin. Around me the inn was quiet, and I stood for a moment on the landing hoping that the peaceful atmosphere would soothe my jumbled thoughts. Aside from Lady Catherine, I was the first one down. Under her watchful gaze, I prepped two trays of miniature blueberry muffins. I had just pulled them from the oven when Aunt Winnie came in. The change in her appearance just since last night shocked me. Lines of fatigue were etched into her face, her eyes were dull, and her movements seemed sluggish. She wasn't even wearing her usual tailored clothes. Instead she had on faded jeans and a red sweatshirt that read SHE WHO MUST BE OBEYED. I couldn't bring myself to burden her with the knowledge that Detective Stewart thought he had new evidence against her. It would be cruel to worry her with it. I would just tell her that I was going to meet him to discuss the necklace and nothing more.

"Aunt Winnie!" I cried. "You look exhausted! Why don't you go back to bed? I can handle breakfast."

She yawned and poured herself a large cup of coffee. Sitting down at the kitchen table, she took a long sip and said, "I'm fine, honey. I'm just a little tired, is all. I didn't sleep well last night." Lady Catherine leaped up onto Aunt Winnie's lap and nudged at her hand. Mechanically, Aunt Winnie stroked her long white fur.

"Why don't you go back to bed and lie down for a while? Do you want me to call Jackie and Linnet and cancel?"

"No," she said, before taking another sip. "I want to go. I have a feeling that Jackie knows something. I want to find out what it is."

"All right, but on one condition. You go upstairs and rest. Peter and I can handle breakfast."

I expected her to fight. Instead, she put a hand to her eyes and gently rubbed them. "Maybe you're right. I'm not thinking clearly and a short nap might help. Thanks, sweetie," she said with a smile. "I don't know what I'd have done this weekend without you and Peter." Still holding Lady Catherine, she stood up. She shifted the cat up over her right shoulder, picked up her coffee, and walked out.

Moments later, Peter came in. Sniffing the air appreciatively, his brown eyes quickly sought out the tray of small blueberry muffins. Reaching out a long arm, he grabbed one and popped it into his mouth. "I just saw Aunt Winnie," he said through a mouthful. "I guess it's just us this morning."

"Yes, I sent her back to bed," I answered, watching Peter eat a second muffin. "She looks completely worn out. I'm afraid that this is starting to take a toll on her. After all, she's not a young woman." I pushed his hand away as he reached for another muffin.

"Elizabeth," Peter said patiently, "she's just tired—hell, we all are."

"I don't know, Peter. I'm really worried."

Awkwardly, Peter put his hand on my shoulder. "Come on," he said, "this isn't like you. What's going on?"

"I called Detective Stewart this morning to tell him about the necklace, but he didn't seem all that interested. When another man came into his office, he thought he put me on hold, but he didn't. I heard him discussing the case. They found a roll of reflective tape in Aunt Winnie's desk. It matches the tape they found on Gerald. I'm supposed to meet him at four. I'm hoping that I'll learn more from him then."

"Wait a minute. You're meeting with him? Why you? If he's going to meet with anyone, shouldn't it be Aunt Winnie?"

"I asked him to meet me," I said. "I don't think I should tell Aunt Winnie about the tape—at least not yet. I'm just going to tell her that I'm meeting him about the necklace."

"Elizabeth," Peter said, "don't underestimate her. She's stronger than you think. I'd back her against Detective Stewart any day. What did Detective Stewart say about the tape?"

"Just that they found it in her office. I told him about the necklace and he said he would check it out and let me know what he found out."

Peter looked thoughtful. "Do you want me to go with you?" He reached for the muffins. Mechanically, I shoved his hand away.

"No," I said. "I need you to stay here."

"You got it," he said, adding, "although I think that a task as boring as that deserves a treat." He stared at the muffins.

"All right." I handed him one. "But don't you worry about gaining weight and all that?"

Peter smiled at me as he popped it in his mouth. "I have a high metabolism."

I looked pointedly at his stomach. He sucked it in and grinned at me. Rolling my eyes, I handed him the coffee tray. "No comment," I said. "Here, take this out and set it up. I'll be right out with the rest." Peter left and I quickly piled the remaining muffins on the tray with sliced melon. Taking a deep breath, I followed him.

Breakfast was a strained affair. Daniel was nowhere to be found, which was fine with me. As I surreptitiously watched Joan and Henry, I noticed a tension between them. They hardly spoke to each other. Henry stared moodily out the window with worried eyes.

I knew how he felt.

CHAPTER 16

Let me tell you about the very rich. They are different from you and me.

—F. SCOTT FITZGERALD

A LITTLE BEFORE noon, coming down to meet Aunt Winnie, I found Peter in the foyer sitting in the green brocade chair normally favored by Lady Catherine. His long legs stretched out in front of him, he was munching happily on an enormous sandwich and reading *The Maltese Falcon.* He waved the book at me. "Thought I might get some ideas on sleuthing."

"Don't tell me you see yourself in the role of Sam Spade."

"Why? You don't?" He pulled his face into an expression I could only assume was meant to suggest Bogart. It failed miserably.

"You really shouldn't make that face. Ever. To be honest, I see you more as a Hastings or a Watson. A kind of idiot savant, but without the savant."

Peter opened his mouth in protest, but Aunt Winnie emerged from her nap then, ending our conversation. She looked much better. She had changed into a bright red wool skirt and a green-and-black cardigan. Black boots with four-inch heels completed the ensemble. There were still faint circles under her eyes, but the spring in her step was back—insofar as there could be a spring given the absurd height of her heels. On the way to Linnet's house, I was so relieved at Aunt Winnie's improvement that I yelled only once—well, twice—about her driving.

Linnet's "cottage" sat high on the dunes and backed to the beach. Designed to look as if it had been gracing the property for centuries, it was in reality only a few years old. A low stone wall ran on either side of the private driveway and along the sloping grounds. The house itself was equal parts white clapboard, black shutters, and sparkling windows. While it was probably in the same price bracket as Gerald's, this house had a charm and grace that Gerald's larger and more ostentatious one lacked.

Aunt Winnie rolled the car to a stop in the circular driveway just as Jackie opened the front door. She waved at us enthusiastically, her smile bright beneath yet another hat. This one was soft yellow cloth with a wide brim flopping down around her face. I realized that I had never seen Jackie without a hat and wondered if she'd been ill and on chemotherapy. That might explain the hat and the apparently dire circumstances that brought her to live with Linnet. Of course, it also might just be a part of her persona—like her insatiable thirst for gossip.

Aunt Winnie and I got out of the car and walked to the door.

"Oh! I'm so glad you two could come!" Jackie gushed, stepping aside to let us in. "Linney is so excited to see you." I was hard-pressed to imagine Linnet Westin excited about anything, least of all a luncheon with two women she barely knew, but I said nothing. After handing over our coats, we followed Jackie down a short stone-floor corridor into the living room, where a faded green-and-gold Oriental rug swallowed up our footsteps. The room resembled a layout from a design magazine. The tall windows were festooned with tan-and-cream-striped curtains that cascaded to the floor and ended in silky puddles. Fresh flowers spilled out of antique lacquered vases. A fire blazed in the great stone fireplace. On a large sofa upholstered in heavy brocade the color of barley sat Linnet Westin. She rose like royalty to greet us.

Just as she had been on New Year's Eve, she was perfectly coiffed. Her flawless makeup, a tad heavy for my taste, and her rose-colored cashmere sweater and cream wool pants gave her an elegant and deceptively modest appearance. The only change in her façade was that she now wore large and frankly ugly tinted glasses. She smiled in full hostess mode and greeted us politely. "Welcome," she said with a slight incline of her synthetic silver head. "Please make yourselves comfortable." Self-consciously, she raised her hand to the glasses and said, "You'll have to excuse my appearance, but my eyes are light sensitive. I have special prescription contacts, but I can't seem to find them anywhere."

In response, Jackie ducked her head. "I've searched for them everywhere, Linnet. I just can't think what happened to them. But I *know* I didn't throw them out."

Linnet pressed her red lips together in a tight smile. "Never mind, dear. I'm sure they'll turn up." She gestured to two identical chairs patterned in gold-and-cream silk. "Would you like a drink? Some white wine, perhaps?"

"Yes, thank you," said Aunt Winnie. "That would be lovely."

"And you, Elizabeth?" she asked.

"I'll have the same, please."

"Fine." She turned to Jackie. "Jackie?"

"Oh, nothing for me now, Linney," said Jackie, starting to sit down on the couch.

Linnet's smile was small and tight. "No, dear. Would you mind getting the drinks, please? I'll have a glass of wine, too."

Beneath the folds of her hat, Jackie's face flushed crimson.

"Why don't you let me get it?" I asked quickly. "I'd be happy to play bartender."

"Thank you, Elizabeth, but that's not necessary," said Linnet. "Jackie knows where everything is."

"Yes. Have a seat, Elizabeth," Jackie said as she stood up. "I'll only be a minute." Without another word she left the room. Sensing my disgust, Aunt Winnie shot me a quelling glance. I took a deep breath and reminded myself that we were here to learn what we could from Jackie and Linnet. The dynamics of their relationship was not our concern.

Aunt Winnie said smoothly, "This is a lovely place you have here, Linnet."

"Thank you." Linnet sat back down on the sofa. "I like it."

Turning to me, Linnet said, "So, tell me about yourself, Elizabeth. I never got a chance to really talk to you the other night. Do you live near here?"

I replied that I didn't and was soon being politely but firmly badgered with every question imaginable as Linnet tried to sketch my character. I could see her snobbish little mind churning as she attempted to discover if I was A Person of Quality or merely the kind of person who has to buy her own silver. When she asked me what my father did, it took all of my restraint not to reply, "Well, Mother *thinks* he was a sailor."

Finally, Jackie returned with the drinks, putting an end to my inquisition. "Thank you, dear," said Linnet, taking her glass from the wooden serving tray. After handing us our wine, Jackie sat down on the sofa next to Linnet.

"I was just saying to Linnet what a gorgeous home this is," Aunt Winnie said to Jackie.

"Isn't it?" Jackie gushed. "Some mornings when I wake up and look out my window at the ocean, I think I must be dreaming. Of course, this whole last week has been like a dream—although more of the nightmare variety."

"Jackie's sure she's going to solve the case," Linnet said, with the faintest hint of condescension.

Aunt Winnie and I looked questioningly at Jackie, but she only shook her head, sending the yellow folds of her hat flapping. "That's not what I said, Linney, and you know it. All I said was that there was something wrong that night." She turned to us. "I haven't put my finger on it yet, but I know it'll eventually come to me. It's on the edge of my subconscious—I just have to be patient and let it swim up."

Linnet took a sip of her wine. "Have the police learned anything more?" she asked.

Aunt Winnie shook her head. "Not that I'm aware of. Although Elizabeth and I haven't had much contact with them since that night."

Jackie gave a birdlike tilt of her head and peered at me from underneath her hat. Taking a sip of wine, I returned her gaze, hoping my face didn't give me away.

"Have either of you heard anything?" Aunt Winnie asked in turn. Her tone was one of casual politeness, but I knew how much hope she had pinned on Jackie knowing something—anything—that would help her own situation with Detective Stewart.

Jackie leaned forward eagerly. "Well," she began.

Linnet abruptly stood up and said, "Ladies, why don't we go in for lunch now? Trust me, once Jackie gets started on this topic we'll not be able to get a word in edgewise."

Jackie closed her mouth and stood up. "She's right," she said, smiling. "This whole thing has consumed me. I can think of nothing else. You all go in, I'll get the lunch." She turned and left the room, waving away Aunt Winnie's and my offers of help.

"Ladies," said Linnet, with a regal nod of her head, "if you'll follow me."

She led us out to an area just beyond the living room. Composed mainly of windows, it overlooked the tumbling blue waters of Nantucket Sound. In the far distance, a ferry inched its way across the horizon. Below us the beach was empty, save for a few seagulls out cleaning their feathers. Their bodies turned into the wind, they stood motionless on the hard sand.

In the middle of this breathtaking room, an elegant table set for four awaited us. Like the living room, it resembled a picture from a magazine. Each place boasted a crystal goblet, several dishes of light blue bone china, a starched replica of a bishop's hat, and numerous pieces of gleaming silverware. In case there was confusion as to where we were expected to sit, tiny silver snowmen held up heavy white place cards with our names on them. Aunt Winnie and I cooed appreciatively, although privately I thought it more than a little silly for a luncheon for only four people. Then again, my usual lunch consisted of a grilled cheese sandwich or a can of chicken soup, so who was I to complain?

We had just taken our seats when Jackie returned carrying a large tray laden with bowls. She quickly set out the first course—steaming, thick clam chowder.

"Oh, my, thank you, Jackie, Linnet," said Aunt Winnie. "Everything looks lovely, especially this view." She gestured to the bank of windows.

"Isn't it wonderful?" Jackie said, taking her seat. "I love to sit out here with my crocheting and stare out at the water. It's a delightful way to pass the time and plan and think."

Linnet gave a light laugh. "And what are you planning, Jackie?"

Jackie ducked her head. "Oh, nothing, really," she said. "It's just a figure of speech. I only meant that this is my favorite room to sit in."

"Do you crochet much?" I asked Jackie.

"Oh, yes," she said enthusiastically. "I love it. It's really quite addicting. I'm crocheting an afghan. Now, where did I leave it?" She turned in her chair. "Oh, there it is." Getting up, she walked over to a wicker basket on the floor.

She pulled out a wide swath of material that was clearly the beginning of a massive afghan or a tent. She held it up proudly. A large white stripe ran across the top, followed by a green one and then a blue one. "I'm almost done with the blue section," she said. "Next I'll start on the yellow." She eyed the afghan critically before adding, "And then I think I'll be done. I'm not sure. I may add a stripe of red after that."

"It's very nice," I said. "I tried to knit a sweater once, but it came out all wrong."

"Sweaters are harder," Jackie said kindly. "That's why I stick with straightforward patterns like scarves and afghans. I made Linney a scarf for Christmas."

Linnet smiled. "Oh, is that what it is? I thought it was a shawl."

"Now, Linney," said Jackie, "you know perfectly well it's a scarf."

"I know, dear," said Linnet. "I'm only teasing. I think we're now ready for the next course."

Like a well-trained servant, Jackie put down the blanket and quietly disappeared. During the ensuing awkward lull we could hear the surf pounding onto the beach below. Jackie returned quickly with poached salmon, new potatoes, and Caesar salad.

Once Jackie had again resumed her seat, Aunt Winnie said, "I imagine the view here is fantastic in the summer."

"Yes," said Linnet. "Well, I'm hoping so, anyway. Of course, I've only been here a month now, so I wouldn't know. But it does have great promise." Her crimson nails lightly tapped the stem of her wineglass. "I always wanted to live on the water, but Martin would never agree to it." She shook her head before adding, "There are so many things I didn't do because of that man. In some ways this situation with Gerald reminds me of Martin."

Seeing the surprise on our faces, she added quickly, "Not, of course, that Martin was murdered. What I mean is that like Martin, Gerald controlled everybody around him. Now that he's gone, Lauren and Polly are free to live their lives the way they want to."

"Yes," said Jackie. "It's a shame how Gerald kept Polly practically locked up. That's no way for a young girl to live. I hope she didn't have anything to do with his death and can go on and live her life now. Speaking of which, I saw her in town today. She was talking with that woman who is staying at the inn—what's her name? Joan? Polly looked quite upset."

"You saw Polly with Joan Anderson?" I asked, surprised. First they had been out in the snow together the night of the murder, and today they had been in town together. It might all be innocent, but then again, it might not be. I made a mental note to mention it to Detective Stewart.

"Yes," Jackie said. "I waved to them, but I guess they didn't see me. By the time I crossed the street, they had moved on."

I'll bet they had, I thought. If I were Polly and had seen Jackie bearing down on me, I would have moved on, too. At a full sprint, if necessary.

"What about Lauren Ramsey? Don't you feel sorry for her?" said Linnet.

"No." Jackie idly turned her gold post earring as she spoke. "I don't. I don't think she's a very nice person. I doubt if she ever loved Gerald. I think she used him for his money. If you ask me, I don't think she cares at all that he's dead." Jackie suddenly blushed uncomfortably. "I'm sorry, but you should have seen her Sunday, Linney." Turning to me for collaboration, she said, "Surely you noticed how completely unaffected she was? I mean, really. She looked absolutely stunning. In fact, I think she looks better now than she did the night of the murder."

"Jackie, you can't blame a woman who looks better for her husband dying," said Linnet mildly. "I wasn't exactly sobbing into my hankie the day of Martin's funeral."

"Now, Linney, don't say that."

"Why not?" said Linnet. "It's true. I wasted so much of my life because of that man."

Jackie flushed at this statement, no doubt upset by her friend's feelings of regret. "You have a lovely life," Jackie said firmly. Struggling to say something positive about the dead man, she added, "And deep down, Martin was a good man."

Linnet smiled at Jackie. "Dear Jackie. You dated him only a few times, so you remember him when he was still worth something. Trust me, he went downhill pretty fast after we were married. Life was no bed of roses with Martin Westin. And besides, remember the plans you and I had? We were going to be famous actresses in Hollywood. We might have had a real shot at something, Jackie. Remember how good everyone said we were?"

Jackie blushed and shook her head. "They said that about you, not me. You were the one with real talent."

"I think that's an overstatement," Linnet said. "But who knows? Had I really taken the trouble to see it through, I probably would have made it. When I put my mind to something, I usually succeed.

It might have all come to naught, but it would have been thrilling to try." She sighed before adding, more to herself than to us, "It's hard to have regrets so late in life, but sometimes I wish I'd never met Martin."

Jackie stared back at her, her pale lips pulled down. "Me, too," she said softly. I wondered how many of Jackie's plans for her own future had been altered by Linnet's decision to abandon their Hollywood dreams for marriage.

Linnet smiled wistfully at Jackie. "But you're right, Jackie. I do have a good life now. And that's what's important." Changing the subject, she said, "So, besides Lauren, whom else do you suspect?"

The question was not directed to anyone in particular, but Jackie quickly answered. "Personally, I wonder about that Daniel. He's very charming and good-looking. I hear that he's always at the house with Lauren." Her lips were pursed as she said this, and although I couldn't see her eyebrows, I was sure they were raised in scandalized disapproval.

"You seem to have gotten very chummy with him, Elizabeth," she said to me. "What do you think?"

I was spared an immediate response by the fact that I had just taken a bite of the salmon. "Chummy?" I finally echoed. "I don't know that I'd call us chummy."

"But you had dinner with him last night at the Seasons, didn't you? From what I hear, that's quite a romantic spot."

"It was very nice," I said weakly. "But I don't know if I'd say it was romantic." Good God, did the woman have spies everywhere? How could she know so much about the goings-on of practically everyone in this town?

"So what do you think, Elizabeth?" she continued with a sly smile. "Is he seeing Lauren? Or are his intentions focused elsewhere?"

I knew my face was beet red; nevertheless, I calmly replied, "Daniel says that he and Lauren are old friends, and I have no reason to doubt him."

"Interesting," she said. "But I guess you never can tell with men, can you? Then you and he aren't—"

"No."

"I see," Jackie said. "Is that because of Peter? He's a very handsome young man."

"Peter?" I replied, aghast. "No. Peter and I are old friends, that's all. Besides, he has a girlfriend."

Aunt Winnie shot me a puzzled look and I realized that I was letting myself be quizzed when the point of our visit had been for us to ask the questions.

"I did hear that Gerald was married twice before Lauren," I said. "Does anyone know what happened to his previous wives?"

"From what I hear," said Jackie, "his first wife, Polly's mother, died in a car accident. Some have even gone so far as to suggest that Gerald was involved. They say she was having an affair at the time. He divorced his second wife. Pam was her name, I believe."

"Does Pam still live in the area?" I asked.

"Not that I know of," said Jackie. "Apparently, it was a very acrimonious parting. Do you think she might have killed Gerald for revenge?"

"I don't know," I answered. "I don't see how she could have. The police have established that no one from outside the inn killed Gerald. If Pam was there on New Year's, I'm sure Gerald would have recognized her."

"Maybe," said Jackie, "but she could have disguised herself. After all, it has been several years since their marriage."

I thought about that. There really had been only one woman

there that night who was the right age for the second Mrs. Ramsey. Joan Anderson. Was the secret of the necklace somehow wrapped up in that?

After lunch, Jackie served a decadent chocolate cake that I recognized as a product of the Flowering Teapot. She ate enthusiastically, the conversation about Gerald's murder seeming to have increased her appetite. It had the opposite effect on Aunt Winnie and me. In fact, Aunt Winnie ate hardly anything at all. Linnet, too, only picked at her slice, all the while bemoaning the unfairness of Jackie's slim frame compared to her own padded one. It took every ounce of my restraint not to suggest that if she got up and helped Jackie once in a while, she might have less of a weight problem.

Coffee was served—by Jackie—in the living room. In her role as hostess, Linnet decreed that we would not talk any more of Gerald's murder, which pretty much ended the conversation. After finishing our coffee, Aunt Winnie and I thanked Jackie and Linnet for the lunch and made our excuses to leave. Linnet smiled loftily at us from the comfort of the sofa, while Jackie walked us to the door.

"Thank you so much for coming," Jackie said. "I really enjoyed talking with you. We should do this again soon. In the meantime, keep me posted on what you hear about the murder investigation. I know it sounds ghoulish, but I find the whole thing quite fascinating."

"I'll let you know if I hear anything," I said.

"Good. I just wish I could remember what I saw that night that bothered me."

"Well, keep trying," I said. "I'm sure it will come to you."

"I hope so," she replied. "I have the feeling that it's important."

From inside the house, Linnet's voice rang out, "Jackie! I need you!"

Jackie called back, "Coming, Linney!" Turning back to us, she said apologetically, "I must go now. Thank you again for coming." And with that, she shut the door.

I turned to Aunt Winnie. "That woman is unbelievable!" I said. We walked quickly down the stone steps to the driveway. The temperature had dropped again and the wind was howling. Our progress to the car was hampered by Aunt Winnie's heels. With each step she sank into the gravel on the driveway and threatened to topple over. I grabbed her arm to steady her.

Aunt Winnie pulled her coat closer. "Which one?"

"Linnet Westin. The way she treats Jackie, it's despicable!"

"True, but we don't know all the ins and outs of their relationship."

"Well, that may be so," I said, as I propelled us to the car, "but I still don't see how she puts up with being treated like a servant."

"I know," Aunt Winnie replied with a small smile, "but you do not make allowance enough for the difference of situation and temper. Seriously, though, we don't know how bad Jackie's situation was before this. Being bossed around by Linnet might be preferable to whatever she had before."

I opened Aunt Winnie's car door for her and ran around to my door while she started up the engine. Inside, I leaned over and turned up the heat full blast. I placed my hands against the vents, waiting for the hot air to warm them. Aunt Winnie sighed.

I glanced over at her. Her eyes were dull and her lips were pulled into a frown. "What's the matter?"

"Nothing," she said. "It's just that I was hoping we'd learn something today, but if anything I think Jackie learned more from us than we did from her. We have nothing more than when we got here. I have to be honest, I don't relish being the police's top suspect.

I had hoped that you'd have something more to tell Detective Stewart when you meet him later." Wearily, she rubbed her hands across her eyes.

"Don't be absurd," I said, with a confidence I didn't feel. My stomach twisted with guilt. I knew I was right not to tell her yet about the new evidence against her, but it still made me feel rotten.

"I don't know, sweetie," she said. "For the first time since this terrible thing happened, I'm worried."

"Well, don't be," I said. "The police will find the killer soon. I know it."

Up ahead the traffic light flipped to yellow and Aunt Winnie gently applied the brake. Watching her slow down for a yellow light was like being kicked in the stomach. I was so preoccupied with worrying over the draining effect this murder investigation was having on her that I almost missed her next words. "I just can't wait until all of this is over," she said tiredly.

My brain froze. I had heard those very same words before. Slowly, my mind thawed and certain facts swirled in my head like tiny snowflakes, until a definite pattern began to emerge.

Suddenly, I felt much better about my meeting with Detective Stewart.

CHAPTER 17

The only time a woman really succeeds in changing a man is when he's a baby.

—NATALIE WOOD

IMPATIENT FOR MY meeting with Detective Stewart, I arrived at the Flowering Teapot early. The atmosphere was tranquil; a fair number of customers sat lingering over their tea, enjoying the soft afternoon light and the scents of banana and nutmeg from the day's special. Apparently the shop's only anomaly amid all the calm, I sat down at an empty table. My stomach was in knots and I nervously picked at my fingernails.

As soon as she saw me, Lily came over. "Elizabeth! How nice to see you again. What can I do for you?"

"I'm meeting Detective Stewart here."

"Really?" Her voice rose. "Why? What's going on?"

I opened my mouth to tell her but thought better of it. Besides, what exactly was I going to tell her? That Detective Stewart thought he had evidence against Aunt Winnie? That I found a necklace with strange initials on it? It would be all over town within fifteen minutes. "Oh, nothing much," I lied. "He just wants to double-check some things about the other night."

"Well, I hope they find whoever did it soon. It's all anyone can talk about around here." She gestured at the other patrons in the shop, some of whom were openly staring in my direction. If they thought I was interesting now, I'd be absolutely fascinating once Detective Stewart showed up.

"Let me bring you some tea," Lily said, as the small silver bell on the door tinkled, announcing a new arrival. It was Detective Stewart. With his presence, the atmosphere in the shop changed. The lazy, relaxed feeling was gone, and in its place there was a charged anticipation as everyone surreptitiously watched his movements.

Looking every bit the bull in the china shop, he lumbered in my direction, leaving a trail of slushy snow in his wake. Behind him, Pansy shook her head disparagingly at the mess before going for a mop. Detective Stewart's heavy black overcoat added at least three inches of mass to his already stocky frame and his bulky snow boots clomped loudly across the floor. With a brief nod to Lily, he sat down in the chair opposite me. "Hello, Ms. Parker," he said gruffly.

"Hello, Detective Stewart," I replied. "I've just ordered some tea, would you like some as well?"

"Um . . . do you have coffee?" he asked Lily hopefully.

"Of course," she answered.

Relief spread across his broad face. "I'll have coffee, please."

"Coming right up." Lily bustled off.

Detective Stewart shifted uncomfortably in his chair, and it occurred to me that my suggestion to meet here had been unintentionally brilliant. Detective Stewart was out of his element and ill at ease. Using this to my advantage, I said, "So what do you think about what I told you on the phone? What do you think it means?"

"You mean the necklace?" He shrugged slightly. "I admit it's odd, but it doesn't prove anything. However, we do have some new evidence that does suggest—"

"What do you mean it doesn't prove anything?" I interrupted.

"Someone is missing a necklace that she—or he—doesn't want anyone to know about!"

Lily returned carrying a tray with two steaming pots. Detective Stewart poured out a cup of coffee for himself and took a sip. His large, blunt hands looked ridiculous holding the delicate cup.

"Ms. Parker, I'm not saying that what you saw isn't without merit, but—"

"Have you checked it out? What about the initials? Whose initials are they?"

"I don't have the answer to that," he said. "But I'm working on it."

"You're working on it? What does that mean? I've been thinking about this, and the only people not already known around here are the Andersons. Are they who they say they are?"

"As far as I've been able to tell, they are indeed who they claim to be." Reaching into his overcoat, he pulled out his scruffy black notebook. Flipping it open, he read, "'Henry Anderson, age fifty-eight. His first wife, Valerie, died seven years ago from breast cancer. Runs an antiques business. Married Joan Baxter, age fifty-six, four years ago. It is her first marriage. Together they run an antiques store called Old Things.'" He closed the book and regarded me calmly.

"I still say there's something going on there. The night after Gerald's murder, I found Joan in the dining room. She said she'd been outside smoking. She said that Henry hated her smoking, which was why she was hiding it. But then I saw Henry outside smoking himself!"

"Lots of couples have secrets from each other."

"I still say there's something going on there," I repeated stubbornly.

"And as I said, we're looking into that."

"Well, you don't seem to be looking very hard!" I leaned across the small table and pounded my forefinger onto the linen tablecloth for emphasis. "This is important! And there's something else. On the morning of the murder, when I was bringing out the coffee, I overheard Joan. I didn't think anything of it at the time—in fact, I forgot all about it until this afternoon. Joan seemed upset and she said to Henry, 'I can't wait until this is all over.' Now, why would she say that?" I asked. "By her own account, she was looking forward to the evening, so what was she afraid of? And there's more. Joan and Polly were seen talking together in town today."

Detective Stewart put down his now empty cup; he had drained its contents in two quick gulps. Wearily rubbing a hand across his face, he said, "Ms. Parker, two people talking in the street isn't a crime."

"No, but you have to admit that it's suspicious, especially when these same two people who are supposed to have no prior relationship were also talking outside in a blizzard, no less! Aren't you curious to know what they were talking about?"

Detective Stewart stared at me. "Are you always this bullheaded?"

"When it's my aunt's life on the line, yes. What's your excuse?"

We glared at each other while being stared at by most of the shop's occupants. Detective Stewart put his head back and laughed. It was a harsh noise, like a car speeding down a gravel driveway in reverse. The few customers who hadn't been staring at us now abandoned all restraint and turned to watch.

"Detective Stewart? Are you all right?" I asked. I was pretty sure he was laughing, but he could have been having some kind of seizure.

"I'm sorry, Ms. Parker. Excuse me. You always seem to take me by surprise."

I wasn't sure if that was a compliment or not. "Detective Stewart," I said, getting back to the topic at hand, "my aunt did not kill Gerald Ramsey. I've known her all my life and for you to think such a thing—for anyone to think such a thing," I said, a shade louder for the benefit of the shop's customers, "is ridiculous."

Detective Stewart lowered his voice. "Your loyalty to your aunt does you credit, Ms. Parker."

"Elizabeth."

He nodded his head. "Elizabeth. As I was saying, your loyalty to your aunt does you credit, but there are facts associated with this case that are hard to overlook."

"Such as?"

He held up his hand and ticked off the items on his beefy fingers. "Well, for one thing, there's the fact that Gerald Ramsey desperately wanted your aunt's inn."

"So?"

"So," he continued, "this wasn't just simple coveting on Mr. Ramsey's part. He was taking distinct measures to force your aunt to sell him the property. We know for a fact that he was using his influence on the zoning board not only to change certain requirements but also to establish new ones, the sole purpose of which seemed designed to drive your aunt out of business."

"I already knew that," I said. "Aunt Winnie told me herself my first night here. And I can tell you that she wasn't concerned in the least about it. My aunt is tougher than you realize. She knows how to handle bullies like Gerald Ramsey."

The eyebrow that I had grown to despise during my New Year's Day interview with him now shot up. "Don't go looking for innuendo where there is none," I said quickly. "She wasn't going to let Gerald Ramsey use the zoning board against her. She had her own plan to retaliate, a plan that didn't include murder. She has a friend on the local newspaper here and she was going to make this story public. You know, corruption on the zoning board, greed run amok, that kind of thing. She was going to fight back, but within the confines of the law."

Detective Stewart had taken out his notebook during my tirade and was jotting down notes.

"Is that all you have?" I asked, although I knew his answer before he gave it.

"No," he said. "There's the fact that other than the actors, your aunt was the only one who knew when the lights were going to be turned off. She herself turned them off."

"But I already told you, you could guess that the lights were going to be turned off after reading the invitation. It said that there would be 'screams in the dark.' I think that's why when the lights did go out no one was really surprised. We were all halfway expecting it. Now, I don't think it's too much of a stretch to assume that if I was expecting it, then so was the murderer. All he or she had to do was keep an eye out and be at the ready."

The traces of a smile—or a grimace—played on his lips. I think he was enjoying this. However, all he said was, "It's a possibility."

"It's more than a possibility," I countered, ready to argue the point more, but he held up his hand.

"I'm not done," he said. "There's also the matter of your aunt's past." His hazel eyes grew serious. "She assaulted a man with a gun, shooting him in the leg." No smile played on his lips now; his expression was deadly serious.

"That was self-defense, and the courts cleared her of any crime," I said. "A fact that you undoubtedly already know."

"I've been with the force long enough to know that being cleared of a crime is not the same as being innocent of a crime. And I don't particularly care for people who mete out vigilante justice."

My stomach twisted, but I pressed on. "She wasn't circumventing the law. She was helping a friend get out of an abusive environment. While they were there, the man came home, drunk and volatile. He threatened them. She was protecting herself and her friend."

"She could have killed him."

"Not according to my aunt." I heard myself blurt out the next words before my brain could stop them from tumbling out. "She told me that she was too good a shot to have killed him. She knew where to hit him so that he wouldn't be able to chase them."

This stupid indiscretion earned me not just one raised eyebrow, but two. His brows were practically parallel with his hairline.

"And that brings me to a point, unfortunately, you already know about," he said soberly. "The reflective tape on Mr. Ramsey's suit coat matched the roll we found in your aunt's office. Add to that the fact that the murderer is not only used to handling a gun, but is proficient at it and—"

I stuck out my chin. "And what?"

"And," he said, his hazel eyes sympathetic, "we have the makings of a very strong case against your aunt."

He might as well have kicked my stomach with his heavy, lumbering boots. I gasped before I could answer. "This is nonsense. Any one of the guests that night could have put the tape in her office." My tone sounded firm, but even to my own ears, I didn't sound convincing.

"I am sorry, Elizabeth. I know that you believe in your aunt's innocence and I promise you that I'll check out what you've learned." He tapped his notebook. "But I really think that your aunt should get a good lawyer."

"This is ridiculous. I haven't been in town five days and I've already met several people who had a reason to kill Gerald Ramsey. My aunt can't be the only suspect!"

"I never said she was the *only* suspect, I just said that she is *one*."

I frantically searched my mind for other options. Grabbing at one, I said, "What about Gerald's first wife, Tory? Wasn't there something about her death that implicated Gerald?"

A surprised expression crept into Detective Stewart's eyes. An appreciative one quickly replaced it. "How did you . . . ?" He shook his head. "Never mind. It doesn't matter." With a sigh he continued. "Yes, as a matter of fact there were questions surrounding the death of the first Mrs. Ramsey. She was having an affair at the time and the police thought that her car accident might not have been all that it appeared. But Mr. Ramsey had an alibi, as did her lover. Nothing ever came of it."

"Didn't she have any family? Could there be someone out there who might have thought Gerald had something to do with her death and . . ."

". . . waited twenty years to kill him?" he finished.

I was saved a response, which I suspected would have included a vulgar suggestion as to what he could do with his notebook, by the jangling of the shop's door. It opened, admitting none other than Ms. Jackie Tanner.

Peering in our direction, she sang out, "Elizabeth! I thought that was you!" She was still wearing the yellow hat. All that was missing from her outfit were the field glasses I was sure she employed to stalk her victims. As she bore down on us, Detective Stewart squirmed in his chair.

Marching to our table with a determined stride, she yanked a nearby chair over and sat down. "What a coincidence this is," she chirped happily. "What are you two doing here?"

Under the cover of the table, Detective Stewart pressed his foot gently on mine. "I was just getting a cup of coffee when I happened to see Ms. Parker here."

I followed his cue. "Yes. Aunt Winnie's told me so much about the wonderful food here that I just had to sample it."

Jackie looked pointedly at our food-free table. "I see," she said. Turning on Detective Stewart, she continued. "Now, Detective, tell me, when are you going to arrest someone for this terrible murder? It just gives me palpitations to think that I stood in that room with a murderer!"

Detective Stewart raised his eyebrow at her use of the word *palpitations.* I wondered if he was thinking the same as I—that a more likely description of her feelings would be "rush of excitement."

"We are working toward a solution," he said, glancing at me.

Jackie did not miss the look. "Are you two working on this together? How exciting!"

Detective Stewart stumbled over himself to clarify his meaning, but Jackie went on. "You sly thing, Elizabeth! You never said a word earlier."

"Ms. Tanner," began Detective Stewart.

"Now, don't you worry about a thing, Detective Stewart. I am the soul of discretion. Your secret is safe with me." From beneath the folds of her hat, she winked at him and without hesitation peppered him with questions intermingled with various comments and observations.

Detective Stewart was no match for her. He blanched when she referred to me as an undercover field agent. He clenched his jaw when she wondered if the killer would ever be found. His face flared red when she suggested that maybe the local law enforcement manpower wasn't up to this kind of investigation.

I leaned back in my chair and enjoyed the remarkably entertaining spectacle of a usually intimidating Detective Stewart being verbally trounced by Jackie. Finally, he could take no more. She wasn't listening to his responses anyway. In a jumbled rush, he pushed his chair back and, muttering something about a previous appointment, bolted from the shop.

Watching him go, I chuckled. Apparently, I had unlocked the secret to unnerving Detective Aloysius Stewart—tea shops and Jackie Tanner. His namesake would have been sorely disappointed.

CHAPTER 18

There is danger when a man throws his tongue into high gear before he gets his brain a-going.

—C. C. PHELPS

I DIDN'T NEED to look out my window the next morning to know that another storm was brewing. The intense pounding in my head told me that. Trying to avoid all contact with light, I stumbled to the bathroom, where I blindly groped for either the aspirin or my sinus medicine. Finding a bottle, I gulped down several chalky tablets and sank back into the comforting warmth of my bed.

While I waited for the ferocious pressure in my skull to subside, I thought about Aunt Winnie. Although she had tried to hide it, she had taken our disappointing interview with Jackie pretty hard—we all had. On a certain level, we had assumed that given Jackie's extraordinary ability to know everything about everyone, she would provide a vital piece for our puzzle. I had wanted to keep Detective Stewart's increased suspicions from Aunt Winnie, but it seemed folly to do so in light of the fact that the reflective tape had been found in her office. It suggested to all three of us that someone was trying to frame her. After I'd gotten back from my meeting with Detective Stewart, Aunt Winnie, Peter, and I had sat in the kitchen drinking coffee and trying to think of who could be behind this. We found ourselves exactly where we had been in the beginning, with a handful of suspects and no real evidence against any one of them.

It was well after midnight when we trudged off to bed, depressed and tired. Our best hope in deflecting the police's attention away from Aunt Winnie had been the necklace. Unfortunately, this appeared inconsequential to the police in light of Aunt Winnie's past. We had been left with two absolutes: that the police suspected Aunt Winnie of murdering Gerald, and that the real killer was still out there. It had made for an unsettling night.

When the light no longer made me wince in pain, I gingerly eased myself out of bed. Normally, I loved watching the cool early morning light play across the glossy wood floor, but not today. Today the light merely seemed intent on tormenting me. I dressed sluggishly and crept downstairs to start breakfast. On the stairs, my foot came into contact with something hard. It was Henry's watch—again. I picked it up and continued down.

Pushing open the kitchen door, grown somehow heavier since last night, I staggered into the kitchen. Peter and Aunt Winnie were busily moving about. "Morning," I said. At the sound of my voice, which even to my ears sounded like a wounded frog, both of them spun around.

"Jesus!" said Peter. I gathered I didn't sparkle. He stared at me, mouth open. A forgotten wooden spoon in his hand dripped batter onto the floor.

"Honey?" said Aunt Winnie, coming toward me. "Are you okay? You look terrible."

"Headache," I mumbled.

"Oh, sweetie," she said, rubbing her hand lightly up and down my arm. "I forgot how this kind of weather affects you. No wonder you feel rotten—they're predicting quite a storm. Here, have a seat."

She gently guided me to one of the toile-covered chairs. The cheerful pattern seemed suddenly garish and loud.

I glanced out the kitchen window. The sky was dark and heavy with low, fat clouds. Paring my speech down to the essentials, I asked, "When?" Aspirin helped some, but the only real relief would come when the storm started.

"Not until this afternoon, I'm afraid," said Aunt Winnie with real sympathy.

Great. I had several more hours of this to look forward to. Aunt Winnie shoved a cup of coffee in my hand—a bright purple cup that blared in pink letters SASSY, SEXY, AND SEVENTY. I tossed Henry's watch onto the table and took a grateful sip.

"Why don't you go back to bed?" she asked. "Peter and I can handle this."

I took another mouthful of the hot coffee and rubbed my hand across my face. "No," I said. "I'll be okay. I think the aspirin is starting to kick in. Besides, didn't we agree last night that you were going to sleep in and Peter and I would handle breakfast?"

"Thank you," Peter chimed in with a weary voice. Pointing the wooden spoon accusingly at Aunt Winnie, he said, "I've been trying to convince her of that all morning." More batter dripped onto the wood floor.

Aunt Winnie shook her head. "I remember *you two* agreeing that I would sleep in. What I don't remember is *my* agreeing to it." She slammed the refrigerator door shut. Sticking her jaw out defiantly, she continued, "What's the point of running an inn if you don't run it? This is still my place, thank you very much, and I'll be damned if I'm going to hide in my room every time something unpleasant happens. I can handle this."

Her words were strong, but they were belied by her appearance.

As debilitating as my headache was, it hadn't prevented me from noticing the dark circles under her eyes or her pale, pasty complexion.

"Aunt Winnie—" I began.

"No, Elizabeth," she said, cutting me off. "I know you mean well—that you *both* mean well," she amended, turning to Peter, "but I don't treat you like children and order you back to your rooms." She stopped and gave me a meaningful look before adding, "Even when you clearly need to be there." She paused. "All I ask is that you afford me the same respect."

Peter spoke first. "I'm sorry, Aunt Winnie. You're right. We didn't mean to be obnoxious," he said, the spoon hanging forlornly by his side. Lady Catherine, never far from the food preparations, snaked around his ankles. Her small pink tongue darted out to lick the spilled batter.

"We're just worried about you," I added.

"I know," she said. "But I'm going to be fine. We all will be. Now, Peter, give me that spoon before you make more of a mess of this kitchen and drip batter onto Lady Catherine's fur."

I really wanted to believe her, but it's hard to be optimistic when your head feels like it's being held together with defective tape.

After cleaning up the batter, the three of us prepped the breakfast. Aunt Winnie put together the cereals, Peter ground the coffee, and I took over the muffins. As I placed a tray of blueberry muffin batter into the oven, I said, "You know, before this weekend, I never really cooked. But I think I'm starting to get the hang of it."

"Yes," Peter said, leaning down to change the oven's setting from broil to bake. "You're becoming a regular pro." He winked at me when he said this and gave my shoulder a friendly squeeze.

Joan and Henry were already in the reading room when I carried in the breakfast tray. So was Daniel. What surprised me was Polly standing next to him. Her jet-black hair was still pulled back into a tortoiseshell headband, but she had traded in her usual shapeless ankle-length dress for jeans and a black turtleneck. Against so much black, her freshly scrubbed face appeared young and vulnerable. Unconsciously, my own eyes slid to the room's mirror to seek out my reflection. The vision that stared back at me was anything but dewy fresh. In fact, I looked like something that sucked the life out of dewy fresh things.

"Hello, Elizabeth," Polly said with a small smile. "I hope you don't mind me barging in on breakfast, but Daniel and I are running some errands today. We want to get an early start before the storm hits."

"Not at all. Help yourself," I said.

Daniel had been staring at me since I'd walked into the room. His expression was not one of admiration. "Don't take this the wrong way," he said, as he lifted a muffin from the tray, "but you look like you've been dragged through the hedge backward."

"I have a headache."

"I'd say the headache was having you," he offered before walking away. Polly poured herself a cup of coffee and followed.

I was setting everything out when Joan appeared next to me. She was dressed in a fisherman's sweater and brown corduroy slacks, and her unruly red hair was pulled back into a simple bun. A stranger would be hard-pressed to guess that this refined-looking woman with the delicate features was involved in a murder investigation. But as she peered at me from behind her glasses, I could see that her eyes were worried. What was Joan Anderson's secret? And how did it relate to Gerald's murder?

My head was throbbing and I no longer had any patience for

subtleties. "I meant to tell you, I found Henry's watch. I also found a necklace. You didn't lose one, by chance, did you?"

Joan stared at me, her expression inscrutable. "A necklace? No. But I'm glad that you found Henry's watch. He'll be so pleased."

Henry joined us. "Dear," Joan said quickly, "Elizabeth found your watch."

"Really?" he said, turning to me. "That's good, I've been looking all over for it."

"I left your watch in the kitchen, Mr. Anderson. I'll get it for you in a minute. I found a necklace, too. But no one seems to know anything about it." Joan glanced at Henry. He shifted the position of his thick arms several times, first crossing them on his chest, then letting them fall loosely at his sides, and finally holding them behind his back. "Really?" was all he said.

"Yes," I said, straightening the breakfast items. "I wonder if it could have something to do with Gerald's murder?" I mused. "I'd better call Detective Stewart."

I ignored their stunned expressions and walked back to the kitchen. I told Peter and Aunt Winnie what I had done. "Quick," I said to Peter, "get out there and see if you can overhear anything between them." Muttering something about a "headstrong idiot," Peter rushed off in the direction of the reading room.

Aunt Winnie turned to me. "Honey, are you sure you should have done that?"

I rubbed my head. "No. But it's too late now. I'm going to call Detective Stewart again. I don't know how, but I'm going to make him listen to me."

Leaving Aunt Winnie in the kitchen, I shoved Henry's watch in my pocket and hurried down the hall to the office. As usual, it was a complete mess. Really, the murderer couldn't have picked a better place to stash the tape, I thought. Given the room's constant state of disorganization, Aunt Winnie never would have found the tape herself. My mind went back to my first night at the inn. Hadn't I heard someone in the office? Could that have been the killer planting the tape? I made a mental note to tell Detective Stewart. As I rummaged through the desk for his phone number, I heard the front door open. Wondering who it could be, I stuck my head out of the office. It was Jackie.

She was certainly dressed for the cold weather. An enormous blue wool hat decorated with tiny white snowflakes covered her head. The little bit of her face not covered by the hat was swallowed up by a giant red-and-white scarf that had to be one of her knitting creations. It was mammoth. I could see why Linnet thought the one given to her was meant to be a shawl.

Jackie looked around the empty foyer with an unsure expression and walked by the office before she saw me. "Elizabeth!" she cried out, turning to face me. "I'm so glad you're here. You're just the person I wanted to talk to."

"Why?" I asked, coming out of the office. "What's wrong?"

"I've remembered! I told you it would come to me and it did! Just as I was falling asleep last night it came to me. The lights! It was the lights!" she exclaimed excitedly.

"The lights?" I repeated. "I don't understand. What about the lights?"

She shook her head in exasperation. "Oh, never mind. I must talk to Detective Stewart. I've been calling him all morning, but I can't get through. If I didn't know better, I'd think the man was deliberately ducking my calls."

Luckily, she didn't expect me to refute this; I doubt I could have done it with a straight face. She kept talking, her voice excited. "But then I remembered you!"

"Me?" I said, confused. "Why me?"

"Because you're working with Detective Stewart and you'll know how to get in touch with him!"

Behind her the Andersons and Daniel and Polly came to the door of the reading room. Seeing Jackie, they paused, their expressions curious.

"But I'm not working with him—" I began.

Jackie waved away my protestations with a gloved hand. "Don't worry, my dear. Your secret is safe with me. But I have to get in touch with him. I must tell him. Once he hears me out, he'll understand. I'd drive over to the station myself, but I've got to get back to the house now. I promised Linnet that I'd find her contacts before I met her at the club for lunch—although truth be told, I have *no* idea where they could be. But I'll turn that house inside out if I have to because Linnet will be furious with me if she has to wear her glasses at the club. Oh, I can't wait to tell her about the murder," she said with a smile. "She'll be so surprised! It's not who we originally thought it was at all!"

"But I don't understand," I said. My headache or the medicine had slowed down my thought process dramatically. "What am I supposed to tell Detective Stewart?"

Jackie let out a frustrated sigh. "Why, I thought that was obvious!" she said. "I know who did it! I know who the killer is!"

At the reading room doorway, a coffee cup crashed to the floor. Jackie whirled around suddenly. Realizing for the first time that she had an audience, she gave a startled gasp. Joan and Henry stood just outside the doorway. Polly was bending down to pick up the pieces of the shattered cup. Next to her was Daniel, with an inscrutable expression.

I couldn't see Jackie's face. Was she staring at someone in particular? When she turned back to me, her complexion was ashen. The snowflakes on her hat trembled as she said in a shaky voice, "I can't say any more now. I didn't realize . . . Just have him call me or come by the house. I'll be there for a few hours." Her lower lip quivered and she added in a harsh whisper, "Linnet's right. I am a silly old fool."

Without another word she scurried out, slamming the door behind her. I stared at the group frozen in the doorway. They stared back at me.

CHAPTER 19

For precocity some great price is always
demanded sooner or later in life.

—MARGARET FULLER

POLLY SPOKE FIRST. "I'm sorry, Elizabeth, I seem to have broken one of your cups." Cradling the wet remains in her hands, she nodded at the front door. "What was that all about?" Her tone was casual, but her face was tense, her green eyes glittering like shards of sea glass.

"I'm not sure," I said. "She wants to talk with Detective Stewart about something."

Polly glanced at Daniel. "She didn't say about what?"

If they hadn't heard Jackie's startling declaration, I wasn't about to enlighten them. "Not so that I understood," I said, shaking my head.

"Well," she said, nodding at her hands, "I am sorry about the cup."

"Don't be." I stepped forward to take the pieces from her. Her trembling hands were ice-cold. I looked at her in surprise. Her eyes were trained on my face as if she were trying to read something from it. But she said nothing more. She signaled to Daniel and they both crossed the foyer and slipped into their coats. "Be back later," Daniel called over his shoulder as they stepped out into the freezing air.

Clutching the wet shards of china in my hands, I ran down the hall to the kitchen. Bursting through the door, I said, "Aunt Winnie, you'll never guess what just happened!"

She was sitting at the table, a plate of toast and a cup of coffee in front of her. Eyeing the mess in my hands, she took a sip of coffee before intoning calmly, "You smashed one of my good coffee cups."

"No, Polly did that," I said, throwing the remains in the trash. I turned to her and in an excited whisper, blurted out, "Jackie was just here. She says she knows the identity of the killer!"

Aunt Winnie slammed her cup down on the table. "You're kidding! Who?"

"She didn't say. She wants to get in touch with Detective Stewart first, but she can't reach him." I looked down at my hands, realized they were covered with coffee drippings, and moved to the sink to wash them. I couldn't seem to stand still.

Aunt Winnie's brow furrowed. "I don't understand. Why did she come here?"

I yanked the faucet off and turned back to Aunt Winnie. Jackie's startling announcement had left me with a rush of adrenaline and I now drummed my fingers nervously on the countertop. "She has it in her head that I'm working with Detective Stewart. Apparently she thinks I've got a better chance of reaching him."

"Did she say anything else? What makes her think she knows who did it?" Aunt Winnie was now standing, too, her foot tapping out a rhythm similar to my fingers.

"She said it had to do with the lights, but I don't know what that means." I paced back and forth between the sink and the table while I tried to make sense of that statement. Lady Catherine appeared. Perching on the chair opposite Aunt Winnie, she nonchalantly tried to steal a piece of toast.

"The lights? What about the lights?" Aunt Winnie asked, her voice sharp. Without looking, she shoved Lady Catherine off the chair.

"She didn't say. Everyone came into the foyer from the reading room and she left." I knew it was silly, but hope began to rise in my chest. Maybe this nightmare was about to end. If, by some miracle of heaven, Jackie had solved the mystery, then Aunt Winnie would be safe. But that said, I couldn't stand this inaction anymore. "I'm going to try to get hold of Detective Stewart," I said. "Jackie said she's going to be home for a bit. Then she has to meet Linnet for lunch."

"I'm going to call Randy." Aunt Winnie quit the kitchen and headed for her room.

I rushed back to Aunt Winnie's office, where I resumed my search for Detective Stewart's number. As I rummaged through the desk, Henry appeared in the doorway. "Elizabeth?" he said. He stepped into the room and, amazingly, shut the door softly behind him. "I'm here for my watch."

With his presence the tiny, cramped office seemed to shrink even farther. Henry had never struck me as an imposing man. But now, alone with him in Aunt Winnie's office with the door closed, he seemed large and menacing.

"Of course, Mr. Anderson," I said crisply. "I have it right here." My stomach was churning, but at least I thought I sounded in control. I reached into my pant pocket and handed it to him.

"Thank you." His thick fingers grasped the watch.

"It's very nice," I babbled. "But I think Mrs. Anderson is right—you really should get the clasp fixed."

"Um. Yes. You're probably right." He nodded quickly, sending a strand of limp brown hair down onto his forehead.

We stared at each other and then he said, "Well, thank you again for finding it." He made no move to leave and I became more than ever aware of that closed door. Glancing at the desk, I searched for something I could use to defend myself should the need arise. A letter opener lay on top of a pile of papers and I palmed it. Granted, it wasn't much, but it was metal. It would have to do. My only other defense in hurting him would be to shout out nasty things about Mrs. Kristell Dubois. I entertained a brief image of him falling, doubled over in pain, as I hollered, "Mrs. Kristell Dubois is a gauche, tarted-up old biddy." Henry still made no move to leave; he seemed caught in some internal debate.

An idea came to me. "Don't you want to know where I found it?" I asked, breaking the silence. It was clear that he did not.

Reluctantly, he said, "Where?"

I was taking a gamble, but given that someone had planted the tape in Aunt Winnie's office, I had to try. "Here," I said, gesturing toward the desk. "On the floor underneath the desk. I wonder how it ended up there."

Henry's dark eyes slid to where I had indicated. With a guarded expression, he said, "I have no idea." He hadn't blanched in shock, but I was sure he was upset. Clearing his throat, he seemed about to say more when the door opened. Peter poked his head around the door frame. "Elizabeth?" he said. "What's going on? Oh, excuse me, Mr. Anderson. I didn't see you." Sensing the tense atmosphere, Peter asked, "Is everything all right?"

"Everything is fine," Henry said. Without another word, he shoved past Peter and out of the office. As soon as he was gone, I sank heavily into the chair.

Peter turned to me. "What the hell was that all about?"

"I gave him back his watch. I told him I found it underneath the desk."

"Why did you tell him that?"

"I don't know. I thought that if he planted the tape here, he might look guilty or something."

Peter cocked an eyebrow at me. "I see. Well, did he?"

"No. But he was upset. For a minute, I thought he was going to tell me something, but then you burst in and he left." I sighed and gestured toward the desk. "Here, help me find Detective Stewart's phone number. I've got to tell him about Jackie."

Peter narrowed his eyes in confusion. "What about Jackie?"

"She came here this morning. She said she knows who the killer is—something about the lights. She wants me to call Detective Stewart for her. She hasn't been able to reach him."

"She said she knows who killed Gerald?" he said in astonishment. "Who?"

"I don't know. Everyone came in from the reading room and she left."

Confusion registered in his brown eyes. "But what did she say—and why did she say it to *you*?"

"I don't know." I rubbed my forehead. "She's got this silly idea in her head that I'm working undercover with Detective Stewart. She probably thinks I can reach him on some secret bat line."

"Secret bat line?" Peter repeated.

"It's just an expression," I snapped. "Just help me find the damn number."

We pawed through the mess that was Aunt Winnie's desk until Peter triumphantly held up a small white card. "Here it is. Detective Aloysius Stewart." He paused and cocked an eyebrow at me. "His first name is Aloysius?"

"Yeah, I know," I said, taking the card from him. "I think his mother was a fan of Evelyn Waugh." I flipped open my cell phone;

there was no signal. I pushed the papers on the desk to one side in the hopes that the phone was somewhere underneath them. It was not.

"You seem to know a lot about the man. Are you sure you're not working undercover with him on this?"

"What?" I said. "Peter, I don't have time for this right now. Just please help me find the damn phone!"

Only by backtracking from the wall cord were we able to unearth it. With shaking hands, I clumsily punched in the numbers. The line rang and rang, until finally Detective Stewart's voice mail clicked on. In a voice so raspy it would have been comical at any other time, Detective Stewart gravely pronounced that he was out of the office but would check his messages and return them promptly. I blurted out a plea for him to call me and slammed down the receiver.

Slumping back down in the chair, I cradled my head in my hands. My head hurt.

From somewhere to my left, I heard Peter's voice. "Elizabeth, are you all right?"

I raised my head. "No, Peter, I'm not. For God's sake, I'm a stupid fact-checker at a newspaper. I studied English literature in school, not criminal justice!" The stress of the last few days broke over me and I rambled on, "I know that the name of Ulysses' faithful dog is Argos. I know that in mythology, Truth is the Daughter of Time, and I know that it's 'such stuff as dreams are made *on,*' not *of.* But what I don't know is who killed Gerald Ramsey! I have a brain stuffed with useless bits of knowledge and I'm in the middle of a murder investigation and I don't know what to do anymore!" Wearily, I dropped my head back in my hands.

After a brief silence, Peter said, "It's not 'the stuff that dreams are made of'? Are you sure?"

I opened my eyes and stared at him. "What?"

"I said, are you sure that it's not 'the stuff that dreams are made of'? Because that's what Bogart says at the end of *The Maltese Falcon.*"

"Yes, I'm sure. And since when is Bogart the last word on Shakespeare?"

"He doesn't have to be," he said with a studied look of incomprehension. "He's Bogart."

"Get out," I said.

"Maggie likes Bogart," Peter began.

"Maggie also likes *you,* so that's not exactly a point in her favor for excellent judgment."

Peter snapped his fingers. "Carly Simon. She thinks so, too. She had that song, you know the one, where she sings, 'It's the stuff that dreams are made of.' I really think you're wrong on this."

I threw the letter opener at him, hitting him in the arm.

"Hey! That hurt!" he yelped, rubbing the spot.

"Good. It was supposed to."

He laughed. "Well, I'm glad to see that you're feeling better. And now that you mention it, I do have some errands to run. I'll be back soon." He left, humming the Carly Simon song.

Taking Detective Stewart's card with me, I walked back to the kitchen. Aunt Winnie wasn't there, so I went to take a hot shower. Afterward, my headache was still in attendance, but in a slightly veiled way, as if it was just offstage waiting for its cue. Glancing out my window, I saw that the sky was an ominous mix of slate gray and dark purple; the clouds were thick and heavy.

Once I was dressed, I tried Detective Stewart again from my cell phone. Again, I got his voice mail. I left him a detailed message about Jackie and the necklace, and then called Jackie. There was no answer. An uneasy sensation crept over me and I had a sudden urge to get to Jackie's house. Running down to Aunt Winnie's room, I rapped on the door. No answer. Peter wasn't back from his errands, so I scribbled a note that I was going to Jackie's and left it on the kitchen table. With a growing sense of dread, I grabbed my purse and coat and ran to my car.

I drove as fast as I dared, but the wind was fierce and it buffeted my car around like a pinball. Holding tightly onto the steering wheel, I concentrated on keeping the car in my lane and not overreacting. Jackie was fine, I told myself. I was being unreasonable. She had probably easily found the contacts and left to give them to Linnet. From the way the hairs on my neck stood upright, I knew I didn't really believe this a likely scenario. I called Detective Stewart's voice mail once more to tell him that I was on my way to Jackie's house and for him to reach me there. I didn't even bother to control the rising panic in my voice.

Pulling into the circular driveway, I could see that the front door was ajar. Running up the front steps, I pushed the door open. "Hello?" I called out. "Is anybody here? It's me—Elizabeth."

Silence.

Cautiously, I slid inside, calling out inane phrases like, "Is anybody home? Linnet? Jackie? Hello?" After checking every room on the first floor for human habitation, I cautiously inched my way up the staircase. From the moment I had stepped inside the foyer, every atom of my being wanted to flee. My heart thudded in my chest and my skin crawled in anticipation of some unknown horror, but I forced myself to continue. Upstairs, only two rooms were in use. One was clearly Linnet's. The furnishings were ornate and expensive. Atop a rolltop desk, numerous pictures of Linnet posing with everyone from celebrities to politicians over the years were prominently displayed. A large four-poster bed complete with tapestries sat regally in the middle of the room. On either side were intricately carved nightstands in the same design as the bed. One held a pitcher of bright fresh flowers; the other a lamp and some books. It had all the warmth and beauty of a museum. All that was missing was a red velvet rope strung across the door and a placard that read "Please do not sit on the furniture." In French.

Jackie's room was less flamboyant. There was a twin bed with a patchwork comforter and a dresser. On a white rocking chair sat a battered and well-loved-looking stuffed elephant. None of the room's furnishings matched; the only thing they had in common was age. But to my taste it was preferable to Linnet's room. It held no pictures, but as I turned to leave, my foot kicked a thin scrapbook by the bed. I picked it up and flipped through its yellowed pages. Unlike Linnet's vast display, the major accomplishments of Jackie's life were quietly preserved: her birth certificate, high school and college diplomas, a certificate of appreciation from Radcliffe's drama department, a letter for promotion to head librarian at Ohio University, and finally a letter of commendation received upon her retirement. I shut the book and replaced it with a sense of sadness that a life spanning over seventy years could be captured in such a slim volume.

A third door off the hallway was closed. I had taken two steps toward it when a low moan filtered through its thick frame. The pitiful sound faded and was replaced by an erratic tapping noise. My mind's eye saw a feeble hand desperately grasping for the door handle. Taking a steadying breath against what I might find on the other side, I yanked open the door. A few suitcases and a pile of boxes were the room's only belongings. As I stood there, the moaning returned. I whirled around and saw the giant tree outside the window sway under the gusting wind, its protesting limbs groaning under the strain. Long spindly branches brushed at the glass.

A quick, and less emotionally hysterical, tour of the rest of the upstairs yielded nothing untoward. The house was empty. I reassured myself that Jackie probably hadn't shut the front door tightly when she'd left and the wind had blown it back open. With my nerves once more intact, I walked downstairs, seriously wondering if I should seek some kind of medical treatment for my tendency to overreact. I was on the landing when I heard a door burst open and felt a blast of cold air.

It was coming from the sunroom. Walking in that direction, I saw that the wind had blown the side door open. A bundle of rags lay just outside. But as I reached out to shut the door, I saw that it wasn't a bundle of rags. It was a body.

Stifling a scream, I edged closer. The body lay facedown. I didn't need to turn it over to know who it was. The blue hat told me that well enough. A small smooth ear peeked out from under its floppy folds. With shaking hands, I felt for a pulse. The skin under my fingertips was cold and lifeless. As I pulled the hat back, my breath caught in my throat. Jackie had been beaten savagely; dried blood was smeared all through her sparse gray hair and her face was horribly bruised and swollen.

Above me the trees moaned again as if in sorrow just as the storm broke, unleashing a torrent of angry snowflakes.

CHAPTER 20

Faith, Sir, we are here today, and gone tomorrow.

—APHRA BEHN

I STUMBLED OUT of the house just as Detective Stewart arrived. He jumped from his car and rushed over. "What happened?" he barked at me, his expression black.

I took several deep breaths before answering. I finally spit out, "Jackie. Dead. Backyard," before collapsing in an ungraceful heap on the stoop.

He raced into the house. I did not follow. The cold and the snow pelted my face with harsh little jabs, but I stayed slumped on the front steps. I had had enough of dead bodies.

Moments later, Detective Stewart rushed from the house and grabbed the radio in his car. He barked out orders for police backup and the coroner. Then he jogged over to me. "What happened?"

I tilted my head back. Snowflakes swirled around his face, making his expression hard to read. "I got worried when I couldn't reach Jackie on the phone," I said. "So I came over here to make sure everything was all right."

He pulled out his notebook. "Tell me again what happened this morning at the inn."

"Jackie showed up shouting she knew who the killer was. She'd been trying to get in touch with you. She still had it in her head that you and I were working together and she asked me to call you. She said she'd be home for a little while, but then she had to go and meet Linnet for lunch."

"Did anyone else hear her say she knew who the murderer was?"

"They could have. Everyone was coming out of the reading room when she was talking to me in the foyer. When she noticed them, she stopped talking and abruptly left. She looked upset," I said, recalling her ashen face.

Detective Stewart's mouth set in a grim line. "Who was there?"

"Daniel, Polly, and the Andersons."

"Did Ms. Tanner say why she thought she knew who the killer was?"

I had been dreading this question, but I knew I had to answer it. "Yes. She said it had something to do with the lights." I faced him defiantly.

"I see." His eyebrow inched up. I knew what he was thinking: Aunt Winnie had been the one who turned out the lights.

Sirens wailed in the distance. A chill that had nothing to do with the weather overtook me and I wrapped my arms around my legs and put my head on my knees. I stayed that way for a long time.

Within minutes the house was overrun with police. They rushed in and out of the house, taking pictures, dusting for fingerprints, and asking me duplicate questions. I was still hunched on the front steps. I could no longer feel my bottom, but I didn't want to go back inside the house. Someone—I think Detective Stewart—gave me a cup of coffee. I think he spiked it with some brandy, too. I held the warm cup between my hands and stared at the snow. It fell in thick white sheets. I was so caught up in watching the swirling patterns that I didn't notice the car pulling into the driveway.

A medium-size bear got out of a gold Jaguar and stared at me. I closed my eyes and tried again. This time my brain correctly interpreted the image. I was not seeing an escaped circus act; I was looking at Linnet Westin. She was wearing the long fur coat she'd worn on New Year's Eve. She had added a fur hat and fur-lined boots. She looked like the poster girl for an anti-PETA campaign.

I set down the coffee, now convinced it contained brandy, and stood up.

Linnet's crisp, haughty voice rang out. "Elizabeth! Just what is going on here?" From her tone, I fleetingly wondered if she thought I had been hosting a small party for the Cape's emergency rescue squad in her absence.

"Mrs. Westin—" I began, but she cut me off.

"And where is Jackie?" She slammed her car door shut in annoyance. "She was supposed to meet me over an hour ago with my contacts. I can't find my cell phone, so I couldn't call her to find out where she went." She gingerly stepped out from behind the car, her normally confident stride hindered by the icy road.

"What is going on here anyway?" she demanded. Her mouth formed a crimson O as she made the connection between the police cars and Jackie's absence. "Oh, dear God!" she gasped, in a tight frightened voice. "Jackie! Is she all right?" She started for the front door. I reached out and grabbed her arm.

"Mrs. Westin," I said gently. "I'm so sorry. I don't know how to tell you this, but . . ."

"Where is she?" she whispered. I couldn't see her eyes behind her large Jackie O. sunglasses, but the panic in her voice was unmistakable.

"I'm so sorry, Mrs. Westin, but she's . . . she's dead."

My words hung in the air and I had a mad thought that maybe the wind could blow them away.

"Dead?" she repeated. "But she can't be! I just saw her this morning! How can she be dead? What happened?"

Where the hell was Detective Stewart? Did I really have to be the one to tell this woman that her oldest friend had been murdered? I glanced through the doorway at the empty foyer. "I'm not sure exactly, Mrs. Westin, but it looks as if she's been murdered."

Linnet said nothing for a full minute. Underneath her heavy makeup, her face was pale. She swayed toward me and I grabbed her. "I think I'd better sit down," she whispered.

She was unsteady on her feet. I maneuvered her into the house and into the living room, where I gently deposited her on the sofa. "Can I get you something?" I asked. "A drink, perhaps?"

She nodded vaguely and I hurried off in the direction of the kitchen. Detective Stewart stood talking to one of the many police officers that had swarmed into the house. "Mrs. Westin is here," I said. "She's in the living room. I told her about Jackie. She needs a drink. Where did you get whatever it was that you put in my coffee?"

"Cabinet next to the refrigerator, second shelf," Detective Stewart said over his shoulder as he marched out to the living room.

I found the cabinet, took down the bottle of brandy, and poured a generous amount into a glass. Back in the living room, Detective Stewart was questioning Linnet. She had taken off her hat and coat but was clutching the latter in her lap like a security blanket. I doubt she realized that she was still wearing her sunglasses.

Her posture was rigid, and her grief was obvious. Her face had lost that hard, cold look; instead she seemed fragile and vulnerable. Her palpable distress made me regret all the nasty things I'd thought about her and her treatment of Jackie. I crossed over to where they sat, wrapped Linnet's hand around the glass, and took a seat next to her on the sofa.

"Where were you this morning?" Detective Stewart was saying.

"I had to run a few errands in town," Linnet answered weakly. "And then I went to the club to meet Jackie for lunch, but she never—"

"Your errands," he said, "where were they?"

"The beauty shop and then some dress shops."

Detective Stewart noted this down. "What time were you supposed to meet Ms. Tanner?"

"Eleven thirty."

"What time did you leave the house this morning?"

"Around nine. My appointment was at nine thirty."

"I see." Detective Stewart paused. "I realize that you've only just arrived, but is anything missing that you can see? We need to rule out robbery."

Linnet scanned the room with a vague expression and shook her head. "No, not that I can see. But I'll check my jewelry box in my room. I'm sure Jackie didn't have anything of value."

"Okay. Did Ms. Tanner have any relatives that you know of? Next of kin, that sort of thing?"

"No. She doesn't . . . didn't. Only me, I guess, and we were only distant cousins." Her face crumpled. She took a drink from the glass, and after a steadying breath she added, "She was an only child and never married."

"No children?"

Linnet sat up straighter on the sofa and said sternly, "Of course not, Detective. As I said, Jackie never married. To suggest a child outside of marriage is offensive!"

A crimson blush stained the back of Detective Stewart's neck. "I meant no offense, ma'am. It's a standard question."

"Well, it's a damn silly one, if you ask me."

"Yes, ma'am." He went on quickly. "Mrs. Westin, it has come to our attention that Ms. Tanner thought she knew who killed Gerald Ramsey." Linnet rejected this statement with a shake of her head. Not a strand of her perfectly coiffed hair moved as she did so. "Jackie said that? But that can't be right. She never said a word to me!"

"It's true, Mrs. Westin," I said. "She told me so this morning. She was trying to get in touch with the police so she could tell them."

Linnet's brow wrinkled in confusion. "But who was it? Did she tell anybody?"

"I'm afraid not," said Detective Stewart. "But she did announce her plans at the inn this morning. We are concerned that she was overheard and that's why she was killed."

"Oh, dear God," moaned Linnet. "Did she say why she thought she knew?"

"All we know is that it had something to do with the lights."

"The lights?" repeated Linnet thoughtfully. "Now that you mention it, she did say something about the lights."

"Do you remember what?" said Detective Stewart, leaning forward. His voice was urgent. I held my breath and waited for her to answer.

She shook her head apologetically. "I'm afraid I don't, Detective. Jackie had a tendency to ramble on and I'm embarrassed to say that I didn't always pay attention." Her face crumpled. "Maybe if I had, she'd still be alive. This is my fault. If I hadn't had the idea to go to the mystery dinner in the first place, then none of this would have happened."

I grabbed her hand. Giving it a squeeze, I said, "That's not true, Mrs. Westin. None of this is your fault."

"That's right," said Detective Stewart. His face was red and his lips were pressed together in a hard, thin line. "I promise you, Mrs. Westin. I will find out who did this."

After a few more questions, Detective Stewart asked Linnet to identify the body. "I am sorry to have to ask you to do this, but as you are probably the closest thing to a next of kin . . ." His words trailed off.

"I understand, Detective," she said, standing up. "I'm ready." She was still holding my hand. From the death grip she had on it, it was clear that she had no intention of letting it go.

Together we followed Detective Stewart to the sunroom. Thrown over a chair was Jackie's gigantic afghan with its cheerful stripes of white, green, and blue. Had she been happily working on it when her killer came? I turned away, sick. As we approached the side door, my throat constricted. I felt as if I were trying to breathe through a straw. Linnet showed no sign of letting go of my hand. I continued forward.

The body still lay where I had found it, although a white sheet now covered it. Detective Stewart walked over and pulled the sheet back. The blue hat fell limply to one side, revealing the sparse white hair that Jackie had so carefully hidden with her hats. I averted my eyes; I simply couldn't stomach another viewing. Beside me, Linnet jerked her hand up to her mouth. "Jackie," she moaned.

Detective Stewart looked up at her. "Is this Ms. Tanner?"

Linnet nodded, her hand still pressed to her mouth and her eyes riveted on the body. I gently turned her away and helped her back inside. "I think I'd like to lie down now," she said, her voice small. I walked her up the stairs. Her movements were slow and unsteady.

At the top landing, she paused as if unsure of her surroundings. Fearing that she might be in shock, I steered her in the direction of her room. She sank heavily onto the bed and flung her arm across her face.

"Would you like me to call a doctor?" I asked.

She shook her head. I sat beside her on the bed for a moment before going back downstairs.

Detective Stewart was waiting for me. "How is she?"

"Okay, I guess, but you probably should have one of the paramedics check her out. She's had a pretty nasty shock." So had I, for that matter.

"What was their relationship like?" he asked. "Did she have anything to gain by Ms. Tanner's death?"

"I don't think so," I said. "This house is owned by Mrs. Westin. From what I gather, Jackie was down on her luck and Mrs. Westin invited her to live here as a kind of companion."

"Did they get along?"

"As far as I could tell. I think Mrs. Westin lorded it over Jackie from time to time that she was here out of charity, and I think she sometimes treated her a bit shabbily. But I never saw Jackie get upset because of it."

Detective Stewart nodded slowly, his mouth a tight line. Lost in thought, he turned and walked away toward the back of the house, slapping his battered notebook against his thigh as he went.

CHAPTER 21

One reason I don't drink is that I want to know when I'm having a good time.

—NANCY ASTOR

It was late afternoon when I got back to the inn. I had called Aunt Winnie and told her about Jackie, so she and Peter were waiting for me. Randy was there, too. Pushing past them, I headed for the drink cart with a determined stride. I had never been much of a drinker, but tonight I thought I could become one.

"Elizabeth! What a hellish thing for you to go through," said Aunt Winnie, trailing after me. "Do the police know what happened?"

"Someone killed her," I said numbly. "Beat her to death. I found her outside in the backyard." I closed my eyes against the gruesome image of her poor battered face. I finished the first gin and tonic and made myself another. A large one.

"Honey," said Aunt Winnie, gently taking the glass from me, "alcohol is a crutch."

"Yeah, well, tonight I could use a wheelchair," I snapped, grabbing the glass. She frowned at me but didn't argue. I sat down heavily in one of the fireside chairs.

Peter sat opposite me. "Someone must have overheard her this morning," he said. I nodded dumbly. "Do the police have any ideas? Anything at all?" He searched my face for some kind of reassurance, but I had none to give. I shook my head. As far as I could tell, we were back where we had started. Actually, we were even worse off. According to Jackie, the "clue" that had led her to the identity of the murderer had to do with the lights. And the only one who'd had anything to do with the lights was Aunt Winnie. I took a large sip.

Peter glanced at Aunt Winnie. "What should we do?"

"Short of getting the hell out of this town, I have no idea," I replied. "Detective Stewart told me that he was coming over here to talk to everyone. You can ask him when he gets here."

"This is just terrible," said Randy, shaking his head. "That poor woman. How is Mrs. Westin doing?"

"I think she's in shock," I said.

"Aren't we all?" murmured Aunt Winnie. "Frankly, I'm scared. There's a homicidal maniac on the loose!" Randy reached out and rested his hand on her shoulder.

"It's going to be all right," he said. Aunt Winnie gave him a brief smile. His words may have given her solace, but they did nothing for me. Neither of them had seen what I had. I took another, larger sip.

Aunt Winnie eyed me worriedly. "I've asked Randy to stay here at the inn until this is cleared up," she said. "I think the more people we have under this roof, the safer we all are."

Depends on the people, I thought, moving on from sips to gulps. A dark suspicion overtook me. Wasn't there something about Gerald and the sale of Randy's bookstore? Could Randy have killed Gerald for financial reasons? He had been around a lot lately. Was he trying to discern what we knew? I studied Randy as he sat, his hand protectively on Aunt Winnie's shoulder. She smiled up at him.

It was obvious that Aunt Winnie trusted Randy. I'd never had reason to doubt her judgment before. Suddenly, ashamed of myself, I pushed the ugly thought away.

Peter turned to Randy. "Did you ever find anything out from your niece, the paralegal, about Lauren?"

Randy straightened his glasses and shrugged. "Nothing more than we'd already surmised through local gossip. Lauren did meet with a divorce lawyer, although no action was taken. Conventional wisdom has it that the prenuptial agreement was ironclad and other than walking away with absolutely nothing, Lauren didn't have any options."

Peter leaned back in his chair. "And from what Elizabeth learned about Lauren and her son, Jamie, it's doubtful that she'd want to take him out of that group house he's in, especially if he's making progress."

Randy nodded. "Right. So we are left with a woman who wanted to divorce her husband but couldn't because of financial reasons."

Aunt Winnie pursed her lips. "Crimes have been committed for much less. And, unfortunately, when there's a lot of money at stake, as there is in this case, it can bring out the worst in people," she said thoughtfully. "And let's not forget Polly. Gerald kept her a virtual prisoner. He wouldn't let her go away to school and she wouldn't be able to touch her trust fund for years. I wonder what happens to it now? Maybe she gets it early." She was silent a moment and then snapped her fingers. "Wait a minute! Wasn't Gerald's first wife, Tory, having an affair when she died? Did anyone ever find out who it was with? Randy, you lived here then, did you ever hear of anything?"

Lady Catherine jumped up on Randy's lap. He gently removed her before answering. "No, I never heard who it was," he said, adjusting his glasses.

Aunt Winnie tapped her finger against her chin. "That's someone with a grudge, I bet."

Randy said nothing.

Peter put his head in his hands. "Let's face it," he moaned, "everyone who knew Gerald Ramsey had a motive for killing him."

As if on cue, Daniel walked into the room. He was wearing a blue blazer and jeans, both of which hugged him in all the right places. His hair was artfully tousled and his smile lopsided. But for once his good looks had no effect on me. I was feeling, to quote Pink Floyd, "comfortably numb," and I planned on staying that way for a long time.

Seeing our grim expressions, Daniel's ready smile faltered. "What's wrong?" he asked. "Why the long faces?"

Peter answered him. "Ms. Tanner is dead. Murdered. Elizabeth found her this morning."

Daniel's eyes flew to mine. Did I imagine a look of panic in their blue depths? "Bugger," he muttered under his breath. "How awful. What happened?"

Everyone waited for me to answer, which annoyed me. I wanted to sit in my chair, drink my drink, and forget. I didn't want to have to keep reliving the nightmare. I took another long gulp. With great effort, I said, "Someone bashed her face in." My voice sounded funny, like I was speaking through a tunnel.

From out in the foyer, the front door slammed. The Andersons' voices floated in. Daniel called out to them. "Mr. and Mrs. Anderson? I think you'd better come in here."

All sound from the foyer ceased. A second later, Henry and Joan warily poked their heads around the corner. "What seems to be the trouble?" asked Henry. His tone was casual, but his stance was not. His body quivered like an arrow ready to be released from its bow.

"Ms. Tanner was murdered this morning," Daniel said. Joan took a step back, her hand flying up to her mouth. She stared at Daniel in horror. Henry reached out to steady her.

"Do the police know who did it?" Henry's voice was harsh.

Daniel turned to me. I shook my head. "Detective Stewart is on his way," I said. "He wants to talk with us." I stared down at my glass. How could it be empty? I got up and made myself another one, studiously ignoring both Aunt Winnie's and Peter's disapproving expressions.

Henry began to argue, with whom I don't know. I was only half listening, anyway. I longed to retreat into myself again. I heard him yelling something along the lines of inconvenience, safety, and deranged killers. Peter tried to calm him down, but it didn't do any good. Henry began shouting something about Mrs. Dubois and I was wondering how I could get him to shut up and sit down when Detective Stewart arrived and Henry did just that. Two uniformed police officers remained in the foyer. Idly, I wondered if the back of the inn was surrounded as well.

Detective Stewart entered the room. "Good, you're all here. I gather you've been told about Ms. Tanner," he said, seeing me.

"Yes," said Joan in a small voice. "Was she really murdered?" Her face was pinched as if in pain. Why? I wondered. We were all upset about Jackie, but Joan looked as if she had received a stunning blow.

Detective Stewart answered her. "Yes. And quite brutally. Now I need to take your statements as to where each of you were this morning." He pulled out his notebook and said, "Why don't we start with you, Mrs. Anderson? Where were you today?"

Beside her, Henry opened his mouth as if to argue, but Joan put her small hand on his arm and gave it a squeeze. "It's okay, Henry."

Turning back to Detective Stewart, she said, "My husband and I drove into town and did some shopping at a few antiques stores. We spoke with Mrs. Dubois by phone regarding some recent purchases. Then we had lunch in town, went to the movies, and came back here."

Detective Stewart wrote this down. "I'll need to get Mrs. Dubois's number to verify your story and the names of the places you went."

"Of course," said Joan. A strand of red hair had escaped from her bun. As she recited the details, she methodically twisted and untwisted the lock of hair around her long fingers. Detective Stewart scribbled away. When she was finished, Detective Stewart turned to Daniel. "And you, Mr. Simms?"

Daniel was sitting on the couch, one arm slung over the back. He gave every impression of chatting at a cocktail party rather than being interviewed for a murder investigation. "I was with Polly Ramsey all morning," he said. "As you know, her father's funeral is tomorrow and I was helping her prepare for it." Behind Detective Stewart, I saw Joan's eyes widen. Her mouth opened as if she was about to speak, but this time it was Henry who put a restraining hand on his wife's arm.

Detective Stewart stared at Daniel for a long moment, using that trick that had reduced me to a babbling idiot. Daniel merely arched his eyebrow and calmly returned the detective's gaze. "Miss Ramsey will confirm this?" said Detective Stewart.

Daniel smiled and bowed his head. "But of course, Detective."

Turning to Peter, Detective Stewart said, "Mr. McGowan, you're next."

Peter twisted in his chair, clearly not as comfortable as Daniel at sparring with Detective Stewart. "I was here most of the morning," he said. "Around ten o'clock, I went to the Internet café in town to do some work. I was there maybe an hour. I don't really know. Afterward, I came back here, and I've been here ever since."

"What were you doing at the café?"

Peter hesitated before answering. "Just some work for my parents' business. They're working on some new properties." I studied him over the rim of my glass. He was lying. I was sure of it. I had heard that tone too many times in my youth not to recognize it now. But why? I wondered. What was he up to?

"I see," said Detective Stewart. "That won't be too hard to verify. Great thing about the Internet; it leaves a record." Peter squirmed but said nothing.

"And now, Ms. Reynolds," Detective Stewart said, "perhaps you could tell me your movements this morning?" The smile he gave her reminded me of a portrait of Machiavelli I'd seen years ago. I needed more of my drink.

Aunt Winnie returned the smile with one of her own. Seeing it, I groaned. I knew that smile; trouble always followed.

"I'd be delighted to," she said. "I was here all morning. After breakfast, I went to my room and showered. I spent the rest of the morning in my office, catching up on some paperwork."

I knew what Detective Stewart was going to say next and I dreaded it. I put my glass up to my lips and drained it, desperate to crawl into my retreat again.

"Well, that is odd," said Detective Stewart, tapping his notebook. "Because Elizabeth here"—he waved a beefy hand in my direction and everyone looked my way—"Elizabeth says that she knocked on your door several times this morning before she left for Ms. Tanner's house. She says that she got no answer." All heads swiveled in Aunt Winnie's direction.

She ignored them and said, "Well, that would make sense, Detective. As I said, I took a shower. I was probably in it when Elizabeth knocked. It seems rather obvious, actually." She smiled that smile again. Bad, I thought. Very bad.

Detective Stewart said nothing for a long time. I looked sadly at my now empty glass. I wanted another drink, but that involved standing. And walking. Both seemed inordinately Herculean efforts. And if I was going to emulate any of the Greek gods today, it was going to be Bacchus. Good old Bacchus. Good old Greeks for coming up with him in the first place. Wait, Bacchus was the Roman name. What was the Greek name? I frowned. Dionysus! *That's* my guy. I sat there full of fondness for both the Greeks and their god of wine. That's when I realized I was drunk. I might be able to think of Dionysus's name, but I sure as hell wouldn't bet money on my being able to pronounce it.

Snapping his notebook shut, Detective Stewart stood up. He seemed very far away. He also looked very stern for a man named Aloysius. I stifled a giggle. No wonder he went by Al, I thought. Nicknames could come in handy at times. Really, there were so many. Winifred became Winnie, Linnet became Linney, Jacqueline became Jackie, and Victoria became Vicky. I stopped. Victoria. A memory swirled in my head. It tried to surface but was hampered by alcohol and the ongoing conversation.

"Ms. Reynolds," Detective Stewart began. The thought was gone. So was I, for that matter. My eyelids lowered. I tried to yank them back open, but they were too heavy. Was it warm in here? Underneath me, the chair shifted and moved. I debated calling attention to the defective chair, but it seemed too much trouble. Detective Stewart kept talking. "I think I should tell you that . . ."

There was a terrific noise of something heavy hitting the floor. I think it was me. From above, I heard someone cry out, "Oh, my God!

Someone get help! She's fainted!" In a wry tone, I heard another voice add, "She hasn't fainted. She's passed out. She's drunk." I think it was Peter.

Strong arms reached underneath me and pulled me up. "No, I've got her," said Peter. He lifted me and carried me up the stairs to my room, where he unceremoniously deposited me onto my bed. He said something about my being a damned idiot, but inasmuch as I already knew that, I ignored him and rolled over, burying my head in the pillow.

CHAPTER 22

The less I behave like Whistler's mother the night before,
the more I look like her the morning after.

—TALLULAH BANKHEAD

It is a truth universally acknowledged that hangovers and funerals do not mix. Unfortunately, on the morning of Gerald's funeral, I awoke—contrary to any wish of my own—feeling as if a small mariachi band had used my head for practice. Even my teeth hurt. I felt like Gregor Samsa on the morning of his transformation, but without all the underlying symbolism.

Concentrating on keeping my head from rolling off my neck, I eased out of bed and observed myself in the mirror. The reflection staring back was reminiscent of a carnival fun-house mirror—puffy face, slits for eyes, and a slumped and twisted body. But that was nothing compared to my hair, which was at once depressing and mildly hysterical.

A hot shower and shampoo helped. Some. If nothing else, I'm sure I smelled better. As I gingerly made my way down the stairs, Lady Catherine pounced at my ankles, her claws drawn. I stumbled but managed to grab the banister before I fell headlong down the stairs. My temper flared and I pulled my leg back to deliver a well-deserved kick to Lady Catherine's hindquarters when a movement in the foyer caught my attention. Sitting in the green brocade chair usually favored by Lady Catherine was an armed police officer. He appeared more like a kid selling high school raffle tickets than a civil servant bent on protecting the peace. His boyish face looked as if it had only recently needed shaving, and his arms and legs had that gangly, not-quite-grown look. His eyes and Adam's apple bulged alarmingly. But apparently he had been able to evict Lady Catherine from her favorite chair with no visible scars, so he clearly had some professional training in hand-to-hand combat.

Seeing me, he gravely nodded his head and said, "Good morning, Ms. Parker." Unthinkingly, I nodded back at him. New waves of pain shot into the base of my skull, rendering me speechless. I was surprised that my face was known by the local police department—not exactly the fifteen minutes of fame I was shooting for in life.

"Were you about to kick that cat?" he asked.

Great. In addition to whatever else my reputation was at the station, low-life cat abuser would now be added. Shit. "I, um . . . well," I stuttered. My mind was a blank. I was way too hungover to produce a convincing lie. I gave up. "Yes. Yes, I was. Sorry."

"Don't apologize on my account," he said, distastefully eyeing Lady Catherine. "Damn thing has already bitten me twice." He glanced almost longingly at the gun in his holster. "Too bad someone didn't put reflective tape on *her*."

While I could sympathize with the sentiment, it didn't seem in my best interest to outwardly agree. For all I knew, this could be one of those psychological tests used to evaluate suspects. I could almost hear the horrified gasp from the jury as the court testimony was read: *"Suspect was observed trying to kick a defenseless cat and later heard expressing a wish to shoot said animal."*

"Yeah, well, I think I'm going to see where my aunt is," I said, moving back down the hall. I left him glaring at Lady Catherine, his hand on his gun. Lady Catherine sat poised on the rug, unconcerned, her tail twitching rhythmically.

Pausing at the kitchen door, I could hear Aunt Winnie and Peter on the other side. My cheeks burned hot at the memory of my behavior last night, but I couldn't put off the inevitable. I pushed open the door and stepped inside. The smell of fresh banana muffins was almost my undoing, but I pressed on. Peter clasped his hands together as if in prayer and sang out, "It's a miracle! Lazarus! Back from the dead!"

"Shut up, Peter," I mumbled, although, truth be told, it was nothing less than I would have done had the situation been reversed. I might not have yelled it quite so loudly, though. Hoping to change the subject, I said, "Why is there an armed guard in the foyer?"

"Detective Stewart has decided that from now on we are to have twenty-four-hour police protection. Although surveillance might be a more accurate term," said Aunt Winnie. Holding out a mug of coffee for me, she asked, "Can I get you anything else?" My stomach lurched, but I took the mug. It was black. In simple white letters it read, THERE'S GOT TO BE A MORNING AFTER.

"Yes," said Peter. "Want some breakfast? I could make you up a big plate of runny eggs if you'd like."

For a brief moment, the contents of my stomach hung in the balance. I swallowed hard and carefully shook my head. Peter chuckled. Aunt Winnie elbowed him and said, "Enough, Peter. How are you feeling, honey?"

"About how I deserve. I'm really sorry about last night, Aunt Winnie. I don't know what to say."

"Don't be ridiculous, Elizabeth. Given the day you had, it's no wonder that you—"

"Got blind stinking drunk and fell out of a chair," Peter finished helpfully.

"That's enough, Peter," said Aunt Winnie.

"No, it's okay," I said. "Besides, he's right. If nothing else, I've learned my lesson. Is there anything I can help with this morning?"

"No," said Aunt Winnie. "Peter and I have it under control. Why don't you go upstairs and get ready for the funeral? We should leave here soon. Randy is going with us."

An image of Randy, his kindly bespectacled face, swam before me. I cringed inwardly. Had I really let myself suspect him of killing Gerald and Jackie last night? I felt a fool. I nodded in slow motion to Aunt Winnie and left. I felt awful for not helping, but I knew that if I didn't get away from the smell of those muffins, very bad things involving my stomach were bound to occur.

I got ready as quickly as my pounding head would allow—which is to say, not very fast. Well, I thought with a sigh, maybe this was one time when pasty skin and bloodshot eyes were suitable; I certainly looked funereal. As I checked my reflection in the mirror one last time, I realized I was wearing the same outfit I'd worn the night Gerald had been murdered. My last thought as I left the room was that I hoped it wasn't an omen. How ironic that thought turned out to be.

The church was a large, graceful structure located in the heart of downtown. We silently walked up the wide marble steps. I was surprised to see that the long wooden pews were filled to capacity. Randy went in first, to little notice. It was when Aunt Winnie stepped into the vestibule that several heads turned our way. Seconds later the church vibrated with the soft buzz of voices passing along the news of our arrival. More heads turned. Aunt Winnie smiled and nodded politely to those who turned to gawk at us, but her jaw was clenched. Finally, Peter spotted space for the four of us in one of the pews near the back and herded us in. Once we were settled, I leaned over to Aunt Winnie and said, "I'm surprised to see so many people here. I didn't think that Gerald was this popular."

"He wasn't," said Aunt Winnie, as she read the service program. "I suspect most are here just to make sure he's really dead."

She had a point. In my short time in town, I had not heard one person say anything nice about the man. He seemed to be universally hated or feared. In the front pew sat Polly, Lauren, and Daniel. Several rows behind them were Lily and Pansy. Farther back still sat Joan, Henry, and Linnet. Why had they come?

As the priest droned on, struggling to say something respectful about Gerald's life, I felt as if I were in the midst of a play. Everyone's dress and movements, while perfectly appropriate, were nothing more than costume and stagecraft. The thought brought a melancholy pang. How sad to go through life with no one loving you. Had that really been the case for Gerald? Had he really been so miserable that his own family felt no sorrow at his death? Then I remembered Lily's—or was it Pansy's?—words: If you were going to murder someone in this town, it would be Gerald. Kneeling in my pew, I said a sincere prayer, not so much for Gerald but for his family.

After the service and burial, there was a reception at Lauren's. Like the service, it was well attended, and again for the same reason, I thought: rabid curiosity. People milled about, eating the food, drinking the wine, and making quiet observations about who had killed their absent host. Lily and Pansy chatted in rapid succession with several other ladies, their excited whispers leaving little room for doubt as to the topic of their conversation. Henry and Joan circled with a professional eye, and Henry commented several times on the similarity of this room to one of Mrs. Dubois's smaller guesthouses.

I also spotted Brooke, the salesclerk, standing with Polly and several of their friends. They stood awkwardly, shifting their drinks and plates of food, all the while eyeing Polly sympathetically. Polly noticed me. She gave a little wave and maneuvered her way through the crowd.

"Hello," she said. Gone was the demure and modestly dressed girl whose comings and goings Gerald Ramsey had dictated. In her place stood a confident and self-assured young woman. Her black velvet dress still covered every inch of her body, but in a way that accentuated those inches. I had never noticed before—I doubt anyone had under all those shapeless dresses—that Polly had a stunning figure. She was alternately small and large in all the right places. The headband was gone, too. Her black hair was pulled into a tight bun, further accentuating her exotically shaped eyes. She couldn't have made it any clearer that she wasn't living by Gerald's rules anymore. Polly was now her own woman.

She smiled politely at Peter and Randy before turning to Aunt Winnie. "Thank you for coming," she said. "I heard about Ms. Tanner. I'm sorry that she's dead. She seemed a nice woman." Her unblinking slanted green eyes gazed at us much like Lady Catherine's calculating stares.

What were we supposed to say? Aunt Winnie rallied. "I'm sorry for your loss, dear, and I wish you all the best. What are your plans now? Are you going to stay here?"

Polly's lips pulled down in a slight frown. "No. Father left the house to me, but I don't particularly want it. It feels more like a prison than a home. I suppose I'll sell it."

"Really?" said Aunt Winnie. "Where are you planning on going?"

"Oxford. I've been accepted into their graduate program for art history."

"What about Lauren?" I asked. "Do you think she'll stay here?"

Polly shook her head. "No. I asked her, but she doesn't want the place, either. I suspect she feels the same as I do." Polly regarded the expensively furnished room with little affection. "It's funny," she said. "I never really liked Lauren. I always thought she was sort of vapid, and after all, she was married to my father, which wasn't exactly a point in her favor." Polly glanced over to where Lauren stood with Denny tucked under one arm. She was trying to manage her cell phone with her free hand. "But now, I think we both understand each other a little better. She's not that bad once you get to know her."

Polly waved her hands as she tried to find the words to go on. "My father controlled everyone and everything in his life. Lauren and I were just pawns in his world and we both ended up doing things we didn't want to. Now that he's gone, well, we can be ourselves."

Someone called to her and she excused herself. I thought about what she had said. She was by all accounts a determined young woman who had hated having her freedom curtailed by an overbearing father. She was young. She was pretty. And thanks to Gerald's untimely death, she was now quite rich.

Aunt Winnie and I walked over to Lauren to offer our condolences. Seeing our approach, she smiled and signaled that she was almost done with her call. "All right," she said into the phone. "I'd better go now. I'll call you later. I love you, baby."

Clicking the phone shut, she turned to us. "Sorry, that was Jamie. He couldn't be here today, which is probably for the best. Having to deal with this would be too much for him right now."

The memory of Lauren's phone call the night of the murder came back. What had she said? "I love you, baby." Of course! Lauren hadn't been talking to a lover—she'd been talking to her son, Jamie. The one she'd do anything for. Would she have killed for him?

Lauren shifted Denny, holding him in both arms. Seeing me, his fat little tail thumped wildly and he strained to be let down. Thankfully, Lauren did not comply with his wishes. I was in no humor to have my only pair of stockings mutilated by a lusty pug. After a few futile lunges, he went limp and merely panted longingly at me.

"Thank you both for coming," Lauren said. Wearing a simple black dress that set off her deep tan to perfection, she looked stunning. Before I could stop myself, I blurted out, "You're so tan!"

Lauren glanced complacently at her tawny arms, saying, "I found a fabulous tanning salon downtown. I've been trying to get my base tan in good shape. I don't want to go to Bermuda looking pasty."

"Bermuda?" I echoed.

Lauren nodded and stroked Denny's fur with her glossy pink nails. "Yes, I leave next week. Of course, I still have to clear the trip with Detective Stewart, but I don't think it will be a problem." She smiled at me, and I wondered if she thought she was going to charm Detective Stewart into letting her go. If that was the case, she had another think coming. Say what you might about the man (and I could say plenty), Detective Stewart didn't strike me as someone who let feminine charms influence his work.

"Are you going with anyone?" Aunt Winnie asked.

Lauren shook her head. "Not this time. I wish I could bring Jamie, but I don't think he's ready to leave South Carolina yet. I hope to take him next year. Who knows, maybe we could even move there. I've never been a fan of the cold. Bermuda might be just the place for us to start over."

Changing the subject, Lauren now said, "I heard about that poor woman, Ms. Tanner. Do they really think the person who killed Gerald also killed her?"

"I think so," I said. Lauren shook her head, sending her blond hair cascading over her shoulders. "How awful. She was a strange little woman, though. A terrible gossip." Linnet passed unnoticed behind Lauren as she said this. I saw a faint blush of crimson stain Linnet's neck as she quickly moved away. "Well, in any case, I hope they catch him soon," Lauren said, oblivious to her insensitivity. "What about her friend, Mrs. Westin. Does she have any idea who did it?" Lauren's tone was light, but her hand was not. Tense and rigid, it hovered above Denny's fur.

"No," I said. The hand relaxed and resumed its affections.

"What are your plans?" asked Aunt Winnie. "Polly says that neither of you are going to stay here."

"That's right," said Lauren. "I want to find a place near Jamie. I'm hoping that he'll be able to come live with me soon. He's really making progress." She smiled. "You know, for the first time, I really think everything is going to turn out all right." A petite woman in a red dress came to offer Lauren her condolences and ask for a phone number of a mutual acquaintance. Lauren shifted Denny into her right hand to write out the number with her left. As she did so, Denny broke free and leaped from her arms. I jumped back, but he bolted past me. Great. No wonder I couldn't keep a boyfriend; I couldn't even hold the interest of a horny pug.

"Denny! No!" Lauren yelped, but he ignored her and ran across the room. Turning to me, Lauren said, "Elizabeth? Would you mind terribly getting Denny? Thanks."

She turned back to the woman, leaving me no option other than to retrieve the wayward Denny. I followed him down the hall toward the back of the house, muttering obscenities under my breath. As I rounded the corner, I walked straight into Peter. His face was contorted with anger. Putting his arm out, he tried to turn me around. I spun out of his grip. "What are you doing?" I asked. "I have to get Denny."

"No, you don't," Peter said briskly. "Turn around."

"Peter! Stop this. What's the matter with you?"

"Nothing," he bit out through clenched teeth. "I don't want you to go in there."

I glanced at him in surprise. Why was he so angry? "Peter! This is ridiculous. Let me go."

Abruptly releasing me, he said, "Fine. But don't say I didn't warn you."

Pushing past him, I said, "Warn me about what? You know, sometimes you can be so . . ." But the rest of my words died on my lips. In the sunroom stood Daniel and Polly. Kissing.

I backed out slowly so as not to be heard, but in truth they were so wrapped up in each other that I probably could have led a marching band in there without either of them noticing. The implications of what I'd seen made my head spin. Daniel and Polly? Not Daniel and Lauren. Not Daniel and me. How long had they been together? When had Polly morphed into a little Lolita, or had she been that way all along? And what did it mean?

As I backed into the hall, I bumped into Peter. His arms came up around me. "I'm sorry, Elizabeth," he said. "Are you okay?"

I was only half listening. I twisted away from his grasp. I had to go somewhere quiet and think. In addition to feeling punched in the stomach, there were more sinister implications I needed to sort out. Peter said something, but I didn't hear him. I walked back to the sitting room where only a few days before I'd had tea with Jackie. It was during that visit that Jackie had unaccountably become upset—but about what? Daniel and Polly had been having what I had thought was a mundane conversation about smoking. But given what I had just seen, maybe nothing between them was mundane. Could Jackie have realized that as well? Could that have been what had upset her?

I was so caught up in the memory of that day that as I entered the room, I imagined I was seeing Jackie again, but it was only Linnet. She was sitting in the very same chair that Jackie had sat in. Her head was tilted to one side and she wore an expression of worry on her face. I closed my eyes, trying to remember every word that had preceded Jackie's flustered behavior and her statement that something was wrong. What were they? If only she had told someone what had bothered her, she might still be alive. I opened my eyes and looked at Linnet. She stared back at me, her expression anxious. Had she lied before about knowing anything? Could Jackie, in fact, have hinted at what she had been thinking?

I walked toward her and she stood up. "Mrs. Westin?" I said. It was evident that Jackie's death had taken a terrible toll on her. Her clothes, usually elegant and stylish, hung shapelessly from her frame. She was still wearing her oversize tinted glasses and her makeup seemed heavier than usual. I suspected her vanity was trying to overcompensate for her haggard appearance.

"Hello, Elizabeth. How are you?" She sounded tired.

"I'm fine, but if you don't mind my saying so, you don't look so good. Can I get you anything?"

"No, I'm all right." Her words came out haltingly, as if she was having trouble speaking. "All this death. It's harder than you realize. And I miss her. We were friends for so long. She could be such a pain sometimes, but now I'm alone, with no one. No one to talk with about the old days. Martin. No one else remembers." Her voice broke and she swayed toward me. I reached out to steady her.

"Mrs. Westin, why don't I take you home? I think all this has been too much for you."

With apparent effort she whispered, "They all think I know something. But I don't! I don't! They keep looking at me, talking to me, bringing me drinks I don't want, just to talk to me." She stared vacantly at the drink in her hand and muttered thickly, "Tastes awful, too."

A prickling sensation ran down my spine. I took the drink from her. She didn't seem to notice. I turned my head to search for Peter. Catching his eye, I frantically waved to him. But it was too late. Beside me, Linnet Westin crumpled to the ground.

CHAPTER 23

Expect the worst and you won't be disappointed.

—HELEN MACINNES

I STARED DOWN at Linnet's inert form and screamed. Peter was at my side in an instant, followed by Aunt Winnie and Randy. Peter gently picked up Linnet and laid her on the couch. Randy ran to call 911.

"What the hell happened?" Peter barked at me.

"I don't know," I said, staring down at Linnet's face. Her lips were slack and beads of perspiration covered her face. She murmured indistinctly. Keeping my voice low, I added, "She said people thought she knew what Jackie was going to say. She seemed nervous and said her drink tasted funny. Then she passed out." Peter stared at me wide-eyed. I nodded at the glass in my hand. "Is that . . . ?" he began.

"Yes. When the police come, I'll give it to them. Maybe they can test it."

Aunt Winnie knelt beside Linnet and grabbed her hand. "Linnet?" she said loudly. "It's Winnie. You hang on. The paramedics are on their way. Everything is going to be okay. Can you hear me? It's Winnie."

Linnet moved her head slightly but did not raise her lids. "Linney?" she said, her voice distant and confused.

Aunt Winnie raised worried eyes to mine. "No. *Winnie,*" she said, a shade louder. "Just relax. The paramedics are coming. You're going to be fine."

Next to me, Peter whispered, "She's delirious."

"I know. She sounded that way before she collapsed."

Lauren pushed through the small crowd gathered around us and stared down at Linnet. "Oh, my God!" she said, her blue eyes wide with horror. "What happened? Did she have a heart attack?"

"It would seem so," Peter said quickly, lightly stepping on my foot. Annoyance surged through me. Did he really think I was so stupid that I was going to blurt out that I thought she'd been poisoned with the drink I now held in my hand? I debated returning the gesture—albeit a lot harder.

"How awful," Lauren murmured.

Polly appeared with Daniel in tow. Her lipstick was smudged. I have no idea how Daniel appeared; I couldn't bring myself to look at him. "We called 911," Polly said. "They should be here any minute. Is there anything we can do for her?"

"I don't think so," said Peter. "We'd best wait for the paramedics."

"What happened?" asked Daniel. He stood tensely, his left hand balled into a tight fist.

"They think it was a heart attack," said Lauren. Staring at Linnet, she said, "Poor thing. It's no wonder, really. The stress of the last few days must have gotten to her. Why, when I saw her this morning, I almost didn't recognize her."

"Yes," said Polly. "I thought she looked ill, too."

I wondered if either woman really had been fearful for Linnet's health or if it merely made for a good cover story. The mournful wail of a siren reverberated through the room and I clutched the heavy glass a little tighter.

As they had on New Year's, two men dressed in white raced into the room with a gurney and quickly checked a recumbent body for signs of life. Thankfully, this time their trip wasn't for naught. In silence, we watched as Linnet was lifted onto the gurney and rushed to a waiting ambulance. The siren faded, only to be replaced with another, more ominous sound—a low, throaty cough. Detective Stewart was standing in the doorway, his bulky frame taking up most of that space. He was staring directly at me. There was little pleasure reflected in his hazel eyes. I suspected that there'd be even less after I explained to him my theory about what I now held in my hands.

I resolutely forced myself across the room to where he stood. "I have to talk to you," I said, my voice low, "in private."

"Imagine my surprise," he said, raising an eyebrow.

I followed him into the foyer. "Linnet Westin was drinking this right before she collapsed." My words tumbled over each other in a rush. "She wasn't making too much sense, but she told me that she thought others suspected her of knowing what Jackie knew. She said that people kept pushing drinks on her and that they tasted terrible." I thrust the glass at him. "You probably should get this tested. I bet there's some kind of poison in it. Check for ones that make you delirious and dizzy. If you want, I could—"

But he didn't let me finish. Roughly grabbing the glass from me and sending the amber contents sloshing violently, he leaned in so close that I could clearly make out each beat of the throbbing vein that ran down his jaw. "What do you think you're doing?" he growled, his teeth clenched.

I looked at him in surprise. "I'm trying to help."

"Well, unless I ask you to—don't!"

"Are you kidding me? A woman collapses on the floor moments

after telling me that people are pressing her for information and that her drink tastes funny, and you want me to . . . what? Mind my own business and just go home?"

"What I want is for you to let the police do their jobs and you to stay out of it. Thank you for the drink sample, *but stay out of this*! Don't you understand that you could be killed? One person has already died because someone thought she knew too much. Now we may have a second. I do not want you to make it a third. Got me?"

I'm not sure what I was going to say, but it was probably for the best that one of the sergeants came into the foyer. He eyed me suspiciously and said, "Detective Stewart? Could I speak to you for a moment?"

Detective Stewart took a deep breath and nodded. He stepped toward the sergeant and then turned back to me. Giving me a level look, he said, "I hope I've made myself clear."

"Crystal," I snapped back.

The throbbing of the vein in his jaw accelerated and I was suddenly afraid it would explode. I wondered if I had pushed him too far. He glowered, but I held my ground and willed myself not to look away. Without another word, he turned and stalked out of the foyer. I sank down on one of the antique chairs that lined the hall, my bravado spent.

By the time the police finished taking everyone's statement, it was late afternoon. We piled into Aunt Winnie's car, none of us saying much. Next to me in the backseat, Peter called the hospital and tried to get information on Linnet's condition. I listened closely to his end of the conversation, even though it was difficult to comprehend anything given his penchant for monosyllabic responses. Up front, Aunt Winnie seemed intent on besting her own personal speed record. Randy sat calmly beside her, apparently immune to her crazy driving. Frankly, I was astounded at the almost Zen-like serenity he exuded in the face of obvious danger. But when he didn't flinch after our near miss with a snowplow, I realized the reason for his composure. He had taken off his glasses. Virtually blind without them, he rode in blissful oblivion. Clearly he had ridden with Aunt Winnie before. After what seemed an eternity, Peter snapped his cell phone shut and sagged into his seat.

"Well?" I said.

"She's going to be fine," Peter said. "She was poisoned—with digitalis, apparently, but thankfully, it wasn't a fatal dose. They pumped her stomach."

"What's digitalis?" Aunt Winnie and I asked at the same time.

"Poisonous plant, I guess, otherwise known as foxglove. It's pretty common around here," Peter replied.

"Which means anyone could have gotten it. Where is Linnet now?"

"Still at the hospital. They're going to release her tomorrow or the next day."

From the front seat, Aunt Winnie swiveled around and stared at Peter, aghast. "That soon? But that's insane! The poor woman was poisoned!"

"I agree," said Peter, "but there's no use arguing with insurance companies. Speaking of which, would you please turn around and watch the road before the rest of us need to file claims?"

"Well, we can't let her go home by herself," said Aunt Winnie, once again facing front. "I'll see if I can talk her into staying with us for a few days. She really shouldn't be alone. After all, someone tried to kill her!"

A black car pulled up beside us. The back window rolled down and I saw a hand launch something toward our car. My scream of warning came too late, and before I knew it, I was covered with glass and a brick lay on the floor. Before I could think to get a look at the license plate, the car was gone. Aunt Winnie slammed on the brakes and pulled over. "Is anybody hurt?" she yelled.

"What the hell happened?" Randy asked, fumbling for his glasses.

Peter grabbed the front of my coat and shook the glass off. Then he brushed his hands over my arms and pulled my hands up to inspect them.

"Hey," I said.

"I think we're both okay," he answered Aunt Winnie.

He reached down and grabbed the brick. In red letters the word *Murderer* was crudely painted on the side. Silently, he showed it to me. "What is that?" asked Aunt Winnie.

"Nothing," said Peter.

"Don't give me that," she said, turning her head to the backseat. "What does it say? I can see lettering."

Peter read it out and Aunt Winnie was silent. Without saying another word, she started the engine and pulled out onto the road.

"Aunt Winnie?" I said.

"Not now, Elizabeth. I need to think."

Nothing more was said until we skidded to a stop in the inn's driveway. I staggered into the reading room, tired and angry. I sank gratefully into one of the chairs and closed my eyes. Aunt Winnie went straight to the office. I heard the click of her answering machine as she played back her messages. A few minutes later, she came into the reading room and headed for the drink cart. "I don't know about the rest of you, but I'm having a drink. Can I get anyone else one?"

Peter and Randy put in their orders. I kept my eyes closed. Finally, I heard Aunt Winnie's voice. "Elizabeth?"

"What?"

"Can I get you a drink?"

"No, thank you."

"Aw, come on, Elizabeth," said Peter, trying to inject an air of normalcy into the tension. "The hair of the dog that bit you and all that?"

"It's more like the hair of the mastiff that mauled me," I replied, opening my eyes. "No, I'm off the hard stuff for a while."

"Whatever you say," said Aunt Winnie, making the drinks. Once done, she sat down on the couch next to Randy. Taking his drink from her outstretched hand, he asked, "Did you call the police?"

She shook her head. "And say what? That someone launched a brick into my car window? What are they going to do?"

"They could at least look into it," I said. "You should report it!"

Aunt Winnie didn't seem to hear me. "Were there any messages?" Randy asked, his voice low.

She nodded. "A few crank calls, but mostly cancellations. It's just as I feared. People don't want to stay here because they think I had something to do with what happened." Randy reached over and took her hand. She stared at the floor. Lady Catherine sauntered into the room and leaped up onto her lap. Aunt Winnie didn't seem to notice.

"Aunt Winnie?" I asked. "Are you all right?"

At the sound of my voice, she raised her head. "I've made a decision," she said slowly. She glanced at Peter. He sat up straighter in his chair. "I'm going to sell Longbourn."

Her words were like a painful kick to my already ailing stomach. In spite of the state of my head, my reaction was swift and explosive. "What?" I yelled, jumping out of my chair. "But you can't! This has nothing to do with you! You love this place too much to sell it!" My voice caught and I realized that over the past few days, I, too, had grown to love Longbourn. The thought of it being sold was a physical blow.

"Elizabeth, please calm down. I've given this a lot of thought and I think it's for the best. Like it or not, I'm going to be forever associated with this tragedy. People are canceling their reservations and really, who can blame them? Would *you* want to stay at an inn where the owner is suspected of murder? While I think I could weather the cancellations, I won't put your lives in danger. We were lucky today that no one was hurt. We might not be so lucky the next time."

"But who are you going to sell it to?" I sputtered.

Aunt Winnie took a deep breath, but it was Peter who spoke. "To me," he said quietly. "She's going to sell it to me."

I whirled around dumbfounded and stared down at him. Unflinchingly, he stared back.

The hate I had felt toward Peter that summer so long ago was nothing compared with the rage engulfing me now.

CHAPTER 24

Now comes the mystery.

—HENRY WARD BEECHER

"It's not what you think," said Peter, warily holding out his hand.

"Don't even talk to me," I shot back. "You have no idea what I think."

"Elizabeth," said Aunt Winnie. "Please. Sit down and listen to me."

"But you can't sell this place!" I said. "All this trouble will pass and people will forget. You can't just give up!"

"I'm not giving up, not in the way you think," she said, but I wasn't listening.

I turned back to Peter. "How could you do this? Your secret phone calls have been about this, haven't they? To get this place."

"Yes, but Elizabeth, just let me explain," he said. "Aunt Winnie is selling me a part of the inn, kind of like a partnership. And it's only temporary. I'll take over, change the name . . ."

I blanched.

"Just so that people forget the association," he explained quickly. "Once people have moved on and the police have arrested the killer, Aunt Winnie can buy her share back."

"That doesn't make sense," I said. "If you're going to buy it back anyway, why sell it in the first place?"

"Elizabeth," said Aunt Winnie, "Peter and his parents are offering me a way not to lose my shirt because of all of this. If I turn over control of the inn to them, people might stay here again. They'll change the name and no one will associate this place with me anymore. The inn can continue. And then, once the police have solved this case and everyone has moved on with their lives, I can come back and take it over again. But I couldn't live if anything happened to you because some crazies think I killed Gerald and Jackie."

"But what are you going to do in the meantime?"

She pulled Randy's hand into her lap and, with a small smile, said, "Travel—with Randy." Randy returned her smile.

"What about your bookstore?"

"I'm selling it," said Randy. "Without Gerald, the plan for the mini–shopping center fell through and I was able to find a buyer."

I was still standing with my fists clenched at my sides. "Elizabeth," said Aunt Winnie, "it's what I want to do. No one forced me into this. It was my decision. It's because I love Longbourn so much that I'm doing this. If people won't stay here, then I don't have a business. But if Peter and his parents take it over, then it has a chance. And like Peter said, once all this is finished, I can buy my share back. I will feel much better with them running the inn rather than some stranger."

I didn't know what to say. Aunt Winnie's mind was made up. I looked at her and Randy sitting together on the couch. I refused to look at Peter. Randy caught my eye and said gently, "From a business point of view, it makes great sense."

Defeated, I shook my head and turned to leave the room. "Where are you going?" Aunt Winnie called out after me.

"To bed." I felt like I could sleep for a week.

Contrary to the popular belief that a good night's sleep is a great cure-all, I didn't feel better in the morning. In fact, as the cold morning light streamed through my bedroom window, I felt worse. I now understood Aunt Winnie's impulsive decision to buy Longbourn in the first place. There was something special about it. The thought of her having to sell it—even if it was only a part of it—made me feel worse than any hangover.

Lying in bed mulling over this recent turn of events, my mind rekindled a thought I'd started to formulate after Jackie had died, something to do with nicknames. When it came to me, I sat upright. Of course! Other facts formed a pattern, and a solution emerged. I ran downstairs, past the armed policeman in the foyer, to tell Aunt Winnie. I flung open the kitchen door.

"Jesus," Peter said. "Don't do that! You scared the crap out of me!"

Still angry, I ignored him. "Aunt Winnie," I said, "I think I figured out something! I'll need to check it out, of course, but—"

Aunt Winnie's face clouded over. "No, Elizabeth," she said, interrupting me. "I've made my decision. I want you to stay out of this. And you, too, Peter," she said, turning to him. "Let the police handle it."

"Are you kidding?" I said.

Peter was equally astonished. "You want us to leave this in the hands of Detective Stewart and Ichabod Crane out there?" He jerked his head toward the foyer.

"In a word, yes," said Aunt Winnie.

"But why?" I asked. "I think I've figured something out—"

Aunt Winnie grabbed my arm. Hard. "Why? Are you serious? Listen to me! Elizabeth, this isn't a game! Jackie is dead because she tried to play detective! And someone tried to kill Linnet because he thought she knew something. I'm not going to let the same thing happen to you. You are the closest thing I've ever had to a daughter and I'm not going to put you in danger!" Her voice caught and tears sprang into her eyes. "And you!" she said, spinning back to Peter. "Don't you get any stupid ideas, either. I may not be related to you, but as far as I'm concerned you're a part of this family. I am pulling rank on the both of you. You will not get involved. We will let the police handle this. I know that they suspect me, and I appreciate what you have been trying to do, but I cannot let you do anything more. It's simply too dangerous. Am I understood?"

Peter and I stared mutely at her. She glared back. "Answer me! Am I understood?"

"Yes, Aunt Winnie," I said, pasting on a meek expression.

"Yes, Aunt Winnie," said Peter with equal meekness.

But I knew we were both lying.

Aunt Winnie knew it, too, because she said, "And to ensure that you do just that, I've taken the liberty of calling your friend Bridget."

"What?" I said. "When?"

"Last night. She and Colin are on their way up." She checked her watch. "They should be here by two o'clock. They've agreed to stay a couple of days. I've already got their room ready."

"Who are Bridget and Colin?" Peter asked.

"Bridget is my best friend," I answered quickly, forgetting that I wasn't speaking to him, "and Colin is her fiancé." I looked back at Aunt Winnie. "But why did you call them?"

"Because I know you. And I can't watch you twenty-four hours a day to make sure that you—the two of you—stay out of trouble. But among me, Bridget, and Colin, the odds are much more in my favor."

"But this is silly!" I sputtered. "I don't need a babysitter!"

"I never said you did," Aunt Winnie answered. "Think of it as a little peace of mind for me."

The arrival of Bridget and Colin might bring peace of mind to Aunt Winnie; it would do anything but that for me. Bridget had an overblown and finely honed sense of loyalty. If she had promised Aunt Winnie to keep me from investigating, then that's what she would do. I glanced at my watch. If I wanted to get anything done before she and Colin arrived, I would have to get moving.

After breakfast, I went into town under the pretext of visiting Lily and Pansy and stocking up on more pastries. In reality, I wanted to go to the Internet café. It was the only place where I'd be able to confirm what I now suspected.

I stopped at the Teapot first, so my outing would not be a total lie. Both Lily and Pansy were agog with questions about Jackie's death and Linnet's collapse. Looking over her shoulder, Pansy said in a hushed voice, "I can tell you it's cast a pall on this town. Everyone is scared and no one wants to venture out of doors. The other day this place was packed—Mrs. Ramsey and that housekeeper of hers, what's her name?"

"Mrs. Jenkins," provided Lily.

"That's right, Mrs. Jenkins. Anyway, they were here placing orders for the reception after the funeral."

"That friend of hers was with her, too," Lily added in a meaningful voice. "You know the one."

"Daniel?"

"That's the one." She nodded. "He's a handsome devil."

"He and Polly were here?" I asked.

"No," said Pansy, shaking her head. "Not Polly. *Lauren.*"

But that meant that he had lied to Detective Stewart when he said that he'd been with Polly all that day. I snapped my mouth shut. I was not about to repeat Jackie's mistakes.

Once my purchases were boxed, I thanked Lily and Pansy and hurried along the snow-covered street to the Internet café. I bought a cup of coffee and settled at one of the computers. The place was empty save for the proprietor, who idly leafed through a magazine, and a lone customer who methodically tapped away at his keyboard. The former, an earnest-looking boy with wire glasses and neatly trimmed blond hair, and the latter, a lumpy man with stringy black hair, paid me scant interest.

I typed in Baxter and waited. In no time, the information I was searching for appeared on the screen. It was just as I had suspected. I reached over and hit the print button.

CHAPTER 25

Keep breathing.

—SOPHIE TUCKER

I DROVE AS fast as I dared back to the inn, although I was hampered by the icy conditions of the roads and the timid progress of the other drivers. On my way, I called Detective Stewart, whose number I had memorized by now. The line rang and rang and rang and rang. My heart sank with each additional chime and I feared that I was going to get his voice mail again. Thankfully, he finally picked up the receiver. With a sigh of relief, I blurted out what I had learned. My words were jumbled and incoherent, but they must have made sense to him because after a brief silence, he simply said, "Damn it! I'll be right there. Don't do anything stupid."

I wondered what exactly constituted "stupid." After parking my car, I raced into the inn. In the foyer stood the Andersons, putting on their coats. I couldn't let them leave. "Um, Mr. and Mrs. Anderson?" I said. "I don't think you should go out today. The roads are terrible. I've just been out myself and it's treacherous."

Henry ignored me and continued to help Joan into her heavy coat. For all I knew, their bags were packed and already in the car. I felt a stab of panic.

Joan shook her head. "It can't be that bad. After all, the policeman was able to drive here." She nodded in Ichabod's direction. Watching us with a wary expression, he did not join the discussion.

"Yes, but they have special cop cars equipped for the snow," I babbled. At this, both Henry and Ichabod turned to me in surprise. Special cop cars? I knew with a sinking feeling that there was no way I was going to convince them to stay, especially if I kept talking gibberish. Aunt Winnie, Randy, and Peter came out of the kitchen. "Hello, everyone," said Aunt Winnie politely. "What's going on?"

"Nothing is going on," said Henry. "Joan and I are going for a ride."

"I don't think it's safe to drive," I said stubbornly. "The roads are sheer ice."

Aunt Winnie glanced at me. "That's very considerate of you, Elizabeth, but I think the Andersons can make their own decisions." Randy said nothing but watched Joan silently.

Joan gave Aunt Winnie a grateful smile and started to pull on her gloves. I had to do something. They were leaving. Taking a deep breath, I stepped forward and pulled out the necklace. It hung from my hand, the long silver chain glinting in the light. "I know about Vicky."

Joan spun around, her eyes riveted on the necklace. Forgotten, her gloves dropped to the floor and her face drained of color so quickly that I thought she might follow after them. Pulling Joan to him in a steadying grip, Henry eyed me with ill-concealed fury. Belatedly, I wondered if this was what Detective Stewart meant by something stupid.

"Detective Stewart is on his way here," I said. "Why don't we wait in the reading room for him?" Joan's face was deathly white. Henry's, on the other hand, was purple with anger. Mutely, they followed me.

Joan sank down onto a chair. "What is this all about?" Aunt

Winnie asked me. Next to her, Randy stepped back toward the bookcases.

"Joan was Gerald's sister-in-law," I answered.

Aunt Winnie gasped. "Are you sure?"

I nodded. "When I first met Joan, she told me her older sister had died in an accident. Her name was Vicky. I didn't think about it at the time, but this morning I was thinking about nicknames and I remembered that Vicky is short for Victoria. Gerald's first wife's name was Tory, which is also a nickname for Victoria. As we all know, she also died in an accident several years ago. I confirmed it today by pulling up information on the late Mrs. Victoria Ramsey from the Internet." I brandished the printout of my discovery. "Victoria's maiden name was Baxter," I said, waving the paper at Joan. "And you told me that your antiques store was named Miss Baxter's Things of Yore. Now I understand your relationship with Polly—you're her aunt." Henry was standing next to Joan's chair. His hand gripped her shoulder tightly. Turning back to Aunt Winnie, I said, "I think we now know who Joan was calling from your office—Polly."

Joan stared at her lap, ruthlessly twisting her hands. I held out the necklace. "The night I found you in the dining room, you were looking for this, weren't you? It's Victoria's, isn't it?"

Joan threw her head back and stared at me defiantly. "Yes. I lost it the night Gerald was killed. But as loathsome as Gerald was, merely having once been related to him by marriage is hardly a reason to murder him."

"It is if he killed Victoria," I retorted.

A terrible silence followed, but Joan did not avert her eyes from mine. "He did kill her," she said finally. "I know it in my heart, even if the police never were able to prove it."

"What happened?"

Joan closed her eyes. "Victoria married Gerald after knowing him only a short time. She thought he was charming, and . . . and I think she really thought she was in love with him. He was very wealthy, which I'm sure helped, too. Vicky wasn't mercenary, but she had struggled so hard after our parents died." Joan opened her eyes and added, "Who knows? Maybe she saw what she needed to see. At first she was happy, but soon enough Gerald showed his real stripes. Vicky wanted to leave him, but then she found out she was pregnant."

Joan shook her head sadly. "She was so excited. She'd always wanted to be a mother and she thought that having a baby might change Gerald. But it didn't." Joan paused. "Gerald was disappointed that Polly wasn't a boy, and after she was born, he ignored them both. Vicky was determined to make a good life for Polly, but she was lonely. And then, well, she met someone."

No one said anything, but Joan continued as if we had. "You have to understand, Vicky was a good person, but she was in a miserable marriage. In the end, though, she couldn't go on with it. She didn't like what she was doing and she thought Gerald was suspicious. That scared her because Gerald was pathological about people lying to him. Anyway, she was coming home from meeting this person for the last time when a car ran her off the road. According to witnesses, it matched a general description of one of Gerald's. But Gerald produced several of his buddies to swear that he was with them all night. I kept pushing the police to arrest him—I knew he had done it—but in the end they just didn't have the evidence. Vicky's death was listed as an accident."

Henry silently watched his wife, anguish etched into his face. She took a deep breath and continued. "Afterward, Gerald got rid of everything of Vicky's, like he was trying to erase any proof of her existence. Tell me, does an innocent man do that? The only thing I had that belonged to her was her necklace. Over the years, I tried to get in touch with Polly, but Gerald always blocked me. He refused to let me have any contact with her."

"Why?" I asked.

Joan shrugged. "Who knows? He couldn't take his anger out on Vicky, so maybe he tried to take it out on me. Maybe he didn't want me telling Polly my suspicions about how her mother died."

"Did you?"

Joan looked at Henry before answering. Something unspoken passed between them. "No," she said.

"But she knew, didn't she?"

This time Joan didn't need to confer with Henry; she knew how to answer. "I don't know," she said. "We never spoke of it."

"What happened to Vicky's lover?"

Joan paused and lowered her eyes. "I have no idea," she said. "I . . . I never met him."

"So how did you and Polly finally connect?" I asked. "It wasn't a coincidence that you came here, was it?"

"No. Polly contacted me about six months ago. She didn't know I existed until she accidentally came across Vicky's obituary. It took her some time to find me—I was married to Henry by then and had changed my last name—but Polly is a very determined young woman when she wants something. She and I spoke on the phone a few times, but we hadn't been able to meet face-to-face. Gerald kept a pretty tight rein on her. When Polly told me there was to be a party here, it seemed the perfect chance for us to meet. Henry and I would come up and stay at the inn and she would convince Gerald to come to the party."

"Weren't you afraid that Gerald might recognize you?" I asked.

"Not really," said Joan. "I was away at school when Vicky and Gerald were married. I saw him only a handful of times. And he wasn't the type to pay attention to people he found inconsequential." Behind her wire glasses, Joan eyed me with a steely expression; Polly's strong will hadn't come only from Gerald's side of the family. "I just wanted to meet Polly. But once Gerald was killed, I was afraid to come forward and tell everyone who I was. I'm sure the police still have the records on Vicky's death. I made it pretty clear at the time that I thought Gerald was involved. Once all that came out, it would look as if I tried to take justice into my own hands. Polly and I agreed it would be best if we just pretended not to know each other."

Without warning, the doors to the room flung open and Detective Stewart stormed in. He briefly glanced at Joan before homing in on me. It wasn't pleasure I saw staring at me in those eyes. He was livid. In case there was any doubt he yelled—loudly. "Just what in the name of God do you think you're doing?"

Startled, I stammered out what I had learned. "Joan Anderson. I told you there was something about her, and there is! She's Polly's aunt!"

Detective Stewart's face was a mask of controlled fury. Through clenched teeth, he bit out, "We already knew that, Ms. Parker. We have been conducting our own investigation—an investigation, I might add, that is now totally blown!" There was no restraint in these last words—they were shouted.

Out in the hall, I heard the front door open and two very familiar voices floated in from the foyer. A second later, Bridget's bright red head popped around the door frame. Colin, looking like a rumpled teddy bear in a tweed blazer, stood behind her. Bridget's smile of greeting faded as Detective Stewart continued his tirade.

"You are not a police officer!" he boomed. "You are a private citizen. A private citizen who has no authority to do anything in this case!"

My temper flared and I shouted back. "Authority!? I don't need your authority to help my aunt. It's absurd that anyone would suspect her even for a moment of having anything to do with this! And yet that is precisely what is happening. My aunt is innocent, Detective Stewart, and I'll be damned if I'm going to sit back and watch her go to jail because you and the rest of the police department want to pin this on her!"

The room was silent as everyone waited for Detective Stewart to respond. He took his time, performing some sort of breathing exercises first. When he did speak, his voice sounded strained and unnatural. "No one is trying to pin anything on anybody. Two people have been brutally killed and a third is recovering in the hospital. We are doing our best to find the killer before he or she strikes again. Your intentions may be good"—he paused, glaring at me as though he found this hard to believe—"but you have interfered with official police business. I am warning you, Ms. Parker, don't do it again, or the only one going to jail here will be you!"

With that, he turned on his heel and slammed out of the room, charging past Bridget and Colin. They watched him go with identical startled expressions. In the foyer, I could hear him talking with Ichabod.

Henry turned to the rest of us, his face tight with anger, and said, "I will not stay in a place where I am going to be spied on and accused of murder. I'm confident that Detective Stewart can suggest a *reputable* inn for us to stay in while he concludes his investigation. And you can be sure that I will relay this entire incident to Mrs. Dubois. When she hears of this outrage, you can be assured that she will make certain that none of her many acquaintances ever come here!" Reaching down to grab Joan's hand, he pulled her to her feet. "Come on, Joan," he said. "We are leaving."

Joan did not meet our eyes as she followed her husband out of the room. In the foyer, I could hear them speaking with Detective Stewart.

None of us spoke. Finally, Bridget turned to me with a smirk and intoned slowly, "And you were just going to catch up on some reading."

CHAPTER 26

No good deed goes unpunished.

—CLARE BOOTHE LUCE

WITH THE INN empty of people who could seriously be considered suspects, we all stayed up late bringing Bridget and Colin up to date on the investigation and swapping murder theories. They were alternately horrified and enthralled by what we told them. And they laughed far too long and hard at Peter's imitation of me falling out of a chair. By the end of the night, Colin and Peter were apparently on their way to becoming bosom buddies, and even Bridget was giving me none too subtle nudges about Peter. At one point, when everyone else was talking, she leaned over to me and whispered, "Peter's gorgeous! Why don't you like him, again?"

"Because as a child, he was the spawn of Satan," I whispered back.

"Well, he's not a child now," she said.

I rolled my eyes at her and merely said, "Once a spawn, always a spawn."

But I knew I wasn't being completely fair. I didn't really hate Peter anymore, although I was still mad about the inn. A psychiatrist might diagnose my feelings as misdirected anger over the injustice of Aunt Winnie's current situation, but I don't really hold much with psychiatrists. And besides, it's just easier to be mad at Peter—after all, it's an emotion I'm familiar with.

Breakfast the next morning was a quiet affair. Daniel was still at Lauren's house, leaving the inn to us. Aunt Winnie, Randy, Bridget, and Colin were drinking their coffee in the reading room when I came downstairs. I didn't know where Peter was and I told myself I didn't care. I got myself a cup of coffee from the kitchen and walked down the hall. In the foyer, Ichabod was again at his post in the green brocade chair. He nodded in my direction but said nothing. The front door opened. It was Daniel. His face was drawn and haggard.

I studied him with a newfound detachment. I had impulsively decided to like him before he'd even said two words to me. I could see now that he had never had any partiality for me. Daniel merely attached himself to anyone who gave him the slightest encouragement. He'd jumped from me, to Susie in the acting troupe, to Polly all in a matter of days. What I *didn't* know was whether his affair with Polly was just another step in his fluctuating affections or had a more sinister explanation. Cool analyses aside, I was still pissed at him. He was, in my opinion, simply one of the most worthless men in all of Great Britain.

"Rough night?" I asked.

He grimaced. "You could say that. I spent most of it with Detective Stewart."

"I see. And how's Polly?"

"About the same, I'd say. He grilled her pretty hard, too."

"That's not what I meant," I said, adding further emphasis to my next words. *"How's Polly?"*

He gazed at me uncomprehendingly before the gist of my meaning penetrated his brain. At least he had the grace to look uncomfortable. "Elizabeth," he began, "it's not what you think . . ."

That was the second time in forty-eight hours that someone had told me that. "Really?" I snapped. "And what do I think, Daniel? That you're a rat bastard? That you used me to keep your relationship with Polly off the radar screen? Or do I think that you and your little girlfriend killed Gerald so you could both get what you want? Now which one is it? A, B, C, or all of the above?"

He stood very still. The only indication that he was upset was the appearance of two spots of red that blazed on his cheeks. He glanced uneasily at Ichabod. Ichabod gazed back with open interest. "I didn't have anything to do with Gerald's death," Daniel said. "And I didn't use you. Polly and I, well, we fell into that after Gerald died. It wasn't planned—"

I cut him off with a harsh laugh. "Oh, it was planned all right. Don't kid yourself on that account. If you do, then you're sorely underestimating Polly. The question I'd be asking myself now if I were you is exactly how much of this was planned."

"What's that supposed to mean?" His eyes again strayed to Ichabod.

I shrugged. "You're a bright boy. Figure it out yourself." Taking a sip of coffee, I said, "Now, if you'll excuse me."

Turning on my heel, I walked into the reading room and bumped into Aunt Winnie and Bridget. They made no apology for eavesdropping. Bridget said, "I'm not saying that I blame you, but are you sure that was wise?" On the couch, Colin sat reading the newspaper. Without raising his eyes from the print, he said to no one in particular, "No, of course it wasn't wise. In fact, it was a headstrong, stupid thing to do." I ignored him.

"I don't care anymore," I said. "Besides, Ichabod was out there and heard the whole thing. I doubt I'm in any more danger than anyone else. And speaking of danger, has anyone heard how Linnet is doing?"

Aunt Winnie nodded. "Peter just went to find out. I want her to come here when she's released. There's safety in numbers."

I took a seat by the fireplace, ignoring Peter as he strode into the room. "I just got off the phone with the hospital," he said, after an uneasy glance in my direction. "They're ready to release her. She's perfectly fine, just a little weak. Her car is still at Lauren's house; she asked if someone could drive it back to her place. She said there's a spare key in the glove box."

"I'll do it," I said, putting my cup down. "Bridget, can you come with me to Lauren's house? I'll get Linnet's car and drive it to her place. You can follow me and we can drive back here."

"Sure."

"Are you sure?" asked Aunt Winnie. "Randy and I could do it."

Peter said nothing. He just watched me.

"No," I said. "I want to go. Getting out might do me some good."

I could tell that Aunt Winnie wanted to say more, but she only nodded. "Okay, then."

Inside my car, I started up the engine with a sigh. "Are you okay?" Bridget asked.

"No, but I'm glad you're here. It's all been so awful and I had no Bridget to comfort me."

"Back to the *P&P* references, I see."

"Well, let's be honest, I'm never actually that far away from them."

"Elizabeth, you know I love you and I'd do just about anything for you, but I have to say, I think you're too susceptible to fictional images. You forget they're just that—fiction."

"Meaning?"

"Meaning, first you were set on finding Jake Ryan. Then it was Lloyd Dobler. Now you're looking for Mr. Darcy. Nothing good can come of it."

"I'm not sure you can compare movie heroes with literary ones. They're different somehow. Actors are . . ." I paused, searching for the right phrase. Finding it, I continued, "Actors are all spirits, and are melted into air, into thin air."

"That's not my point and you know it. And stop quoting Shakespeare at me. Who does that, anyway? You know, that actually may be part of your problem. You attract a certain type when you do that."

I laughed. "A certain type? What type would that be? Well-read?"

"No, pretentious assholes. Which, now that I think about it, is a perfect description of your last three boyfriends. In any case, my *point* is that Mr. Darcy is an unattainable ideal, and in the meantime you're missing out on decent guys. Let me explain it in terms you'll understand. Remember Marianne in *Sense and Sensibility*? She almost missed Colonel Brandon because of Willoughby."

"If I'm not mistaken, Colonel Brandon is also fictional."

"You know what I mean!"

"This is about Peter, isn't it?"

"I just don't see why you're so set against him."

"You would if you knew him. Peter is not Colonel Brandon. Peter is more like Tom from *Mansfield Park*—self-indulgent and thoughtless."

"True, but Tom becomes ill in the end and redeems himself."

"Okay, how about this? The minute Peter falls gravely ill, I'll forgive him."

"You can't mean that!" Bridget turned to me, scandalized.

"No, of course not. I'd just rather not talk about this right now. And anyway, we're here."

We pulled up in front of Lauren's house. Linnet's Jaguar was the only car in the driveway so I assumed no one was at home. I got out and made my way to the car. As Linnet had said, there was a spare key in the car's glove box. I climbed behind the wheel and started the engine. "Follow me," I called out to Bridget. "It's just down the road."

As I drove, I heard a faint beeping noise. It seemed to be coming from under the driver's seat. Once in Linnet's driveway, I parked the car and leaned down to peer underneath the seat. A cell phone—no doubt the one Linnet had lost—lay there. I pulled it out and flipped it open. The readout indicated a new message. My heart skipped a beat when I saw that it was from Jackie. With shaking hands, I opened the text message, not caring that I was reading someone else's mail. The message ran: "Linney, I'm going to see Dt. Stewart. I figured it out. It was Lauren!"

The words swam before my eyes and I was only dimly aware of Bridget calling my name. I looked up, dazed, my head spinning.

"What's the matter? You look like you've seen a ghost."

"No, just a message from one."

"Huh?"

I handed her the phone. Her eyes grew wide as she read. "Holy shit."

"Yeah, that about sums it up. I guess I should call Detective Stewart. Somehow I doubt he's going to be happy to hear from me."

"Who cares? He'll just be happy that the case is solved."

"I guess." I pulled out my phone and called Detective Stewart.

As predicted, he did not sound happy to hear from me. However, his tone changed considerably when I told him of my discovery.

Two hours later, I was back at Longbourn, sitting in the reading room. Based on my discovery, Lauren had been summarily brought down to the station. A search of her house had turned up a vial of ground foxglove. It didn't seem likely that she'd be leaving for Bermuda anytime soon. Around me the mood was celebratory. Aunt Winnie had been cleared and the inn was safe. I still wasn't happy with Peter, but at least he would no longer be buying the inn.

While I was glad for Aunt Winnie, my mind couldn't wrap itself around the fact that Lauren was the killer. Granted, I had initially wondered about her because she had married Gerald for his money and was no doubt relieved to be rid of him, but a murderer? The more I thought about it, the less it made sense. I kept my thoughts to myself, however. Lately I had had such lousy judgment where people were concerned that it was probably an indication of Lauren's guilt that I *didn't* think she was guilty.

I slept badly that night. My mind kept probing at the question of Lauren and at my own dissatisfaction with it. Was I nothing more than a modern-day Don Quixote, titling at nonexistent windmills? By morning, my brain was a foggy jumble. After two cups of hot coffee, I was no better. I needed fresh air and exercise. I went upstairs, pulled my hair back into a ponytail, and threw on my jeans and a sweatshirt. After glancing at my reflection in the mirror, I added the new earrings I'd gotten on my shopping spree. I don't know why, but the soft jangling noise they made and their bright colors cheered me. Should I run into any of Aunt Winnie's friends,

I could at least hold my head up with the knowledge that while my outfit was sloppy, at least my accessories were nice.

Downstairs, Peter was waiting for me in the foyer.

"What do you want?" I said, as I yanked my coat out of the closet.

"I want to talk to you," he said. "I didn't take advantage of Aunt Winnie. I was trying to help her!"

"If that was the case, then why all the secrecy? Why didn't you tell me what you were planning?"

"Because Aunt Winnie asked me not to. She wanted to be the one who told people. It is *her* inn."

"Yeah. Thank God *that* hasn't changed," I said. Peter's face fell. I knew that I wasn't being fair. But I had been angry. I was angry that Jackie was dead and Linnet had been in the hospital. I was angry that Peter and Aunt Winnie had been right about Daniel using me. "I've got to go," I muttered. "We can talk about this later." I didn't wait for his response. Jamming my arms into my coat, I left, slamming the door behind me.

I tried to reconcile Jackie's text message to Linnet with the facts as I knew them. I couldn't. I tried to visualize Lauren slipping on the glove and shooting Gerald. I couldn't do that either. And then there was the lie I'd heard told to Detective Stewart. What was the reason for it? A niggling in my brain told me that I was missing something. I drove to the beach. I walked along the hard sand, my head bent low against the wind. I pulled out my gloves from my coat pocket and slipped them on. And then it came to me. I had seen Lauren write out a number for her friend with her *left* hand. Like most blondes, Lauren was a southpaw. The glove found at the murder scene was for a *right* hand. Someone *had* tried to frame Lauren! But who? Lauren might be annoying and vapid, and she had clearly never loved

Gerald, but it took a special kind of hate to frame someone for murder. Slowly a fantastic idea took form in my brain. I froze in my tracks, thinking about Lauren. There *was* someone, after all, who might have hated Lauren, someone who would derive satisfaction at seeing her in jail. But that would mean . . .

My mind raced with the events of the last few days, replaying scenes in my head. Of course! I had been looking at everything upside down. Once the pieces fell into place, it all made sense. However, my only proof lay in the details of a lost love and a seemingly white lie told to Detective Stewart. Could I even get Detective Stewart to listen to me? I knew better than to try. I needed more evidence, evidence I would simply have to get myself.

I raced back to my car, left a message for Aunt Winnie as to where I was going, and drove to the Linnet's house. Thankfully, no one was home. Now that I was here, though, the question of how exactly I was going to get in presented itself. Smashing a window would no doubt set off an alarm. I peeked under the doormat in the faint hope that I'd find a key. There was none. I dragged my hands through my hair in frustration. I simply had to get in. Without the evidence, Detective Stewart would never listen to me.

I ran around the side of the house, all the while petrified that I'd be spotted by the neighbors. Despite the cold, a clammy sweat broke out on my neck and back, and I realized I could never lead a life of crime. Not due to any superior moral fiber on my part; I just didn't have the stomach for it. The mere idea of breaking into someone's house had rendered me sweaty and queasy. If I actually got in, there was a very good chance that I'd throw up and then pass out. Still, I kept searching for a way in, holding on to the hope that I'd find a spare key outside. My weak stomach aside, I couldn't let Lauren hang for Gerald's and Jackie's murders. Finally, luck smiled on me.

Hanging from a nail near some plants was a gray house key. I was no gardener, but I would bet money that these were the foxglove plants from which the murderer had prepared the poison. I grabbed the key and ran around front. With shaking fingers, I slid the key into the lock and pushed open the door.

The stillness inside amplified the pounding of my heart. I darted up the stairs and into Linnet's bedroom. A quick search provided what I was looking for. I lifted the lid of the jewelry box and enjoyed a moment of triumph as my hand closed around the glittering earrings. I had been right!

I thought of Gerald, who was hated by nearly everyone he knew, a man who most likely caused his first wife's death. I thought of Jackie and her ridiculous floppy hats and insatiable thirst for gossip. In spite of her silliness, she had been likable. She hadn't had an easy life. Her dreams of moving to Hollywood were ruined by a friend who opted for marriage instead. What had Linnet said? *"Jackie, on the other hand, has always had a real talent for mimicry—more of a gift, really, than a talent. She was amazing."*

Another memory slid into focus—the night of Gerald's murder. I had been in Aunt Winnie's office, hearing the front door open. Two voices floated in. One was Linnet's. *"This is a horrible night to be out. Really, Jackie, I don't know why I let you talk me into coming to this. I hate these things."*

Next came Jackie's voice, all breathy and excited. *"Oh, don't be that way, Linney. It'll be lots of fun. You'll see."*

But that wasn't what Linnet had told the police. She told Detective Stewart that going to Aunt Winnie's had been *her* idea. And with Gerald's death a chain of events had been set in motion that would end with Jackie's death. Gerald, a man who was universally hated, a man who no one was surprised to hear had been murdered.

In quick succession, other facts fell into their correct place: a sudden weight loss and a smooth, unpierced ear beneath a floppy blue hat.

I was so caught up in my reverie that I didn't hear the footsteps on the stairs. Too late, the hair on my neck stood up, telling me that I was no longer alone.

I spun around.

"Hello, Jackie," I said, once I got my voice back.

CHAPTER 27

Everyone is a moon, and has a dark side
which he never shows to anybody.

—MARK TWAIN

STILL DRESSED IN Linnet's clothes and wearing her wig, Jackie tilted her head to one side and peered up at me. With a flourish, she pulled off the wig with one hand, revealing a head of fluffy white hair. She looked like somebody's sweet old grandmother. The only jarring note was the unwavering gun in her other hand. It was a Derringer just like the one that had killed Gerald. "They released me from the hospital early. I took a cab home," she said conversationally. "But when I saw your car outside, I had a bad feeling." She shook her head from side to side, clucking her tongue disapprovingly as if at an errant child who had been caught with her hand in the cookie jar. She saw me glance at the gun and nodded. "My father collected them. I grew up practicing with them. If I do say so myself, I'm an excellent shot. They were the only things of value that he left me." She turned the small gun in her hand so that the light caught the shiny white pearl handle. "Seemed a silly inheritance at the time, but they actually have come in handy."

I was ice cold. My mind screamed at me to say something, to keep her talking until I could figure a way out of this, but I couldn't move, let alone talk. Fear ate at me, leaving nothing but a quivering shell. Finally, I managed to get out, "You loved Martin."

She looked up at me again with that birdlike tilt of her head. "He was my world," she said simply. "And then Linnet saw him." She spit out Linnet's name as if it were an insult. "She wanted him like a child wants a piece of candy. Martin loved me, but . . . but when Linnet came around, I disappeared, the way the moon eclipses the sun. Once Linnet set her sights on Martin, he didn't have a chance. She never loved him; she just loved his money. All this," she said, with a wide sweep of the gun, "came from Martin's money. And Martin belonged to me. The way I look at it, this is how it should always have been—me living in this house with the things that his money bought. I've only righted the wrong Linnet created."

"So you killed her and assumed her identity," I said carefully, trying to keep my voice neutral, as I thought one should when dealing with crazy people. I warily contemplated her and the gun. I looked around for something to use as a weapon but could see nothing. I was certainly bigger and could probably tackle her, had she not had the gun. A tiny part of my brain registered that it was, in reality, a small gun, but a gun is a gun, and when you're staring down the barrel of one, size doesn't matter. To my shattered nerves, she might as well have been holding an AK-47. My only hope was to keep her talking while I tried to maneuver my way toward the door to the hallway. I remembered what Detective Stewart had told me: Derringers have only one shot, two at the most. If I could take her by surprise, I might be able to make a run for it.

"It was easy, really." Jackie became eerily conversational. I began to feel an unreal sensation creep over me. This couldn't be happening. "When I read of Martin's death, I wrote Linnet a letter of condolence and, amazingly, she invited me to visit. Seeing her preen around her grand house, touching her grand things, all the while spitting on poor Martin's memory made me hate her as I never had before. That's when I first thought of killing her. But how could I do it without getting caught? While I contemplated a murder plan, Linnet decided to sell her house and move to the Cape, and she asked me to come live with her. Of course I agreed. Neither of us had any living relatives or knew anyone on the Cape. How easy would it be for me to become her? After all, we were cousins and we resembled each other. I was always good at imitating people. Linnet wore a lot of makeup and a wig and—"

"And you always wore big floppy hats to hide your face. You wanted everyone to think they were meant to cover thinning hair, but it was Linnet who had the thinning hair, Linnet who wanted to hide it. That's why she wore a wig."

She smiled at me like a proud parent. I remembered Linnet's battered body lying in the snow that day and how I'd seen the sparse hair and assumed it was Jackie. And Linnet's sudden need for her tinted glasses—hadn't she insinuated that Jackie was to blame for the loss of her contacts? At the time, I'd thought Linnet was being unfair, but no doubt Jackie *had* hidden the contacts, forcing Linnet to use her glasses. It was just a prearranged prop for Jackie to obfuscate differences between her and Linnet. As I slowly edged toward the door, I asked, "So you killed Gerald for nothing? Just to divert attention from your real crime."

"Exactly. I couldn't have asked for a better target. Why, I hadn't been here three days before I realized that everyone in this town hated Gerald Ramsey. And really, it's not as if anyone minded his dying. In fact, I think I did several people a service. With so many suspects, the police were far too busy checking motives to worry about anything else."

"And then you showed up pretending to know something about his death."

"Yes." She laughed. Her laugh had a strange edge to it. Unstable was one way to describe it. Scary as hell was another. "You should have seen your face," she went on. "It took all of my self-control not to burst out laughing. From there on it was simple. I just became Linnet. I'd studied her closely." She shifted her posture slightly, rearranged her facial expression, and suddenly she *was* the proud and haughty Linnet Westin. Then her face crumpled and the illusion was gone. Her mouth twisted. "Killing Linnet gave me a great deal of satisfaction, but later, when it was over . . . well, she was the only one who remembered the past. She may have sneered at Martin, but at least she remembered the sound of his voice. Now no one does, only me." She trailed off, staring at something unseen in front of her. Cautiously, I took a few steps toward the door again. "But what's done is done," she said, snapping back to the present. I stopped my slow inching. "It's for the best," she added firmly. "Linnet deserved to die. She stole Martin from me. It would have been different had she really loved him. She made his life a living nightmare and she drove him to drink. He barely touched alcohol when I knew him. Linnet killed him just as she killed my dreams."

"I can see that," I said. I was still at least twenty feet from the hallway.

"So tell me, dear." She smiled her friendly, Jackie smile. "What tipped you off?"

"When you tried to frame Lauren. It was clever of you to text a message to Linnet's phone and leave it in her car. You asked Peter to have someone drive the car back to the house, hoping that person would find the cell phone and read the message. But it made me wonder. Why a text? A voice message made more sense, but you couldn't be sure of anyone hearing it. After all, you probably didn't even know Linnet's access code and chances were no one else would figure it out, either. I imagine it was easy to plant the foxglove at Lauren's house during the funeral reception. But I couldn't believe that Lauren was the killer. And then I remembered that Lauren is left-handed. The glove you used when you shot Gerald was right-handed. So I asked myself, who hated Lauren enough to frame her? And I thought of you the day of the luncheon. You sat at the table, twisting your earring and telling us of your dislike of Lauren."

"So?"

"So you have pierced ears. Linnet didn't. She wore clip-ons, expensive ones. The kind that Jackie would never own." I held up the diamond clip-on earrings I had taken from Linnet's jewelry case. "The body I found outside did not have pierced ears. I saw it. It was a smooth ear. There was no hole in it. That's when I realized the body I found must have been Linnet's. Was Lauren like Linnet? Is that why you hated her? Because she also married for money and not for love?"

She sneered. "Aren't you clever today? Yes. I sent the text to Linnet's cell. Lauren is no better than Linnet and she deserves to rot. And it all worked, too. Aside from you, everyone thinks that Lauren is the murderer and Linnet Westin is nothing more than a beastly snob. I'll sell this place and move away. And no one will ever be the wiser."

"I'm afraid that isn't true," I said, taking a deep breath. "I already called the police. Detective Stewart and his men should be here any minute."

She laughed; it had a high-pitched resonance that made my skin crawl. "Oh, come now. You can't possibly think I believe that." I knew what she was going to say next. "Your face gives you away every time, my dear.

"Now what am I going to do with you?" she asked pleasantly, as she casually surveyed the room. "I can't do anything here—I don't want to risk leaving a trail. I'll have to move your car and then when it's dark, I'll . . ." I slowly slid my foot toward the door again. She pointed the gun squarely at my chest. With deadly determination, she cocked the hammer. "I don't think so, my dear. As much as I like you, I didn't come this far just to get tripped up by a silly girl. Move this way. Downstairs, please. Slowly. And don't be an idiot."

Her eyes gleamed like blue steel and the hand that held the gun neither shook nor quivered. My feet backed away from both her and the gun on their own accord, reversing my earlier progress to the door. My mind was in a panic but not so much that I didn't know my fate was sealed unless I did something, and fast. Jackie hadn't told me all of this to let me go. She was going to kill me, just like she had killed Gerald and Linnet. Do something, I thought. Don't just stand there! Move! The only problem was, I didn't know *what* to do. All I knew was that I did not want to die. A vision of Gerald's dead, staring eyes swam before me, increasing my terror. As I saw it, I had two choices: A, I could let myself be shot, or B, I could not. I opted for option B.

Lowering my head, I put my hand on my stomach and sagged against Linnet's dressing table. "What are you doing?" Jackie asked suspiciously.

"I . . . I think I'm going to be sick." I placed my hand on the table for support.

"Well, don't," she snapped.

"That's what I'm working on." I pawed at the table as though to keep myself upright. My hand snaked toward Linnet's heavy metal jewelry box. I leaned my body forward, taking deep breaths. With a quick prayer, I grabbed the box and flung it at Jackie's head.

She saw it coming and jerked backward, but not before the box grazed her. The impact sent a shower of diamond and pearl baubles through the air. "You bitch!" she screamed as she stumbled, clutching her cheek. Taking advantage of her imbalance, I shoved past her and scrambled for the stairs. She lost little time in taking up the chase, and I could hear her close behind me. At the base of the stairs she caught up with me, grabbed my ponytail, and yanked me backward. Her strength surprised me and I inwardly cursed the local senior fitness program. I spun around to strike her, only to have her claw at my eyes and face. Tears blurred my vision and I yelped in pain as I felt one of my earrings ripped out. I balled my hand into a fist and swung at her head, but she was faster, and had the advantage of sight. A blinding flash of light burst behind my eyes as she slammed the gun into my left temple. The floor swam up to me and I knew no more.

When I awoke, my legs and arms were bound with some sort of clothesline and a rag was jammed into my mouth. The left side of my head was on fire and my right leg ached. Frantically, I struggled against the ropes, but to no avail. The gag in my mouth cut my air intake to a mere trickle and my throat spasmodically retched, trying to force it out. Waves of panic overtook me. Then I did what I always do in stressful situations. I started counting.

By the time I hit 325, my breathing had calmed down and my pounding heart no longer sounded like a jackhammer in my ears. I was lying on a smooth cement floor, apparently in the basement. From the way my body felt, Jackie must have sent me tumbling head over ass down the stairs. At first, it seemed pitch-black around me, but slowly my eyes adjusted. A quick inventory wasn't encouraging.

In one corner of the basement there appeared to be a few discarded painting supplies. In the other, white cardboard boxes were precariously stacked on an old kitchen table. Luggage and a dirty mop took up the third corner. The fourth corner was bare except for a few cobwebs and dead flies. Across from me stood a hatchway to the outside, a large metal padlock hanging from the latch.

I decided to start with the boxes—they might contain something sharp that I could use to saw at the ropes. I rolled myself over toward the table, whimpering in pain as my leg dragged with each turn. Finally, I was able to pull myself up to my knees. I was upright, but my head was spinning and my leg was throbbing. The room swayed and I feared I might pass out again, but thankfully everything came back into focus. Straining my eyes, I peered at the boxes on the table. They were sealed and, according to the neat lettering printed on each one, held nothing more than old sheets and towels.

Time for Plan B, I thought, as I dragged myself like a wounded crab in the direction of the painting supplies. Here, my efforts were more rewarding. On one of the paint trays lay a painting razor blade, one side covered with a protective plastic coating. With my hands tied behind my back, I backed into the supplies and blindly groped for the razor. Once I had it, I jabbed at the thick ropes. I was glad that at least my left hand was tied over my right, so I could hold the blade. My movements were clumsy and weak, and the razor fell from my uncooperative fingers twice, but it finally sliced through my bonds and the ropes loosened and slid from around my wrists. Yanking the rag out of my mouth, I greedily sucked in the damp air before I started sawing at the clothesline around my ankles.

When that fell to the floor, I collapsed back onto the ground. My arms felt like rubber and my legs felt even worse. Any attempt to put weight on my right leg made me see stars. Other than the door at the top of the stairs, the only way out of the basement was through the padlocked hatchway. My only hope was going up the stairs and trying the door, but in my current condition those stairs might as well have been Mount Everest. Nevertheless, I rolled over and crawled to the bottom. My progress, one step at a time, was slow and painful, but finally I was on the top step. I grabbed the knob. It was locked. I pulled myself up and switched on the light. A bulb at the bottom of the stairs blazed forth and I blinked several times at the sudden brightness.

I saw a large metal flashlight hanging from a hook on the wall by the door. I grabbed it and sank onto the top step before I eased back down the stairs. At the bottom, I reached up and twisted the bulb out of its socket. The inky darkness was claustrophobic, but at least when Jackie returned, she wouldn't have light to guide her. It wasn't much, but it was something. Clicking on the flashlight, I searched every inch of the basement. I found nothing, and my efforts to smash the lock on the hatchway were futile. A razor and a flashlight were all I could muster to defend myself against a gun. I would just have to make do and ambush her as best I could. I lay back down on the floor where Jackie had left me and waited.

After what seemed a dark eternity, I thought I could hear her moving around upstairs. I don't know how long I had lain there—it seemed like hours. The pains in my leg and my head were draining my energy. Eventually, the house fell silent. I struggled to remain awake, but my eyes grew heavy. The next thing I knew there was a hand on my shoulder. Disoriented, I jerked awake, my heart pounding. This was my only chance. I rolled over and slammed the flashlight as hard as I could into Jackie's head. She fell back with a thud.

My flashlight did the job, all right, but I stared in horror at the crumpled form that lay beside me. It was Peter.

CHAPTER 28

Is not general incivility the very essence of love?

—JANE AUSTEN, *PRIDE AND PREJUDICE*

"PETER!" I YELPED. "Oh, God, Peter! Speak to me!" I scrambled to his side and clicked on the flashlight. Blood poured from a nasty gash on his right temple and his face was a terrible shade of gray. The thought that I had actually killed him produced a sharp and sickening tightening in my chest, the intensity of which took me by surprise. The memory of my jest to Bridget that the minute Peter fell gravely ill, I would forgive him rushed over me and I felt sick. I cared for Peter, I *really* cared for Peter! I had let my anger from events fifteen years ago spoil everything. It figures, I thought bitterly. I finally meet the perfect guy and then I go and blow it by smashing his head in. He might have forgiven me for the dead fish in his bed, but this was different. Blood was involved. Cupping his face, I said, "Peter! It's me, Elizabeth! Can you hear me?"

He moved his head and moaned peevishly. "What the hell did you do that for? I risk my neck to save you and this is the thanks I get?"

I sagged back with a rush of relief; he was alive. "I thought you were Jackie," I whispered. "I'm sorry, I'm so sorry. Where is she?"

"Jackie? Jackie's dead," said Peter, groaning. "And I was the one who got hit in the head?" Gingerly he raised his hand to his head and tried to sit up. He made it only halfway.

"Jackie's not dead. She killed Linnet and is pretending to be Linnet. Where is she? Is she still upstairs?"

"Are you okay? Did she hurt you? What happened?"

"I'm fine. Well, I think I did something to my leg, but other than that, I'm okay. Is Jackie still upstairs?"

He took a long time answering. "Peter!" I repeated, shaking him. "Is she here?"

"Please stop that," he said, wincing. "She left."

"Peter, listen to me. She's going to kill us. She has a gun. We have to get out of here, but I hurt my leg and I can't walk. You've got to call the police."

"Police," he repeated, but his voice sounded faint. I shook him again. Hard. He tried to slap my hand away, but he was so weak it felt like the brush of a feather. He sank back onto the floor. I had to keep him talking. I had to keep him awake. "Peter, listen to me. How did you know I was here?" I heard the panic in my voice.

He was such a long time in answering that I thought he had passed out, but finally he opened his eyes. They were unfocused, but his voice sounded stronger. "I didn't," he said. "When you didn't come back to the inn, I got worried. Aunt Winnie said you'd come here, so I came looking for you. But Linnet said you left hours ago. I saw your earring on the floor. Something seemed wrong, so I left and then doubled back. When she went out, I broke in." The effort of this short speech drained him. He closed his eyes. The right side of his head was now covered in blood.

I reached down and cupped his face. He leaned his head into the palm of my hand. "Elizabeth," he muttered, "don't be mad. I was only trying to help."

"I'm not mad at you, Peter, but we have to get out of here! She could be back at any minute." As I said this, the basement door creaked open. I shrank back and clicked off the flashlight. Jackie's silhouette appeared in the doorway. "What the hell?" she said, reaching for the light switch. She flipped it several times. "What's the matter with the lights?"

I did not answer.

She slowly came down the stairs toward me, the gun out and aimed in my direction. Halfway down, she stopped in surprise at the sight of Peter. I grabbed his limp hand. Jackie's eyes went from Peter's recumbent form to the flashlight now clutched in my hand. Her mouth twisted into a cruel smile. "Well, well, well," she said. "What do we have here? Did the gallant hero try to save the damsel in distress only to get bashed in the head?"

Coldly regarding Peter's crumpled heap, she said softly, "This does complicate my plans somewhat, but no bother. It won't be too hard to rig this so the police think Peter was behind the killings. I imagine a tragic fight to the death between the two of you ensued when you learned of Peter's guilt. Yes, I think this might work out quite nicely." Seeing the remains of the rope on the floor, she reached into her coat pocket. "I had a feeling that those wouldn't hold, so I bought these." She pulled out a pair of heavy metal handcuffs and threw them at me. They clattered across the cement floor, coming to a stop at my feet. "It's amazing the things they sell at those adult video stores," she said, with a shake of her head. She pointed the gun at me again. "Now move away from Peter, roll the flashlight to me, and put those on."

I was still holding Peter's hand. He gave it a squeeze. I glanced at him in surprise. He was lying back with his eyes closed, appearing for all the world unconscious.

"Move it!" Jackie demanded crossly.

I rolled the flashlight to her and reached out and pulled the handcuffs toward me. They were cold and heavy. Sliding away from Peter, I made a show of trying to put them on. While I did so, I palmed the razor. I had to stall her. If she just moved a little closer to me, I might have a chance. "Hurry up!" she barked again.

"I'm trying," I said, as I continued to fumble with the handcuffs. "But I think I broke my wrist when you pushed me."

She considered me suspiciously. "Don't play games with me, Elizabeth. You'll lose. Again." Her eyes narrowed as her finger tightened on the trigger of the gun. "I can make your last hours painful or quick—it's up to you. Now, do as you're told and put those damn handcuffs on!"

"I'm trying!" I burst out, "but there's something wrong with the clasp!"

She watched me doubtfully and cautiously crept a few steps toward me. She glanced once at Peter. He lay motionless on the floor. As she moved past him, he opened one eye and slowly raised himself up. Jackie was standing directly in front of me with the gun in closer proximity to my person than I was comfortable with. "Push the handcuffs to me," she said. I dropped them to the floor and kicked them toward her. Putting the flashlight down, she grabbed them. "Hold your hands out in front of you," she commanded. I did so, still clutching the razor. She edged closer to me and snapped one of the bracelets around my wrist. I jerked my other hand around and slashed her on the arm that was holding the gun. Blood sprayed and the gun clattered to the ground. "Jesus!" she yelped, stumbling back. I flung myself at the gun while behind her Peter leaped up and pushed her to the ground.

"You bastards!" she screamed.

A voice at the top of the stairs boomed out, "Police! Nobody move!"

Peter and I ignored the command. He threw his body onto Jackie's while I picked up the gun and trained it on her. I heard the sound of several pairs of heavy boots thudding down the stairs, but I didn't dare take my eyes off of Jackie. She squirmed and pushed against Peter as he pulled her arms behind her back. He was weak and shaky, but she was no match for his bulk. Detective Stewart's voice rang in my ears. "You can put down the gun, Elizabeth. It's all right now. We've got her."

I lowered my arms and dropped the gun. "How did you know to come?"

"I called them," said Peter, as he surrendered Jackie's struggling form to one of the uniformed policemen who swarmed the basement.

"You called them?" I sputtered. "But when?"

"Before I broke in, of course. What kind of an idiot do you take me for?"

CHAPTER 29

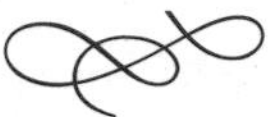

That would be the greatest misfortune of all!
To find a man agreeable whom one is determined to hate!

—JANE AUSTEN, *PRIDE AND PREJUDICE*

SO NONE OF this was about Gerald after all?" asked Aunt Winnie, shaking her head in disbelief.

"No," I said, settling back onto the couch. "Jackie just used the fact that most everyone hated him to her advantage. Remember, no one was really surprised when he was murdered. All Jackie had to do was pretend to know something about his murder and then when 'Jackie' was found dead, everyone would assume that the two crimes were related."

It was almost midnight, but none of us were tired. After the police took Jackie away, they had taken Peter and me to the hospital. I had a twisted knee and a sprained ankle. Peter had a concussion and needed stitches. From the way he carried on about it, it seemed unlikely that he would ever let me forget it. "We are now officially even, do you understand?" he had yelled at me in the hospital. "Nothing I ever pulled on you compares to this!" He had a point, but I wasn't about to admit that—to him.

"Does it hurt?" I had replied sweetly, actually feeling vast relief at how quickly he was returning to the Peter I knew. "Do you want me to kiss your boo-boo and make it all better?" He responded with a gesture that I interpreted as a no.

Now, sitting next to me on the couch in the inn's reading room, his mood had improved. We weren't alone. Aunt Winnie, Randy, Bridget, Colin, and Detective Stewart were with us. We had discussed the details of the past week in more than enough detail, but still no one was ready to call it a day.

"I can't believe that Linnet was Jackie all along. I truly believed her as Linnet!" said Aunt Winnie.

"That's not too surprising when you think about it," I said. "None of us knew either woman very well, and Jackie always wore those enormous hats that covered half of her face. But physically, they were very similar—I think Linnet herself told me that they used to pass for sisters when they were younger. After she killed Linnet, Jackie donned Linnet's wig and clothes and made up her face the same way Linnet did. What we all thought was a recent weight loss due to grief was really the thinner Jackie wearing Linnet's clothes. And then there's Jackie's talent for mimicry—she probably would have made it had she gone to Hollywood all those years ago."

"But to fool everyone the way she did just seems amazing," said Randy.

"I know, but remember before 'Jackie' died, Linnet's special contacts mysteriously disappeared and she had to wear those enormous glasses. I'm sure Jackie threw the contacts out, knowing that Linnet would have to wear the glasses. They were simply part of her disguise. And she constantly seemed unsteady on her feet. We chalked it up to grief, but in reality she was just masking the differences in their gait. With those minor alterations, Jackie was able to offset the differences between the real Linnet and her imitation."

"And all because Linnet stole Jackie's boyfriend over half a century ago," mused Randy. "That's a long time to nurse a hate."

"Yes," said Detective Stewart. "We've gotten some medical history on Ms. Tanner and apparently she's struggled with this anger a long time. She'd seen several psychiatrists over the years, but without success." He paused. "Obviously."

"Could she really have gotten away with it?" asked Bridget. "I mean, just taking over someone's identity like that?"

"She might have," said Detective Stewart. "Neither woman had other living relatives and there was no reason to doubt who she said she was. You can get away with a great deal if you have enough audacity."

"So Joan was . . ." said Randy.

"Polly's aunt, nothing more, nothing less," intoned Detective Stewart.

"But what about Daniel?" said Peter. "He lied about being with Polly. Why?"

"Because Polly was actually with Joan. They didn't want that known because they were afraid that people would start to wonder why they were spending time together. If their relationship as aunt and niece was discovered, they feared that Joan would fall under police suspicion. Daniel gave Polly that cover."

"And we all know how uncomfortable suspicion is," said Aunt Winnie to the ceiling.

Detective Stewart shifted awkwardly in his chair. "I am sorry, Ms. Reynolds," he said, "but . . ."

Aunt Winnie waved away his apology. "But I look like a crazed killer. I know. Don't worry about it. I get that all the time." She leaned forward and winked. "Now, I don't know about the rest of you, but I'm hungry. How about you all come help me in the kitchen?" Next to me, Peter moved to stand up. "I didn't mean you, Peter," she said. "You sit here and rest. Keep Elizabeth company."

Within seconds, the room was empty, the result of Aunt Winnie's none-too-subtle maneuvering. Peter and I sat close together in silence and watched the rhythmic leaping of the flames of the fire. My heart beat a little faster.

Peter took a deep breath and gently took my hand in his. "Elizabeth? I hope you know that I wasn't trying to put one over on Aunt Winnie with the inn. I was only trying to help."

"I know. I'm sorry. I was just upset about her having to sell it in the first place. It really didn't matter whom she sold it to."

"There's something else you should know," he said. His face was flushed, but whether from the fire or emotion, I couldn't tell. "I was going to rename it the Inn at Lambton."

"Peter, it doesn't matter what . . . wait a minute, what were you going to name it?"

His amber eyes glowed in the soft firelight. "From *Pride and Prejudice,* the Inn at Lambton."

"But . . ." The Inn at Lambton was where Elizabeth was staying when she and Mr. Darcy realized they loved each other. Peter leaned toward me and kissed me. I didn't stop him—for a long time. Then I reluctantly unwrapped myself and eased away. His eyes sought out mine in confusion. "What's wrong?"

"Are you sure you want to do this? I mean, after all I am a girl on the rebound."

"I don't understand."

"I overheard what you said to Aunt Winnie on New Year's Eve. You told her that you didn't want to date a girl on the rebound."

Peter looked embarrassed. "Oh. I just said that to save face. You'd made it pretty clear that you didn't like me. I knew that if I asked you out, you'd say no."

"But what about Maggie," I replied. "I don't like . . ."

He laughed. "Maggie is my dog. I made up the rest."

I reached up and touched his bandaged head. "It's a lucky thing you have a head injury," I said, before pulling him back toward me.

Later, as we sat together with everyone again eating crackers and cheese, I thought about my New Year's resolutions: to have inner poise, not to let Peter McGowan get under my skin, not to allow myself to be locked in a dark basement, and finally to have a calm and relaxing New Year's.

In a week, I had broken every single one of those resolutions. I grabbed Peter's hand and smiled. He squeezed my hand and smiled back.

It was going to be a great year.